I0639322

PATH OF THE
TITANS

BOOK 3 : SYSTEM CONSOLIDATION

A LITRPG EPIC FANTASY
TIMOTHY McGOWEN

PATH OF THE TITANS - SYSTEM CONSOLIDATION

A LITRPG EPIC FANTASY

PATH OF THE TITANS
BOOK 3

TIMOTHY MCGOWEN

ILLUSTRATED BY
CHRISTINA P. MYRVOLD

EDITED BY
CANDACE MORRIS

RISING
TOWER
BOOKS
Fantasy · LitRPG · Camelit

OTHER BOOKS BY THE AUTHOR

Copyright © 2024 by Timothy McGowen

All rights reserved.

System Expansion, Book 3

Path of the Titans

Ebook ISBN: 978-1-956179-45-3

Paperback ISBN: 978-1-956179-46-0

Hardback ISBN: 978-1-956179-47-7

First Edition: May 2024

Published By: Rising Tower Books

Publisher Website: www.RisingTowerBooks.com

Author Site: AuthorTimothyMcGowen.com

No part of this book may be reproduced in any form or by any electronic or mechanical means, including information storage and retrieval systems, without written permission from the author, except for the use of brief quotations in a book review.

For permission requests, email to timothy.mcgowen1@gmail.com . This is a work of fiction. All characters, organizations, and events portrayed in this novel are either products of the author's imagination or are used fictitiously.

REVIEWS ARE IMPORTANT

Every review matters, get your voice heard. Follow me on Amazon to get informed when my next book is released!

https://www.amazon.com/stores/Timothy-McGowen/author/B087QTTRJK

Join my Patreon for early Chapters!

https://www.patreon.com/TimothyMcGowen

Join my Facebook group and discuss the books

https://www.facebook.com/groups/234653175151521/

SPECIAL THANKS

I wanted to give a special thanks to those that helped bring this book to its current state.

Candace Morris - Editor and Super Hero.

Dantas Neto, Sean Hall, Hugo Morais. (Elandar) - Proofer

I dedicate this book to my fans. Without your loyalty and dedication I'd never be able to craft so many wonderful stories.

CONTENTS

CHAPTER 1
NEW ARRIVALS

"AETEX! WATCH OUT!" Knox called as a dark figure blurred and appeared before him. He didn't seem to notice or care. Instead, he began speaking with the figure, and neither attacked.

"Frederick, see to Ramses and keep him safe," Knox said, jumping from the wall and using Ethereal Step to appear on the ground unharmed from the fall. He needed to know what was being said and why a new army had appeared.

Was this the cumulation of the dark oozes and the attacks of the darkness-infused girl? There was no telling; so, he would get his answers. Despite the ever-growing mass of troops, he felt confident approaching because Aetex let off a power that trumped any of the dark figure's own.

Knox's sense had been confused at first, taking in the mass of energy from them all and assuming that it was an individual power level, but as he got closer, he felt that these people weren't as powerful as he'd first assumed. The one speaking with Aetex had power that much was for sure, but she was more around Knox's level and not quite Aetex's own.

"And here he is now, allow him to speak for himself, but I can assure you he is a man of honor," Aetex said as Knox approached.

Knox truly saw her for the first time as he came closer, and his jaw hung open a measure.

As the first light of dawn began to paint the horizon with hues of gold and crimson, the figure of a female stood in stark contrast to any other elf Knox had encountered. Her obsidian skin caught the early light, creating an ethereal shimmer that contrasted sharply with the darkness from which she stepped. The sun's nascent rays played upon her white hair, turning it into a radiant halo around her, while her striking purple eyes absorbed the burgeoning light, reflecting with a luminous intensity that seemed almost otherworldly.

She stood for a moment, considering Knox, and allowing the first touch of sunlight to caress her face—a rarity for one of her kind, he assumed, as she'd come from under the ground. The rising sun cast long shadows that danced around her, mirroring the complex interplay of darkness and light that defined her existence. With a grace that belied her formidable presence, she stepped fully into the light, her gaze fixed on Knox, a regal power seeming to surge within her.

"You speak for your people?" She asked, her words were understandable, but she had an odd accent that Knox hadn't encountered before.

"I do," Knox said, his own Mystic Armor shining blue light in contrast to her own armor that seemed to pull the very light around her into itself.

"I seek audience with a Titan and have brought my people here to ask for asylum against the Dark One," she said, then seeming to remember something], she added, "My name is Sintra'reah T'sarran, but please call me Sintra."

"I am Knox Trelling, Titan of the Light. Are you telling me you are here for asylum and not to attack us?" I asked, a weight ready to release upon hearing her words.

"We've risked life and limb to find one such as you, and our home is no longer safe for our kind. The Dark One, the Titan of Darkness, seeks to subjugate not only our kingdom but the surface as well. I come for asylum, but also with a warning. Her influence has reached the surface, and even now, she plays for power. Will you aid us in throwing her down and ending her evil reign?"

"Of course, we will," Aetex answered before Knox even had time to fully process what had been said.

"I'm willing to hear you out, but if you aren't attacking, then I suggest you gather your people together and come inside," Knox said, far less worried about them as he scanned them individually with his sense. There were injured and weak among them as much as Knox's own people.

"Very well," Sintra said, she turned and signaled to her people, some two or three hundred if Knox had to guess.

Knox walked ahead of the group with Aetex at his side.

"You missed the entire battle," Knox said, eying the large man and wondering where he'd been.

"I had my own role to play," Aetex said as if that settled the matter. "Besides, you defeated your foe and drove out the undead; the last bit was a mystery to me. I was on my way to aid you with them, but our visitors arrived the moment I did."

"Where were you?" Knox asked, not wanting to let him out of it so easily. "I needed you."

"These folk needed me more," Aetex said. "They'd found a few enemies below that they couldn't handle, so I intervened."

"Did you know they were friendly?" Knox asked, shutting his eyes in frustration for a moment.

Aetex smiled down at him. "I'd hoped, and speeding along their surfacing would have brought them here in time to help deal with the army we fought, it is my great pleasure that they did not need to fight, as they are much weakened from the magics they had to employ and their long journey."

"We will talk about this more later," Knox said as they made it to the broken gate and entered Luminar, the Titan Complex.

Knox spoke with the Ahtora King, who left in peace and with the promise of trade. His people had received minimal losses, and they took their dead with them. He tried to get them to stay longer, but they insisted that they must withdraw back to the waters from whence they came. It was all for the better, as Knox had his own dead to deal with. They'd lost dozens of men and women in the fight, perhaps even a hundred, but it was hard to tell with so many undead corpses to worry about.

Knox gathered together all those he felt should have a say in the matter and summoned forth the dark elf Sintra.

"Tell us of your journey and why you left to the surface?" Knox asked. He was more curious to learn about a civilization that lived within the ground and obviously had access to levels and such, but he would take things slow and for the benefit of everyone, start from the beginning.

"I will tell my tale, and in return I hope you will assist me in my quest," Sintra said, launching into her story from the beginning.

They called themselves Noctrae, which she said roughly meant 'walkers of the night'. They lived deep within the caverns of the dark underground and there she ruled as a princess to her people. However, some two hundred years ago—her people were very long lived—a force known as the Dark One began to influence the Noctrae people into worshiping her. She told them she was a Titan of old and their sacrifices were necessary to grow her power.

Her people took this in stride, giving this powerful being much of what it asked for, until the queen of her people was requested as sacrifice some ten years back. This caused a civil war between those loyal to the crown and those loyal to the Titan of Darkness. It ended with the queen's death and a small force of her loyal followers fleeing to the surface for help. They'd heard word of an ancient Artifact that could magnify power beyond that of its wielder's wildest dreams, however it is said to only be able to be wielded by another Titan. So, they followed the signs toward the surface and for ten years they searched.

Now they'd found Knox and wanted his help to find this device which they called, the Aura Prism.

"I've heard of such a device," Draven said, interrupting the tale. "How you know of it is beyond me, this is a matter I should speak to you privately," he said, narrowing his gaze on Knox.

"Follow me," Knox said, grabbing the man by the shoulder and taking him to a side room. "Speak quickly, what is so secretive that you can't say in front of everyone."

Draven looked conflicted suddenly, as if perhaps he shouldn't have said anything to begin with. "I've said too much already," he said, rubbing at the back of his neck. "But if my guess is right, you've a right to know."

"Then tell me," Knox said.

"The device she calls the Aura Prism, we call the Aurorapex," he said. "It has been guarded by my family for many generations. My family holds the seat of power in Lumisar, the city state in which your mother is our High Magi. I know more than I ought to, but in this situation my prying ears have done you a favor."

"I know all this, well, most of it," Knox said, shaking his head.

"What you don't know is that your mother is key in suppressing the power of the Aurorapex. We fear the day our true ruler would return, so we hide the power. You see, once the Auro-rapex is claimed, with it comes the throne of Lumisar. Though we exist within another kingdom, our city-state has always been sepa-rate. Should we crown a new king, it would most certainly mean war."

"I'm going to share all this information with the others," Knox said flatly. Draven sighed but seemed resigned to the infor-mation getting out.

Knox returned and shared what he'd learned, then Draven left the meeting, offering no new information.

"And we are to just trust these newcomers and get aboard with their quest?" one of the Elders asked, voicing a concern Knox already shared.

"We will consider it, but the safety and rebuilding of Luminar comes first, before all other considerations," Knox said. "With that in mind, let us speak of supplies."

The meeting turned to more pressing matters and Sintra listened without interrupting.

"We need to talk," Dernal said, pulling Knox aside at the end of the meeting. Everyone knew what they needed to do, much of it involved cleaning and repairing work along with the maintenance golems, but Knox had no specific task assigned to him, besides caring for Ramses.

"About what?" Knox asked, walking to the guest cabin that had been set aside for Ramses. Dernal walked along with him, seemingly uncaring in what direction they went.

"Your mother hired me to protect you, you should not return to Lumisar, for you will share her fate if you do," Dernal said.

His words stopped Knox dead in his tracks, and he looked at him with steel in his eyes. Did he just admit to being hired by his mother?

"You knew how much I yearned to know of her, you knew how much I wanted to be like her," Knox said, his words much quieter than he meant them to be, but so fierce were the tangle of emotions going through him that he could barely get out what he wanted to say.

"I went against her wishes after I got to know you, she implored me to keep you out of the Adventurer life, but I knew how much it meant to you," Dernal said; clearly disclosing this was having an effect on him, but Knox didn't care.

"You," Knox said, tears coming to his eyes as he regarded his old friend. "How could you?"

"Without me you'd never have walked this path and taken on the power you have now," Dernal said, heat entering his voice. "I wish now that I'd followed your mother's warnings. You'd be safe; we'd all likely be safe."

His words stung and suddenly Knox felt himself withdrawing. He could do whatever he pleased, what did it matter to Knox anymore? He had a greater mission to accomplish now, and he would see it through to the end. His people would be safe, even if that meant he had to go to Lumisar and put himself in harm's way.

"I can't right now," Knox said, turning and dismissing Dernal with a look. The short man didn't resist, instead he hung his head and turned to walk the other direction.

Of all the people Knox thought might betray him, never had it occurred to him that Dernal could be the one.

CHAPTER 2
AFTERMATH

"Are you feeling up to talking?" Knox asked Ramses. The man had lost much of his color again and looked frail. They were in a small hut, furnished because it belonged to one of the fallen.

It was a spherical design and the walls rose up to an impressive twelve feet at the highest, much higher than was needed for Knox and his people. Even Terrim could stand in one of these smaller huts and not hit his head. The bed took up a quarter of the space and a water basin had been set beside it to give Ramses a way to bathe himself if needed. It looked like someone had helped him because he was clean, and Knox couldn't imagine him having the strength to do it himself in his condition.

"I'm fine," Ramses said, sounding anything but fine. His voice was more a croak than anything resembling coherent speech, but he cleared his voice and spoke more clearly. "I'm fine," he repeated, sitting up and gazing up at Knox.

"Here is your journal," Knox said, handing over the book he'd grabbed on his way here. "I read some of it, sorry I didn't mean to intrude on your privacy."

"It revealed some of my entries to you?" Ramses asked, his expression one of shock.

"Only a small handful, enough that I know what you've been through, and I'm surprised that you made it as far as you did with no one around," Knox said. He put a friendly hand on Ramses' shoulder and the man flinched but didn't pull away.

"Yes," Ramses said, his eyes going distant. "I've had a time of it, that's for sure. Are you here to listen to my request for aid?"

"I'm listening," Knox said, after everything that had happened, he was more than a little apprehensive about hearing what else was about to be added onto his plate, so to speak.

"I wish to stay among you for a time while I rejuvenate, then when the time is right, I want to connect our Titan Engines. You are the closest of our brethren, but not the only other Titan. Eventually, I see a world where the System is once again the law of the land, each Titan Engine working together as a network of power."

"I'll need to speak with Mic about what that would entail, but you are welcome to stay among us for as long as you need," Knox said. "Can you tell me the upsides of connecting Titan Engines or why we'd want to do it?"

Ramses seemed shocked by Knox's question, sitting up taller and groaning from the effort it took. "Power my boy. The more connected we are, the more power we will be able to channel, making us that much closer to the real thing."

"The real thing?" Knox asked, confused by what he meant.

"Yes, like a real Titan," Ramses said, then seeing Knox's face remained confused he continued. "We are Titan Born, but that doesn't truly make us like the Titans of legend. They were beings of great power and creation. Not until we've connected our engines and put the entire world under the thrall of the System can we even hope to match their power. And trust me when I say we will want to, because I fear there are greater threats out there than other Titans growing in power."

"What kind of threats?" Knox asked, his hand fidgeting on the hilt of his axe at the thought of more powerful enemies coming down on them. He'd been facing each threat as it came to him, unable to even consider that there might be something greater than the darkness to deal with.

"Gowlen my boy, have you not questioned the simulacrum of the Titan? He will weasel out of most questions, but if you know how to ask you can learn much," Ramses said, taking a deep breath he launched into it.

"I've learned much, but what I'm willing to share is the most basic concepts. As far as I can tell this entire world, maybe even our entire dimension, was an experiment of this Titan Gowlen, one of the original Titans to rule over humanoid kind.

"What's more, I think he's abandoned us for the past several centuries, whether that is because he wanted to give his experiment time to age or he's given up on us, I cannot say. What I can say is that if he returns, we better be strong enough to deal with him, otherwise he might choose to wipe the slate clean and we'd be powerless against him."

Knox pinched the bridge of his nose as he took in the new information. "So, we have a potential threat that holds enough power to create this world, or perhaps the entire, what'd you call it, dimension? And we are supposed to be able to fight it?"

"Eventually. It requires that we walk the Path of the Titans, so we can go from Titan Born to true Titan. Only then will we be able to wield the cosmic forces required to fight back against our creator," Ramses said, growing more animated as he spoke, and some of the color seemed to return to him. "Will you stand with me against such an impossible foe?"

"Not today I won't, but I'll speak with Mic about what can be done. How sure are we that these Titans can even die?" Knox asked, curiosity over the new situation overriding his better sense.

"I have to believe that as we Titan Born can die, so can the ones that created us. And who is this Mic you keep speaking of?" Ramses asked.

"He's a golem that survived from the last Titan Born to take up the mantle of Titan of Light," Knox said. "He doesn't remember everything, but he knows enough to be helpful. He's been a sort of mentor or guide to me during these past months. Him and your journal have been helpful in understanding what I am."

"My grimoire is no simple journal," Ramses said, hugging the book to his chest as if it were a child in need of comforting. "But I am glad you were able to gain some measure of comfort and knowledge from it. I imagine the magic must have synergized with you to show you glimpses into what I've written inside of it."

"Why are you so weak? The last I read, you'd begun to fight great sea monsters and you were strong enough to spread your system," Knox asked the burning question that had been on his mind since the man's collapse.

"The sea is a vast place of life, however the strongest of the monsters were also the smartest. They began to roam further and further out until I had only the simplest of life forms to deal with. We, as Titan Born, can sustain ourselves purely off of essence if we wished, but when both food and essence are taken from you, it begins to take its toll. I tried hibernating, letting my body run on low resources for years on end, but eventually it caught up with me. The memories of the great sea monsters are great, and they still have not returned."

Knox nodded along. "So, how'd you get here then?"

"I used what little power I had to fuel the portal, it took more than I had anticipated, which left me in this state. If I hadn't been able to transfer a measure of your essence over to me, I'd have likely died. Do you have any Cores that I could consume? I am sorely low in my reserves."

Knox sighed. "I can give you some, but food and drink will do you as much good, I think. What level are you to have killed so many undead like that?"

"Levels? Bah, they are a sore measure of my power, and you shouldn't concern yourself with them. We are beyond levels, the longer we walk the Path of the Titans the more levels will be meaningless to us," Ramses said, a smirk on his face.

"You stole an entire level from me when you joined with me

to attack the undead, so while I can appreciate that you think we will eventually not need to be concerned with levels, right now I am. So please, tell me your level and I will share my own," Knox said.

Ramses surprised him by waving his hand and showing a translucent screen that showed off his status. Knox had never known that you could share such a screen with others, but he looked over the man's screen with interest.

-Personal Status-
  -Name: Ramses-
  -Level: 62-
  -Health: Extraordinary Tier 9-
  -Mana: Extraordinary Tier 9-
  -Stamina: Extraordinary Tier 9-
  -Mind: 240-
  -Body: 240-
  -Spirit: 240-

"All is fair, now show me yours," Ramses demanded, sitting even straighter in his bed as he waited to see Knox's status.

With the loss of levels from using his ring and the one that Ramses took, he wasn't in a hurry to see what level he was now, but he did as requested, pulling up the status and focusing on sharing it visually. A sigh of surprise from Ramses told Knox it had worked; he'd shown his status to another.

-Personal Status-
  -Name: Knox-
  -Level: 41-
  -Health: Excellent Tier 9-
  -Mana: Excellent Tier 9-

-Stamina: Excellent Tier 9-
-Mind: 180-
-Body: 180-
-Spirit: 180-

It wasn't as bad as he'd imagined, he was still within what he'd consider B Ranked, so his attributes hadn't fallen. But he had lost close to three hundred thousand essence, that was going to be a hard journey to recover.

"You are around below where I started as a Titan Born. How is it you've been able to hold your Titan Complex from attackers with such low levels? You must truly have shone forth on the Path of the Titans to leverage such a low starting point into what you are now," Ramses said, he sounded a bit smug, but Knox didn't know if that was because his level was so incredibly high, or he just always sounded like that.

"Have you heard of an artifact called the Aurorapex or the Aura Prism?" Knox asked, eager to change the subject from his low level.

"Ah yes, the Aurorapex, an object held by a foreigner king that prevented several invasions. My order long suspected it was an ancient Titan device but all of our spies we sent to investigate were found out and disemboweled in the most unfortunate manner. We stopped sending our acolytes after the first dozen died," Ramses said, a wide smile crossing his face as if he spoke of something as casual as what he was having for dinner and not the deaths of over a dozen of his students.

"It is said to be kept in a city named Lumisar," Knox began to say, and Ramses interrupted him.

"Lumisar," Ramses said, his voice questioning. "I thought you said this place was called Lumisar?"

"No, this city is named Lumi*nar*, not Lumisar," Knox said, then shrugged. "I took the name from what it used to be called, no idea why they are so similar."

"Perhaps they were ruled by the same king, with what I know now I'd say that the king of old that rules the city of Lumisar, as you call it now, was very much a Titan. I'd even have suspected that the city had a Titan Complex, if I hadn't found you here in the middle of nowhere."

"Whether or not that is the case," Knox said. "I've got a new quest ahead of me, to retrieve this artifact and take it to deal with the Titan of Darkness."

"You should be trying to recruit them, not attack them," Ramses said, folding his arms.

"I can try that," Knox said. "But I want to go in knowing I have a chance to win. Will you, when you've recovered, stand with me against them if they refuse to cooperate?"

"I've a long road of recovery ahead of me, but if I am able, I will come to your aid under one condition," Ramses said, his face stern as he stared down his nose at Knox.

"I'm listening," Knox said.

"If we pull her down, we must put someone new in her seat of power and get them to connect their Titan Engine with our own," Ramses said.

"Fine," Knox said. "We are in agreement."

Knox met with Murdoch privately and they went over the list of the dead. Among them were two names that hurt to hear, both Sarah and her sister Angie had died along with the rest of their party. Knox felt a great weight in his stomach at hearing the news and he just sat in silence while Murdoch went on to speak of other matters. By the time he finished, Knox nodded that he'd heard, and Murdoch went on his way.

He didn't know how long he sat there in his quarters, but a

gentle knock pushed him out of his reflection. Wiping away a stray tear, Knox stood and greeted the person at his door.

"Come on in, Beth," Knox said, doing his damnedest to keep a straight face.

"I heard the news of the fallen," Beth said, her own eyes watery with tears. "I'm so sorry Knox."

She took him into an embrace and the warmth of her touch was enough to send him overboard. He began to cry like a child, unable to help himself. He'd experienced loss before, everyone living out this far did, but poor Sarah and young Angie. Why hadn't he insisted that they leave with those that had left to avoid the battle, the children and the weak.

He knew strong-willed Sarah wouldn't have gone along with it though. She wasn't the strongest of the Adventurers that they had, but she was damn well near the top. Together with her sister and their party, they'd been a group he could rely on. Now they'd all fallen along with eighteen others, their names burned into his mind as he considered the events that led up to it.

Was there something he could have done to have prevented it? Should he have taken all the power or given more of it when the time came? So many questions and doubts rolled through his mind, but then something Murdoch mentioned brought his grief to anger.

He'd commented that their losses weren't all that bad considering the scope of the battle they'd waged. That they should count themselves lucky that more hadn't fallen to the undead force they'd fought against. How could he be so cruel and dispassionate? Lives were lost and he couldn't do anything about it.

They held each other and cried for several minutes before the tears just wouldn't come anymore. A weight that Knox knew would never truly go away settled in his gut and he knew for the first time in his life, true grief.

Recovering himself enough, he left his cabin in search of someone else to speak with, anyone else. He cared for, perhaps even loved, Beth, but it felt too much like a betrayal to spend time with her right now. So instead, he went in search of someone else and who he found, almost made him turn back.

In fact, he did begin to turn away, in search of Terrim or perhaps Henry, but his father put a hand on his arm, turning him back.

"You've heard about your mother," Askar said, a look in his eyes that Knox couldn't quite identify. "Maybe you can understand now. Let's talk about it."

If not for the image of his father risking his life to save Knox on the battlefield he might turn the man away immediately, but he owed him something and if this was what he wanted, to talk, then it would be payment enough for Knox.

"I have and I'm not sure how I'm supposed to feel about it," Knox said, speaking honestly. "She abandoned us, but that didn't give you the right to treat me like a piece of shit all my life."

"Didn't it?" Askar said. "You are a constant reminder of the woman I loved leaving me for some duty that she couldn't even tell me about. She wrapped me so tight in oaths that I couldn't have told you any of this until you found out on your own. I originally slipped you her journal in hopes you'd figure it out and I could be open with you for once. But no, you started to idolize the woman that betrayed me, betrayed us."

"I found her journal in spite of you," Knox said, but then thinking back he'd always wondered why his father had kept the journal at all, now he knew.

"She took my boy from me when she wrapped me in those oaths. I couldn't be myself, forced to live the life of a commoner, cutting trees for a living. Then, despite my strength, I lost an arm.

17

It was too much for me. I broke and I haven't been the same since. I wish you could have known me before; I was much like your friend Dernal, slow to open up but fiercely loyal."

"Dernal betrayed me. Did you know about him?" Knox asked, his mood still somehow calm despite the topic.

Askar looked taken aback, his mechanical arm coming up to scratch at his chin, he was truly getting the hang of using it. "Sent by your mother?" Askar guessed, Knox nodded. "Damn him, but why did he encourage you toward the life if she forced me to keep you from it? When you left to go be an Adventurer, I struggled against all my oaths to not drag you back by your neck. Of course, once you got started it wouldn't take you long to grow more powerful than me, you are like your mother in that, obtaining power so fast and easy. Back when I was an Adventurer, the first time, every little bit of growth was difficult for me. I fought for every inch I got."

"You'd have me believe that she got you to swear oaths that made you be a shitty person, to drink your life away, to treat me like a piece of garbage?" Knox asked, heat entering his voice with every question.

Askar hung his head, his fists clenched and shaking. "You don't know what it was like," he said, then shaking he turned and left. Knox let him go, not bothering to go after him or try to ease his pain.

Knox was in pain with no way out, so why shouldn't his father share the same fate.

CHAPTER 3
VENTING FRUSTRATIONS

Two days went by, and Knox had done all that he could to help the repairs, but his grief refused to settle. He needed to let loose and get into some action to help blow off some stress. With that in mind, he gathered his party and asked them to be ready to do a dungeon run.

Eleanor Dawnbringer gave them a writ that could be taken to the Mire's Gloom Dungeon to allow them to skip the line. She'd fought bravely and had stuck around after the attack. The influence of the darkness was still rampant, but the dark elves had helped in that regard, taking time to hunt down anything infected with the ooze. Everything was operating fine, and when repairs were complete, a task that would take another two weeks or so, they would leave to try to recover the artifact from his mother. Until then, Knox had time to kill, so he was going to run a dungeon with his team.

Dernal stayed behind, meaning they'd take Henry with them, but Leo and John both wanted to go. Knox hadn't said so much as a word or two to Dernal since he'd discovered his betrayal, still working out how he felt about everything as he was, but he was beginning to feel like he didn't resent the man after all. He had, in the end, gone against his mother's wishes and helped him become an Adventurer.

Leo and John knew nothing about his actions, so Knox didn't hold any blame on them. That left him with a group slightly too large, so he'd asked Murdoch to stay behind, busy as he was in the restoration of the city; he hadn't even complained about missing out.

That left Beth, Terrim, Leo, John, and Henry healing to go with them, Frederick was busy as well and Knox didn't want to push the topic as they already had one more than was normal for a dungeon run.

John being who he was, started flirting with Beth the moment the group left to journey to the dungeon town. Beth took it in stride and flirted playfully back, something that Knox found didn't bother him at all, still stuck in grief as he was for Sarah.

"You really think we shouldn't worry about the pirates anymore, a good portion of them escaped," Terrim said, getting Knox's attention as they walked through the forest toward the dungeon town.

"We will know shortly," Knox said.

Knox had thought long and hard about this, speaking with the three pirates turned golems—Edgar, Borris, and Vlad—he'd determined that the remaining pirates would leave the port and not likely return any time soon. However, to be safe, they were taking a long way to the Dungeon Town to check out the deserted port town. According to the Command Chair, the area was empty of any threats, but Knox wanted to verify with his own two eyes.

"How you holding up?" Terrim asked.

"How do you think?" Knox shot back, immediately regretting how sharp his words came out. "I'm sorry, it's just not been easy."

"I know a part of what you are feeling, when Danielle was sick and I thought I'd lost her," Terrim said, shaking his head.

Knox met his friend's eyes and for a moment felt like perhaps he did know what he was feeling. "Thanks man, how is Danielle doing?"

The children and the weak, Danielle included, had returned a day or two ago and were helping in the rebuilding efforts. Terrim, of course, had been over the moons to see her back and getting him to agree to come to this dungeon run had actually been more difficult than Knox would have guessed. But in the end, Terrim was a good friend who knew his buddy needed to smash things, so he came along to help.

"She's doing great, she even helped kill some monsters on her way back, so she didn't feel so useless. Her level is increasing steadily," Terrim said, then pausing, he seemed to consider something before continuing. "I might even invite her to do a dungeon run at some point."

"That sounds nice," Knox said, hearing his friend but his own mind going to the time he told Sarah that she couldn't come with his group. Why hadn't he allowed her to come on a run? Sure, she was at a lower level, but she could have learned and perhaps gotten stronger or more skilled.

They continued in silence after a while, and Knox wondered what they'd find when they reached the pirate lands. They followed the coast currently, adding at least a day to their journey to the Mire's Gloom Dungeon town.

What they ended up finding was nothing short of shocking. Piles of dead bodies lay strewn about here and there. The ocean breeze was the only thing keeping the scent of the stink of dead smoldering bodies from being overwhelming.

All the buildings were smoldering wrecks, everything they left behind had been put to the torch, even a few larger ships lay in burning wrecks, only one looked like it might be salvageable. Knox didn't know what he expected but this wasn't it at all.

"Why would they burn it all when they left?" Knox asked the party and Leo answered.

"Why wouldn't they?" he asked in turn. "Whatever extra supplies would just be helpful to others and these pirates are a selfish bunch. If I had to guess, they won't be returning to this port any time soon."

"Still, let's look around and see what we can find before we set off," Knox said.

They began their search of the mostly burnt-out ship that still floated at the water's edge. Knox could see holes where it had taken cannon fire and the sails had all been burnt up, but the boat was otherwise in great shape. John went ahead looking for traps and good thing he was with them, because he found several. Each trap was meant to explode a large section of the ship or perhaps the entire thing. They had a black powder filled to the brim in barrels and a flint and steel contraption that would ignite it.

They did what they could to salvage the traps and prevent any explosions. With a bit of work, they got the barrels of the stuff onto the shore for later use. Knox would send Mr. Tome to secure the location, as he could be trusted with such a substance. What was more, the ship looked in decent enough condition that Knox was going to see about having it fixed up, one never knew when a ship might come in handy.

John took the task of going back to town and delivering a message about the pirates while the rest of the team went on ahead. With the black spheres the pirates had, they'd captured many over the months, John would be safe to travel alone. He could also move a good measure faster on his own, so he hoped to catch up with them before they made it to the dungeon town.

With the matter of the pirates settled and one threat crossed off his list of many, Knox took a deep breath and wished they'd run into a monster or two already. But as luck would have it, they had a very uneventful trip to the Mire's Gloom Dungeon town, arriving late in the night on the third day.

John joined them the next morning as they prepared to go into the dungeon.

The town seemed almost ordinary on Knox's return to it. Gone was the mystical sense of excitement that he'd first felt when arriving. He no longer worried about any of these Adventurers being stronger than him, even the gate guard at the dungeon didn't have an aura as powerful as Knox's own. It was almost disappointing in a way.

"Here to run the dungeon," Knox announced, passing over the writ to the dungeon guard.

"Lots of changing going on here, we've been allowing groups in but honestly with the new levels and abilities, we've lost more than our fair share inside. Be careful and mind your pace while inside. Seems like the dungeon is hitting a bit harder than she usually does; something has her out of sorts," said the armored gruff man that Knox didn't recognize.

"Noted," Knox said with a curt smile and a nod.

The group walked up to the dungeon pillar and placed their hands on it. Before they disappeared, Knox heard the gate guard say something about him, but he didn't catch it. Something like, "Wasn't that that Knox fellow?"

Light flashed in his eyes and once more he found himself in a cavern area inside the dungeon. They'd resupplied and were ready for several days inside. Setting up camp, Knox was moving fast and was very eager to start clearing out the dungeon.

"Should we jump to the end for more of a challenge?" Knox asked, smiling wide as he cracked his neck to the side in preparation for some physical exertion.

"We can vote on it," John suggested. They did so and Knox was overruled, most wanting to take out each path of the dungeon before going forward.

So, they found themselves in the easiest wing of the dungeon, killing monsters barely worth his time. He did note that they hit harder and faster than he remembered, but that could just be time blurring the lines for him.

It only took a few hours to clear the first path, the boss being no issue as Knox went full power at him, killing him within minutes. The loot was good, at least for lower-leveled folk; Knox suggested that they save all the loot and give it away to lower-leveled members of Luminar later; Leo and John seemed hesitant, but they agreed, asking only that they still get dungeon points to spend later.

Path after path fell before them until they reached the final themed path forward. Here he had slain upstart sheriffs, killed dragons, and more, so he wondered at what adventure awaited them now.

"It's been a long day," Leo said, Henry seemed more worn out than the rest of the group and Knox knew Leo was speaking on his behalf. "Let's rest before finishing the final path."

They'd cleared all the paths in a day, maybe two, but they hadn't stopped to rest the entire time. Seeing as most of them didn't need much rest, it was fine, but Knox had been so narrow minded in his pursuit to kill monsters that he hadn't noticed how tired Henry had become.

"Sorry," Knox said to Henry, before turning to the group at large. "Let's rest for the night and we will challenge the themed dungeon path first thing tomorrow."

"And let's eat, I'm starving," Terrim said, stuffing some dried meat in his mouth. He'd been eating the entire time, but Knox forgot how not everyone could survive on just essence alone.

"Okay, let's eat then sleep," Knox said, nodding to his friend as they headed back to the base camp to rest.

Beth had been unusually quiet during the run, ignoring most

of John's flirting advances. But now she came to stand beside Knox and fixed him with a glare.

"What?" Knox asked, unsure what he'd done to attract her ire.

Beth cleared her throat and stared him down, saying nothing at first. Then, after a solid half minute or so, she spoke low enough that only Knox could hear but with anger clear to be heard in her voice.

"You trying to kill yourself?"

Knox blinked at her and matched her gaze. "No, I don't think so."

She pinched at the bridge of her nose, something she rarely did before continuing. "The way you keep throwing yourself headlong into the fights, you've taken more damage than all of us combined, and you are the reason Henry is so worn thin."

"Oh," Knox said, thinking back he hadn't really seen it like that. He was the strongest in the group and the monsters were so weak that he just wanted to get it over with so he could find a real challenge. Sure, he'd taken a few hits here and there but was it really so bad as she made it out to be?

"Some of us still care if you live or die, remember that won't you?" Beth asked, her voice softening as she spoke. When she'd finished speaking, she turned and joined the others for a hot meal over the fire.

Knox hadn't realized he was being so reckless, but now as he thought back, he truly had been throwing himself into battle without regard for his injuries. He would do better, he decided. He'd fight with his team instead of ahead of them, he had too much that could be lost still if he weren't careful.

CHAPTER 4
THEMED DUNGEON

THEY STEPPED through the threshold and into the last branch of the dungeon, expecting anything. What they got was a cold breeze and an area filled with trees that swayed with the wind. A single large moon hung high in the sky, lighting the way and shadows spread out rampant and odd in their formations. It was as if there was a whisper in the wind and Knox could almost make out what was being said.

"Greetings," came a voice from behind them and they all spun to find a dwindling old man in rags, holding a map, along with a round orb that glowed a dim blue light from runes carved into the surface. "You have come to seek the treasure of the Wizard's Tower?"

"We have," Knox said, not missing a beat. These themed dungeons always had some scenario they wanted you to play out and he'd found by hard experience that it was best just to roll with it.

"Then map and key I have for thee," said the glowering old man. "Be ye ready for such a challenge, only time will tell. Take this now and be ye well."

Knox nodded along, taking the map and the sphere from the

old man, then turning, he saw in the distance lit up by the large moon, a Tower rising up high into the sky.

"That's it?" Terrim asked, sounding a bit confused. "We just accept random stuff from an old guy and go headlong into that Tower?"

"If ye seek answers you may ask three questions and I will answer them," came the old man's voice.

Knox shrugged. "We go in and kill stuff, it won't be terribly difficult, I'm sure. Let's just go and end this."

"If we follow your map, will it lead us to the end of this adventure?" Leo asked, ignoring Knox as he began to walk forward toward the Tower.

"Wise questions, there is a path that must be followed exactly on the map. Stay to that course and ye will find your footfalls relatively safe, though monsters do walk the halls, only the strongest ye will avoid."

"What waits for us on the top?" Knox asked, turning back and playing along.

"A terrible fate for those that can't withstand the gift giving nature of power. Give and you shall conquer."

"How does the key work?" Terrim asked, drawing sharp looks from Leo and Knox as both had questions they wanted to ask.

"Keep it at your side and doors will open for ye as ye proceed ever forward. Lose it and tempt the fate of the Tower's guardians. Three questions asked and answered, goodbye."

And with that, the old man shifted into mist, disappearing from sight. It was more than a little creepy, but Knox steeled himself and signaled for his group to follow him through the woods toward the Tower.

The Tower lay at the center of a grove of trees, some as tall as the very Tower itself. It had a base some hundred paces wide with a single wooden door that glowed with a faint show of power. All up and down the Tower were runes that glowed so fiercely that they were visible even without his sense. Knox recognized some of the symbols but was surprised to find some that he didn't even remotely remember seeing in all his study.

Odd that he was still encountering runes and formations he'd never encountered before, it was like the system of runes was as endless as the power they could call forth. At the top of the Tower, it flared out and held tall windows that shone with white light from within. An indication of life inside or just the glow of the power that they were meant to find, Knox didn't know which.

The moon, not their normal moons that they were used to, was huge behind the Tower, its light almost seeming to lend its own power to the Tower. Where was this dungeon getting this image of a world with only a single moon, and so large? It boggled the mind to think that perhaps the dungeon knew of other worlds, or perhaps Knox was overthinking it and it was just a made-up world that the dungeon created.

Up to this point, Knox had felt little rush from the battles he'd faced, and very little offering in the way of peace from his emotional burdens. He knew, of course, that no matter how hard he fought or tried, that Sarah and her sister wouldn't be coming back, so why even bother to distract himself?

These questions lay heavy on his head as he approached the door, sphere held out before him. He didn't know what he expected, but the door swinging wide as he approached wasn't on his short list of expectations. No, in fact, he'd assumed the sphere would offer some sort of puzzle making it harder to gain entry, perhaps a code phrase or a working of runes. To have it open so freely sent trigger alarms throughout his head, but still he kept the lead and walked right through the door, his party following behind him.

The first thing that he noticed was the size of the interior, it was bigger on the inside. The next thing was the floor glowed under his sense, triggering his alarm bells once more. He held out a hand stopping anyone from entering any further than he had, his foot only a pace away from the nearest of the glowing vines on the floor.

Light streamed in from a window that definitely didn't exist on the outside, falling on a large figure standing stone still and wielding an axe nearly as tall as Knox.

"John," Knox whispered, pointing at the figure that still stood motionless. "Check the ground for traps, but I have a good guess of what we are about to face. I'd bet my lunch that if we touch those strands of magic on the floor, we will have to face big ugly over there."

"Let me have a look," John said, kneeling down and running his hand dangerously close to the glowing on the floor.

"Perhaps we ought to put the big guy in front," Henry suggested, nudging Terrim forward, but Knox stopped him from going much further.

"I'll be fine," Knox said. "For now, I'm taking the lead, but if we wake up the big guy, I'll step back and let Terrim tank it."

"Good, I'm not sure I'm ready to heal you through whatever he could do to you," Henry said, a touch of reproach in his voice that Knox ignored.

"Traps, or rather one huge trap, covers most of the floor and I see no way of disarming it," John announced, stepping back and shaking his head.

"The spots between the lines I can see are big enough for two of us at a time, so perhaps we try and make it to that door without triggering them?" Knox reasoned.

The door he spoke of was barely visible behind the titan-sized monster. It stood as tall as Terrim times two with the ceiling being three times Terrim's height.

"Dog and I will go last," Beth said, Knox turned and gave her a nod.

She stood proudly with her massive wolf in the back with a bow drawn and arrow nocked. She was ready to fight and would likely be the first to strike out when and if combat began, but Knox worried that her ever-growing wolf would be too big to fit in the spaces that would only fit two people standing abreast.

"Have Dog hang back, I doubt the two of you will fit in a

space together, just have him follow one step after you," Knox suggested.

"You heard him, fat boy," Beth said, stroking Dog's head, he leaned into it and eyed Knox with all too intelligent eyes.

The wolf had grown to the size of a small bear in the weeks following his taming. It was like the creature grew stronger along with Beth, which meant there was no telling how big he'd eventually get. He was already big enough that she might be able to ride him, which gave him an interesting mental image of her sitting astride him while jumping from spot to spot.

Knox went first, jumping to a spot and indicating where Terrim should land. His large friend made it perfectly into the spot he'd meant for him and soon they were four spots in and halfway across the floor. Dog finally jumped into the first spot, and he was just small enough to fit, his feet narrowly missing touching the edges. The way he adjusted his feet gave Knox pause, it was almost as if he could sense where the lines were as well. Smart Dog, or uh wolf.

They were only five feet from the mighty guardian, a being made of thousands of strands of wood with thorns coming out in odd angles and wielding a mighty axe. Now that they were so close, he could make out that the creature was almost entirely made of vines and thorns, which oddly enough looked similar to the patterns they were avoiding on the ground.

"Shit," John said, and suddenly a flash of light went off behind Knox.

He turned just in time to see vines reach up out of the ground and cover John's leg that had hit one of the invisible lines they'd been avoiding. Of all the people to trigger the trap, John was the last on Knox's list, but there they were.

A mighty roar echoed, and the ground flared, the light seemed to retract as the trap faded. The strands of power pulled themselves into the guardian and suddenly it had eyes of white flaring with as much power as had been on the ground, trapping them.

John was just getting his leg free when the golem of vines and thorns came to life, swinging his axe in several slow testing motions. It lumbered forward, letting off another shout as it came forward.

"Terrim," Knox shouted, but Terrim was already moving forward, his shield raised.

The battle was on, and they took their normal formation as they prepared. Knox, for once during the dungeon, let Terrim take the lead against the mighty foe.

Before the monster could so much as take another step, a half dozen arrows blazing with fire smashed into it and set it ablaze. The vines withered at the touch of fire, and it let out a mighty scream of pain, but that didn't stop it from attacking, its axe lifted and ready to strike.

The vine guardian, what Knox had named the monster in his mind, lunged forward. His mighty swing smashed against Terrim's shield and Knox heard a faint cracking sound from the crystalline shield that Terrim used, but it held. He pushed back and the monster staggered.

Taking the opportunity to attack, Knox cast Lustrous Chains, hoping to slow down the already lumbering monster. Chains of golden and white light sprung up and wrapped up the monster. It roared again and Knox brought a hand up to his head to shield his ears from the overbearing sound. The spell held long enough for another barrage of arrows to ignite the vines on the monster, Beth using her special abilities to burn into it.

Dog came lumbering around the right side, catching hold of the vine guardian's weapon arm, wrenching the weapon free from its grasp.

Leo took this opportunity to strike out with his powerful flame attacks, each one heating the air around them as it came spiraling up from the ceiling and down on the unsuspecting monster. Henry could be heard in the distance, chanting healing spells as the fight progressed. John appeared behind the massive monster, his daggers slashing out with powerful strokes, attempting to hamstring it.

The monster thrashed back and forth under the restraints of the chains, each movement breaking a strand here and there. Knox launched out a powerful Luminous Surge just as the final chains broke away, and the beast shook itself free. The power gathered around him like a veil of energy before releasing in a blast, knocking the monster back a step.

A sudden yelp of pain brought Knox's attention to Dog, who'd been covered in vines and thorns, slowly being crushed to death. Pulling free his axe, Knox rushed forward, using Ethereal Step to teleport forward and strike down with all his power. His strike rang true, and he cut the arm free, just below the elbow, of the monster and freed Dog.

As if in thanks, another half dozen arrows rained down all over the vine guardian, each one infused with power and blowing away sizable chunks. Beth called out, and suddenly, Dog howled. There was an energy surrounding him as he grew even bigger, if only for a moment or two. With his newfound size, the wolf smashed back into the fray.

It was a testament to each of their power and accuracy that they avoided hitting each other as they traded blows back and forth with the monster. Dog would jump back just as fire consumed the monster, John would appear at Dog's side slashing out with his powerful daggers as the wolf dug into the vines and thorns with his teeth.

It was a dance of death and Knox's party was winning. That was, until the vines of the monster seemed to relax, and the creature turned into less of a humanoid figure, and more a tangle and blob of vines and thorns. It spread out, entangling each of them, slamming their bodies against the walls and pillars that made up the room.

Then, just as quickly as it had lost form, it solidified back into a humanoid shape, leaving all of them tied up in vines that had separated from the main body. However, Knox noticed something in that moment, the creature had lost much of its height, as if getting attacked and using that attack had diminished it in some way.

Half the party had already cut themselves free, Knox was the first, just teleporting out of the snare, but Dog was struggling, and the monster moved to bisect the wolf with its axe.

"Not today," Knox said, rushing forward and using Dimensional Shift to switch places with Dog. His own axe came up and he caught the mighty blow from the monster as it came down. The weapon rang in his hands, and he struggled to keep his grip as the attack rattled him to the core.

Not wasting a moment, he used Nexus Shift to put himself behind the monster, leaving behind a flash of white light, disorienting his opponent. He slashed down with his axe, taking the monster right in the back and slicing through its ever-weakening vines and thorns.

Jumping back as heat grew ahead of it, Knox cast Reality Ripple to slow his opponent just as Leo's powerful flames consumed it. With the slowness affecting the monster, it struggled to put out the flames.

Suddenly, something gave, and it spread out once more, trying to entangle them. But with the slow effect activate, it didn't expand fast enough. Knox activated Solar Wings to get height, slashing away vines as they reached for him and readying another spell.

His Radiant Glyph spell took only a second or two to activate, and he used it to call down flames and control what was already there. The fire that Leo called down continued to flow and Knox empowered it, condensing it to a heat so powerful that the monster didn't stand a chance. It withered and died only moments later with a slow groan of pain.

Landing lightly on the ground beside his party, Knox checked that everyone was okay. Henry was struggling to untie himself, but otherwise everyone was doing good.

"Where's the map say to go now?" Terrim asked as he examined his shield for permanent damage. It was a powerful artifact that could reflect magic, but in this situation, it was only useful as a generic shield, as the monster hadn't had any projection magical spells.

"Oh, the map," Knox said, remembering that he had a map that they were meant to follow.

He drew it out from his side pouch, along with the key, and looked down at it. It was a magical map, that much was for sure, as it showed six little ink dots and a basic layout of the room they were in, including a red dot that had been crossed out just in front of them where the monster lay. A series of small dashes led to the side, away from the door that Knox had assumed was the way forward.

"Well shit," Knox cursed, looking up sheepishly from the map. "According to this there is a hidden doorway over here," Knox moved to the wall and began to feel on it for any signs of a door, his hand slipped through solid stone a pace or two into his search. "And here it is. We didn't have to fight that guy after all."

A series of exaggerated sighs and a few curses followed, but Knox just shrugged. He'd enjoyed the challenge and in the moment of combat he'd all but forgotten his loss.

They fought off smaller versions of the vine guardian as they went, following the map, but nothing that was a difficult challenge. It seemed like the dungeon Tower wasn't going to be very difficult if they just followed the map, which really tempted Knox to go off course, at least a little. But he held his temptations back and led them higher and higher, until finally they reached a room filled with mirrors.

"The map says we should go in, but my sense tells me that those mirrors are powerful artifacts. Should we have Beth shoot them from afar before we enter?" Knox suggested.

"If they are as powerful as you claim, I doubt an arrow would do the trick, but give it a try," Leo said, shrugging.

"Beth," Knox said, she sighed as she walked forward, taking aim.

A single arrow shot forward and hit the nearest mirror, bouncing off harmlessly.

"Looks like we are doing this the hard way," Knox said, stepping forward and entering the room.

The floor was made of stone, but it reflected almost as well as the dozens of mirrors on the walls, reaching up some thirty paces. Each mirror was ornate with curls and curves of silver metal. The light in the room came from candles all around and a single bright white light that came from the moon outside, flowing through a massive window in the ceiling. It was like they were at the top, but according to the map they still had a ways to go. This was a tricky Tower, that much was clear.

The map said to go straight through the room to a massive reflective door that was almost as much mirror as it was door. But as Knox stepped forward and into the space where two of the mirrors could see him, he noticed movement. Out of the two closest mirrors stepped out two copies of himself, each one with a wicked grin on their face. The fact that Knox himself wasn't grinning was the first thing that caught him off guard, the second was the fact that the figures had walked free of the mirror and pulled out axes.

According to his sense, these copies weren't at all as powerful as he was, but they had a measure of his power and he needed to be careful.

"Here to drown your sorrows, silly human. Don't you know that pain is an eternal and beautiful emotion?" One of his copies said, but not in his voice, instead it was a menacing, slightly nasally voice. Who could this be, Knox immediately wondered.

"Careful," Knox said over his shoulder as his party members entered to see what was happening. "The mirrors will copy you, so be careful or we might be overrun."

"I can see that," John said, rushing to the front of the group. "Let's get copies of me," he declared, stepping up next to Knox.

The first two mirrors didn't shift or change, each one not even reflecting his image at all. Knox reasoned it must only copy the first person to come in contact with it or perhaps it had some kind of recharge time.

"Let's kick my ass and finish this Tower," Knox said, raising his hand just as blue armor appeared around each of his copies.

Knox's twins pulled out their axes and immediately disappeared. Knox couldn't help but groan in frustration as they reappeared in front of him, swinging down at him. He used Dimensional Shift on one of them the moment they appeared, causing one to get axed right in the chest while the other smashed his axe down harmlessly. That hit alone was enough to do the trick and the figure shattered into pieces before them.

Knox turned and hit the attacking target the moment he'd shifted positions, and he ended its short life as well. That ended up not being such a big problem as he thought it might be, Knox mused.

"Guess they are pretty weak," Knox said, then the mirrors shimmered and two more copies of him appeared. "Shit."

Realizing the mirrors must have a short recharge period, Knox signaled for his group to charge forward toward the door, all of them reacting instantly as he ran forward triggering all five of the mirrors at once. Instead of ten sets of Knox, like he'd thought might happen, it picked John, Leo, Beth, and Dog to copy next.

Surrounded but out of range of the mirrors after a short run, the battle was on. Outnumbered as they were, Knox felt a rush enter him at the thought of how challenging it might be.

Two copies of Dog rushed for him just as Beth got attacked by a teleporting copy of Knox. The battle was chaos and Knox had to focus on what was in front of him if he wanted to stay ahead of it. The only real plus side to this fight was how easy these copies went down.

Knox held out a hand and cast Luminous Surge, thinking to

take two down at a time, but he learned something about mirror copies in that moment, they reflected magic. His attack came rushing back at him and if not for his natural defenses against light, it might have really hurt. As it was, he needed to call this new information out to his group, but he struggled to find a moment to do it as four figures, two canines and two Terrim's came for him.

Knox heard Leo scream in surprise and pain as one of his spells backfired and soon came a call for no magic.

"No magical attacks!" Leo cried out, swinging his staff in an expert display of finesse as he shattered a mirror version of Beth to pieces as she leveled her bow at the real Beth.

Back and forth they fought, Knox throwing back Terrim's giant form and following up with a slash that it caught on its shield, preventing it from shattering. It was a fierce fight, but Knox was winning as he shattered the final Dog copy and faced off against the two Terrim's.

"Hold onto your pain," said the same voice as before. "In it you will find true peace."

"Just die!" Knox screamed back at the Terrim copy, slicing low and shattering its foot. From there it was an easy slash to the side to end it. But this gave the next one an opening and it slammed its very solid shield right into the side of Knox's face, throwing him backward in a daze.

Recovering just as Terrim's mirror weapon came down on his head, Knox was surprised and relieved to find the real Terrim appear and take the blow on his shield.

"You got nothing on me," shouted Terrim, slamming his own shield against the mirror copy and shattering it. He followed up by striking out with his own axe and ending the replica.

From there, it was just a matter of cleaning up as Terrim and Knox went from copy to copy and ended them before too long. Leo's was tricky, throwing fire here and there, but with Terrim's shield absorbing it, there was an opening that Beth took, killing the fragile glass copy.

"I think we are nearing the end," Knox said, the map showing them a corridor beyond and what looked like might be a staircase, the first one they'd encountered so far.

Knox was mostly right as it turned out. They fought more monsters, dealt with some traps, but eventually reached a staircase that led them up and up and up. Eventually, they reached a magnificent door covered in runic carvings and glowed with a fierce light.

Holding the key out in front of him, the door flashed and slid slowly open, revealing the room within.

It was massive, that was the first thing that Knox saw, but as he stepped in and really looked, he was taken aback by the overwhelming magic that lay within, his sense feeling overwhelmed by it.

At the top of the Tower on the ceiling was a swirling vortex of power, blue energy so dense and lively that it was creating little arcane figures that swirled around with it. All over the room on the walls, floor, and even the parts of the ceiling that could be seen, were runic formations that glowed with a powerful blazing blue light.

"Get in here and be ready," Knox said over his shoulder as the figures swirling above by the vortex began to swish through the air slowly down toward them. They were some type of arcane elementals with immense magical powers behind them, though it was hard to be certain, Knox admitted to himself, as his sense was so overwhelmed by the central vortex.

One of the arcane elementals, swirling with its own blue power and in the shape of a cloaked figure, swished lower and Beth let loose an arrow at it, but the arrow passed right through it.

"Might be resistant to physical attacks," Beth said, shooting again but infusing her arrow with one of her special abilities. It flew out and exploded just as it made contact. However, instead of dissipating the arcane elemental, the spectral beast grew larger.

"They can absorb magic," Leo announced as he saw what had happened.

"Then what do we do?" Knox asked. Physical and magical attacks were all they had.

"I don't know," Leo admitted. "But someone better work it out quick."

Terrim raised his shield as one swooped low and activated its special ability. It sucked in the arcane elemental, or at least a portion of it, before it broke off, leaving it smaller than it was before.

"Get behind Terrim," Knox called out. They had a single item that could absorb magic, but it had a limit before he'd have to expel it, so it wasn't the fix he was looking for.

What could he do? There had to be a way through this, the dungeon always provided a way.

Dodging back and forth, Terrim did his best to fend off the arcane elementals, but Beth took a hit and was thrown bodily back into the wall. When she touched the wall, the runes flared, and she screamed. Henry chanted to heal her as she took a double dose of intense arcane damage.

"Think," Knox said, speaking to himself as he racked his brain. He looked at the map, but it didn't show anything of use, so he thought back to what the mysterious man had said. Was there anything in his words that would be useful now? He'd said something about giving and conquering...

"What did that old man say about the top floor?" Knox asked Leo as he teleported around a stray arcane elemental—they were multiplying now and getting harder to avoid.

"Give and you shall conquer," Leo said. "But what must we give so that we can conquer?"

"Stupid riddles are going to get us killed," Knox said, taking a glancing blow and being thrown back a step or two.

Leo cried out as two of the arcane elementals came at him at once, he had no choice but to attack them to get them to back off and they gladly sucked up his fire power, converting it to new mass that they could use against the party in further strikes.

"Let's try to overload one of them, you ready Leo?" Knox asked, meeting his friend's eyes.

He nodded and Knox pointed to an already large arcane elemental, indicating that it was to be their target. He summoned up his power and cast Luminous Surge with as much power as he could manage, short of taking a restraint ring off. It blasted forth and enveloped the target just as flames poured down from the ceiling onto the same arcane elemental. There was a screech of what Knox could only call pleasure as the arcane elemental grew several times its normal size.

"Give it all you can!" Knox screamed, casting the spell again and again, while maintaining each cast for as long as possible.

The specter grew and grew until it was a massive formless blob of power nearly as large as the vortex above. Only then did they finally cut off the power. Something had happened during their attack that caught Knox's interest. Some of the fire and his own light attack had hit the vortex. The effect of which had an opposite effect than the arcane elementals, the vortex seemed to shrink in power just a tiny bit. It was so small that Knox almost disregarded the fluctuation, but now he wasn't so sure it was worth ignoring.

Wanting to test his theory, he shot forth an Arcane Pulse into the vortex and, sure enough, it began to close, if ever so slightly.

"We had it wrong," Knox called out over the din of battle. "Throw everything you have at the vortex, anyone with anything remotely resembling magic, you too Beth, hit it hard!"

Now it became a dance for time and against death as the arcane elementals went into a frenzy, striking out each chance they got.

Strike after nasty strike, they took hits and Henry healed, even going so far as to summon his Guardian to help him heal when

Leo took a really bad hit from the massive arcane elemental they'd created. But slowly, one spell at a time, the vortex began to close until it was only a single pace wide. Then it began to suck back in the arcane elementals, growing bigger as it did so. But Knox knew that they were a match for the expansion, and they continued to hit it with their own spells until they couldn't cast even a single spell more. It had done the trick, the vortex closed with a tiny popping sound and the room went from a wild winding sound to an eerie silence.

CHAPTER 5
PREPARATIONS TO LEAVE

THE LOOT they got wasn't worth mentioning, despite the fanfare of the last room. They'd cycle it to others and call it good when they returned to the village, except for a pair of earrings that John was keen on keeping that allowed the user to slip into shadows and teleport to another shadow on a short cooldown. With the loot settled and the dungeon finished, they made their way back to their basecamp at the start of the dungeon.

"Shame we didn't get much decent loot," Terrim said, his first time through this dungeon hadn't provided him much of anything worth keeping. Knox did see him eying a shield that had a way to stick into the ground with a small trigger, but his magic reflecting shield was just too powerful to switch out right now.

"We've just grown too powerful for this dungeon, despite how hard a time we had with the last room, I think we need to find a more difficult dungeon if we want to progress much more," Leo said, his voice warm and friendly.

Knox heard them but wasn't really listening. He'd hoped that going through the dungeon would allow him to vent some of the emptiness he felt inside from the loss of Sarah and the others that fell, but it didn't. He felt the same, but he made a decision right there while looking at Beth and the rest of his friends. He couldn't do everything to save everyone, but he'd try his damnedest to make sure no more of his friends fell.

If nothing else, he had to accept, as he'd always been taught, that death was just a part of life. With that mental confirmation of the events and his part to play in them, he felt something give. It was slight and it wouldn't be a perfect fix, but he allowed himself to feel the grief and pain that came with their loss. He wasn't ashamed to admit that right in that moment he cried silent tears in remembrance of those who had fallen, while swearing an oath to himself that he would do all he could to save those he still could.

Life was not easy, sometimes it seemed damn near impossible, but he was alive and so he could do something about it. The meaning of their saying, 'to death' really hit him now as he considered his life. He would do all he could to the end, to death, nothing would stop him from protecting those he loved and cared about.

"Let's get back," Knox said, covertly wiping away his tears. "I've got a trip to plan and preparations to attend to."

"You feeling okay?" Beth asked; her question was spoken in a bare whisper of her normal volume, making sure Knox was the only one to hear her.

"I am," Knox said confidently. "Thank you." He put a hand around her and pulled her into a welcoming hug.

They held each other for a long moment, each one enjoying the warmth of the other.

The packing of their little camp took no time at all and soon they were exiting the dungeon. The guard gave them a polite nod as they left, and Knox gave out instructions for supplies to purchase. Each of them left to do their part to prepare for the two-day trip back to Luminar.

The trip took less time than it should have, Knox pushed the group hard, resting less than they had on the way there and running at faster speeds than before. In a day and a half, they arrived outside the gate to see that it had all been repaired. Mic found Knox almost immediately, pulling him aside to talk.

"You must do something about Ramses," Mic said, he'd barely let Knox enter the complex before assailing him.

"What about?" Knox asked, remembering the conversation they'd had before he left.

He'd told Mic all about Ramses' idea to merge their Titan Engines and do the same with the Darkness Titan if she would cooperate or after they installed a new Titan Born. Mic had been for the idea, saying that the spread of the system wasn't meant to just be a generalized area of effect, that at least six Titan Engines needed to be active to cover the entire planet. This had come as a surprise to Knox, to imagine that there were six other Titan Born out there someplace, or at least there had been at some point.

How many had died like the previous Titan of Light? That just brought more questions to his mind that he needed answers to, like who had killed the last Titan of Light and how? A sword to the chest hardly seemed like a proper way to kill such a powerful being. If Mic hadn't destroyed both the armor and the sword for materials without asking him, he might have a better way to investigate the murder, but as it was now, it might remain a mystery.

According to what he'd learned in the Labyrinth, there were at least six types of Titans or at least the guardians appeared to be those six types. Life, Light, Death, Darkness, Water, and Fire, but that didn't mean there weren't even more, according to Mic. Each Titan revolved around a concept of divinity or elemental power.

Mic had answered Knox, but he'd missed it, so he raised his head and focused on the golem. "Say that again, sorry."

"He's been making more changes to our Titan Engine than I think is necessary, trying to focus the expansion in a single direction. I told him that with time and power it'll spread naturally, but he's intent on it connecting to his within a month or less. He must know that you can't push the Titan Engine too hard without enough power!"

"Is it going to be damaged?" Knox asked, feeling a touch of worry himself. If Ramses broke his Titan Engine, what would that mean for the system and his connection with it.

"Well, no, the Titan Engine is an artifact of the Titan Gowlen, even a fully-fledged Titan would have trouble undoing its purpose, but he is upsetting the balance, and I don't like it," Mic said. "Besides, he's not telling me everything he's doing. I'm the resident Titan Engine expert, not him."

"So, he's leaving you out and it's upsetting you?" Knox said, a smirk forming on his face. It was such a human petty thing that he'd almost thought Mic might be above it, being a golem and all. But no, just like everyone else, he had feelings that could get hurt.

"Yes!" Mic said, agreeing with Knox completely. "Make him stop."

"If he isn't hurting anything, I don't mind the waters being converted to the system before we reach further inland. In fact, it might be good for now. Gives us time to grow stronger before more people learn of the system," Knox said.

It was true that he'd been worried about the system expanding into a more populated area and the chaos it might create, but he'd assumed that there wasn't another way, so this was actually welcomed news.

"But, but—" Mic said, but Knox walked past him, eager to get the preparations started for the journey that lay ahead.

He had decided on his trip back that a smaller group would be best to accomplish their goal, he just had to decide on how many he'd bring with him. Obviously, he wanted to bring his closest friends, but he had to think about who had the skillsets that would be needed on this quest.

To that end, he began speaking to all of the people around to find out any who might have connections within the city. Clearly, he had Draven and his family as a potential connection, but he also learned that John was from the city as well. Ultimately, he decided on taking Draven, John, Dernal—because the man refused to be left behind—and the dark elf Sintra.

She claimed to have an object of her own that would help to contain the power of the artifact, a sort of covering, and Knox took her on her word about it.

With a party decided they made preparations and set a day to be off. Knox avoided saying any long goodbyes, fully intending that they should return before long. Instead, he sought out John to ask him more about his experience with the city and what he offered the group.

"I'm in tight with several local business owners," John said, smiling. "I mean, they know of me at least. It had been a few seasons before I went to the city, but I was born and raised there, and you never forget the place you come from."

"So, how much trouble will we have slipping in unnoticed, do you think?" Knox asked, getting to the crux of why he wanted to ask about the city. "What can you tell me about their defenses?"

"I mean, besides a guard at the gate doing cursory checks, I doubt a few travelers will be noticed. Besides all that, we are Adventurers, and we are given a fair bit of latitude when traveling," John said.

Knox nodded along, not knowing that about Adventurers but understanding it all the same. When you had a civilization that had folk who could do miraculous things, you might tend to treat them with a touch more respect and leeway. They could also go the other way, which is why Knox was asking and finding out as much as he could. He'd already spoken to Draven and gotten some information, but despite court gossip and the movements of his noble house, he knew precious little.

"What about the war going on? Will that likely make traveling, even for Adventurers, a bit harder?" Knox asked, remembering what he'd learned in the past months leading up to his village splitting and half becoming refugees.

"There's another war on?" John asked, seeming legitimately

surprised. "That is a whole different beast. They'll be wanting to recruit Adventurers and offering steep rewards for us to fight in their armies. I'm sure we will still be alright, but don't be alarmed when they start offering you thousands of gold to fight on the front lines. One of us is at least as good as several dozen fighting men." Then, looking Knox up and down, he amended his words. "For you, likely a good hundred or more fighting men."

"Doesn't the guild stop Adventurers from interfering with conflicts? I thought Dernal said that at one point?" Knox asked in return.

"They discourage us, but they can't outright forbid it—too much money in the endeavor. So instead, they tax the hell out of our earnings. It's a good half they want to keep whenever we take a contract," John said.

"Squeezing their earnings seems like a good way to stop all but the most determined from participating," Knox said, understanding a bit more.

"That's just it," John said, smirking as he spoke. "Over the years they've increased the amount paid to make up for the costs, so it still isn't half bad work. If you can stomach the killing."

"That just brings me back to my first point," Knox said. "How easy will it be or won't be to get into the city now?"

Another voice from behind Knox, he'd felt him coming, spoke out over the buzz of conversation in the mess hall. "With me at your side you needn't worry." It was Draven who spoke, and Knox turned to regard the man.

He wore polished armor that shone with the glow of enchantments, even a few that's only purpose seemed to be to glow and look flashy. It was impractical in battle or any type of stealth quest, but it did put on quite a show.

He had dark purple eyes and black hair cut close on the sides with the top left long and pulled up into a bun, not all too dissimilar to how Dernal wore his. When he looked at you it was always with a sternness that didn't fit his overall tone of voice but seemed his natural way of looking at people.

"Even so," Knox said, "I'm not sure I want to announce to the noble house that I'm here to take away their prized artifact."

Draven snorted at that, sitting beside John and leaning over to speak. "Any can challenge the Tower, it'll be a surprise to all if you return, as none have in the recorded history of the city. But none will bar your path to making an attempt. In fact, they might throw you a feast in preparation for the attempt."

That was news to Knox, and he needed to know more. Before he could speak, John interjected.

"He's right, my second cousin attempted it, and he was far stronger than I ever could have hoped to be. They threw him a party and everything before he vanished inside. He never came out of course, no one does," John said.

"Then how does my mother fit into all of this?" Knox asked, looking specifically at Draven as he spoke.

"She's the guardian of the door, so to speak," Draven said. "Her blood or her bloodline at least, is required to open the door, but don't go spilling that to just anyone." Draven shot a look at John that said, 'keep your flaps shut' and John just smirked all the harder.

"So, my blood will open the door?" Knox asked, trying to understand.

"Not your blood, but it has something to do with your bloodline," Draven said. "When her father passed, she took up the mantle. It is a great honor, but one my uncle is worried about, as she didn't have any known children and she's refused to take any suitors. Court gossip says that soon she'll be forced to wed and produce heirs if she doesn't make the choice herself soon. Not sure how they'll manage that, as only my uncle is strong enough to challenge her now. If only they knew that she had an heir, and he was likely stronger than her, or close to it now."

"You'll keep my secret?" Knox asked, hoping he knew the answer to the question.

"You've earned my trust several times over, but I'm afraid court gossip has gotten out to a certain extent since our last meeting. You look so strikingly similar to your mother in so many ways. You are all but expected to arrive and take over her mantle at this point."

Knox put his head in his hands for a moment, thinking. Perhaps he could use this to his advantage, perhaps he ought to lean into the 'taking over the mantle' business. Or perhaps none of it mattered because whatever he would face within this 'Tower' they spoke of, might be too much for him after all.

"Can a challenger for the Tower bring a party in with them?" Knox asked, looking for further clarification.

"No," John said, speaking before Draven had a chance to say a word.

"He's right," Draven said. "It is meant to be a challenge that only one can take, but there have been a few instances of parties entering, however, their fate remains the same, missing in action."

"And when I successfully remove the artifact from the Tower?" Knox asked, though both of them only shrugged at that question.

"Never happened before, so I couldn't tell you," John said.

"In theory, you'd be set up as the reigning king of Lumisar and none should be able to stand against you or your power. In fact, I don't know that the noble houses, my own included, would hand over power so easily," Draven said.

"We leave at dawn. Draven, I am trusting in you to keep my identity a secret, for now. Please don't break my trust," Knox said, eying the larger man with searching eyes.

He seemed to be a man of honor, as far as Knox had experienced, fighting alongside them when the pirate horde had come. You could learn a lot about a person when battling beside them during the fight of their lives.

"You are sure you want to go?" Knox asked Sintra for the second time.

"It is my duty to my people, I do not fear the uplanders' cities or the light," Sintra said, her voice defiant as if Knox had asked her something extremely personal and she was offended to answer.

"We've had little chance to get to know each other yet, but I am relying on you," Knox said, he'd come to try and work out what exactly they had that would 'contain' the artifact, but so far, he'd not been able to get to that topic of conversation.

"As are we," she said, inclining her head. "My people have left the safety of the dark to stand in the light with you. Though it is uncomfortable, we will do all that is required to bring peace to our people and overthrow the evil that has taken root in the heart of my kingdom."

Not for the first time, Knox wondered if he was doing the right thing, believing her and helping her people. He knew she was being truthful, he could just feel it, and he trusted his instincts, but still, basic reason told him there was probably something he wasn't being told, some part of the story being left out.

But he also knew that she wouldn't be the one to tell him, not yet at least, and that was part of why he wanted to bring her along. If he could get to know her more, learn to trust her word and her actions, then he'd know whether or not she'd be safe to fight at his back.

"The item you said can contain the power of the artifact; you are sure it is up to the task?" Knox finally just asked the question that had been burning into his mind. "Perhaps you'd let me examine it?"

Her eyes flicked over Knox but lingered on his eyes. She sighed and nodded. "I believe I can trust you, do not touch it, but you may gaze upon it if you truly wish. But be warned, this device can only withstand the power of the artifact for a period of time, you'll need to master it before we come against the great darkness."

With that, she pulled out a simple sphere from her pouch at her side and Knox examined it with his sense. There was a distinct lack of anything around the sphere and Knox strained his sense to the limit, trying to piece whatever veil the object had, but failed. It was like staring into nothingness, not a single runic formation or drop of power could be felt from the object. So much so, that it even seemed to draw in power from around it, blacking that out as well.

"Fascinating," Knox said, reaching out to try and touch it.

She pulled away at first, but then seemed to think better of it, holding it out for him to touch. When his hand touched the surface, he felt a great coldness wash over him and he immediately drew back. That was when he noticed she wore a glove that shone with powerful magical runic formations, but it had been hard to notice against the sheer pull of the nothingness.

"You truly are as you say," she said, seeming surprised as Knox withdrew his hand and shook it, the coldness vanishing a moment later. "Anything less than a Titan touching it would have been laid out for a day or longer. You are the answer to our prayers."

"It tried to sap away my power," Knox remarked, realizing what had happened.

"It is made of an extremely rare mineral found within our kingdom," she said. "So rare that it doesn't have a name in our tongue, only called nothing or the nothingness. I am its guardian for now, but should I fall, do not let it touch your skin for very long, for even a Titan has limits."

"Why not use this metal against the Dark Titan, drain her of her power and kill her?" Knox asked the question that seemed like an obvious answer to their dilemma.

"We tried, but she is powerful beyond imagination," Sintra said. "Arrows and spears made of the metal were not enough to do more than anger her. I lost my army to one such attempt, their souls taken to feed her ever growing power."

"What hope do I have to take her down then?" Knox asked more to himself than to her.

"I found not one but two Titans," Sintra said, smiling softly, a gesture Knox had not seen from her before. "Have faith in your power and I believe you will succeed."

There were two of them now, but Ramses had been very vague in his answers when asked if he'd help take down the Dark Titan, saying only that there needed to be one at all times, so that if she was overthrown, someone new would need to take her place. With that thought in mind, Knox bid her farewell and sought out Ramses for a final question or two.

"Are you sure you won't come?" Knox asked, he'd found Ramses in the Titan Engine room, tinkering away as he'd done since awakening.

"I'm very busy and if I'm understanding the situation correctly, you'll need me here to defend your Engine from assault while you are away. Who knows who might try and usurp your power while you are gone. The Titan of Light must not fall again," Ramses said, barely looking over his shoulder as he worked.

"Take a break and really talk to me," Knox said, putting a hand on the frail looking old man's shoulders. "The complex will be safe enough under Mic's watch, we could really use a being as powerful as you."

"My power," Ramses said, turning to look Knox full in the face, "is severely limited this far from my own Titan Engine. You will do good to remember that fact when you leave your own seat of power. Our Titan Engines have a multiplying effect on our power output, though, from what I've seen you've barely tapped into that potential. So, you might be alright since you don't rely so heavily on that power as I do."

"And that will be fixed once you connect our Titan Engines?"

Knox asked, leaning against the Titan Engine and feeling a warmth push into him while doing so.

"In part," Ramses said. "More than that, it will enable me to transport myself back and forth with ease. I'm operating at less than half my original strength, but even so, I could match you in power. You would do well to stay here and learn your true potential, instead of chasing fairytales and myths."

This was new, Ramses hadn't asked him to stay behind before and Knox wondered at what had changed in his opinion of him.

"I have to go," Knox said, and he meant it in more ways than one. He needed to go to retrieve this object that Sintra had spoken of, but also because he needed to see his mother. It was a deep and raw need for answers that pushed him forward.

His own emotions about what or how he'd react when actually finding his mother were mixed, but he knew that it was something he had to resolve. There was a measure of excitement, but also sorrow and pain. She'd basically abandoned him, and whether or not it was for his own good, as she might have seen it, it didn't take away the pain of the abandonment.

A part of him had always wished that perhaps she was still alive, and she had good reason for staying away. Perhaps fighting an endless war against a force that meant him harm or some other fairytale ending, but to learn she was in a city only a month's journey away, through the pass, and into the flatlands, it hurt to think about.

"You alright?" Ramses asked. "You zoned out there for a moment."

"I'll be alright, but if you aren't going, I should leave. I've got preparations to make," Knox said, turning and leaving the room.

CHAPTER 6
JOURNEY TO CIVILIZATION

AETEX, despite not being invited along, stood waiting for the small group as they gathered outside the wall to depart with a pack of his own on his back.

"You thought to leave without me?" Aetex asked and Knox avoided his intense gaze.

"I need you to stay here and keep the city safe," Knox said, finally looking up to meet Aetex's intense stare.

"I go where I am needed and I have only a single master that I serve," Aetex said cheerily. "In this, I can see clearly where I must go."

"Fine," Knox said, shaking his head. He couldn't stop the man from coming any more than he could stop water from seeping out of his cupped hands. Aetex was an inevitability that he should just learn to accept, so he did so.

"I will scout out ahead and rid us of any interruptions," Aetex said, and with that, he turned and shot off into the sky. How the man managed to fly was a continuous mystery to Knox, but he did it with such ease that it must be some innate ability he possessed and not a skill that he activated.

"That... man, is powerful in a way I can't quite understand,"

Sintra said, standing beside Knox looking more nervous than he'd have imagined her getting.

"Are you sure you want to come along?" Knox asked for a final time. Sintra had talked long and hard with her people to convince them, they'd wanted to send guards with her, but she insisted that Knox was all the guard she needed.

In answer, Sintra just looked at him and leveled a heavy gaze. Knox put his hands up and made a show of closing his mouth. He wouldn't ask again, at least not today.

"Wait up!" Came a voice, and Knox turned to see Terrim and a decent-sized group of people behind him. "We wanted to say goodbye, but you snuck out before we could throw you a proper party."

Frederick, Beth, Murdoch, Henry, and a few others trailed behind Terrim and Knox smiled at seeing his friends wanting to see him off.

"I don't have time for a sincere goodbye for all of you, so, see ya!" Knox called out, then made a show of turning to leave.

Terrim wrapped him in a powerful bear hug from behind and Knox lost the breath in his lungs as he was picked up and placed in front of his friends.

"You don't get away that easy," Beth said, stepping forward as Terrim released Knox. She put her hands on Knox's chest and leaned in, giving him a sweet but gentle kiss on the lips. "Be safe." Her words were breathy and slow as she stared into Knox's eyes.

"I will," Knox said, grabbing hold of her hands and squeezing them.

"I won't kiss you, but trust that the spirits around you will see you safely returned," Frederick said, chuckling a bit as Beth stepped aside.

One at a time, everyone said their goodbyes and Knox gave them each the time they deserved, thanking them and waiting for the final one before he could leave. Terrim made a joke about this or that and left Knox laughing until he saw the person in the back that he hadn't noticed, his father, Askar.

"I'm shit at this stuff," Askar started, but Knox was barely listening, his emotions toward his father so uncertain. "But when you see Scarlet, tell her I tried my best. That I kept you safe for as long as I could. That I miss her."

Knox looked at his father and for once he saw not the man that had been his father, unruly and filled with anger over what he considered a bad lot in life, but instead, he saw a man who'd loved a woman and had been, in his own way, betrayed by her. A bitter man who had only wanted to live his life but was forced to give it all up for a child he'd never asked for. Knox felt a measure of sympathy for the man, but as he was that child that hadn't been wanted, he couldn't fully empathize with him.

"I'll give her your regards," Knox said coldly, barely looking at the man for fear that he might lose his temper.

"And boy," Askar said, his voice turning a touch harsh as he spoke, getting Knox to look up glaring. "Be safe." His voice not matching the words he spoke at all.

Knox couldn't help but smile at the ridiculousness of it all. "I will," he finally said, turning and bidding his friends and family farewell.

The journey into the Shadowfall Swamp's borders was swift, as all present could run at a speed and maintain it that would have a horse panting for breath. By the end of the first day, they'd reached the edge of the swamps, or what was left of them, and into the forest surrounding them. Truth be told, the swamps were slowly becoming a lush green forest, filled with minor monsters and solid ground, all the water being soaked up by trees that grew much too fast.

Knox knew that it had to do with the Titan Engine and the spread of the System, turning the area around the city into a more hospitable place for training-up those within it. Truly, it was amazing how the very ground could be changed to meet the requirements of the System. Aetex joined them as they made camp for the first night, finding a grove of trees that would provide sufficient cover from the on and off again showers of rain they'd been getting.

Realizing that he didn't really know what season it was anymore, he turned to John to ask him that very question.

"What season are we in now?" Knox asked. "Luminar seemed to be in a perpetual spring of sorts, but these rains speak otherwise."

Dernal answered before John could speak.

"Hhrmm," Dernal said. "Nearly summer by my reckoning."

"He's right," John said, twirling a dagger in his hands. "And I've got several missed appointments with my summer maidens down in the flatlands. You know I normally take all of the summer off to relax, so I hope you had a decent payment in mind for my help."

Not knowing if John was just teasing or being serious about payment, Knox took out his coin purse and jingled it. "I've plenty of coin to pay you if that is what you wish?"

"I jest, I jest," John said, then eying the purse he motioned that Knox ought to toss it over. He did so and John poured out a dozen or so coins into his hands. "For the essentials that I might require during the trip, nothing more."

"Hhrmm," Dernal said, and for a moment, Knox thought John might put the coins back, but instead, he purposely didn't look at Dernal when throwing the coin purse back to Knox.

Knox had a combination of gold coins and Runemarks, as well as his fair share of Monster Cores, so there was little he doubted he couldn't pay for, even Draven had looked at his wealth appreciatively and he knew the man had as much, if not more, coin on his person.

They continued chatting over the fire, each one telling stories of dungeons they'd dove or monsters they'd killed.

Draven had a particularly hard to believe story about fighting a flying sea creature with more tentacles than he could count. Knox shared his most recent adventure in the Mire's Gloom Dungeon and the Wizard's Tower, but John stopped him halfway saying he was telling it wrong. He then went on to describe a series of events that were more ridiculous with each section of the story he told.

"You were not on the verge of death, and I never unleashed the beast as you said," Knox said, shaking his head. Dernal actually chuckled at this, and Knox stole a glance at the man.

"Stories always get bigger with each retelling," Aetex said. "I remember a time when the young one I'd trained came back to me, telling how they'd fought off a giant flying beast, saying that they themselves had learned to fly as well, not an easy feat mind you. I learned later that it had been almost every bit as dangerous as they'd described, but I imagine when Nick tells his tales to his children they will grow, as do all tales."

There was a sadness in Aetex when he spoke of home, one that Knox hadn't really noticed, as the man rarely spoke of his life, but he seemed in a particularly sharing mood, so Knox tried to get more information out of him.

"Tell me of your home, do you wish to visit it again someday?" Knox asked, wondering where exactly the man was from in the first place.

"My home is no more," Aetex said, a deep sadness permeating his words. "But my people live on and that is what matters. They spread throughout the stars, bringing order among the chaos. One day, I hope to return to them, but that day is far off and I've a mission of utmost importance to see to."

"This mission," Sintra said, breaking the silence she'd kept during the retelling of tales. "You are the guardian to the Titan of Light?"

"I am," Aetex said proudly. "He is my ward and I've been sent here to do what I can where my master cannot. This pocket dimension is hard for even him to access without pressing his full concentration to the task. This Titan Gowlen was a clever being, far beyond much of his other kind."

"You speak many words I do not understand," she said, looking at him with a slight tilt to her head. "What is a 'pocket dimension' for instance?"

Knox leaned forward, eager to hear more about this as well. Aetex took a bite of the meat he'd been cooking over the flames and continued on as if it were common knowledge.

"Best I can understand," Aetex said, "is Titan Gowlen was able to use his ability of creation and take a portion of normal spacetime and bend it into an entirely different section of space. Creating a small pocket world outside of normal existence. Doing so limits the other Titans' abilities to interfere with him, but also the very gods that created them. I doubt he knew it but in doing what he did, he cut off a small portion of their power and made it his own. He is as much a god here as any true god. It is doubtful still that he could stand to my master's might, and he is the least among the greatest."

"It is as if you speak in riddles meant to frustrate me," Sintra said, rubbing at her temples.

"What does that make me?" Knox asked, his attention fully on Aetex now. "If I am walking the Path of the Titans to become as he is, then will I have this power to create eventually?"

"That is a mystery that hasn't been revealed to me," Aetex said, giving Knox his full attention. "But I imagine Titan Gowlen is doing as was done before, trying to recreate the greatest of the first ones' achievements, making Titans. Many of their kind have attempted to do so before, but in all previous attempts they've only been able to create beings that can match a portion of their power. They lack a true ability to replicate, so it remains their greatest goal."

"So, there is a chance we aren't ever going to be true Titans, like the Titan Gowlen?" Knox asked, a measure of relief coming with the realization, though he couldn't put his finger on why. To him, true Titans had always been this mythological unknowable force, to think that he was to become one had given him pause since finding out.

He would, of course, continue to walk the Path of the Titans, but knowing that the end of the road didn't lead to him becoming something he couldn't even comprehend, gave him a measure of confidence and comfort.

The next day saw them further into the woods and closer to his old home, or what remained of it. They planned on skirting around that location, no one wanting to lay eyes on the ruins, most of all him. As they traveled, running through the woods at speeds that most could only dream of maintaining, Knox had much time to think, and he went over how the situation might play out time and time again.

Would his mother accept his return, his mission to retrieve the artifact? Would she tell him he was being silly and wish for him to remain and do as she had done, some responsibility that he couldn't bring himself to care about? There were so many questions he had and only time would tell where it would land.

After about a week of travel, they reached the pass that was nearly impossible to venture through during the winter and still held snow, despite how far they were into the summer. The actual road was cleared, but the piles of white could be seen as you traveled the road that cut straight through the mighty mountains. This was officially the furthest Knox had been from home and he felt an odd weight lift from him as he passed through and onto the road.

His entire life had been in a specific part of the world, and his entire world had changed over a year ago when he'd first taken the steps to leave his town and challenge a dungeon. He spared a glance at Dernal, they were walking at a more normal pace now as the road into the flatlands was busy enough that running wasn't an option.

Dernal, the man who'd made all this change possible, had been the very agent of his stifling. Though he'd changed his mind and been the one that helped him realize his dream, he couldn't help but feel a fissure form in their relationship. Dernal, one of his closest friends and mentor, had betrayed him by not telling him the moment he'd changed his mind. Knox's entire life might have taken a different course if he had and suddenly, he wondered if he truly would have wanted to know before?

The emotions were hard to work through and he needed to talk with Dernal if he were ever to work them out, so he slowed his pace and took to walking beside the older, short man.

Dernal wore his usual armor, leather with metal plates and various runic formations enforcing the armor. His hair was tied up in its usual bun, dark with a few strands loose from their day of running before arriving on the road. He'd been talking in a low voice to John, but upon Knox's arrival beside him, John sped up and started talking with Draven, while Sintra spoke with Aetex at the head of the group, despite neither of them knowing the way they tended to walk toward the front, both natural leaders.

"Hhrmm," Dernal said, when Knox stole a glance at him.

"We need to talk," Knox said, sighing as he tried to find the right words. "What you did..."

"Was not right," Dernal said. "But I had a duty to my friend."

"So, you know her pretty well?" Knox asked, surprised by this.

"I've known her on and off most of her life," Dernal said. "I wasn't around when she met up with Askar and went on wild adventures despite her father's warnings, but I was there to pick up the pieces when she was forced to leave you."

"Why?" Knox asked, unsure what he even meant, just so full of 'whys' that he couldn't ask anything else.

Dernal seemed to sense what he meant and continued. "She needed someone she trusted, even more than that fool partner of hers, to watch over you. I'd been an agent under her father, doing this or that for him, so I took up the life of being an Adventurer again, found a group and started to watch over you while around. I couldn't always be around, but Askar—his failings as a father aside—was strong enough to keep you safe from most dangers."

"You could have told me," Knox said, looking pointedly at Dernal.

"I couldn't," Dernal said. "It wasn't my place. Besides that, I was also bound by oaths, your mother is rather skilled in employing them, so until you found out on your own, I literally couldn't speak a word about it."

"Yet you helped me become an Adventurer?" Knox asked. "That wasn't something an oath bound you from doing?"

"Quite the contrary, actually," Dernal said, shaking his head. "I was bound to keep you safe over the safety of my own self. As I saw it, you being an Adventurer, despite not being what Scarlet wanted, was exactly the way to keep you from danger."

"It hurts to find out how much my life was just a thing for others to toy around with, what decision was my own? How can I trust anyone again?" Knox asked, pinching at the bridge of his nose.

Dernal began to answer but stopped himself and they walked in silence for a time.

Knox just couldn't understand why his mother had done what she'd done. To him, she'd been a mystery and something for him to aim for, being a powerful Adventurer like her, seeking answers in runes and magic. But to learn that his very foundation in how he saw himself was a lie, it shook him to his very center.

"I don't even know who I am, because of her," Knox said. Then turning, he stopped and waited for Dernal to answer.

Dernal for his part stopped as well, the road had thinned enough that they weren't directly in anyone's way for now, but if they stood for long enough a wagon might run them down.

"You know who you are," Dernal said, his voice stern. "You are the same thoughtful, kindhearted, and powerful man you've always been. You do what is right because you know it is what needs to be done. This entire adventure we are going on proves that, despite what you might be going through right now, you are still true to yourself and your ideals."

"Ideals seem petty when faced with the truths I am learning," Knox said, but even as he spoke the words, he felt that they were wrong. He did have ideals and a truth that he followed, that remained him despite all of the uncertainty. "But you are right. I am Knox, Titan Born of the Light. Perhaps I am no longer Knox Trelling or even Knox Blackwood, but something of my own. Perhaps I am just Knox and that is enough."

"Hhrmm," Dernal said as they began walking once more.

It wasn't perfect, but Knox was more confident in who he was now than he had been before. It wasn't his drive for knowledge or his desire to do right that defined him completely anymore, but something deeper, something he had a hard time defining in his thoughts. But he was Knox, and he would do his damnedest to do what he thought was right and seek out any knowledge he could. Not because of his mother, or his father, or even Dernal, but because it was who he was.

He was Knox.

CHAPTER 7
STRANGE ENCOUNTERS

THEY WERE HALFWAY through the long pass through the mountains when they encountered trouble.

Up ahead was a force of what looked like soldiers blocking the path forward, turning some people back while allowing others to pass. Those that were turned back had expressions of anger and disbelief on their faces and Knox called out to one to hear what had happened.

"Can you tell me what's going on?" Knox asked, stopping a man who walked with a woman and young child.

"Only those with trade are being let through, and only after a tax is paid. We don't have but what we've got on our backs, so they turned us away," the man said, turning and going his way after speaking.

Knox wanted to call back out to them and tell them to come with them, but he didn't know if they'd be let through without violence, so he held back.

"What's our play here?" John asked, looking warily at the soldiers.

"Hhrmm," Dernal grunted.

"We can crush them under our boots," Sintra said, a touch of violence reaching her voice.

"Nonsense," Aetex said, folding his arms. "We will simply request passage and they will grant it."

"Let's find out," Knox said, and they went forward, a strange party indeed.

The closer they got the less soldier-like the group appeared, more like a rag-tag band of dirty and rough looking armored men. Doing a rough count, he found there were a total of twenty-five men, well within what he could handle himself if none of them were Adventurers. Walking up with his hand on the hilt of his great axe, Knox caught the eye of the one that stood at the head of the group.

"Halt," the man said. "This passage is closed to refugees and vagabonds. Turn back or be taken into custody."

"We're Adventurers, no passage is closed to us," Dernal said, his voice more a growl than anything else.

This caught the man's attention, and he did a double take on the group, then seeming suspicious, he narrowed his eyes and drew his sword.

"The hell you are," he said, spitting at Dernal's feet.

The spit barely had a chance to hit the ground before Dernal moved, pulling a dagger out and pressing it hard on the soldier's neck.

"How's 'bout you disband your little group of runaway soldiers, or we will kill you all," Dernal's words were barely above a whisper and if not for Knox's increased ability to hear, he'd have missed them.

The man proved to be more stupid than brave, yelling out despite the dagger pressed to his throat. "Cut them down!" He yelled.

Dernal growled and punched the man so hard that he went flying ten feet back.

"Kill if you have to, but incapacitate if you can," Dernal yelled, and the fight was on.

Knox focused in on his sense as a dozen crossbolts were fired into the crowd. Moving with as much speed as possible, he cut down four of them midair, hoping none of the rest hit any innocent civilians.

Next, he used Ethereal Step to appear in the back line and cut outward with the flat end of his axe, bowling over three of the archers in a single swing.

Another bolt was loosed but Knox switched places with the shooter with Dimensional Shift. It had the desired effect of sticking the man with his own shaft, causing him to fall down in pain, clearly out of the fight.

Knox realized with grim satisfaction that these soldiers were nothing compared to the might of his group. They fell from a single blow, and their blunted strikes broke bones more often than not.

Within a matter of minutes, they'd taken down over twenty men, trained soldiers meant for battle.

Finding the leader, Dernal already had him back up and he was sporting a shiner where he'd taken the hit to the face, Knox listened in on their conversation.

"You will pay for this," coughed the soldier, but the man refused to look Dernal in the face.

"Disband and stop terrorizing the locals. We will be coming back through here soon and if we catch you, I'll make an example of you all and put your heads on pikes," Dernal said, his voice a dangerous, low growl.

Knox was surprised to hear such ferocity come from Dernal, but it was just as well, because the man seemed about to piss himself now.

"Two dead, and they are all injured," Knox said, making sure the captain of the little band of soldiers heard him.

"Couldn't be helped," Dernal growled, dropping the man on the ground again and turning his back on him. "Let's go."

Leaning in close, Knox whispered to Dernal. "Did you want to heal any of them or not?"

"No," Dernal growled the words, stomping off at the head of the group.

The trip remained boring up until they left the pass and entered a low valley of open hills and small villages. One in two of these villages were burning remnants of what they once were and the ones that hadn't burned to the ground appeared worse for wear. They just so happened to come across a village as an attack of some kind was happening, soldiers fought soldiers, and there was even a flash of magic here and there.

"Do we skirt around it or see what we can learn by getting closer?" Knox asked.

"Not our fight," Dernal said.

"We should investigate and lend aid where we can," Aetex said, crossing his arms.

"I'm with Dernal," John said, looking down at the ground as if ashamed to say it.

"We don't have time to put our noses in every conflict, we will skirt around it and try to stay out of the battle if we can," Knox said, Aetex shook his head at that but didn't offer any rebuttal.

"I sense the darkness close by," Sintra said, pointing toward the battle that raged some few miles away.

"That changes things," Dernal said.

Knox nodded and Aetex smiled.

"John, can you scout ahead and look for the signs of the darkness infection?" Knox asked, already walking in the direction of the fighting.

John nodded and sprinted ahead, disappearing only feet away as he activated his skills.

Now that Sintra had mentioned it, Knox sent out his sense as far as it would reach, and he too felt the strange darkness that he'd become all too accustomed to feeling. It was like a sickness that, as he sensed it, made him feel ill. So, he withdrew his sense a touch, instead focusing on moving forward at full speed. Aetex stayed with him while the others lagged behind several steps.

John returned just as they were approaching the town.

"Several villagers and soldiers are fighting and killing the rest, they have black eyes, and they are shrugging off mage fire from a few Adventurers that this army brought," John said.

During their trip John had explained that the armies tended to lean toward using ranged Adventurers like mages and wizard types more often than not, whereas physical fighters could make a difference, mages could make a massive difference by the sheer power they could call down at once.

"We get in, neutralize the threat and get out without inter-fering if we can," Knox said, not wanting another fight with soldiers to break out after they finished with the true threat.

"Oh," John said, looking at the ground. "I've contacted the mages already and told them we were going here to aid them; I'd have been back sooner, but I was working out the terms of our assistance."

"Fine," Knox said, rolling his eyes. Of course, John found a way to get paid to help. "Let's move!"

As one, they took off into the battle, the ruined village in flames all around them. An army of no less than a hundred men were being fought and killed to a standstill against twenty-two black-eyed people. Some had wounds where black ooze poured out, but most looked like they'd not taken a single hit or attack, despite the onslaught that was being thrown against them.

Fire appeared from above and one of the black-eyed villagers, a small boy of only ten or twelve years, waved a hand and a black energy shot out, intercepting the blast. The ground shook under the weight of the explosion as it was diverted into an already burning building.

It made Knox sick to his stomach to think he'd likely have to kill the boy, but he knew that most, if not all, of these people would be beyond saving. Regardless, he rushed through the troops, using Ethereal Step to reach the front lines and blasted out with a Luminous Surge.

The light from his hands seared flesh away and dropped three of the darkened souls to the ground, where they screamed in agony. The boy, Knox's sense told him he was the strongest of all of them, turned and laughed.

"We are come, none shall stop the spread of darkness," he said, then focusing on Knox, he sneered. "You travel far from your home, Titan of Light, are you confident that it will not fall without you?"

This stirred up a storm of emotions in Knox, but he had to stay focused in battle, so instead of thinking on the very thing he'd been worried about, he turned and cut the darkened soul behind him that attempted to attack him from behind.

That was when Dernal, John, and Aetex entered the battle. Each flashing with power and might as they slammed into several darkened souls, taking them down with ease.

Aetex moved with the fluid grace of a dancer as he punched his way through the group, one dark-infused person at a time. Where they'd been able to fight off these lower-level Adventurers before, they were no match for Knox and his team.

Sintra suddenly appeared behind the young boy, slashing out with her thin black blade. He turned in time to see her and a blast of dark energy sent her flying backward. But not before she slashed out and sent a stream of black slashing into the boy, leaving a red line that was soon filled with black ooze.

Knox entered the fray then, using Luminous Surge once more on the boy and searing flesh from his face as he screamed. He didn't wait to see what the boy would do next though, swinging his axe in a deadly arc. It connected with a weapon of pure black as the boy manifested it out of nowhere.

Knox repositioned his feet and raised his hand to release an Arcane Pulse, throwing the boy back a few steps. There, Sintra was to intercept him, slashing here and there. But the boy was fast, catching her blows and forcing her onto the back step. She raised her own hand, muttered words Knox couldn't hear, and her blade began to pull in the light around it as she struck out.

As the two blades of sheer blackness met, the boy's shattered under the weight and force of her own strike. She let her weapon fall out of her hands and for a moment, Knox couldn't tell what had happened, then he saw the dagger in her gut. Somehow, the boy had struck out with his other hand, hitting his right in her exposed stomach.

Before Knox could release another Luminous Surge, Sintra screamed, pulling free the dagger and throwing it back at the boy. It took him in the throat, only dissipating into smoke after the damage was done. The boy gurgled and spat black ooze mixed with red blood and suddenly his face looked very much like one of a scared little boy, confused at where he was.

"Dernal!" Knox cried out, rushing forward with an Ethereal Step and casting Luminous Surge on the boy, hoping to purge what darkness was left in him.

He screamed in obvious pain, but Knox knew he had only moments to save him, and this was the way. Casting it again the boy began to shake and convulse. Dernal arrived just as Knox hit the boy for a third time, his body going still.

"Can you save him?" Knox asked, readying up another Luminous Surge.

"That's enough," Dernal said, pushing Knox aside and chanting over the boy as he focused on the wound on his neck. Though he closed all the wounds, the boy still didn't move.

Knox checked with his sense and sure enough, the darkness was gone, but he didn't sense any life in the boy and with a sudden realization, he stood and took a deep breath.

"He's gone," Dernal said.

Knox looked down at the young child's eyes that stared right at him with an empty hollowness. Dernal closed his eyes and only then could Knox look away. This life was not one for the easy going or faint of heart. Knox steeled himself and turned to find the soldiers closing in around them, caution clear on their faces.

"You took down the demons," said a larger man in armor with a feathered plumage at the top of his helmet, perhaps a leader among them?

"They weren't demons," Knox said. "They are people infected with a sickness, one that I'd hoped hadn't spread this far."

"Call it what you will, but we are grateful to have had your aid. Outnumbered as they were, I still didn't like our chances against them," the armored man said. "My name is Uther, please stay and aid our wounded, I will see to it that you are compensated for your time."

Knox suddenly felt very tired, like he hadn't slept in days, so he nodded and took Uther's offer of hospitality. Aiding in the healing as best he could, he found several that had been infected with the darkness, but it was in the early stages, and he purged them clean. If this issue with the darkness spreading wasn't dealt with soon, it might truly be the end of civilization as they knew it.

"So, tell me," Uther said after everyone had been healed and tents were erected. Knox and his group were in a tent with Uther, sitting atop rugs that had been brought out to cover the ground. "What brings you Adventurers through these parts? With the winter melting, most are out to experience the more exotic dungeons in the borderlands.

"We are on our way to Lumisar," Knox said, seeing no reason to hide his destination from this soldier.

"I'm familiar with it, though it has been some time since I've been behind her walls," Uther said. "We are just one of many of King Wilham's armies trying to deal with unrest in the kingdom. Though it would appear you know something about it, this darkness that takes people has caused him no end of trouble. You came down the pass out of Feralease, I'm sure the chaos out there is as bad as it is here in the lower realm?"

Knox had lived his entire life in Feralease and in the small town of Keenlen's Vale, so while he knew of the rest of the kingdom by story, this was the furthest out he'd ever been so hearing it called the lower realm was new to him.

"Many have sought refuge and been turned away, but my people have survived as best we could," Knox said.

"Being as powerful as you seem to be, I can see why," Uther said, just then someone else entered the tent, one of the Adventurer mages in bright purple robes. "Ah, welcome Istereal, come sit with us. He is from the city of Lumisar, where you are headed."

"My lord," Istereal said, inclining his head to Draven, who just looked startled and shared a glance with Knox.

"Lord?" Uther said. "I'm sorry for such casual behavior, if I'd known you were nobility." Uther began to stand but Draven held up a hand to forestall him.

"Please, treat me only as an Adventurer right now, as that is the capacity I am filling," Draven said. He didn't seem too excited that he'd been recognized, but Knox couldn't tell why it mattered.

"Thank you for saving us," Istereal said, his words directed right at Draven, despite how little the man had actually helped during the battle, being the last one there and taking out the fewest of the darkened souls.

"It was nothing," Draven said. "Please, join us for a meal."

There was a tray of assorted fruit and nuts, with some hardened crackers added in laid out before them. Knox hadn't been eating, feeling as tired as he was, he wanted nothing more than to sleep.

"Could we stay the night with you, perhaps borrow a tent or two for the evening?" Knox asked, this got him surprised looks from the rest of his companions, who knew they'd just slept the day before, meaning they'd be good for at least another two to three days. Knox just couldn't explain it, he was tired, and he needed rest.

"Why of course," Uther said. "After our meal, I will see to it immediately."

Knox nodded and stopped listening to the exchange of words as he drifted into a state of near sleeplessness. It was during the in and out of this almost sleep state that he began to hear someone calling out to him as if from a great distance.

True sleep came quickly when he was finally given a tent and he laid out on his bed roll. Almost immediately, he began to dream of the Titan Gowlen, the metallic being known to him now as a Titan and a powerful one at that. In his dream, he looked out into the vastness of the sky and beyond, he saw the workings of the Titans, both small and large. They were building up to something, a goal that they'd sought for endless millennia.

But overshadowing all of that was a great darkness, a void in the endlessness of space. And from it, Knox could tell the Titans were not ready to face what was coming. All the power they wielded would come to naught against a force so great that even the makers of this universe could not kill it, and instead were forced to lock it away.

All of this vague awareness came to Knox in his dreams, and he wondered what it meant. As he pondered over the state of Order and Chaos, he saw what the future might hold for all of creation if this great void were to escape its bonds. Planets, his included, would become dead and cold, the flame of creation extinguished wherever it went.

"Why do you gaze into our futures?" Came a booming voice so great that it seemed to shake reality itself as it spoke.

Titan Gowlen loomed over Knox suddenly, and he couldn't escape his gaze no matter what he tried.

Finally, after what felt like eons, Knox found the strength to speak. "I am dreaming," he said as if that were the simplest response to a question he couldn't even begin to answer.

"You are one of mine," Titan Gowlen said, his voice vibrating the very existence around him. "Then I have begun to make progress after all. You are connected to the weave that we Titans use to see eventualities, but you have not done this alone, someone or something has aided you. Show yourself, creator."

"Relax," Mah'kus said, his voice a comforting soothing experience when compared to the fierceness of the Titans.

Titan Gowlen suddenly had an expression of severe annoyance, but he dared not look directly at the humanoid figure that had appeared beside Knox.

"You have found my secret space," Titan Gowlen finally said at length. "Then it is time I purge it and collect my things before you undo all my hard work."

"Do as you feel fit," Mah'kus said. "But your work is to be commended. You have nearly replicated a small portion of the work we did in creating your kind. This is unexpected and perhaps unwise. But I will use your tools and together, when you are called upon, you will fight at your creator's side. Now leave before you upset me."

"As you command," Titan Gowlen said, but not before stealing a glance at Mah'kus and then a long look at Knox. "I am come, be prepared."

Then the heavy presence dissipated, and Knox felt alone once more, despite Mah'kus standing beside him.

"What does that mean for my home?" Knox asked, looking at Mah'kus and not feeling the great fear that Titan Gowlen seemed to feel when looking at him. To Knox this Mah'kus character, god or not, seemed like a regular person to him.

"All things will come to an end eventually," Mah'kus said, then turning to look right at Knox he gazed into his eyes.

In those eyes Knox felt the weight of a thousand words pressing down on him and an endlessness that he couldn't begin to understand settled around him.

"I won't allow this Titan to end my world," Knox said, a growing fierceness coming forth as he spoke.

Mah'kus smiled and held out his hand. "Have a donut, relax, for you have more pressing matters to attend to. Follow the Path of the Titans, grow in power and you might find yourself able to defend against Gowlen when the time comes. But that is far in your future, first you must survive the threats all around you. Remember, when the time comes, choose the *right* path." He emphasized the word right and suddenly Knox sat up, fully awake and the dream seeming to fade somewhat from his mind.

He remembered it all, if only vaguely, but he knew he needed to choose the right path when it came down to it, whatever that meant. Was he meant to literally chose the right path or was it meant more generally, as he should follow what he felt was right? Knox didn't know but he couldn't get the words out of his head.

He bit into the pastry that he found sitting on his chest without even realizing it until the taste of it came over him. It was good, if a bit overly sweet.

CHAPTER 8
ARRIVAL AT LUMISAR

DERNAL AND JOHN took the lead from here on out, they knew the lands better than the rest of the party, even Draven, who'd traveled through but only because they'd been searching for a hunting ground to grow stronger. Apparently, in the more populated areas there were fewer dungeons and wild monsters to deal with since the king had declared the heart of his kingdom to be safe.

How that would stop dungeons from appearing, Knox wasn't clear, but he was only listening to the buzz of conversation with half an ear anyway. His mind was enraptured by the dream he'd had and his interaction with Mah'kus. Of course, he knew it was more than a dream and now he had more to worry about. They still had many weeks of travel ahead of them, but the roads were clear and safe, with only the occasional outbreak of the black sickness causing them to help out where they could.

Only days from arriving, Knox finally worked himself up enough to talk to Aetex about his dream. He started by filling him in on the entire dream to hear what he had to say.

"Mah'kus works in mysterious ways, and rarely does he tell you everything you ought to know," Aetex said, like that was enough.

"But I'm meant to choose the right, what does that even mean?" Knox asked.

"When the time comes, I'm confident that you will understand," Aetex said, still unbothered.

"What about you?" Knox asked. "You were sent here to help me by an all-powerful god, but why am I important?"

"We are all important to the plan of our creator," Aetex said. "Look." He stopped his steady walk and put a hand on Knox's shoulder. "I don't understand all he has meant for us to do, but I know and trust him as much as anyone can know their creator. Trust that he has a plan, and you are an important part of it."

"How can I trust what I can't understand!" Knox said, his voice rising a bit higher than he meant it to.

"Has he led you astray yet?" Aetex asked. "Have my actions not proven that I am here to help you? There comes a time when you will need to have faith in his plan, but now isn't even that time. You have proof of his plan for you, I am here to guide you young one. Be at peace and know that I will do all I can to keep you safe. For one day soon, I believe you will be strong enough to protect me and my kind."

"I just don't understand," Knox said, frustrated at it all. "If he is all powerful-"

"I never said he was all powerful," Aetex said, cutting Knox off.

"Okay if he is as powerful as he appears to be," Knox said, "then why is he going to let the Titan Gowlen come here and 'collect' his things. It sounded very much like he meant to destroy this planet and collect the Titan Born as if we were just pieces of a puzzle for him to collect and use."

"I cannot begin to understand the motivations of someone such as Mah'kus," Aetex said, "but I know him to be a true friend and he has helped me find new purpose when I had none. Even death is not outside of his purview."

"You are saying he can restore people from death?" Knox asked, surprised that anyone could manage such a feat, god or not.

"I died in battle against a brother of mine who'd lost his way," Aetex said, lowering his voice several degrees. "Mah'kus chose not only to restore me to life but give me greater power than I could have ever managed in my past life. But giving life comes with a great cost, even to him. He must be recovering if he is contacting you directly."

"I'm sorry to hear that," Knox said, and he meant it. "I can't imagine fighting one of my friends and having to take his life or vice versa. But if he can give life, even with a cost, does death even matter? If I fail, he will just bring me back."

"He won't," Aetex said, looking downcast. "I was a special case; my own fate and path was at an end. You are a part of a great destiny that is yet to be decided. You may live, you may die, but whatever your fate, know that he is helping as much as he is able. Sending me to this pocket dimension was more than he thought he'd be able to do, so to hear he is speaking to you directly, it is good news."

"I understand," Knox said. Truth be told he didn't, but this conversation wasn't getting him anywhere. Aetex was far too invested in Mah'kus and his goals to see clearly, that much Knox understood.

Knox would keep the words Mah'kus said close, but in the end, it would be his own decisions that would dictate his future. If he were to become a true Titan and wield power equal to Gowlen's, then perhaps Ramses' plan had more merit than he first thought. Perhaps together they might face off against the threat that is the Titan Gowlen, perhaps they could keep their world intact despite his efforts.

The time came when they finally crested a hill and caught sight of the city, Lumisar. It was beyond anything Knox had expected to see and several times bigger than the half dozen cities they'd crossed through on their way here. Sure, the others had walls, and some tall buildings, but nothing compared to the massive layout that lay before them.

This was truly the gem of the lowlands, only matched by the capital city, according to Draven, that held almost twice the population. Knox couldn't quite wrap his mind around what he was seeing though.

There were three sets of massive walls, each a massive ring and each one filled with buildings rising up several stories. And even outside the city there were villages, it seemed, all around with massive fields of crops and such. This far out there didn't seem to be any soldiers fighting darkened souls either, which wasn't as surprising as they'd encountered less and less as they traveled. It was almost like Keenlen's Vale was the starting point of the spread of the darkness and it was slowly expanding outward.

Lumisar was so far out as to be immune to the problems of both the darkened souls and the soldiers at war, whatever or whoever they were fighting. Uther had spoken at length about it, but Knox had been so tired that he'd barely caught a word, just something about an invading force from the Northwest border of the Kingdom.

At the center of the massive city that sat higher than the rest, was a single Tower. It shone with a golden light against the sunlight that reflected against it and toward the base was all manner of Towers and constructions that didn't match the same golden color.

Pointing, Knox was about to ask about it when Draven spoke.

"That is the Tower that holds the Aurorapex, but most just think that challenging the Tower alone will give them the chance to rule over Lumisar, but it is in fact the artifact held within that grants the holder that right. I must warn you that if you do intend to challenge the Tower and you do retrieve the artifact, my family isn't likely to play nice when they learn they will no longer be in power. Our entire seat of power within the city is built around the Tower and should it fall, which is what historians say will happen if the artifact is removed, then you will be setting forth a series of events that might lead me to fight against your goals. A future I don't want any part of, for I know my death would soon follow."

Knox couldn't tell if it was meant as a warning or a threat, but so far Draven had been nothing but helpful, so he took it as the warning it was and turned to him.

"You build your castle, your ruling seat, around the Tower's base?" He asked, knowing full well that it was the case as he focused his eyes on the location and saw the differences in materials.

"My ancestors did, yes," Draven said. He didn't seem at all put off by Knox dodging his comment about having to turn on him, so Knox let it be.

As they traveled down the large road toward the city, Knox went over what he was feeling and tried to understand why he felt more excited than anything else. He was finally going to meet his mother, of course that was the easiest answer.

When all else was put aside, the grand quest, the world-ending threats, he was finally going to meet his mother. Then, as he thought about it, a weight filled his gut and he started to feel sick.

He was finally going to meet his mother.

But she'd abandoned him, she'd been the cause of his grief with his father, she'd also been the very reason he'd first started wanting more out of life. The reason he'd wanted to become an Adventurer and seek more learning. She was both his inspiration and his bane, in a sense.

"What is she like?" Knox asked as he hurried ahead to stand beside Dernal.

"Scarlet?" Dernal asked. "Hhrmm. She's strong-willed and caring. Resourceful and clever."

"Do you think she expects me?" Knox asked. "I mean, she sent for me, but what if I'm not what she expects?"

Dernal stopped then and looked Knox in the eyes.

"I've told her much about who you are, and I can tell you without reservation that she not only expects you, but she looks forward to seeing you," Dernal said. "She is much like you, inquisitive, extremely intelligent, brazen, and resourceful."

"I'm not sure how I feel about all this, but I just wanted to say..." Knox paused as he prepared himself to say something that wasn't easy for him. "Thank you. Despite the betrayal I feel, if you hadn't gone against her wishes I'd have never gotten to be an Adventurer in the first place. Never had realized my destiny."

"Let's not remind her of that," Dernal said. "I haven't spoken with her since I started you on the path and she won't be happy about it. Especially when she thought you lost to the dangers of being an Adventurer."

"But she knows I'm fine now, I'm sure she'll forgive you," Knox said, then thinking about how he'd felt when he learned of the betrayal he added, "Eventually."

With that, their conversation went into silence, and they continued their walk toward the city. Every part of Knox wanted to run out ahead and get there as soon as possible, but that would draw extra attention to themselves, and they were trying to avoid that. So much so, that Draven had taken on a cloak to hide who he was. He assured them that he'd done the same thing on several occasions and with how busy the ins and outs of the gate were, he wasn't likely to be noticed, at least getting into the first ring of gates.

The internal ring or most central ring, he said, wouldn't grant them access unless he were with them. Which was good because Knox wanted to go straight there and get this over with. His stomach still had the heavy weight in it, and he almost felt sick from the anxiety of it all.

The road before them was cobblestoned, but so well kept that there wasn't a single one out of place the closer they got to the city's entrance. All types of people, some clearly Adventurers, walked along the road in armor and some in peasant's clothing as they went about their daily duties and chores. The sky above shone bright and clear, no clouds in sight, and Knox had a hard time imagining the dark sickness coming here, so lively and fresh the land seemed.

It had even been weeks since they'd felt the ground shakes that he'd now aligned with the movement of the dark ooze underground. Lumisar was a peaceful city, filled to the brim with more people than Knox had ever seen, and he was more than sure that he loved it.

The wind blew here and there, a pleasant cool breeze that gave relief from the heat of the day. Not that it was overly hot, just warm enough to enjoy the breeze as it cut through the lower part of the road.

The road began to rise as they walked, the entire city sat on a massive plateau of sorts, whether man-made or natural, Knox had no way to know. Regardless, they began to walk toward the side of the road as wagons and carts slowed their ascent upward. Knox was feeling so chipper, yet nervous, that he almost wanted to reach out and help a poor older man pushing a cart but decided that he was doing alright himself. He just wanted to act, to do something, and all the people around him just made him want to help all the more.

Eventually, he couldn't stand it and he found a clearly pregnant woman and asked if he could help her push her cart through the gate. She looked at him as if he'd just asked her to borrow her unborn child, lowering her head and ignoring him, walking all the faster for it.

The gate loomed over them as they neared, a massive affair with a portcullis allowing them over a hundred-foot expanse. As they walked across it, Knox looked over the side to see a several hundred-foot moat had been dug around it and filled with water. This truly was a city that would take a miracle to conquer, he absently thought as they walked past the guards without incident.

"Even our mightiest cities do not have populations so grand as this," Sintra said, she walked beside Knox and spoke in a hushed tone. "Our capital city came close, but the people here seem to have no end."

"What is it like living underground?" Knox asked. "I can't imagine never seeing the suns and moons."

"We have many sights to behold down beneath, but I do admit that since seeing the many moons, I'm intrigued," she said, dodging a pair of children that nearly ran into her.

"Lumisar is the pride of our kingdom," Draven said, looking proud despite having most of his face cloaked. "In ancient times, this city was a nation of its own, but such talk isn't something you'll hear often as King Wilham keeps a strong hold on his subjects."

"As long as the people are safe and happy, then I am in support of this ruler," Aetex said, joining in on the conversation.

"Should we visit and make a report to the Adventurer's Guild?" John asked, looking at Dernal as he spoke.

"I'm sure someone else will make a report," Dernal said, shaking his head. "No, we stay on mission and see about getting to that Tower and meet with Scarlet."

"How are we going to do that exactly?" Knox asked. "Do we just walk right up to the gate and announce ourselves, or are we going to try and sneak in?"

Draven laughed at that, lowering his hood a bit. "My face will be our ticket into the most inner-section of the kingdom and into an audience with my uncle. From there we can announce your intentions to challenge the Tower and Scarlet will be free to meet with you in the meanwhile."

"And they'll just stand by while I try to steal their artifact?"

Knox asked, still a bit unclear at how all this worked, despite having it explained to him before.

"Of course," Draven said. "There is a long tradition of challengers, despite not having one in some time, they won't deny your request."

"And when I actually retrieve it?" Knox asked, knowing what came next.

Draven coughed. "Then we might have a tiny problem, but I'll be working with the court to try and prepare them for that eventuality. I doubt I can sway my uncle on the matter, but I can possibly get enough people behind the idea that he won't be able to act openly against you."

"But he'll be able to try and take care of him in the dark," Sintra said. "I understand such matters and I don't like our chances of escaping his clutches if all of us are included in his hospitality."

"Hhrmm," Dernal said, considering. "She's right. John and I will stay out of the noble court and make ready to flee when the time comes. Give Scarlet my regards."

"Oh, I've got the perfect place," John said, smirking. "You'll love it."

With that, the two bid them farewell and departed with promises to be on the lookout for Knox and his possible escape. This was John's home city, so Knox was sure that he'd find a way to get information about his Tower climb. If not, Dernal had contacts in the city as well, so one way or another they'd meet back up.

Aetex, Sintra, Knox, and Draven all headed through the next gate and onward toward the final inner-city gate that would bring them that much closer to Knox meeting his mother.

"We should stop off at a bathhouse so I can get cleaned up, otherwise I'll have a hard time convincing the guards I am who I am," Draven said, turning a side street and leading them off from the main road. "I've got a change of clothes, but it'll do to rid us of the smells we've gathered over the last few weeks of travel."

Knox nodded along, the idea of a bath sounding good to him as well. Though the pit in his stomach wanted nothing more than to go meet his mother, he didn't want his first impression to be one of bad smells and dirty attire.

"You'd also do well to polish up that armor," Draven said, motioning to the tarnished looking enchanted armor Knox wore. "While I know by hard experience that it is hardy beyond measure, looks play a big part in my family's court. Perhaps we can purchase you some fashionable attire, like a cloak or something to go around it."

"Lead the way," Knox said, finding no objection with what he was saying. He was alright with spending a few coin to get dressed in better looking clothes. Perhaps he might even get a shave and a haircut, his face was covered in a month's worth of growth and his hair more than a bit unwieldy.

"I have no need of such accommodations," Sintra said. Knox gave her a once over and sure enough she was the cleanest among them, her scent that of the ground after a rainy day, refreshing and new.

"How does that work?" Draven asked, making a show of sniffing Knox and pinching his nose. "I mean we've all skipped the same amount of baths, I'd figure you'd be just as ripe."

"I've a passive spell that tends to my personal cleanliness and that of the attire I wear. It was passed down in my family for generations, one of the first I learned as a child," Sintra said.

"So, it isn't a System spell?" Knox asked, eager to learn more about magic and how it operated in a System-active environment.

"Not all magic is, but such learning is possible outside the system," Sintra said.

They'd had many such small conversations about her people and the System over the weeks of travel, but Knox stayed fascinated by such topics.

"How many generations did you say the System has been active for your people?" Knox asked, trying to remember if it were five or six generations of her people.

"Six," Sintra answered. "Even our oldest scholars can't remember the day when the Dark Titan began her rule. Our histories suggest she started much like you, a small area of effect that spread through our nation like a plague, infecting us and changing the ways we operated."

"Fascinating," Knox said, but Draven cut them off with a sign of his hand and a gesture toward a building ahead.

CHAPTER 9
MOTHER

BATHED, armor cleaned, hair and face trimmed, and a new bright yellow cloak with gold trim, Knox felt as ready as he'd ever be to face what lay ahead. Draven had cleaned up nice as well, leaving only Sintra in her dark clean armor looking plain against the overly styled clothing of the two men. Aetex, on the other hand, wore his same armor, cleaned but plain in its construction, and he looked as ordinary as one could look when being a non-human in a very human centric city.

"Will them being non-humans be a problem?" Knox asked, gesturing over his shoulder.

"What?" Draven said, barely glancing at their two partners. "No, of course not. My family may be many things, but they are accepting of all the races of the world."

Knox nodded along, glad to hear that at least wouldn't be an issue.

Draven led the way to the gate and Knox was proud to say they turned quite a few heads as they walked. He thought he looked pretty glamorous, more so than he'd ever had before and it felt nice to be wearing something so comfortable under and over his armor.

A part of him couldn't stop thinking about how he'd be able

to enchant the cloak to add layers of protection later. He knew so much about runic formations now and how helpful they could be even on ordinary clothing, that he'd almost tried to thread a few into the cloak the moment he'd purchased it. However, they hadn't the time or the thread to do it.

"Announce yourself," said the closest of the guards as they approached.

The road leading up to the final inner wall was all but cleared of traffic and a surprising number of twelve guards stood ready with hands on weapons. The gate itself was closed and Knox could make out several dozen arrow slits cut into the wall with arrows poking out of them. This was a heavily guarded gate and Knox had no doubt that they'd have Adventurers wielding magic standing above waiting to rain down death. He did a check with his sense and sure enough, he counted four such beings of low to medium power levels.

You didn't have to be much stronger than a normal person to kill them when you could call down the elements on their head from a distance. Knox wasn't so worried about them or the arrows, despite the damage they might do, his party far outpaced them in terms of raw power and speed.

With the sun shining at their backs, Draven answered the guard, giving him his names of all present as best he knew them. The guard seemed to relax and squinted at Draven before nodding his head.

"Alright, step forward and enter. Remember Adventurers," the guard looked pointedly at all but Draven. "No using your magics within the walls, doing so is punishable by not only the Adventurer's Guild, but by our law."

They all nodded; Knox wanted to smirk but held it together. If Aetex and Knox wanted to really cut loose, there would be none here strong enough to stop them. Or at least that is what he thought as his sense swept through the area looking for any threats above B rank. He found several, suddenly, and felt a bit more worried as his sense penetrated the veils those further in the city held over themselves.

"How strong is the noble family here?" Knox asked as they passed through the gate and into the final circle of buildings.

"I've got a cousin that is one of the few A Rankers, but I doubt even he could match you after seeing what you can do," Draven whispered back.

That set Knox at ease a little, but still, he wasn't invincible, and neither was Aetex, so they'd have to be careful not to let themselves get overwhelmed should it come to a fight.

The inside of the wall was like walking from one world and into another. Where the buildings had all been finely crafted before, of stone and wood, the inside section was built of stone that glistened in the sunlight and was smooth to the touch. Even the streets here were made of the material, whatever it was, with small grooves cut into it, like lines down a paper.

"The streets are laid out with marble from the mountains," Draven said, seeing Knox stare in awe at the sights before him.

Even the people here wore fancy clothes of many colors. Where the outside had variety, this place was an altogether different beast. Knox watched in awe as powerful horses drew fancy black lacquered carriages to and fro, with only a few people actually walking to where they needed to go.

"This way to my father's court," Draven said, pointing down the main road leading directly to the Tower that hung above them like a sentinel of power.

Knox turned to see that even Aetex seemed in awe of the sights, he slowed himself a measure to walk alongside the man. "Fascinating, isn't it?" Knox asked, then before Aetex could answer Knox added, "You see the grooves in the street, they have runic formations in them to create motion or something. I think it is meant to push rainwater off toward a specific location."

"I've seen many mighty cities in my day, but this one is a wonder and a marvel that reminds me of the ancient cities that my people once built. Though they stood in ruins in my day, I could still imagine their splendor when I first lived," Aetex said, folding his arms as he regarded the massive Tower, his head tilting to take it in fully.

"The Tower is a beacon of power," Knox said, his sense burning anytime he focused too hard on it. "It hurts to even look at with my sense." He sometimes wondered if he made any sense when talking about his special sense. To him it was like feeling and seeing at the same time, a mix of sensory information that his brain translated to thought and sight and even smell sometimes.

"I can feel the warmth of it even from this distance," Aetex said, nodding. "If that power could be harnessed and released, I don't know of many beings that could withstand such a blow, Titan or otherwise."

"Do you think that is the trick of the artifact?" Knox said, his eyes tracing the Tower while he kept his sense localized around himself.

"All I've heard speaks of it being a force multiplier, not as something used to store and release power," Sintra said, she looked as amazed by the sights as the other two, but she kept her composure much easier.

"Regardless of how it works, I'm certain now that it holds great power," Knox said, his gaze still locked on the Tower.

Because of this, he didn't notice when they stopped, and he nearly bumped into Draven.

They stood just outside one of a dozen castle-like structures built around the massive Tower. They clung to the structure, rising into the air, some several hundred paces. Guards stood outside, though not as many as the outer gate, and Knox sensed that each of these guards were in fact ranked C Adventurers, so who knew what abilities they might be hiding.

"You are expected," said the largest among the men in matching silver armor. "Your uncle is in his hall awaiting you. But your friends may not enter at this time."

Draven looked over at the group and Knox shrugged. "I'll be out to fetch you in minutes, I just need to explain to my uncle why you are here," Draven said, then turning back to the guards, he entered through a smaller door set next to the massive doorway big enough to let in an entire row of carriages.

The wait was awkward with the guards refusing to chit chat, even when Knox tried to ask them how their days were going. But as promised, only minutes later Draven appeared and ushered them into the keep.

They entered into a fortified hallway, with more kill holes in the ceiling and side of the walls. After going through it, they were led through a heavyset wooden door with metal bands reinforcing it and several lines of runic formations hidden under the metal that Knox detected easily with his sense. Once through that door the defensive emplacements stopped.

Instead of arrow slits and kill holes, there were tapestries, statues, suits of armor, and even weapons on display. Some of which even had enchantments on them, though most appeared to be ordinary in form and fashion. Aetex looked at one particular piece of weaponry and frowned.

"I swear this design is from my home planet, it is almost exactly as I remember it," Aetex said, reaching out to touch it, but Draven held out a hand to forestall him.

"Though not all these weapons are magically enhanced, all of them are important and put out for display for a reason. My uncle would not be happy about us messing with them," Draven said as he walked on ahead.

The floor was covered in a bright red carpet that showed no signs of wear. It was enough of a curiosity that Knox focused in with his sense and sure enough, noticed that the threads had the tiniest amount of runic formations woven into it at seemingly random points. This keep, despite already being the most lavish place he'd ever visited, was a magical marvel with all its runic formations. He could spend the next week at least studying the methods and uses of such formations.

Knox gave a passing look at the weapon that Aetex had been attracted to and noticed that it did indeed have an odd look to it. The blade curved at the top half but was otherwise straight and it had what looked like runic formations cut into it, but they were just different enough to be nonsense. The weapon itself gave off no measurable energy that Knox's sense could identify, yet looking at it, he felt a pull to pick it up that he couldn't quite explain.

He resisted the urge, whatever it was, and turned to follow the group, softly nudging Aetex away from it as well, though the man wasn't easy to nudge when he didn't want to move.

"Odd," he finally said, then moved on his own accord back to the group.

"Could you read those runes on it?" Knox asked, catching Aetex glancing back at the weapon as Draven led them through another door at the end of the hall and into a larger, and if possible, even more elaborately decorated room.

"Almost, it was nearly Ki'darthian in formation but lacking at the same time. Perhaps from a previous age or perhaps it was nothing and it just seemed similar," Aetex said, shrugging his way into the door.

Before them lay a vast room some hundred or even two hundred paces long and fifty paces wide. Tapestries of grand battles and other random scenes covered the walls, with statues of armored figures and a few busts of people Knox didn't recognize filled the edges. Toward the back was a lifted area and a single throne made of a solid black rock that seemed almost glassy in appearance, different from anything he'd seen before.

On that throne sat a man wearing a full suit of enchanted armor, along with a flowing red cape. On his head, instead of a helmet to match the black and gold armor he wore, he had a crown made from the same black stone as the throne.

He had eyes that seemed to blaze with power and his aura gave off that of someone close, but not quite, to A Rank. He had purple eyes, dark brown hair that came down past his chin, and a neatly trimmed beard. His expression was hard and his eyes sharp as he took each of them in; his eyes lingered far longer on Knox than the others.

"You've an impressive aura, I believe you must be the one called Knox," the man said, tilting his head slightly as he spoke. "My nephew has told me how you saved, twice now, my own kin and I owe you my thanks."

He didn't sound thankful, Knox thought. In fact, he spoke each word as if it were an accusation of some kind. But Knox didn't let that skew his impression of the man, he was obviously Draven's uncle and a man of great power.

"No thanks is needed," Knox said. "I was just doing what I could when the opportunity arose. I would do it for anyone."

"May I introduce you to my uncle, Silas the Keeper of the Tower, Steward of Lumisar and a powerful evoker," Draven said, bowing his head as he spoke.

Knox followed suit, but noticed with a grimace that neither Aetex nor Sintra bowed their heads.

"Introduce your friends, nephew," Silas said, waving his hand toward Aetex and Sintra.

However, instead of starting with them, he looked to Knox and spoke. "This is indeed Knox, the one I told you about. He is what is known as a Titan Born, Keeper of the Light of Luminar, and friend and loyal ally."

He'd thrown in a title Knox hadn't heard yet and it made him grimace once more, but for another reason. He hadn't really talked about keeping his Titan nature a secret. In fact, he'd been quite open about it during their trip, answering Draven's many questions, but he hoped for a touch of discretion when they arrived.

Oh well, Knox thought, meeting the Steward's purple-eyed gaze with his own steeling look and nodding his head respectively.

Draven continued his introduction a moment later. "This is the great warrior known as Aetex. He has also proven himself a great ally and friend, though if he has a surname or title, I am unfamiliar with it."

Aetex took that time to bow his head to the steward, if ever so slightly, but never did he take his eyes off the man during the entire exchange.

"I have no need of titles nor a surname any longer," Aetex said, interrupting Draven as he was about to continue. "I do, however, have questions about some of the weaponry you have on display in your hall. Can you tell me where you got the blade of a Ki'darthian warrior?"

Draven looked like he was going to be sick suddenly, his eyes flashing from his uncle to Aetex, but his uncle just smiled—though it never touched his eyes—and spoke.

"I'm not familiar with that term, but I could have you speak with the court historian about any number of the artifacts and weapons on display, when the time is right," Silas said, his smile fading as he looked to Sintra with curiosity in his eyes.

"And this is Sintra, heir to the throne of her people, the Noctrae. While I know her less than the others, over the last few weeks she has proven herself to be a wise and fierce warrior," Draven said, and Knox let a breath of air out that he'd been holding.

For a moment there, he was sure that the man might give away their entire point of their quest. Although Draven said a challenge to the Tower would be welcomed, if he let loose what they planned on doing with the Aurorapex once they'd gotten it, he wasn't sure introductions would go as smoothly. But Knox worried for nothing, introductions were finished, and the room fell into an unsteady quiet as they waited for the steward to address them once more.

After a time, he did so, standing as he spoke.

"You must be tired from your journey, please accept our hospitality and be our guest. We can discuss your challenge of the

Tower at a later date, but for now, please rest," Silas said, holding out a hand in a way that seemed to suggest he'd like them to leave.

Knox looked to Draven, who nodded his head ever so slightly and began to lead them from the room. Following, Draven didn't speak until after the door was shut behind them, servants inside doing the work of shutting the doors.

"I think that went well," Draven said, clasping his hands together.

Knox sighed. "It went fine," he said after a short pause. "How long are we going to have to wait until we can challenge the Tower and uh," Knox hesitated before finishing his sentence, "when do you think I could meet my mother?"

"I'll take you to her right now," Draven said, smiling brightly. He was so much more friendly in his smiles than his uncle, that it was almost as if they couldn't be related. Though demeanors aside, they did bear a striking resemblance, especially the eyes.

Knox's vibrant blue eyes flashed, and he grew both excited and nervous at the same time. A lump formed in his throat that prevented him from responding, so he just nodded.

Draven first set up both Aetex and Sintra in rooms, as well as showing Knox to his own room where he took off his armor, not wanting to meet his mother dressed for battle. He kept the cloak; he was fond of it as it was one of the nicest articles of clothing he owned. After a quick splash of water from the basin, Knox turned and indicated that he was ready. From there he was led through a number of halls, each one going deeper and higher into the keep.

Draven spoke conversationally as they walked, but Knox barely heard a word, except that they were headed to his mother's favorite place and where she could be found most days, a library.

Servants moved here and there in black and white livery, one such pair stood at the entryway they approached and opened the massively tall doors with the barest of touch. Inside, light poured out from dozens of magical soft white lights, different from the blue fire that lit the hallways, though no less fascinating.

The torches had Knox nearly stopping when he'd encountered them, Draven called them mage fire, a simple runic formation that created a smokeless fire that refused to light anything aflame without long exposure. But all that was forgotten as he looked into the massive library with its three levels of books. Walkways, ladders, and more made it possible to access the thousands of books, but none of that caught his eyes so much as a single figure sitting at a table surrounded by books.

She wore a red dress, her hair up in a messy bun, and when she looked to see who had entered, she did so with Knox's eyes, the same vibrant blue that seemed to sparkle even from a distance.

Scarlet Blackwood stood suddenly, her hand going to her mouth. His mother, the woman he'd so desperately wished to meet, looked over to her son and saw him for the first time as a man and not the babe she'd known.

"Knox," she said, her words barely a whisper but easily heard by his enhanced ears. "My boy." Tears fell as she heaved a breath of air and began to run toward him.

Knox didn't know what to do, so shocked at seeing her that he just let tears of his own fall down his face as he waited for her to walk the twenty paces between them. She covered the distance with the speed of an enhanced person, easily a match for his own speed, he thought as she crashed into him.

Her hug was warm, and he still had no words, but he hugged her back, squeezing her and wishing in that moment that she would never leave him. All the anger and confusion in his emotions were gone when put against the moment they were sharing. He could feel the raw emotion she felt for him like magic itself, washing over him and for a moment, he thought he could understand what a mother's love truly meant.

"I'm so sorry," she said, crying all the while. "I never wanted to leave you." She was sobbing but her words carried weight as she spoke.

"I'm alright," Knox said, his own tears continued to fall, and his words were spoken with raw emotion. "I'm okay." He didn't know why those were the words to escape his lips, but his mother sobbed all the harder upon hearing them.

For a long moment, they just held each other and stopped speaking. At some point, Draven left, but Knox still didn't want to release his mother, fearing that he'd wake and find it a terrible dream meant to tease his sanity.

After a period of time, uncountable by Knox or Scarlet, they released each other and Knox gazed into her eyes, so much like his own that he felt as if he were looking in an odd mirror. Her eyes were stained red by the crying and some dark face makeup she'd had now smeared her cheek. She coughed suddenly, pulling a white handkerchief up to her mouth and Knox recoiled when he saw red stain it.

"Are you okay?" he asked, his lips ready to begin the casting of his Luminous Surge to try and heal whatever damage she might have. His hands came up to make the signs, but she put her hands on his, lowering them.

"You're a healer," she said knowingly, regaining her composure she straightened and continued. "But no healing can restore me, none that I've encountered at least. I'm dying just as my father did and just as his mother did, just as you will one day. I'm so sorry to bring you here to your death."

Knox tilted his head to the side in confusion, not willing or able to understand the words she'd spoken. What did she mean she'd brought him here to his death? How could she be dying when he'd finally found her, finally been reunited with the mother he'd never gotten to know outside her journals.

"I read all your journals," Knox said, blurting out the words before thinking. "I got to know you from them, but please, you can't be dying?"

After a time, Knox got control of his emotions and remembered his mission. Despite the grave news he'd heard, and hoping it wasn't as bad as his mother feared, he pressed on to try and convince her of his mission.

"I'm here for the artifact in the Tower," Knox said to that end.

Scarlet just smiled. "I know, you are here to guard it now, just as always has been our family's curse. I hoped to have separated you from your fate, but the wheels are in motion now and I cannot stop them."

"No, you aren't understanding," Knox said, frustration leaking into his tone. "I'm here to challenge the Tower, not become its guardian."

This had the effect of making his mother's eyes go wide in understanding and then even wider as the implications hit her. "But you can't, it is a death sentence and one that will take you the moment you enter that vile place."

"I've challenged places like it before," Knox began to say but Scarlet cut him off.

"This is no mere dungeon," she said. "If you are anything like me, then I know you are going to be stubborn about it, but I beg you, do not enter the Tower. None have done so and lived."

"I'm different," Knox tried to say but it didn't appear she was listening anymore, just shaking her head and looking at him as if he were insane.

"It isn't about being different or stronger, this place was built for legends of old to challenge, it has been too long, and the threats inside have grown in power. Even during my short period over them I've felt it grow and shift," she said, pacing back and forth as she spoke.

"I'm the Titan of Light," Knox finally said, then to prove his point he fully unshielded his aura for her to witness, not just the little bit that leaked through for all to see, but the entirety of it.

She took several steps back with her hand on her mouth. For a long while she said nothing, her eyes shifting from confusion to astonishment then back to confusion.

"Mask yourself," she finally said, and Knox did so, as best as he still could under the influence of the system. "You've reached impossible heights, but what does it mean that you are the 'Titan of Light'. Surely, you don't speak of the Titans of old, the very beings said to have made this artifact and the Tower it resides in?"

"I do," Knox said. "I've got a lot to tell you, can we sit and talk?"

Scarlet nodded her head and they sat. Knox started at the beginning, telling her about his obsession with her journals and learning about runic magic. Next, he went on to tell his tale in full, sparing no details and getting her up to speed on the most important topics, ending with his current quest and need to obtain the artifact.

"I don't know," she said, shaking her head. "On the one hand you might be one of a few beings now that can enter and get the artifact, but on the other. Why didn't this Ramses fellow come with you? Surely, two of you up against the Tower would be better than one, tradition be damned."

"What of the steward?" Knox asked. "Will he stand in the way of me challenging the Tower?"

"He will," she said without hesitation. "Normally to do so would be socially unacceptable, but you are the last heir of our bloodline and the Tower without a guardian is a threat to him. It has been many generations since such a time has occurred, but the last time it was said to have brought chaos to the land."

"Then I have to figure out a way to get into the Tower without him knowing," Knox said.

Suddenly, noise from behind caught Knox's attention as several guards rushed into the room.

"You are under arrest," one of them declared.

CHAPTER 10
REJECTION

"STAND DOWN!" My mother growled from where she stood, Knox could feel the power building around her as she spoke. "You touch a hair on his head, and you'll not make it out of this library alive."

The dozen guards all took several steps back in obvious fear from the powerful Adventurer. What they couldn't know was that Knox could match her power, point for point, but he chose not to, instead resting a calming hand on her arm.

"I'll be alright," Knox said, then leaning in he added. "I've got a plan."

Of course, that was a lie, but Knox didn't want his mother to get in trouble on his account and it worked. She powered herself down and gave him a searching look.

"Are you sure?" she asked.

"I'm sure," Knox said.

Knox allowed himself to be taken, his weapons were removed and even his cloak pulled from his shoulders. He didn't care, he'd met his mother and he found that he was quite fond of her, even loved her and he wouldn't allow her to ruin her life for him when he had options.

What were the chances that Aetex, Dernal, and John would

stand by and allow him to be imprisoned? Not likely, he knew and with his own power he could easily liberate himself whenever he wanted. Or at least, he thought as much as he allowed them to take him deeper and closer to the Tower.

Through winding hallways and spiraling staircases they went ever lower until finally reaching a dark and dank prison. Rows upon rows of cells were filled with folks of all colors, sizes, and types, from elves to men. But the cell they took him to was covered in magical runes to the point that Knox was actually glad to be taken there, as it would give him a chance to study said runes.

"What am I being charged with?" Knox asked casually to one of the guards as he locked him behind rune reinforced bars that Knox was sure he could still break through given enough time.

"Not my business to say," the guard said, almost as casually as Knox had asked. Seemed like it was just a normal day for him, nothing too special going on. "But I don't envy you, these cells are unforgiving to your type."

"My type?" Knox asked, trying his best to keep the man talking for a chance to get more information.

"Adventurers," he said, then gesturing to the walls he continued. "They say these scratches on the wall drain away what makes you special and leaves you weak like us normal folk. For what it's worth, I'll see that you are well fed and watered."

"Thank you," Knox said. "Name's Knox, what's yours?"

"You can call me Micky," the man said, smirking. "I've got to go but hang in there and I'll see about getting you some water."

Pleasantly surprised by the kindness of the guard, Knox watched him go. He had light blonde hair, an odd accent, light skin that appeared to be left out in the sun too long for it had gone several shades darker and looked more like leather than smooth skin. Then there were his eyes, they seemed to glimmer a light shade of blue that reminded Knox of the ocean.

True to his word, Micky returned with water about an hour or so later with the promise of food in a few more hours. The effects of the prison cell soon became apparent as Knox studied them, more by his understanding of them than any sign of them actually working. If he understood it correctly, then the runes could siphon off magical energy to someplace else, but the problem was, Knox's aura was far too powerful to be affected by such mundane methods.

So instead of becoming any weaker, Knox felt just fine. In fact, he enjoyed his stay so far, doing his best to memorize the few runic formations that he thought he might be able to use himself. The draining, for instance, could be handy against weaker foes if he incorporated it with his Radiant Glyph spell and figured out a way to increase the pull.

He studied further and determined that if he took off certain protections, he could indeed increase the flow of it. Around this same time, he heard a voice from the cell to his left, another magically guarded one that Knox had assumed was empty.

"It tears at your very soul, doesn't it?" came the voice. "I know a trick or two to help fight off its effects, if you are interested in a trade."

Going up to the wall so as to better hear the man's voice, Knox responded. "I've no need to trade, the runic formations are too weak to bother me. This entire cage was meant to hold someone much weaker than me."

After a short pause, the man responded with a touch of humor in his voice. "Then why stay? Break free and release me as well, together we can bring justice to all the wrongly imprisoned."

"You were wrongly imprisoned?" Knox asked.

The man laughed. "Well, no, but I'm sure a few people here were and we can bring justice to them," he said.

"What's your name stranger?" Knox asked.

"Names aren't important, not in here. But you can call me Jack, for that is all you'll learn from me, Jack squat," Jack said.

"Alright Jack," Knox said, smirking. "What are you in for and how long do they plan on keeping you here? I've never been to a prison before and I'm unsure what to expect."

"Well," Jack said, drawing out the word. "There's the torture, the starvation, oh and the beatings on Tuesdays."

"They do all that?" Knox asked, surprised since Micky had been so nice to him.

"No," Jack said, seeming taken aback. "That's what I'm in for. As to when I'll be released, they've got me set up with a date with the executioner when he comes back to town. They do so few executions that they've had to call to the next city over to borrow someone able to do me in."

"Are you guilty of the crimes you've been accused of?" Knox asked, wanting to feel sorry for the guy but having trouble empathizing with his plight.

"Guilt is a funny thing," Jack said, laughing as he spoke.

"In what way?" Knox asked, this man was beginning to give him the creeps.

"In that I don't feel any, so why should I be guilty of the crimes they say I've done?"

"I mean," Knox began to say then paused to consider his words, "whether or not you feel guilty, if you did such horrible acts, then you deserve the sentence you've been handed."

"What about you?" Jack asked. "Are you a horrible murderer and defiler of the divine? Perhaps you eat children and murder helpless folk without our great gift? Oh, let me guess, you killed one of the nobles and tore their skin off so you could wear it to one of their balls?"

"What? Gross, no I'd never do that," Knox said.

The man laughed. "Oh, right, that was me," he said, his laughs continuing to echo through the halls.

Knox turned just in time to see Micky returning with a tray of food. He fit it in a slot and waited for Knox to grab hold before releasing it.

"Don't mind him," Micky said, thumbing a finger over to the man who called himself Jack. "He talks big, but he's actually in here for disturbing the peace repeatedly and will be out before the week is out." Leaning in, Micky whispered the next words, "He's a bit insane, but he's harmless."

"I heard that," Jack said, his laughing cutting off abruptly. "I'll be sure to kill you first, Mick my boy."

"And I'll be awaiting the day," Micky said, not missing a beat. Looking back at Knox, he took him in, looking up and down. "You are still looking pretty well. Usually, folks we put in here get pretty pale after a few hours, might have to have the High Magi come in and check the runes. Wouldn't want you escaping before they can tell you what you did wrong." Micky winked at him with that and then scratched at his chin. "Yes, I'll have Scarlet stop by and inspect them, just to be sure."

Several hours later, while Knox tried to nap, despite the near constant laughter that came from Jack's cell now, Scarlet appeared, wearing much the same she'd had on when he'd met her in the library, but her eyes were red around the edges.

"Are you alright?" Knox asked, but she gave him a look and began to chant runic phrases. The door opened and she came in, but the entire area went still and quiet.

"I've cast a sphere of silence, we have true privacy now, not like we did before," she said. Then going over to the wall, she inspected some of the runic formations scratched into the wall. "These are fine, yet you remain unaffected, you truly are stronger than even I, aren't you?"

"I believe so," Knox said, he'd made it to his feet and walked over to pull his mother into a tight hug. She welcomed it and he whispered into her ear. "Have you any word from my friends, the ones that came to the keep with me?"

"They are fine for now," she said, not whispering as she pulled him back out of the hug. "I've stayed Silas's hand from moving any further by threat of leaving. He knows he needs you to maintain the seals on the Tower, but he doesn't want to lose you to the Tower or, if you were to succeed, want to bend the knee to you as Lumisar's new king."

"I don't want any of that, but I need what lies within if I'm to save the world," Knox said, trying to be as blunt as possible. "I could leave this prison at any time, I doubt there are any here that could stop me from fighting my way to the Tower's entrance."

"Then why have you not done so yet?" she asked, her tone implying that Knox should do just that.

"I wanted to ensure my friends were going to be safe, which means they need to get out of the keep and into the city. If anything were to happen to Sintra, her people wouldn't react kindly, I think. And Draven has been a huge help, but I imagine he could handle himself in the politics of the nobles."

"He does and he is," she said with a grin. "Even now, he is turning the tide of the nobles' support to your favor, speaking of the Titan System and how it will enable a new age of powerful people that, if they act fast, they'll be able to direct and harness. He speaks of you as if you were the coming of a new age."

"I just might be," Knox said, shaking his head. "The Titan System is spreading far through the Endless Sea right now, but eventually it will begin to encompass all of the kingdoms, not just this one. People, weak and strong, will be able to harness power like never before. And not only that, but the influence of the Titan System changes the land as well, making it fertile and filled with monsters that will need to be slain."

"You are so much more than I'd have ever imagined," she said, brushing a hand across his cheek. "I didn't want this life for you, because I knew it would mean you'd be forced to be a warden of the Tower one day, but now it seems like you might actually have what it takes to defeat the challenges of the Tower."

She stayed quiet for several long seconds, just gazing into his eyes while he did the same, so happy in the comfort of a mother that clearly loved and cared for him.

"I will walk the halls of the Tower with you," she said finally. "Before you disagree, I am the only one who has studied what little knowledge we have of what lies within. I can help guide you through the five challenges and when the time comes for you to defeat the champion, you'll be ready."

"I could ask for nothing else so wonderful as having you by my side for this," Knox said, not planning on disagreeing with her at all. "But first, we must see to it that Sintra and Aetex escape the keep and find my friends, Dernal and John."

"Dernal, that rat bastard," she growled the words. "I'm glad for how all events have worked themselves out, but you'd be safe and sound living a normal life if not for that man's influences." She got thoughtful for a moment before continuing. "Tell me of Askar, he was such a wonderful man and I loved him so dearly, but I can't imagine how my betrayal would have affected him. Dernal has told me much, but tell me the truth, was the noble man of honor I'd grown to love, was he truly replaced by a drunkard?"

Knox found himself struggling to find the words to describe Askar, his father. He'd cared for the man after his accident and before that he'd been almost bearable, if a bit moody. But he found himself more recently respecting the man and the sacrifices he made, dealing with events as best he knew how.

"He's a complicated man," Knox finally said. "He lost an arm and fell into the drink as a way to comfort what he felt was a life of failure, but I know now it was more than that. He spoke of oaths you bound him with to keep him from speaking the truth. Why did you do that to him?"

Scarlet turned red in the cheeks and looked away. "A mother's love for her child outweighs all else and from the moment I saw you, your tiny pure face, I knew I couldn't let you become what I would eventually have to become. In a fit of, well I don't rightly know, but in the emotional state I was in, having to leave you and learning of my father's death, I did things I'm not proud of."

"He's doing better now, and he sends you his regards," Knox said, meeting her eyes as she finally took her gaze off the floor.

"I miss him," she whispered the words more to herself than to him.

"You can come with me when I retrieve the artifact," Knox said. "There will be no point in being here afterward, will there?"

109

"I suppose not," Scarlet said, brightening. The idea seemed to build in her, and she smiled wide. "Yes, I will go with you and see this city you are building. Doing so will allow me to become a part of the system that you have access to?"

"You'll love it," Knox said. "There is a structure to it like nothing else you've experienced, but at the same time it is flexible so all you've learned won't go to waste. Plus, I'm sure I could learn so much from you about runes and runic formations. Oh, here watch this."

Knox activated his Radiant Glyph spell and did a simple runic formation to create a ball of light using only his runes. It flickered into life, and he grabbed it out of the air to show her.

"You can do that without hand signs, words, or scribing into an object? Can I learn this power?" she asked, excited by the prospect.

"It's a Titan spell, but I can try to teach it to you. You'll know more once you pick a path of your own and you will see the limits and breadth of the power."

"I should go and see to it that this Sintra and Aetex is given leave," she said. "Once I've done that, I'll come here and together we will storm the Tower!"

CHAPTER 11
INTO THE TOWER

At least a day passed, Knox growing ever more worried about Sintra, Aetex, and his mother. All the while, he listened to the mad ravings of the prisoner beside him, unable to block it out. A few times he tried to replicate the spell his mother had used to create an area of silence, but he hadn't remembered each phrase right, so couldn't work out the corresponding runes.

Just when he felt his sanity had reached its peak, his mother returned with Micky by her side.

"Here to escort you to a meeting, though I think she has other plans," Micky said, thumbing over toward his mother.

"Silas wants to speak with you, but I'm taking you to the Tower before he gets a chance. Come, we must act now," she said, waving a hand and speaking words of power over Micky.

He looked at her as calm as ever, then slumped to the ground, snoring loudly.

"Was that necessary?" Knox asked, figuring the man to be just fine with them escaping if he'd been given the chance to speak on the matter.

"Here, take your things, I've collected your armor and weapons. And for his own security, it was," she said, then waved a hand and the door swung open before her, her arms full with Knox's things. "Time to leave."

"Take me with you!" Jack cried, but she ignored him, Knox doing the same.

He grew quiet as they left, weaving further and further out of the prison and deeper into the keep. Several times they encountered servants and even a pair of guards, but Scarlet had woven something around them that hid them from view. She was a powerful Adventurer and caster, that much was plain to see.

It wasn't until they reached the Tower's entrance that she spoke, her words old and ancient. "Gorith nathar tian gosh row."

A pair of double doors, covered in golden laced runes and hiding even more beneath the surface, cracked open and they rushed forward.

"Stop them!" came a familiar voice. It was Silas and he'd brought company. Cross bolts were released, and balls of fire thrown within moments.

Knox turned and cast Prism Ward just as the attacks hit. However, he needn't have done anything as his mother cast out her arms and a wave of force turned away all the attacks.

"Go on ahead," she said. "I'll take care of them."

Among the group, Knox sensed several C Rankers but nothing more. However, he had no plans on abandoning his mother, so he cast Solar Wings and zoomed forward, punching out two guards within seconds of his wings appearing. He turned to the strongest of the C Rankers and cast Luminous Surge, blowing him backward and taking him out of the fight. Next, he cast Void Grasp, tying up the remaining guards and Silas.

Using Ethereal Step, he teleported back to his mother's side.

"Let's go, that'll keep them tied up for at least a minute," Knox said, smiling at the look of disbelief on his mother's face.

"Okay," was all she managed to say as they turned and walked through the door.

"You'll regret betraying me!" Silas screamed, but his words

were muffled as the door shut behind them and loud words spoke out in the plain square room all around them.

"Welcome Challenger, you have one among you that is able to challenge the Tower, therefore you will not be purged. Speak your name and enter."

Ahead, a doorway appeared with runes around it that looked strikingly similar to a dungeon path door.

"Knox," he said, hesitating before adding, "Blackwood."

"Scarlet Blackwood," his mother said, taking his hand and squeezing it.

"You may enter, prepare yourself for the challenge of Darkness, find yourself and the path forward. Speak the truth to pass."

With that, the sides of the room shrunk and suddenly they were in a hallway, with no way out but forward. Onward and forward they went, stepping through the shimmering portal into the first challenge.

"What can you tell me about the challenges?" Knox asked, turning to his mother as the world around them shimmered into existence much smoother than any dungeon he'd entered.

Before she had a chance to answer, voices sounded ahead.

They stood in a forest, one that Knox could swear looked like the one surrounding his home, Keenlen's Vale. Scarlet looked around with wide eyes as voices neared and three figures appeared before them, stopping to wave.

One was clearly Askar Trelling, and the other two were unknown to him, but one was an elf and the other a human with dark skin and a surly look on his face, he spoke first.

"You've had us thinking you were lost, are you ready to challenge that dungeon, or aren't you?" He looked right at Scarlet as he spoke, only noticing Knox as he neared. "Oh, you've found us a fifth, that's wonderful."

"This is the day I find out I'm with child, the day I leave the group," Scarlet whispered to Knox, cupping her hand to keep the sound from traveling. Then, looking right at the man, she said, "Let's do it, the dungeon will be an easy one."

Then Knox realized where they were, some mile or so outside of the Mire's Gloom Dungeon, a place he was rather familiar with.

"Knox, this is Dale," she pointed at the muscled dark-skinned man. "And that is Askar and Gil." Pointing to Knox's father and then the elf.

"Well met," Knox said. "I'm Knox."

Askar smiled wide at that and came forward to shake his outstretched hand. "Nice to meet you bud, I have a grandfather named Knox, good name. He was a bit of a timekeeper, loved watches and the sort. You wouldn't happen to have the time, would you? Because I do, and we are late."

"Oh, don't listen to them," Scarlet said, playing along. "They are just sore that another person is here to share the loot."

"She isn't wrong," Gil said, her voice high-pitched even for an elf.

Knox just smiled and followed Scarlet as they headed for the dungeon, unsure what the Tower was challenging them of here.

"After this dungeon I felt the first signs of pregnancy sickness, but why are we here?" Scarlet asked, and suddenly, as they walked the world around them shifted and they stood inside a cavern, a dead dragon the size of a wagon in front of them.

"That was close, but you really came in clutch there, Knox," Askar said, slapping him friendlily on the shoulder.

"We need to talk," Scarlet said, putting a hand on Askar's shoulder.

They walked off to the side, but Knox could hear them even though they whispered their words.

"I need to tell you something important," Scarlet said, Knox looked away from them to appear to give them privacy.

"What's going on?" Askar asked, sounding more concerned than Knox had ever known him to be.

"I'm with child, I'm sure of it now," she said.

"That's wonderful news," Askar said, not missing a beat. "Scarlet, I'm so happy and I can't wait to meet them!"

"What?" Scarlet asked. "You didn't react like this before, what lies are these?"

"I don't understand," Askar said, glancing toward the group and seeing Knox, clearly watching them despite trying not to. "It is my child, isn't it?"

"That's closer to how I expected you to react," Scarlet said, putting a hand on his shoulder. "I can't be an Adventurer anymore, not till the baby comes. And we have to keep it a secret from my father, I don't want him growing up to be..."

"To be what?" Askar asked. "You speak so little about your family and past, what secrets are you hiding from me?"

"It's nothing, let's get our loot and leave," Scarlet said and as she did so, the world around shifted once more.

They were in a home that Knox recognized, his home, but it was newly built, and everything looked in good condition. Even now, he could sense a dozen or more runes throughout the house, but only half as many as he knew there would be one day.

"Today is the day that I leave," Scarlet said, looking down at her stomach. She was fully pregnant now and a now bearded Askar stood close by with a younger looking Henry.

"Why is he here?" Askar said, gesturing to Knox. "It's bad enough that you insist on naming our child after him, but to keep bringing him around."

"He is a friend and nothing more," Scarlet said, then whispering to Knox she added, "I don't know what this challenge is meant to be, but events are different from what I remember, having you here, for instance, changes things plenty."

"Well friend or not," Henry said. "I've work to do, so I'll need him to wait outside with Mr. Trelling. Please come lay down Scarlet, you shouldn't be up in your condition."

Askar and Knox left the room, going to stand outside, and Knox looked out over his home. The neighborhood wasn't so bad here, a few rundown looking houses, but Knox's own was well-built, as well as a few others. Time had drawn this section of the town down to the slums it became later.

115

"You excited to have a kid?" Knox asked, illusions or not, he was intrigued by the chance to speak with a younger version of his father.

"I think she means to leave," Askar said, his expression dark. "We got news her father is ill and will be dead soon, but she says she can't go until after she's given birth. She tells me her family can't ever know she's had a child."

He turned to Knox and to Knox's surprise he had tears in his eyes. In all his life, he'd never known Askar to cry.

"I'm sure she is doing what she feels is best," Knox said, unsure what the proper response should be. If this were a test, he ought to be looking for a way to beat it, but just seeing his father weep openly about possibly losing the love of his life was more painful than he thought it would be.

"I don't want to choose between them," Askar said, shaking his head. "I want them both, I want to love and protect them, but she's going to leave, and I'll have to fend for our child myself. What if I'm a shit father, what if I can't do it?"

"Y-you," Knox stuttered his next words, before closing his mouth all together. This was almost too much to bear, the emotions of the moment rolling over him like crashing waves. He had tears of his own in his eyes now and he looked at Askar in a new light.

A father, unprepared and left alone to fend for a child he knew nothing about how to raise. A man prepared to do anything for that child but mourning the loss of his love.

"I know it isn't the fault of the child that she's leaving, but I can't help but feel resentment toward him and I haven't even met him yet. Am I a bad father? Am I going to be a bad father?" Askar asked, looking Knox full in the face, tears streaming silently down his face.

Knox's thoughts raced as he thought what to say. Sure, he thought, he would be a shitty father, but telling him that wouldn't help. Then the words of the Tower's ominous voice 'speak the truth' hit him and he prepared himself to do one of the hardest things he'd ever done.

Clearing his throat, he looked up at the young Askar and prepared to tell him the truth.

"You are both a terrible father and at the same time, the best parent I had," Knox said, putting a hand on his shoulder. "You let your resentment darken your mood. You drank too much, you broke things around the house, and you hit me, but you did something that my mother never did for me. You were there, and for that I am thankful. You aren't perfect, but I forgive you."

The world around them wobbled and shifted, Scarlet appeared beside him, tears of her own running down her face.

"I should have never left you both," she said, sobbing out the words. "I thought it was the best way forward, but I let duty come before my family."

"And I suffered because of it, but I'm here with you now, and together we will defeat this Tower and claim the artifact," Knox said, trying to keep his emotions in check.

Ahead of them a doorway appeared, and they found themselves in a familiar hallway.

"We can move forward," Knox said, taking the first step. "Together." Knox held his hand out and she took it, tears still streaming down her face.

CHAPTER 12
CHALLENGES OF A DIFFERENT KIND

"You didn't get a chance to tell me what you know about the challenges," Knox said, trying to get them back on track and not lingering on the emotional punch in the face he'd received.

"Right," Scarlet said, still dazed by the contents of the first challenge. "Uh, so from what I've read, it challenges you in different ways. It could be physical, emotional, or mental, but we've all but confirmed the emotional attacks, haven't we?"

"Appears that way," Knox said, the room they were in solidifying.

Before them, in a room approximately one hundred paces wide and long, was a single giant rat. No new voice came to give them a greeting or a hint at the challenge, but when the rat saw them, it began to run forward, and Knox had an idea what kind of challenge this floor would hold.

"This must be the physical one," Knox said, pulling free his axe as he walked. He had both Scarlet and his battle axe and chose to use the smaller of the two for this opponent.

"That is a gift I gave your father before I left," his mother said, noticing the axe. "I was going to ask you about it. Has it served you well in both mundane and other situations?"

"Quite well," Knox said, twirling the familiar weight in his hands and striking out at the rat as it came within range. With a single precise blow, the rat was finished. "It saved my life more times than I can count, a deadly weapon reinforced by powerful magic."

"A formation to keep it sharp and several to increase its durability, as well as a hybrid formation meant to draw in power to fix minor blemishes on the metal and wood. That one was something I was very proud of when I did it. I've done more magnificent runic formations since, but this was the first of some very interesting line of work," she said.

"To the next room?" Knox suggested and they walked into a wide-open doorway and into the next room.

The next room held a wolf, it died in a similar fashion, and then a Nolic, an Owlbear, and finally a magic-wielding goblin. After those more physical fights, Knox was wondering if the challenge would either end soon or become more difficult. He'd yet to use his magic once and relied only on his axe.

"I named the axe Scarlet," Knox said, the thought making him smile as they walked toward the next room.

"Oh?" Scarlet said, smirking at her son. "So, I'm a weapon and a tool? That is oddly fitting for the situation I find myself in here in Lumisar."

"This axe was my best friend and companion through several phases of my life. I've replaced it since," Knox said, nudging the more powerful axe at his side. "But that doesn't mean I've forgotten it."

With that, he put away the smaller woodcutter's axe and pulled out his battle axe. "Let me show you what it can do."

The axe could suck in the essence of the monsters he fought, and he ought to have used it this entire time, but he wanted to show his mother he still had a use for the tool she'd crafted for Askar and eventually him. Perhaps he ought to give the axe back to Askar, the thought had always repulsed him up until now.

Now he thought it might be a good idea.

The monster, or three this time as it were, that awaited them in the center of the next room was more of a black shadow than anything else. It seemed to fade in and out of existence.

"A shadow wraith," Scarlet said, energy surging around her as she spoke. "They are beings of magic and can only be slain by such, allow me."

Knox held out a hand. "This is my challenge and I've got magic to spare," Knox said, mumbling a few words and holding out his hand to cast Luminous Surge.

The attack hit the first one full in the face and it screamed as it was torn apart by the light. However, the other two phased out of being and appeared right in front of Knox. He teleported out of the way using Ethereal Step just in time to avoid being touched by one, but his mother wouldn't be so lucky.

She screamed as the ice-cold grasp of one encircled her neck. A moment later, she was lashing out with blue energy that repulsed the wraith back but failed to kill it.

Knox ran forward, grabbed his mother, and activated Dimensional Shift to swap their places with one of the wraiths. Then he ran into the two of them, casting Nexus Shift he returned back to his mother's side and left behind an explosion of light that consumed both of the remaining wraiths.

"You have such a variety of magic at your disposal," she said, shaking her head in disbelief. "I thought I was versatile, but you."

"I haven't even shown my full utility yet," Knox said, casting Mystic Armor on himself. It shone a golden color after he took the time to add some of his spare points into Lightforged Armor. It increased his resistance to Physical and Magical Damage by a whopping 15% and was worth each of the five points he'd used. He would need to sit down and really go over his talent trees and points he'd gained soon, but now wasn't the time.

Next, he cast Mystic Veil on the pair of them, further reducing the damage they'd take.

"Also, check this out," Knox said, casting Astral Projection and splitting himself into two.

"You are a true marvel," Scarlet said. "Now stop showing off and let's continue."

They did so, pushing forward and into the next room where they met another challenger. This time it was a team of three Spectral Knights, ghostly warriors clad in ethereal armor, wielding spectral swords that seemed to pull in the light around them.

"Watch out for those swords," Scarlet said, but Knox was already paying close attention to them as the three came to encircle them. "I'd be willing to bet they have life draining properties on top of being able to cut you in two."

They moved slowly and deliberately, so Knox allowed himself to breathe and focus on his sense, tracking their movements and getting ready to strike out. His axe was up and ready to block the first strike as it came, nearly as fast as he could move. These spectral knights were no joke; a strike slammed into his back, glancing off his armor. He felt a portion of his energy drain on contact with the sword, weakening the armor more than a normal blow would have.

Knox's axe passed right through the knights, only seemingly able to make contact with their weapons, but either way, his own weapon did its job of pulling essence out of the creature and weakening it. They were fighting with similar weapons and Knox absently wondered if he'd be able to take a few of the swords out with him for study and eventual use by someone in Luminar.

His stray thought cost him another strike on his back and he turned in time to see his mother pull out a weapon of her own to deal with the third knight. It looked to be just a sword hilt, but as she held it a beam of bright blue power formed into the shape of a blade. She cut low, slashing the Knight's arm clean off.

Knox slashed out with his axe and took one of the Knights in the head but took another blow that shattered his right pauldron into sparks of magical debris. Having downed one, he was able to give the next his full attention. They'd been moving so fast that two-on-one meant he was forced to take hits, but now that it was one-on-one, his speed was a match for the knight.

Weaving in and out of combat, he struck at the knight until finally getting a blow through his defenses. The cut opened a wide groove on his chest and Knox followed up with an Arcane Pulse, knocking its weapon from its hand. Then, using Ethereal Step, he appeared before the knight and drove his axe down hard, killing it. They went up in a poof of ghostly smoke, weapons and all.

Knox cursed under his breath, and he turned to see his mother finish off one by taking its head clean off, she was a far superior fighter than Knox had realized.

"You handle a sword pretty well for a caster," Knox said, seeing her blade fizzle out and return to being just a hilt and handle. She stowed it away with a smirk and a wink.

"There is much about your mother you've yet to learn," she said teasingly.

They fought several more spectral types before reaching what must have been the final room, for the door was three times the size of the others and inside Knox could hear pounding as something massive walked around the center of the room.

Walking up to the door and stepping through the swirling smoke that kept them from seeing inside, just as all previous doors had, they got their first glimpse of their final challenge of the floor.

It was a stone golem the size of a two-story house, or perhaps a rock elemental, Knox was unsure of the proper designation. It looked like someone had taken several boulders and stuck them together to shape a vaguely humanoid shape. This wouldn't be an easy fight, Knox realized instantly as he caught the A Ranked aura coming off of it. It was time to give it all he had and hope that he could keep his mother in one piece while doing so.

They squared off against their new opponent and Knox did his best to keep his thoughts clear. This was going to be a challenge like no other, but he'd beaten worse odds before, and he'd beat this rock golem.

"Stay as far away as you can and hit it from afar," Knox said. "The less I have to worry about protecting you, the more effective I'm going to be in battle."

"I'm no pushover, you know," Scarlet said, but all the same she nodded to his words. "I'll do my best to stay out of the way."

Knox understood that she knew that her son, despite his age and inexperience, was a far greater threat to the golem than she could ever be, magic or no. But in this case, perhaps he could use her wisdom.

"Any ideas on the best ways to defeat this thing?" Knox asked, his spells were ready to be cast but so far, the lumbering elemental didn't make a move to attack.

"Elementals draw in a good deal of magic to give them form, so magical attacks will be limited in their usefulness, but not totally ineffective. I imagine it is pretty slow and might react slowly as well, so speed will be your greatest weapon. If you have a blunt weapon I'd say, try that, but as that axe appears to be your only weapon, use it but expect that it will take significant damage to its durability during the fight, maybe even break," Scarlet said, shooting off facts rapid fire.

"Go fast, use force and magic with limited success. It has to have a Monster Core someplace, any idea where I should look?" Knox asked, stepping forward and twirling his axe with his left hand while reading a spell in his right.

"I don't, but from what I've read the base of the spine is the most common place, so perhaps under the rocky bit that looks like a head?" Scarlet suggested.

The rock elemental roared despite having no visible mouth, a sound like the crash of boulders running down a rocky hill. It lumbered forward, slow, but not as slow as Knox expected with its bulk. Still, he was faster and rushed forward with weapon ready, mumbling the words of a spell as he closed the distance. With his right hand he let loose a Luminous Surge, the spell hitting the rock elemental, but doing no noticeable damage besides rocking it back a foot.

The rock elemental got within striking distance and Knox leaned into his sense to position himself in a way to miss the strike while connecting his own. It worked, his weapon clanging hard against the stone and chipping small pieces free. The smash of its attack was so powerful though that, despite missing, it forced Knox to reposition his feet.

This had the undesirable effect of putting him in the path of a second strike, which he took on the forearms. He felt his bones nearly give under the blow and his entire body was flung backward like a rag doll. His mother cast a spell that slowed him, and he rolled to a stop some ten paces away and got to his feet in time for the rock elemental to reach him, swinging its huge boulder fists for another attack.

Dodging and rolling, Knox put all his energy into avoiding attacks while Scarlet pelted the rock elemental with arcane attack after arcane attack. At one point she chanted for several seconds and cast a beam of water that cut off an entire shoulder section.

"Do that again but aim for the head," Knox called out between dodging and getting in a few strikes of his own.

"I was aiming for the head," Scarlet cried back between panting breaths. "I can't manage that again for a bit, I'm running low on energy already."

"Time to get serious then," Knox said, mostly under his breath to himself.

Knox ran, putting distance between him and the rock elemental, throwing a Luminous Surge at it to get its attention, then he laid his trap. First, he cast Void Grasp to slow it. Then, slamming down his foot, he cast Radiant Ground. Next, he activated Radiant Rush over the same area of ground, ending his spell with a Nexus Shift on the rock elemental so that he landed right in his damaging spells. But he was far from done.

Casting Lustrous Chains, he felt himself dip below half Mana, but he pressed onward. With the chains tying up the giant of a golem, it took a slow steady beating from the ground effects. Casting Solar Wings, Knox put himself out of reach and began to use Radiant Glyph to do his multiplier runic formation that he'd been perfecting.

One second passed, then two, then three and his chains gave out. Next his wings began to fade, but he did it, finishing his runic formation. It floated above him, and he cast Luminous Surge into it, filling it with as much power as he dared. He could feel the multiplying effect beginning to take hold as the power folded in on itself.

A beam of brilliant and blinding white light shot out for the rock elemental like a ray of unstoppable sunlight. It crashed into the arm that the rock elemental raised to block and completely obliterated it. The attack continued for another two seconds, all the power he'd given it being sucked out and powered even more so by his expenditure of Mana.

The rock elemental cried out as its chest took a hit, but it didn't go down. He'd hit it with his hardest attack, and it had lost an arm and that was it.

Then, right before his eyes, the rock elemental began to shift, and the rocks folded within itself as it changed. Suddenly, it had lost about half of its mass and height, but it had an arm again and showed no signs of any damage. It was sleeker and more slender than before, as if they were fighting an entirely different foe.

As Knox landed on the ground and readied his axe, the rock elemental moved forward. Slow at first but gaining speed in a way it hadn't been able to do before. Like a rockslide that grew in intensity and speed as it went, this rock elemental hit Knox with the force and speed of a true A Ranker.

Knox barely had the forethought to lean into his sense and use it to outstep the rock elemental. He could just barely stay ahead of it, receiving a few glancing blows as he danced around it and pain throbbing through him, threatening to slow him down. If he slowed now, he'd be dead, for this new rock elemental was no pushover in speed or strength.

Right when Knox was getting the hang of its attack pattern, it roared, and the arms shifted, becoming two long, sharp swords at each end. Suddenly its attack patterns were different, slashing here and there like an expert swordsman. Knox was forced to parry with his weapon and use Reality Ripple to slow the attacks enough for him to dodge. But Reality Ripple only worked for a small amount of time, and he didn't know if he could keep ahead of such attacks.

Not knowing what else to do, he used Arcane Revelation, after Ethereal Stepping away to a safe distance. This spell allows him to copy a spell from a different path by merely thinking about it, if only for a short duration. All he could think was that he wasn't a match for this creature and that he needed help, so he cast a spell he'd seen Dernal and Henry cast before, summoning forth a Celestial Guardian.

Knowledge, foreign and strange, filled his head for only a moment and he suddenly knew what he had to do. He cast the spell, and the world tore open to allow a Celestial being into exis-tence before him.

"I come to aid you, young one," it said, its voice booming yet comforting. This particular Celestial Guardian was easily two heads taller than the biggest he'd seen summoned before and it wore armor far more majestic, even sporting a crown on its head. "I am prince of my people. Stand down Elemental or be torn asunder."

It rushed forward, wings beating behind it and a magnificent golden sword wielded in its two hands. Knox ran to his mother and checked on her. She was on her knee and breathing hard as she tried to recover enough Mana to fight back.

"It won't last long," Knox said, panting and out of breath himself. "But I bought us a few seconds to come up with a plan. This version of the rock elemental is too fast for me, I might need to remove a restraining band to defeat it, but I don't want to lose my hard-won progress."

"What do you mean—no, it doesn't matter," she said, shaking her head. "I'm nearly to the point that I can cast my water jet again, and with how skinny this new form is, I think I can sunder it into two. Go help your friend and be ready to do that tele-porting step when I yell for it."

"Right," Knox said, nodding his head and hefting his axe.

He watched the fight progress and was surprised to see that his summoned Celestial Guardian was pushing back the elemen-tal. It wasn't without damage, though; the angelic creature had cuts and bled shimmering white light in various places as the rock elemental did its best to shred him through his armor.

The Celestial Guardian slashed out with its sword and took a chunk off the rock elemental's chest, but it was clear he was slow-ing, his strikes coming less and less for each strike he received.

"Coming from behind," Knox yelled to his Guardian, and it looked, sparing only a moment to acknowledge him. Between the two of them, the rock elemental's speed began to mean nothing. He struck out low when the rock elemental attacked high, but the Celestial Guardian was there to catch, and parry blows that would have taken Knox's head off.

Relying on his sense he saw the movements the rock elemental meant to make before it made them and cut chunk after chunk out of it. He was low on Mana, so he used his spells sparingly, casting Astral Projection and using Ethereal Step only when necessary to keep himself ahead of death.

Together, they fought like ravenous wolves, sensing their prey's weakness.

"I'm sorry, but my time has ended. Have faith, and you will defeat your foe," the Celestial Guardian suddenly said; a rip of a portal appeared behind it, and he was sucked back in.

That left Knox in a one-on-one fight that he knew he couldn't win. A slash came down for his face and he could sense without trying to use it that he didn't have the Mana for another Ethereal

Step for at least another few seconds, so close he was scraping the bottom of his Mana pool.

Suddenly a sword of vibrant blue appeared, stopping the blow, and Knox turned to see his mother, a look of fierce determination on her face as sweat poured down her brow.

"Get away from my son, you piece of shit!" she screamed at the rock elemental; while holding the sword arm in place, she began to chant. Knox caught the next blow on his axe and used his tiny bit of mana to cast Lustrous Chains, both arms were taken in a multitude of chains, giving them a chance to escape melee range.

Scarlet finished her chant and dropped her sword, raising both hands together, she chanted a final word of power.

A beam of narrow water shot out and bisected the golem and shattered chains. It didn't stand a chance against her attack with its new slim form. The top half fell to one side and the bottom to the other.

"We did it!" Knox cried, but just as he allowed himself a breath of fresh air, the two parts began to shimmer and change.

"Smash it to bits!" Scarlet cried, grabbing up her sword and rushing forward. Knox did the same with his axe and followed her example, smashing the top half as hard as he could with no regard to the damage his weapon's edge was receiving.

The shimmering and shifting stopped suddenly, as Knox cracked against something softer in the middle of the chunks of stone.

"I think I found its Monster Core," Knox said as a torrent of energy was sucked into his weapon, and he felt himself receive a flood of new essence.

"You are such an essence hog," Scarlet said, eying him with a touch of humor in her tone. "I've not gotten a lick of essence from any of these monsters, it's like you have a tornado inside of you pulling it all in and leaving none for me to pull inside."

"Benefits of the system," Knox said, shrugging and catching his breath.

They'd done it, defeated a nearly impossible foe, but this was only the second floor of five. Would they have what it takes to conquer three more floors, and how much more difficult could things get? Sure, there were different types of difficulty, but if they faced off against anything stronger than this rock elemental, then they'd be in some serious trouble.

Besides all that, Knox remained confident in his ability to overcome and though she hadn't said it, his mother was even more confident that her son had what it would take to obtain the legendary artifact.

CHAPTER 13
RIDDLES AND MIND GAMES

"How DID you manage to summon that," Scarlet paused as if she were trying to think of the right words, "golden thing?"

"I have a costly spell that allows me to tap into other Paths and copy a spell, this was really the first time I had a need to do so, but it took much more mana than I realized it would," Knox said, shaking his head at the thought of how drained it had left him. "If I'd known I might not have cast it or perhaps I'd have led with it. It gives me a crazy amount of utility, but it isn't something I can just use for each fight."

"Well, it worked," she said, her breath was finally coming in evenly again and her color appeared to be returning to her face. "Too bad you couldn't copy my water technique; we'd have ended the fight before it had a chance to change."

"If you'd learned it from a path, I might be able to, although I haven't seen anything like that yet. But there is an elemental magic path that might fit you pretty well," Knox said.

Scarlet nodded, then looked up at him as if remembering something. "That runic formation you did that multiplied the output of your spell; can you teach me that?"

"Sure thing," Knox said, happy to know something that she wanted to learn.

They spent the next half hour going over the formation and adjusting it to make it more efficient based on some notes from Scarlet. It was a moment Knox enjoyed, both of them being able to flex their academic minds and magical knowledge. In fact, they had so much fun doing it that for a while they both forgot where they were and the grand quest that awaited them.

When they finished, Scarlet was looking much better and Knox felt like his resources had filled themselves up, restoring his health and mana. He'd be more careful in their next fight not to bring himself to the brink so fast, but looking back in the fight he really couldn't nitpick too much considering the opponent he was up against.

A door had appeared in the back of the room, and they went through it and then up a staircase to the next floor. What awaited them was a single mirror in the center of the room, the rest of the room was the same old square stone of the previous floor.

"What do you think?" Knox asked, sensing nothing magical from the mirror and seeing no other way forward, not even a door on the far side, though he suspected one would appear when they figured out the challenge.

"Only one way to find out," Scarlet said, shrugging. "I've reached the extent of my very limited knowledge of what to expect, so this could be anything."

They walked up together but as they got to a point where they could see their reflection, Knox immediately knew something was off. Instead of the armor reinforced with his magical glowing golden armor, he saw himself wearing some plain clothes similar to what he'd wear when working as a woodcutter, brown slacks and a tan tunic.

On his waist, instead of the battle axe, he saw only Scarlet, the axe. His hands were worn and his face tired, much as he felt after a long day of work. But what was more confusing was he didn't see his mother's reflection. Instead, he stood alone as he once was, staring back at himself.

"What do you see?" Knox asked, confused at what the mirror could be showing them.

"I-uh, I see myself as I once was," Scarlet said, her words coming out as a whisper. "An Adventurer, and by my side, Askar. What do you see?"

"I see myself as a woodcutter," Knox said simply. "What does this mean? Is it showing us our past?"

"No," Scarlet said. "Askar and I are older, and battle scarred from a life of Adventuring. This is some illusion on what might have been or what could have been, perhaps?"

"Look, runes on the edge of the mirror, I recognize some of them as the Titan Language," Knox said, focusing on them and trying to work out their meaning. "It says, and this is a rough translation but, 'Reflection of what could have been, find strength in what is.'"

"What could have been," Scarlet said, reaching out to the mirror and tears filling her eyes. "Why not show me a life with my child, why show me alone with Askar by my side. Is it saying that there is no life where I could have lived with my baby boy by my side?"

"I stand alone," Knox said, thinking about what that could mean. "I see no one else around, but myself at the end of a long day of work. What does that mean, what am I to learn from this 'could have been'?"

As Knox stared into the glass it shifted and he saw himself as he was, battle worn and wearing armor, but a moment later it shifted to the old him. Was it somehow showing him a possible self—but what was the point?

As he looked at his old self, he felt an emotion he didn't think he would feel, a longing for the life that he'd once had. Was there possibly a part of him that still wished he'd stayed as he was and not taken the path of an Adventurer, the way forward that led to him walking the Path of the Titans?

Something about that felt right and so he latched onto it.

Sure, he wasn't always happy with how his life had gone, but he definitely didn't want to go back to that life either.

"I'm satisfied with my life as it is, I don't need to see what might have been," Knox said, practically shouting at the mirror now.

He heard something click and suddenly he was looking at himself in the mirror as he was now, just a simple reflection.

"I'm not," Scarlet said, once more tears streaming down her face. "This isn't exactly the life I imagined, but oh my sweet Askar how you've changed." She reached out her hand to the mirror and as she touched it, the mirror rippled and began to suck her in.

"No," Knox said, grabbing hold of her and pulling. "Make peace with your past, reject what cannot be!"

"I'm trying," Scarlet said, her breathing coming fast and hard as it sucked her in all the way to her elbow. "I don't want this life! I want a life with my son, give that to me and I'll let you take me!"

"Stay with me now and you can have that! I'm here now!" Knox fell backward as suddenly the mirror stopped sucking her in.

"I'm here," Knox said, holding his mother as she cried. "I'm here now."

The next room held a statue of a beast with a wolf's head, wings of a crow, and the body of a bear. Light poured in from windows high up in the spherical room, falling in a line leading up to the beast. It was as if the very light wished for them to walk the path up to the monster, but Knox resisted the urge to walk in the light. Instead, he stayed at the door and readied his weapons. Surely, this would be another test of strength and battle prowess.

"Come near so that you may hear," came a voice from the beast's wolf-like head. "Do not fear, for I shall adhere."

"Adhere to what?" Knox called out, walking forward with Scarlet just behind him but staying out of the light.

"To my oaths of nonviolence," came the voice. "Should you attack, I will respond in kind, but speak to me and all I shall do is speak to you."

"Speak about what?" Knox asked, wary of the beast.

"I've a riddle that I wish to present to you, answer correctly and you shall pass, fail to do so and you shall not pass," came the response.

"We're listening," Scarlet said as they stepped into the light before the majestic beast.

"I am not what I was yesterday, and tomorrow, I will not be what I am today. Seen in seasons and in the sky, felt in hearts and in the blink of an eye. What am I?"

"Are you any good with riddles?" Knox asked, but he could already tell by the look on her face that she was as puzzled as Knox felt.

"Normally, I'd say I was. In fact, I was the go-to person in our dungeon group years back that handled most of them, but I'm not sure about this one," Scarlet said, her head tilted to the side a measure as she pondered over what the answer could be.

"How many times can we try to answer?" Knox asked, wondering now if it were a one-and-done kind of deal.

"I'll allow three attempts, but no more," came the response, a wolfish grin on the monster's face.

"Is it time?" Scarlet asked and Knox nodded eagerly as that seemed like it could fit.

"Incorrect," responded the beast.

"The present?" she asked a moment later.

"Incorrect."

"Those could all fit to a degree, but if it isn't any of those then I'm not sure what it could be," Scarlet said, rubbing at her nose.

"Let's think about what this floor has been about so far," Knox said. "It has focused on our past, perhaps that could be the answer?"

"No," Scarlet said immediately. "It has been more than that, almost as if it were focusing on... I have the answer!"

"Are you sure?" Knox asked, biting his lip as he waited to hear her answer.

"I'm sure," Scarlet said, a wolfish grin of her own spreading across her face. "The answer is change."

There was a long pause while the wolf head just stared at Scarlet before it let out a loud sigh. "I'll accept your answer. You are free to continue."

And with that, they were free to go. Knox stepped carefully around the mighty beast and found a doorway awaiting them on the other end. Surprisingly, it led up and to the next floor. This particular challenge had been difficult and short, but for a very different reason than the previous one.

"Thank you," Knox said, regarding his mother. "I'd have been forced to fight that beast if not for you."

"You'd have figured it out eventually," Scarlet said, brushing a hand lightly on Knox's shoulder.

CHAPTER 14
TEMPTATIONS

THE MOMENT they made it to the new floor, they found a room filled to the brim with magical items that practically screamed power to Knox's sense. A voice rang out as it had at the start of the Tower.

"You seek power to destroy your enemies," the voice said. "I offer you greater power and weapons here if you would only turn back and leave the Tower afterward. Choose wisely, for I shall not grant such a boon again."

Knox looked over to Scarlet, but she looked as puzzled by the words as he felt. So instead, he tried to talk to the voice.

"The artifact I seek is said to be unparalleled in power, why should I settle for less?" Knox asked.

"Not all you seek shall you find, nor will it quite be as you imagine. Choose here and leave, great warrior."

"It wouldn't hurt to look," Knox said, shrugging.

Each piece of magically enhanced gear, weapons, and trinkets had a plaque that explained what it would do.

There was a spear that could inflict a wound that could not be healed. A staff that called fire that had the ability to erase you from time, not just kill. A bracelet that was said to give the power of the gods, enabling creation and destruction in equal measure. The list went on and on, each of them Knox imagined could get the job done of defeating the great Dark Titan, but it made him lust all the more for the greater artifact, the item he'd been sent here to gather.

"Can I test the weapons, perhaps if I saw them used in combat I'd be tempted," Knox said, speaking to the disembodied voice and hoping for a response.

"Choose a tool and step through to face a challenger."

A door appeared and Knox could see a golden armored figure with a simple great sword in his hands awaiting him. Knox picked up an axe, which was said to be able to cleave the very fabric of space with its slices, and he tested the weight. It was light, but heavy enough to have a good feeling to it.

The weapon was ordinary, if practical, in design. A simple small axe head with a spike on the other side. It radiated power, yet no runes could be seen on the surface or beneath it. A simple tool of destruction.

Walking toward his opponent, Knox focused on the simple sounds of his own footsteps and his breathing. The room was lit by some unseen force, and he found himself searching for the source of the light, but there was none, just an ever-present glow filling the room.

His golden armored opponent stood still as death as he approached. Knox noticed with a measure of thankfulness that his mother stayed out of the room, looking through the portal at them instead. There was no telling the destruction this weapon might cause, so he wanted to be sure she'd be safe.

Raising the axe and saluting his opponent, the golden knight did the same, signaling the start of the battle.

With speed to match an A Ranker, the knight shot forward, its weapon going wide and swinging down in an upward arc, heading right for Knox's face.

He was ready with his own strike though, swinging to meet the weapon and turn it aside. However, as he swung, the air rippled and the force of his swing intensified to the point that a bar of distortion shot forth and hit the knight's blade, shattering it on contact.

Stumbling backward, it had no way to defend itself as Knox sliced down and tore it into two pieces as easily as if he were cutting a tender steak with a sharpened knife. One single slice and the Knight succumbed to his mighty weapon. Before he could celebrate, two more appeared to take its place, each rushing forward to avenge their fallen comrade.

Knox parried the first blow, shattered another sword, but he was too slow to catch the next. However, to his astonishment, his axe moved on its own accord, placing itself in line to intercept the blow. It didn't shatter the blade, as Knox hadn't swung it, but it stopped the sword dead in its tracks.

His next blow took the two knights apart in a single swing. Then three knights appeared, and the battle raged on. It continued like this, his weapon proving to be perfect for him in every way and making him an unstoppable warrior of death for hours. Until finally, he faced off against literally dozens of knights and still found himself victorious against them.

If the disembodied voice was trying to prove the worth of these weapons he was offering, he'd done so. Turning his back on the newest army of knights, Knox walked for the door. As he'd hoped, the knights did not attack after he disengaged.

Sweat pouring down his face and his body having been pushed to its physical limits, Knox smiled at his mother.

"Have fun, did you?" she asked, grinning at him as he approached.

"I did," Knox said, returning the smile with one of his own. "This weapon is incredible, and I'm truly tempted to take it. How much more effective could this artifact truly be?"

"If you are tempted by such a weapon, I can only imagine what the true prize at the end would be," she said, eying him with amusement. "Whatever you choose, I will stand beside you."

"All I know of the artifact is that it will magnify power. What is the point of that when I can take this weapon and defeat any foe? And if not this axe, then perhaps those gauntlets that are said to give you the power of creation and destruction? Would I be able to simply unmake the Dark Titan?"

"I wish I had the answers," Scarlet said. "Again, I'll stand by you no matter what you choose."

Knox considered all the foes he'd faced and how he'd used a magnifying item before, though it crumbled to dust after use. What if the artifact turned out to be much the same and he found himself without a means to effectively fight off any after he defeated the Dark Titan? No, it was clear to him that he should take this axe, perhaps a few of these items, and leave.

But then a whisper of doubt entered his mind. If such grand prizes are offered to tempt you away from the true prize, then it must be worth it. Perhaps it wasn't simply a magnifying device, but something more. It was almost as if this entire place was built to challenge only those like him, Titan Born. So perhaps it was an item that would help him walk further down the Path of the Titans.

His mind, made up for the moment, solidified around this new idea. He would take a risk and hope that he wasn't going to be let down.

Setting the axe aside, his fingers lingering on the wooden shaft, Knox spoke to the disembodied voice. "I refuse your gifts and your offer."

"Very well. Proceed to your final challenge."

A new door appeared much like the ones before, and they found themselves in a stairwell leading up to a brightly lit room.

As they took the staircase, silence between them, Knox hoped he'd made the right decision. The very echo of his footfalls seemed to mock his foolishness, but he ignored them. He had made the right decision, and he would prove it when he won the artifact.

The room they entered was massive, with ornate golden runes carved into every square inch of the walls and a single golden figure standing in the center of the room, a pedestal barely visible behind him.

But what truly caught Knox's attention was the appearance of the figure before him. He recognized it as the being that had been stabbed through the chest, standing ten feet tall and wearing clockwork style armor, a halo of gears around his head. Except, instead of a skeleton within the armor, a figure with skin as gold as Knox had ever seen, filled it.

"Who are you?" Knox asked, afraid of the answer he'd receive.

"I am merely an echo," came a voice Knox recognized as the disembodied voice he'd been hearing this entire time. "But I was once as you are now, Titan Born, Titan of the Light."

"You are the guardian of the artifact?" Knox asked, the massive man nodded his head in one slow nod. "And I'm meant to fight you?"

"You are," came the response, "but I am in no hurry to spill the blood of a brother. Ask me what you will, and I will slay you when you've quenched your thirst for knowledge."

"You will kill us both?" Knox asked, moving to stand before his mother, ready to defend her.

"No," the voice said. "I seek only your blood, that it might restore me to a fuller version of myself. Perhaps with your core I might cease to be an echo, you are strong, but perhaps not strong enough for such a task."

"Who are you?" Knox asked, his body still tense and ready for tricks.

"I am an echo of the former Titan Born of Light. My name is not yet for your ears, lest I reveal to you secrets you're not yet ready for."

"How'd you die?" Knox asked, he was walking closer to the man despite the situation, he felt drawn to him.

"I was created before that event occurred, but if what I feared came to be, the Titan of Darkness got her way and ended my life despite my best efforts to hide from her wicked power."

"I seek a weapon against her, will this artifact make me strong enough to face her?" Knox asked, gesturing behind the man toward the pedestal that he hoped held the artifact he needed.

"Come no further," warned the voice as Knox got within twenty paces of him. "The artifact will help you realize your full potential as a Titan. It was a creation of mine that would have enabled me to cast her down, but I could not bring myself to do it."

Knox scrunched his brow in confusion at the Titan's words. "Why?" he asked.

"For we shared much before she became obsessed with the idea of conquering this world. But I was not so kind to her, I broke my power against hers, weakening us both to the point that hibernation and repair was our only recourse. She obviously awoke first and is drawing power to herself much faster than ought to be possible. If you hurry, you might be able to defeat her, but no artifact will guarantee victory."

"You didn't tell me why," Knox said. "Why not just cast her down and kill her when you had the chance, or were you too weak?"

"I was sufficiently strong, or with the help of my devices I would have been. Instead, I chose to hide my greatest tool here in this Tower, the former base of operations for the Titan of Light before I moved it in an attempt to hide. I chose not to kill her because we shared blood. In the time before our finding of the Titan Complex, we were kin. In fact, the Titan of Strength and the man who became the Titan of Death, also shared a distant relation to us, but none were closer than us, Light and Dark."

"I've met the Titan of Water, he resides in the Titan Complex now, wanting to link our engines," Knox said, seeing if the Titan knew anything about the process.

"It would be wise to do that before you attempt to fight off my dear sister," the voice said. "Perhaps with your combined might and the focusing lens you will be able to overcome what she has become. I've tested you in several ways to make sure you were worthy, and I judge that you are, but before I can give you the focus lens, you must destroy me. I do not wish for death, but as I am only an echo, my master or former self can never truly rest until I've been dealt with. If you can defeat me, you may take the focusing lens. It will unlock your full potential and no longer will you need those rings or to worry about gaining additional essence."

"What does that mean, I'll just be as strong as I can be?" Knox asked, not sure that he was understanding.

"You will still want to grow more powerful by increasing your System Levels, but no longer will you have to worry about suppressing yourself. You will begin to become the Titan you were meant to be. But more power will always be available to you, and you should seek it if you truly wish to ascend to greater heights."

"I guess I'm ready then," Knox said, pulling free his battle axe and taking a step back, putting himself into a fighting stance.

"Then let it begin, it is my truest hope that I will not slay you."

He moved like a blur, Knox's eyes unable to even track his movements. Diving to the side, only his sense working fast enough to give him any warning, he dodged the first strike, but the follow up one sent him flying through the air, holding his ribs in pain. Several had been cracked for sure, and Knox couldn't even say if he'd been punched or kicked, so fast were the echo's movements.

As Knox slammed into the wall and began to tumble back down toward the ground, he ripped the first of his restraining rings off his finger and looked with new eyes. He could almost see the echo move now, but it was still so fast. It stopped, seeming to consider Knox, then raised a hand. Light shot out and seared into him with pain more intense than he'd ever felt.

Before he realized it, he was screaming and wishing for it to end, which it did some moments later, but the skin on his face was boiled and ruined, Knox knew without looking. Gasping in pain and panicking, he ripped free all the restraining rings and felt his body begin to tear itself apart as it sucked essence from him to stabilize his form.

Suddenly the pain stopped and Knox, at a level far beyond anything he'd ever faced before, stood and faced his opponent. He noticed, though he didn't dwell on it, that his skin had turned a sheen of golden metal, but he felt like flesh and blood as he had before.

When the Echo moved next, Knox could track his movements and he rushed forward to finally fight back. His axe came down, but the Echo casually raised his arm and batted it away, the blow scoring his armor but leaving him intact.

Back and forth they fought, Echo was faster, but he obviously hadn't taken the sense talent that Knox had, because he couldn't dodge the blows so much as parry them. He showed use of so mundane a path after only seconds of battle, a whip of water appearing in his hands. So, he'd be an Elementalist, that could be problematic. The whip of water lashed out and he used another ability to harden, creating a spear of magical ice.

With his reach and that of the long spear, Knox was back on the defensive, doing all he could to not get skewered. He caught a few blows of his axe on the ice shaft, but whatever magic had formed it gave it an immense amount of durability.

Knox used Ethereal Step to get distance and lined up a Luminous Surge. It left him with so much power that he thought he'd over done it, but upon checking his mana was only down a fraction. He was operating with so much power that he could feel his very being struggle under the weight of it.

"Each second that passes," the voice said, not at all out of breath while he continued to attack while speaking, "is a victory for me. If you wish to strike me down, you ought to hurry."

His words enraged Knox in a way that he'd never felt before, but he had a trick up his sleeve that he'd used once and figured he could use once more. Using his ability, Arcane Revelation, he called upon the ability to summon forth a Celestial Guardian once more. Hopefully with his suppression rings off the one he could summon now would be all the more powerful.

Imagine his surprise when a portal opened and a four-foot-tall boy walked out, a simple golden crown on his head.

He spoke in a boyish voice, but with authority that belayed his external age.

"I am the King of the Celestials. Here to aid you, but I caution you, my might is to be used for worthy causes only. Tell me why I should strike down this opponent for you?"

The Echo didn't relent, his attacks aimed at Knox and ignoring the small child that looked no older than eight or nine.

"I seek to strike him down," Knox said, breathing hard. "So that I can restore the balance to the world and drive back the darkness."

"And you," the boy said, holding up a hand, bands of gold surrounded the Echo and stopped him dead in his tracks. "Do you believe you ought to be slain for the greater good?"

Without hesitation, the Echo responded while breaking the golden bands at the same moment. "I do, being of the Celestial realms."

"Then I shall aid you," said the Celestial boy King.

What happened next surprised everyone in the room. The boy held up his hands and armor appeared from the portal, covering him and growing his height into that of an equally large ten foot being. Then a massive sword appeared, and he took it, lifting the weapon as if it weighed no more than a feather.

The Celestial King moved like a blur, but somehow Echo caught his sword strike on his spear and pushed him back. Knox took that opportunity to cast Lustrous Chains, just as Echo smashed his spear into the Celestial King's gut, the armor stopped any penetration, but the king was thrown back a few feet. He recovered and sliced downward with his sword, sending out an arc of white light.

Knox used Aeon Gaze on Echo and saw that when he attacked, he left a moment's opening on his left that he could exploit. Using his instant teleport spell Ethereal Step, he appeared right where he wanted to strike. So focused on his fight with the king, Echo failed to notice him in time as his axe came down, shattering armor and drawing the first blood of the fight.

Echo screamed out and fire exploded all around him in every direction. Knox and the king were sent flying back, but not far. Touching where Knox had drawn blood, a golden substance that matched his skin began to form a layer of hard rock over it as if mimicking the armor he'd lost.

Then, as Knox and the king recovered themselves, Echo raised his hands up and lightning began to smash down all around the pair. The king raised his sword and took strike after strike, while Knox ran forward to engage Echo.

Slashing for his midsection, he dodged a spear strike and hit him hard in the chest. Letting his momentum carry him past the giant of a man, Knox turned just in time to catch a fist in the face. Staggering backward, he activated Dimensional Shift with the king just as the spear came for his chest.

It worked, putting the king in the way of the strike, the Celestial able to bat it away at the last moment, and giving Knox the chance he needed to begin a Radiant Glyph. He worked hard and fast, putting up the newest version that his mother had helped him work out. Then as he finished it, he summoned forth all the power he could into an Arcane Pulse, figuring that light-based attacks might not be as effective against an Echo of the Titan of Light.

His raw wave of arcane energy shot out with so much power that it rippled reality as it went, throwing debris all over the place and striking Echo square in the back. Echo was sent sprawling into the Celestial King's sword, blood spraying as the blow took him right through the middle.

Knox couldn't and wouldn't stop when victory was so near, so he used Reality Ripple to hold Echo in place and cast Aethereal Step to dash forward. Then just as he reached him, he activated Radiant Rush, giving himself a speed boost. His axe came down on the Echo's neck and cut clean through, ending the fight.

"The deed is done," came the voice of the Celestial King as his armor faded away revealing the same small child within it. A portal opened and the kid looked back to say a final thing before leaving. "Do not summon me again for some time. I need to rest."

Knox inclined his head in answer and turned to regard his mother. She stood by the exit, a look of worry on her face.

"You are falling apart!" she yelled, and Knox looked down at himself.

Sure enough, specks of golden skin were floating off him and turning to dust, revealing only light beneath it. He'd pushed himself too far too fast and now he wasn't sure if he could recover. He found the rings, discarded on the ground, but putting them back on did nothing. In a panic and with mounting worry, he went to the pedestal and found the artifact.

It was a simple bracelet, a thin band of gold that could fit someone twice his size. Reaching out to pick it up, the item shrunk and opened. He placed it around his left wrist, and it snapped shut. Suddenly the pain and draining stopped, leaving a warmth on his wrist. He felt fine, better than fine, he felt powerful.

The wounds on his golden skin began to shut, but his normal complexion didn't return. "That'll take some getting used to," Knox said, and he realized his voice was a bit deeper than it had been as well, how odd.

"Are you alright?" Scarlet asked, she'd sneaked up on him and Knox realized that for a moment there he hadn't been connected to his sense. He had to force back the connection with a moment of focus, but when it returned it was like his eyes were open for the very first time.

He saw not only the world around him but the stitching that kept the world together. Magic beyond magic that wrapped the very fabric of reality, and they were all done with complex runic formations. But the language of the runes was just a mask over an even more complex webbing of energies. He could almost reach out and grab those energies, tugging on the strings of creation and destruction.

This artifact had unlocked him and pushed him further down the Path of the Titans than he could ever have imagined.

CHAPTER 15
A NEW WORLD

It was like stepping into a new world. Knox felt the twists and turns of magic all around him, how the system worked and how he could manipulate it even further. Then he saw that focusing this hard was straining his connection with it, his core was just too weak to handle this much power right now. He needed to strengthen it.

Reaching out with his arms, he began to pull essence in, he absorbed the Echo on the ground and began to consume the entire Tower, a construct of intensely powerful essence. Until finally he'd stabilized himself, having only taken a small portion of the Tower's essence since if he took more, it would risk the stability of the Tower itself.

"Knox?" came a voice that he remembered.

Knox had to focus, purposely drawing his sense inward a good measure and allowing himself to only see through his normal eyes. With that accomplished, he opened his eyes and felt much more like himself, despite not looking like it. He had an internal sense of himself, and he knew that even his hair had turned golden, making him look like some sort of freak, but there was no magic he knew that could hide it.

Sure, he could learn to cast some type of illusion, but it would have to be mighty powerful to hide his true self, this version of him. The more he thought about it, the more he realized that perhaps it wasn't true after all. Sensing the weaves of power that made him, well him, he drew on them and weakened himself just enough to pull back the effects of his golden presence.

It worked, suddenly he looked like his old self, even shrinking several feet back to his normal height. He hadn't realized he'd grown nearly as tall as Terrim, but he liked feeling more like himself, even if it cost him some measure of power. Eventually he'd take his true form, but not now.

"There you are," Scarlet said, relief evident in her voice.

Knox looked at her and smiled. "Sorry about that," he said, shrugging. "Suddenly had access to more power than ever before, not something that I was able to easily work out. But I'm back, mostly myself." Knox noticed that his left arm remained golden, and he wasn't sure why, but a quick check showed that it stopped just below the elbow. Oh well, he'd done as much as he could for now and it would have to be enough.

"You ready to leave?" Scarlet asked and they looked around, seeing no exit.

"I killed the Tower's controller, the Echo," Knox said. "Give me a moment and I'll see about making an exit."

Knox closed his eyes shut and let his sense drift to the runes around him, the runic formations that no one else could see, then deeper into the threads of power behind them. He plucked one and sent his intentions into it. A surge of power later and what felt like someone punching him in the gut several times, a door appeared that he recognized.

He'd brought them a way out.

Opening the door, Knox and Scarlet were met with dozens of C Ranked Adventurers and even a few B Rankers, spells already beginning to flare as they prepared to annihilate them.

Knox cast Prism Ward and caught multiple attacks before they could so much as singe a hair on his head. These Adventurers were nothing compared to him now and they needed to learn their lesson. Using Ethereal Step, he appeared next to the strongest of the group and picked him up by his collar.

"Stop the attack or he dies," Knox said, shaking the man as he tried to cast another spell.

Suddenly all eyes were on him, teleporting wasn't a common technique and he'd just weathered every one of their attacks at once with a spell meant only to slow down incoming spells. They grew quiet really quickly, all but the one he held aloft by his collar.

"Stop the attack," he cried out. "Look at his arm! He has the mark. We should be bowing before him, not following orders to kill him."

Knox let him down and immediately the man went on a knee, startling him by the reverence he was showing.

"We should get moving," Scarlet said, eying the group warily. "You are powerful, but your friends are not. Let's go."

"Do not follow," Knox said to the crowd, half of them were kneeling and the other half just looked confused.

"The mark?" Knox asked as they jogged down the halls toward the exit. His mother finished casting a spell to hide their presence as they moved and Knox glanced behind, noticing the door to the Tower remained open, but he didn't stop to try and shut it.

"Metallic skin was said to be a mark of the one that once ruled the nation, now you have it. It's like what Echo said, this city used to be the Titan's home," Scarlet said.

"And now it is a month's travel away," Knox said. "We need to find my friends and get out of here."

"You could be king here if you wanted," Scarlet said, giving Knox the side-eye as they moved further out of the complex.

"I don't think so," Knox said. "It is obvious that Draven failed to turn enough people to his side by the welcome we got after leaving the Tower. I don't want to leave a trail of bodies on my way out, so we need to sneak as best as possible."

"I understand," Scarlet said, then looking behind her and stopping, she said, "A shame to leave all my research behind. Think we have time to grab a few notebooks?"

Knox sighed but he understood her dilemma. "Yeah, we have time, let's go get them."

They reached her quarters minutes later, but instead of being empty, a single person stood in the room, Draven.

Scarlet let her veil drop and Draven jumped.

"I knew you'd be able to do it!" he said excitedly. Walking up to Knox he pointed at his arm. "You even have the mark. You are the true leader of Lumisar."

"I'm the ruler of Luminar, not Lumisar. Sorry, but we are just here to collect some notes and then we are leaving," Knox said, Scarlet was already filling a pack with as many papers and notebooks as she could.

"Then I will follow you to the end, I've failed to turn the courts against my uncle, but I am loyal to our true king, you." He took a knee and Knox wanted to groan.

"We don't have time to argue," Knox said, helping the man up. "If you want to come, then let's go. We are sneaking out of the city and heading back at full speed."

"As you say," Draven said, tilting his head.

They escaped the keep with such ease that it surprised Knox, but he had no complaints. They took up cloaks, Knox in his glamorous golden cloak once more, and his companions in nondescript black ones. Using Scarlet's stealth magic, they made it through to the middle level of the keep, but it was clear that Silas was after them, guards by the dozens were going street to street accosting people.

But with the aid of her magic, they avoided them all, until finally reaching a place where Draven said he'd sent Aetex and Sintra. It was an inn with a dancing pig sign on the outside and plenty of patrons coming in and out of it.

The sun shone above illuminating their path forward. It was midday by Knox's reckoning, and he was sure that they could get out of the city by nightfall if they just tried hard enough. The gentle buzz of conversation filled his ears as they entered the pub, eyes searching for their friends among the diverse group of people. From elves to humans to a few races Knox didn't recognize—with rock-like skin and big ears—his party still stood out like a wolf among sheep.

Sitting at a corner table, Aetex's massive form could be seen rising a head above the rest and as they neared, they saw Dernal, John, and Sintra all awaiting them with meals and drinks set before them.

Knox was silent as he approached, not by any attempt to be so, but his movements just felt so much more graceful than ever before. Despite this, Aetex turned before he'd made it within ten feet and acknowledged him with a tilt of his head.

"Come, have a seat," he called over the din of conversation.

"How did he see through my veil?" Scarlet muttered to Knox, but he just shrugged, not having even realized she'd kept one up after they entered. His sense was on the fritz as he tried to find a good balance between seeing the very fabric of creation and sensing as he had before.

The group quieted as Knox, Draven, and Scarlet found a seat around the table.

"You got it," Aetex said, a wide smile on his face. "And you've grown immensely already, this bodes well for your mission against the Dark Titan."

"We need to flee the city and get back as soon as possible," Knox said. "I'm afraid going after the Dark Titan must take second seat to helping Ramses connect our Titan Engines. If we are able to connect them, I believe together we might be enough to face off against her and win."

"What's the rush?" John said, sipping his drink.

Just then, a pair of guards entered, and they were clearly not looking for drinks.

"My veils can't hide so many," Scarlet hissed. "We need to start moving, tell your friends to meet us outside the gates." She placed a hand on Knox shoulder, and he stood, following her meaning. She could disguise the pair of them, and the rest should be fine to escape on their own.

"We leave at nightfall, get outside the city before then," Knox said, looking at each of his friends in turn, then to Sintra, who looked out of place even among the diverse group. Her bearing and general look being that of royalty or at least someone who thought highly of themself.

No one spoke as they went back through the tavern and headed for the door, though Knox did notice a few traded glances from Dernal and Scarlet. She was obviously still not happy with him and he with her, though why he'd have reason to be sour toward her, Knox did not know.

They nearly made it out of the city when they encountered Adventurers with enough power to make Knox stop and pay attention to them. Two A Rankers stood atop the wall and by the way they were looking down at the pair of them, they saw right through Scarlet's veil.

"What are they doing in the city, they ought to be miles away right now," Scarlet said, gesturing to them and stopping. A moment later the two figures, twins Knox realized as he looked them over, came floating down to the ground.

"Tress and Terris," Scarlet said, looking nervous for the first time since they'd left the Tower. "Has Silas paid for your services? He must truly be desperate."

They were so similar looking, but as they stopped before them, Knox realized one was clearly a female and the other a male. The female spoke first, her voice sweet as honey.

"Scarlet my dear, what a clever masking spell you used there, it is a shame that boy is blazing like the noonday sun. I'd say that even my brother, with his weak eyes, could spot him under that veil."

"I could," came the response.

Turning to Knox, the female bowed deeply and cleared her throat as she stood, her brother followed suit a moment later.

"I am Tress, one of only half a dozen in this kingdom right now that might be able to match you in raw strength. This is my brother Terris. Together, I believe we are your match, but it need not come to blows," she said, her voice still as sweet as ever.

Knox regarded each of them, then looked deeper with his sense, peering into their very beings and connection with the magic. They'd both reached A Rank, but just barely. The amount of taint they'd taken in meant they would make it no further, and despite Knox still being B Ranked by level, the Aurorapex or focusing lens, he wore on his arm was giving him access to attributes far above that of even an A Ranker.

He smiled and showed them his golden arm. "I'm not looking for a fight," he began to say, but Terris interrupted him.

"Good, because I had a big lunch and kicking your ass will definitely work up a sweat." Terris smirked and traded a look with his sister, they truly thought they had this in the bag, Knox realized.

"Let me finish," Knox said, command filling his voice. Both of them took a step back at his command, it was like they'd been forced to resist his words, so powerful they were when laced with magic.

Finally, they both nodded that they would and Knox continued. "I will kill you both if needed, but I'd rather not. Perhaps a show of strength to prove that you are completely and utterly outclassed?"

"They are both A Ranked," Scarlet hissed. "I know you are strong, but perhaps retreat is the best option."

"I don't retreat anymore," Knox said, letting the power flow through him was intoxicating but he summoned up enough to truly show them what they were dealing with.

Then with a simple thought, he unleashed his aura.

Scarlet cried out first, holding her hands up to shield her face as she fell to a knee almost instantly. Next Terris fell down as if worshiping Knox, though he was sure he just happened to fall that way. Last to fall was Tress, her grim expression that of someone who didn't like to lose.

Knox let his aura fade and hid it back behind his carefully prepared defenses. He wasn't A Ranked, not with his rings off. No, he was an S Ranker at least. This was a level of power that had remained the thing of myth and legend for the last thousand years and there would be no denying his power now.

Knox waited as everyone stood, doing his best to keep a smirk off his face. However, instead of being cowed like he'd hoped, Terris and Tress looked hungry for battle suddenly, both of them flaring their powerful auras and causing Scarlet to take several steps back.

"Get back and don't interfere," Knox said to his mother, and she nodded, slipping back into the shadows of the buildings.

The area had been cleared of everyone, his blast of aura knocking out the few that had remained, like the guards. They'd be alright of course, but it would be a few hours before they awoke, and they'd be sore as hell when they did.

"Let's take this fight someplace less populated," Knox said, letting his sense wash outward and feeling for a place mostly abandoned. He found a farm that had no people and a large enough space for the quick battle that was likely to follow.

"Fine," Tress said. "Where did you have in mind?"

"Follow me and we will do battle," Knox said. He jumped using more force than he'd ever used before, the very ground shook and cracked from the force of it. But it worked, he was sent flying through the air toward the farm. Just as he was about to land, he used Ethereal Step to appear on the ground already, effectively cancelling out his momentum with a quick adjustment to how the spell worked.

Behind him, running on the ground, Tress and Terris quickly made their way to his location. Sure enough, the area was cleared, and the farm appeared abandoned, so Knox felt no guilt about what was going to happen here.

"You know," Tress said, appearing before him in a blur of speed. "You are clearly strong, but I still don't think you can take us both. Give up and let us take you in. I'll guarantee that Silas won't be able to hold you and after he's done paying us, we could go do some of the A Ranked dungeons this country has to offer. It is so very hard to find people strong enough to form a full party."

"I'm afraid I have my own quest that I must follow," Knox said, cracking his neck to the side. "However, if you are open to it after I put you both back in your place, I'd be willing to run a dungeon with you in the future."

"Enough talk," Terris said, twin daggers appearing in his hands. "Let's make him bleed."

A staff appeared out of nowhere in Tress's hands and she shrugged. "Fine, but don't kill him. He'll make a great dungeon buddy after we teach him some manners."

They were quick, but Knox was on an entirely new level, even suppressed as he was at the moment.

The thinnest beam of fire shot forth from Tress, just as Terris stepped into a shadow and appeared behind Knox, ready to deliver his famous backstab.

Knox used Ethereal Step to appear next to Tress, snatching her staff from her hands and throwing it to the side. Then just as she slashed out with an arm chop that would likely be able to take down a tree with ease, Knox used Dimensional Shift on Terris.

He went down hard as the attack smashed into his chest, coughing blood.

"Good job," Knox said, taunting Tress. "You drew first blood."

"Shit," Tress said, grinding her teeth as she spoke. "I hate that technique. Perhaps you can teach it to me later?" Her voice turned sweet at the end as if Knox would actually care to teach her anything after this entire ordeal.

Terris was back on his feet and his aura surged as he pulled free all the power he'd been holding back.

"You'll do well to just attack me with everything you have," Knox said, though ironically, he wasn't planning on doing the same.

"He's right," Tress said, holding out her hand, her staff appeared back in her grasp. "Enough holding back, let's show him our true power."

"Already?" Terris seemed alarmed but fished something out of his pocket. It was a simple ring with powerful runic formations on it that Knox immediately tried to commit to memory. He would need to write it down, but he was sure he got the gist of it, though he wasn't sure yet what it would do.

Tress pulled out an identical ring, formations and all, and at the same time they put on the rings. Suddenly, their A Ranked auras began to pull closer and closer, then suddenly it surged and became something more.

It glowed with an intense red color, almost turning purple. If Knox didn't know any better, he'd say they'd somehow merged and become an S Ranked singular entity. But the complexity of doing such an act would only be possible by some extremely high-level dungeon loot and it would likely be temporary.

Dust had been kicked up during the process, hiding them from view, but as it settled a single person stood before Knox.

In a voice that was a mix of the two, neither fully feminine nor masculine, the being spoke. "You've forced us to use our trump card. Prepare to bleed."

When this new being moved, it was with speed that Knox at his current level could barely track. He took a punch to the face before he could move himself aside, then barely dodged a slash from the being's weapon, a staff with blades affixed to each end.

Back and forth they traded blows and Knox had to admit they were nearly as strong as he was, but he wasn't even operating at his full capacity, nor did he plan to. He caught a blow from the staff on his armor, muttering a few words his Mystic Armor appeared around him, giving him extra protection. Next, he dodged an attack that dug a ten-foot trench in the ground and was filled with fire a moment later.

The combined being of Tress and Terris yelled in frustration, stepping into a shaft of light and appearing behind Knox, ready to strike. Knox activated his Solar Wings, slapping the being aside and destroying the old cottage and barn from the impact. He could feel his body wanting to do more, move faster, act with more power, but Knox held back.

"Just die!" the combined being said, unleashing a torrent of flame and shadow, twirling together in a dance of death.

Knox decided to take the attack head on, raising his hand and doing a quick Radiant Glyph, then transitioning into a Luminous Surge. His attack magnified sevenfold, smashed into the incoming attack.

The resulting explosion actually blew Knox back as it decimated the landscape all around them, burning the very ground to ash and glass.

Surprisingly the being stood, smoke trailing up every inch of it, ready still to make battle.

Knox was happy to oblige it, rushing forward with speed unmatched, the very ground shattering under his footfalls. Despite his hesitation to fight them at first, he was having a good time, he just hoped they didn't do any irreparable damage.

They stopped with their techniques, or in Knox's case his spells, and fought hand-to-hand. Knox's axe stayed at his side, a weapon would just be an unfair advantage for him at this point, while he allowed his opponent to use their fused weapon as they would.

Surprisingly Knox took a hit every now and then, this combined entity moving with bursts of terrible speed, but never did Knox feel threatened by them, yet he fought on, drawing blood with his punches and backhands. One such attack hit with enough force to blow back the ash and glass all around them, shredding any remaining trees still standing.

Still, Knox had stamina to spare, this fight being nothing to him but a workout to warm himself up. The combined being attempted to use a technique, probably tiring of getting slapped around, and Knox allowed it.

Fire spun around them, mixed with shadowy purples and lashed out like a snake toward Knox. He caught the attack with his bare hands and felt his flesh burn, but he'd heal before too long. Surging his power into the spell, he overloaded it and the technique fell apart in a spray of sparks and drops of shadows.

The combined being screamed in pain as they were hit with the full backlash of the power and suddenly, they split. One rolling to the left and the other to the right. The rings, the powerful artifacts that Knox wanted to replicate now, stayed in the middle, sitting still and whole despite the forceful separation.

Knox moved like a gust of wind, picking up the rings.

"You are a monster," Tress said, all the sweetness gone from her voice.

Terris spoke next, his voice filled with reverence. "Nothing has been able to withstand us in that form. You have to take us as your apprentices. We will do whatever you tell us, just please allow us to train under you."

Knox held out his hand to them, helping first Terris then Tress to their feet and handing back their rings. "I will consider it, but first you have to know about the Titan System and how it will change what you can do."

They nodded and Knox gave them the short version of what he was and the power behind the Titan System. They both promised to return with him and join their community, but Knox was hesitant.

"What of your contract with Silas?" Knox asked.

"If what you tell us is true, even our membership with the Adventurer's Guild will be pointless soon. You are change in the most violent form, Knox. The entire world will be remade before things like contracts matter again. Also, fuck Silas and his pile of gold. We've got a way to get stronger now, and we are going to take it," Tress said, looking at her brother he nodded his assent.

"Fine, but if you cause any trouble then I will deal with you personally," Knox said, each of them looking downcast under his gaze. It was funny how quickly their attitudes changed when meeting someone that could exceed their power. With their ability to combine with those rings, they are or were probably the strongest beings on the continent, not counting monsters or dungeon creatures.

"As you wish, Master," Terris said.

"Don't call me that; just Knox is fine," Knox said. "So, tell me, are there really A Ranked Dungeons we could visit? Any on the way we are going?" Knox filled them in on the basic direction they'd be traveling.

"Yes, one, but without a healer, we might be in trouble. Any chance you want to take a two-day detour to pick up Zhul? I bet he'd be willing to let you kick his ass and learn under you as well. It isn't every day that people at our power level learn of a way to get even stronger. In fact, most of us are set in our ways because we know there is no path to greater power, but with this Titan System in place... I bet he'd come," Tress said.

"I'll think about it," Knox said. He was in a hurry, but getting more powerful allies and running a dungeon that could produce loot like those rings wasn't something he could pass up lightly. A plan formed in his head, and he let them know his thoughts.

"With our speed, we could go on ahead and still make it back around the same time as my companions, even spending some time to check on their progress," Knox said, musing over the idea. It would mean they'd be unprotected by him personally, but with the likes of Scarlet and Aetex, Knox would be surprised if they couldn't handle all that they'd encounter.

"Let me talk with my companions, and I will meet you back here in an hour; gather any supplies you need and be ready to go seek out this Zhul person," Knox said; both of them nodded but said nothing.

Knox was going to run an A Ranked Dungeon and he was positive that the treasures he'd find within would be worth it.

CHAPTER 16
NEW DUNGEON

TURNS out no one was thrilled with Knox's new proposed idea, except for him.

"You can't just go put yourself in danger with people you just met," Scarlet said, Dernal and John nodded along with her.

"There isn't any danger from them anymore," Knox tried to reassure them, but he could tell it wasn't a winning battle. "I'm going regardless. I have to get stronger, and this focusing lens—or Aurorapex—is working overtime to keep me at peak functioning condition. But I still have to grow stronger if I'm going to face off against the Dark Titan."

"He's right," Aetex said, coming to support him and surprising Knox. "He has grown powerful, but he is not strong enough for what awaits him yet. He has the speed and power to see that he is safe, even in the dungeons he dares to dive into. I support his decision."

"I'm his mother and I will not let him just run headlong into death," Scarlet said, her face going shades closer to her namesake.

Knox stepped forward and pulled her into a hug. Whispering in her ear, he said, "You'll not lose me so easily. Follow them back, and I will meet up with you all before you even arrive, I promise."

With tears rolling down her face, she nodded, accepting that her son would do as he needed to do to grow stronger.

Aetex looked Knox in the face and repeated the phrase that Knox and his friends had been using more frequently. "To death."

"To death," Knox repeated back.

"Though that doesn't mean you ought to seek death out," Aetex said. "Remember what that phrase truly means, and you'll be fine."

Knox checked his status page to see where exactly he stood progression-wise; despite having access to much more powerful attributes, he hadn't progressed much since he'd last checked.

-Personal Status-
    -Name: Knox-
    -Health: Godlike Tier 9-
    -Mana: Godlike Tier 9-
    -Stamina: Godlike Tier 9-

Finishing with his goodbyes, Knox left to join Terris and Tress at the farm he'd left them at. They'd returned already, each of them with a pack on their back, matching the one Knox carried now, filled with supplies.

"So, where will we find this Zhul fellow?" Knox asked, wondering what direction their journey would take.

"Last I heard, he was working under the king as a personal bodyguard, but I think he'd rather come with us," Tress said with a devious smile on her face.

"You want to go to the capital city of Laurdenar and poach the king's personal bodyguard?" Knox asked, disbelief not hidden on his face.

"It's probably best I go alone," Tress said, smiling now at her brother. "He's got beef with my brother and doesn't take kindly to surprises, so I'll have to work at him until I can get him to come. It won't take longer than a day, two tops, plenty of time for you two to make it to the dungeon and get us registered."

"So, I don't have to go?" Knox said, feeling relief wash over him. He'd only had limited contact with nobles and their kind, but he'd seen enough to last him a lifetime.

"I'll lead the way, try to keep up," Terris said, but Knox just smirked because he knew he could outrun the man with his hands tied behind his back.

Terris took off at a blazing pace, kicking up debris as he went, and Knox followed after him. It had been a long time since he'd been able to cut loose while running, and his speed was something altogether different now. Several times, he nearly fell. His footfalls were so wide that he was practically skipping across the ground, leaping over buildings and wagons that got in the way.

Terris was fast, but not as fast nor did he have the strength to jump as high or far as Knox, so he caught up to him in no time. At this pace, the monthlong journey would take no longer than a few days; at least, that was what Knox thought after doing a quick bit of calculations.

By the end of day one, they'd traveled countless miles and left his friends in the dust. Terris and Knox were both winded from going all out for so many hours, but Knox recovered first, and shortly after that so did Terris. It was amazing what you could do when you really cut loose, Knox mused.

By the end of the second day, they'd already reached the dungeon, and Knox marveled at how different it was from the Mire's Gloom Dungeon. Instead of a town, it was a simple building with a single guard. No shops or buildings were built around it, only the ruins of a long-deserted city. Stone foundations were left bare, and the remains of a Tower some two hundred paces south of the dungeon hut that hid the dungeon pillar.

"What can I do for you, gentlemen?" asked the guard, who sat reading a book without looking up. He gave off some impressive power for a B Ranker, but he was still a ways from reaching A, and by the look of his aura, the taint that blocked progress wouldn't allow him any further.

"We are here to register for a dungeon run," Knox said, and this got the man's attention enough that he lifted his gaze off the book and examined them closer.

"You need at least four party members at A Rank to attempt this beast. The Infernal Labyrinth isn't given its name because it has kittens inside," the guard said, returning his eyes to his book.

"Yes, we know. We have two more people coming. Now do your job and put us down for a run starting in a couple of days," Terris said, then looked around and added, "Any decent place to sleep and get some ale around here?"

The guard looked up, sighed, put down his book, and stood up. Squinting his eyes, he looked at them again and his eyes went wide. "Well, I'll be. Two A Rankers—and you say you've got two more coming? I'll put you down for the next week—whenever you are ready, come on down—but there really isn't any need; this dungeon hasn't been attempted since the last A Ranked group was wiped inside of it some hundred years ago. You sure you'll be up to it?"

"I'm sure," Knox said, his new power giving him all the confidence he needed to challenge the impossible. What glorious loot would he find inside that might give him an edge over the Dark Titan? So many ideas rolled through his head as he waited for the sign-up process to play out.

It turned out there was a town about twenty miles away, which would only be about an hour's jog, so Terris and Knox made their way there for a warm bed and cold drinks. They left messages with the guard to tell Tress and Zhul to meet them there when they arrived, letting him know that it might be a day or two until they did.

"What does it feel like?" Terris asked Knox after he downed his fifth ale and his third meal.

"What's that?" Knox asked, sipping at his first still.

"This whole being a Titan thing?" he asked.

Knox had been filling him in on the basics of what he was as he grew to trust him a bit more the longer they were together. He'd mostly listened up to this point and asked very few questions, so Knox didn't know how well he was taking the idea that he'd always be more powerful than him, no matter how high he climbed. It was a thought that made Knox feel awkward, so he tried not to think about it too much.

"That's hard to answer," Knox finally said. "Before getting this," Knox lifted the long-sleeved shirt he'd started wearing to cover his arms better and showed off the focusing lens, as Echo had called it, "I felt pretty much the same as I had my entire life, but you know, with everything enhanced. I was still basically a normal B Ranker who was on the cusp of A, but now that I have this..." His words trailed off as he tried to think of how to put it.

"You are pretty damn powerful for a B Ranker," Terris said, laughing.

"Well, I'm hoping this dungeon run will put me over the peak and into the A Rank range," Knox said, "but I have the attributes of something beyond A or even S Rank. I feel connected to the very fabric of the world around us—I think I'm truly beginning to understand what it means to be a Titan."

"To think," Terris said, waving for another refill of his drink from the bar maiden, "that I live in an age where literal Titans walk among us. My sister and I are old, nearly three hundred years now, but if you'd told me a hundred years ago about any of this, I'd have laughed you off."

"I didn't realize you were so old," Knox said, looking at the man and seeing the agelessness of his features, but his light grey eyes held something within them that spoke of time untold.

"We were already going to be long-lived; we have elven blood from our mother's side, but hitting the B Ranks slows aging a good bit and A Rank stops it altogether from what I can tell. I can only imagine what happens to your body when you reach as far as you have," Terris said.

"I feel normal," Knox said, lifting his hand and taking a hard look at the golden flesh that had consumed his entire left arm now and up to his shoulder. "But if I hadn't suppressed the power, I'd be much taller and very golden."

"I think it's a good look," Terris said, laughing as he did so. "If you let that look take over your entire body and just stand real still, I bet you could go years without anyone realizing you are anything but a statue."

"Yeah," Knox said, smiling at the thought. "I'm sure that would be a great way to pass the time."

"Better than the boredom that comes with living this long," Terris said, his tone suddenly going serious. "Until we fought you, I thought that my sister and I had surpassed all challenges together. There hasn't been a monster or a challenge short of dungeons like these that require coordination between multiple A Rankers, which have given us any pause. You are doing us a favor by letting us come with you. The idea that I'll be able to progress and grow stronger—it excites me like back when I was first entering the B Ranks."

"Sounds lonely," Knox said, glad that he had his friends and family around him. Not only that, but they'd all progressed to the point that getting to B or A Rank status would definitely be happening for them in the future. In fact, so many people would grow strong because of the System and the endless progress that it seemed to unlock. The entire face of the world would change over the next hundred years and Knox was excited to see it done.

"Aye, it is," Terris said. "It truly is."

Tress appeared with a dark-skinned child an entire week later and Knox took them in with a confused look.

"Where is Zhul and who is the child?" Knox asked.

Terris snorted and the child looked perturbed.

"This is Zhul," Tress said, laughing all the while. "He was a young prodigy some five hundred years back and hit B Rank before his body had even finished developing. But you'd be wise to respect his talents as he'll be the one healing us."

"I meant no disrespect," Knox said, looking at Zhul with new eyes. He undoubtedly had power and he appeared to be on the cusp of A Rank and S Rank. Though his impurities would never allow him to go any further, he must have been so close.

"She tells me you can take me to S Rank," Zhul said, he had an interestingly odd accent that Knox couldn't really place. His words were very abrupt as if each word were his last.

"And beyond," Knox said. "You are close, I can tell."

"Stop that," Zhul said. "Your eyes glow golden and I feel as if you are stripping me bare."

"Do they really?" Knox asked, looking at Terris—he'd grown more comfortable talking to him now than his sister or this newcomer.

"You didn't know?" Terris said. "I see it happen all the time, sometimes randomly, but usually when you are looking around at stuff."

"Well, that's something," Knox said, making a face.

"Let's go check out that dungeon," Tress said, reaching down and drinking up what was left of Terris's drink.

"I am eager to see this city you claim will unlock my potential. Is it not wise to go and do that first, then challenge the dungeon?" Zhul asked.

"It'll take too long," Knox said. "First, we run the dungeon and collect rare loot; then I'll take you to the city. Is the King going to be a problem?"

"I took a leave but gave an oath that I would return; that isn't a problem, is it?" Zhul asked.

"Nah, as long as you don't go telling everyone where to find me and the city, then I'll be happy. Besides, it'll be nice knowing someone close to the king when the System sweeps down and takes over the area. I'm sure he'll be surprised," Knox said.

With that, they left the tavern and inn to head for the dungeon, some twenty miles away. Zhul was slower, whether by choice to limit himself or just a limiting factor, but not once did he draw a heavy breath. Meanwhile, Terris and Knox cut ahead, racing to see who could get there the fastest. Knox won, of course, but he'd been holding back to make sure Terris always thought he had a chance.

"So close," Terris said, panting hard. "I almost had you."

"You almost did," Knox lied, his breath coming out even and not at all winded.

The single guard was still there waiting for them, and they got entry to the dungeon hut after the other two caught up. Placing their hands on it as they all had many times before at other dungeons, the feeling of pulling started, and suddenly they were in the dungeon, a familiar empty cave with several doors and runic formations above them.

Knox smiled as he took in a deep breath. This would be the most challenging dungeon he'd ever attempted, but he was so much more than he'd ever been.

"What do we know about this dungeon?" Knox asked, turning to the other three.

"It is demonic-themed. You know, kobolds, demons, and infernals. Lots of fire and shit," Terris said.

"Why are there only three doors? Usually, there are at least four to five," Knox asked, brushing himself off and casting a few buffing spells on himself and the party.

"Dunno," Terris admitted, his daggers appearing and disappearing from his grasp. "But each path is said to be twice as hard as the next, so let's just get through the first, and then we can worry about doing a full clear."

With their hearts set on what was to happen next, they all finished buffing themselves and casting defensive spells. They entered the first path and the dungeon adventure began.

CHAPTER 17
FIRE AND BRIMSTONE

KNOX'S first sense when entering was the overwhelming heat. Like a furnace blowing hot air into his face, it hit him with overwhelming strength. It took only moments for his sense to sweep out and take in everything in the room, his eyes taking a second longer.

What awaited them was a room filled to the brim with red-hot lava streams and the occasional platform that, if they were careful, would get them to the other side of the room.

"It's hot," Tress said simply, fanning her face as if the tiny bit of air would help banish the incredible heat.

"I'm creating a barrier around us that should lessen the heat," Zhul said, and he began to chant with his odd accent.

Suddenly, an orb formed in his hands and then expanded to encompass the entire group a moment later. It was like a ball of water; as it made contact with them, the heat lessened by an incredible degree.

"I don't see any monsters," Terris said, looking at Knox as he spoke.

"I can sense several awaiting us inside the lava," Knox said, gesturing to the closest stream.

As a unit, they moved forward, weapons ready. When they got

within a dozen paces from the spot, a red and black creature with curled horns jumped free of the lava, wielding a spear with a wickedly sharp tip that glowed cherry red.

Terris moved first, appearing behind it and slicing its throat. However, the demon, for that had to be what it was, didn't go down. Instead, it twirled and slammed the dull end of its spear into Terris, sending him spinning backward into the lava. Knox Ethereal Stepped beside him, grabbed ahold of him, and cast Dimensional Shift on the demon.

It splashed into the lava while Terris and Knox appeared safely on the ground.

"I had it," Terris complained, then looking around he added, "Maybe, it's hard to find shadows to slip through in a room so damn bright."

Knox saw plenty of shadows because the room was so bright, but he decided not to mention it.

"He's back," Tress said, twirling her staff and summoning a globe of water. She shot out a jet stream similar to Scarlet's technique, but this one cut with a ferocity unmatched, bisecting the demon and a stone formation behind it before losing strength.

Knox appeared before the bisected demon and crushed its head for good measure.

"Shall we pull them all and take care of them all at once?" Knox asked, bored by the dungeon's slow pace so far.

"Oh, I like him," Tress said, nodding.

"Let's do it," Terris said.

"You are all fools," Zhul interjected.

Knox ran to each of the twelve demons he knew were hiding in the lava and pulled them out. He then ran back toward the group as fire and brimstone crashed around him from their combined attacks. They were fast, but not nearly as fast as Knox.

Several were cut into two by Tress, one lost its head from Terris's daggers, and the rest were blown to bits by a Radiant Glyph reinforced Luminous Surge. In all, they cleared the first room within minutes, and Knox hadn't even broken a sweat, the globe of coolness keeping him from doing so.

"This is going to be a cakewalk," Terris said, leading the way into the next room and more combat.

Terris was right; the following eight rooms leading up to the boss room for the path were basically child's play. Before receiving the focus lens, it might have been near impossible, but with it, he could bring to bear his true self, though he hadn't needed to yet. It was exciting still, how easy opponents fell to the might of his axe and magic. Tress and Terris were doing good as well, but they were definitely being challenged here and there, while Zhul seemed utterly bored by their lack of wounds or damage taken.

The boss room was much like others Knox had witnessed: a large demon, some ten feet tall with a dagger and a whip, standing on a raised platform with stairs running over with hot lava being the only way up. The fight started off normally enough; Tress threw down water to make a path through the lava and Knox engaged with the boss, thinking he'd two-shot it.

A whip, moving as fast as Knox could track, wrapped around his leg, throwing him off balance and surprising him. Before he could make it to his feet, he was going to fall into the lava. Activating Ethereal Step, he slammed down next to his party with a sheepish grin on his face.

"So, boss fights might be a little more difficult," Knox said, smirking weakly up at them.

"Let's try that again, but together," Terris said. "Oh, who is going to be on add duty? Because here comes, like, twelve demons."

Sure enough, when Knox turned and reached out with his sense, he felt nearly a dozen demons leaving the ring of lava around the edge.

"Tress can you," Knox began to say, but Zhul raised a hand to quiet him.

"I'm bored," Zhul said. "I will take the adds and heal you if you get injured."

Until this point, Knox hadn't seen Zhul do anything other than keep the heat off them, so he nodded, eager to see what the man-child could do.

Zhul began to chant as the demons closed in. Suddenly, roots appeared through the stone and ash, stabbing and entangling the demons. He would be alright, Knox decided as he turned and rushed the boss, but this time with his teammates right at his heel.

"I am B-," the demon began to say, but Knox punched him in the face, and he shut up.

The whip lashed out, but Knox was ready this time, cutting at its length with his axe. The whip fell into two parts, and the demon growled in fury.

Terris appeared behind it, slashing at its neck while his other dagger cut into its side repeatedly. Meanwhile, Tress unleashed a stream of water that cut a deep line into the demon but didn't cut him in two, as it had the lesser demons.

Knox regained his footing and slashed down with his axe, light glistening off the weapon as he went. The demon caught his attack on its dagger, pushing his blow aside, before turning and elbowing Terris hard in the face. Then, as a final act of defiance, his axe came down on its head. It spewed forth fire that consumed the location Tress had been.

His axe did its job, killing the boss and cleaving right through its horns. But Knox couldn't believe what had happened. Was Tress going to be okay? He wasn't sure, as he ran to the smoldering body that lay on the ground.

"Stand aside," Zhul commanded, his hands pulsing with green light as he placed them on Tress's barely moving crisped body.

Vines appeared to wrap her up and Terris pushed through to see what had happened.

"Damnit sis," Terris said, shaking his head. "Hurry and heal her so we can keep going."

Zhul just shot him a look that said, 'Shut the hell up while I work,' and both Knox and Terris kept their mouths shut.

The healing took a solid minute before the vines went away and a naked Tress appeared before them. Blushing, she moved to cover herself. Knox quickly offered his cloak, and she took it.

"Damn boss burnt away some expensive freaking gear," Tress said, frowning.

A chest had appeared, gleaming an orange color that Knox hadn't yet encountered inside a dungeon before.

"Ah nice, an epic chest," Tress said. "You better have some loot that I can use inside that chest!" She seemed to yell out at the dungeon as if it could hear her.

But as odd as the request seemed, when the chest was opened, inside was a red and black robe that fit her perfectly.

"Fire-resistant robes that give me full immunity to heat-based attacks and amplify my own fire-based magic. Simple yet effective," Tress said, focusing on the item before dropping Knox's cloak and putting it on.

Knox recovered his cloak and swung it back over his shoulders. This dungeon was turning out to be a different experience than he'd expected. He just might be challenged before the end of it.

The next path was much of the same, but noticeably harder to deal with. It surprised Knox to realize that these were meant to be defeated by A Rankers, as the threats they were coming up against truly strained his abilities and powers. Even with his increased attributes, he wasn't as strong as he'd like, but he refused to go full metal man just yet, forcing himself to make it work.

There was a touch of worry in letting himself physically change that he wanted to avoid. It was as if he let himself change, he might also change what lay within, and that wasn't something he was ready for yet. Power had a way of changing people, and he was doing all he could to remain the same person he'd been from the start—the one who wanted to help his friends and support the weak.

Besides all that he still had so much to discover, not only about himself and the Titan System, but the world of magic in general. There were secrets to be unlocked, and he would be the one to do it.

The boss here had a variety of ranged attacks that were challenging but eventually overcome by the group. After they collected the loot, only a final path was left.

The loot they got from this last fight was the same quality as before, but they presented themselves as a scepter that Zhul claimed as his own. From what Knox could tell by looking at it, it amplified magic in some way, specifically, healing magic. With the loot taken care of, they approached the final path, and Knox spoke up.

"Will this one be themed do you think?"

"Most definitely," Terris said, rubbing his hands together. "And if we clear it I bet my shiniest dagger that we will get multiple chests as well."

Stepping into the swirling doorway they entered the final path of the dungeon, ready to face off against any foe.

A cheer rose up from all around them and Knox took a surprised step backward as he realized they were surrounded by thousands of people. Well, not quite surrounded, as the people were in the stands of a great arena, and they stood on the arena's cobblestoned floor.

A voice, powerful and sinister spoke out from all around them.

"Welcome to the abyssal arena! You will face off against stronger and stronger foes until you either fall in battle or succeed in beating our champion. Prepare yourselves!"

Instead of a fiery demon who spat lava like some of the previous bosses, a thin man wearing blue ice armor walked out into the field. His skin was that of someone who'd been out in the cold too long, decaying and yet still pristine at the same time. His sword was a thin icicle of ice with a rounded hilt and thin handle.

"This is a bit different," Knox said, readying his weapon and his spells as he stepped forward to fight.

"You will find me no easy target," came a surprisingly feminine voice.

Knox Ethereal Stepped forward mid-swing of his axe in response. The ice man blocked the attack with frightening speed, and blasted Knox in the chest with a ball of ice that shattered on contact with his reinforced magical armor.

Stumbling backward, Knox lifted his chin to his opponent, acknowledging that he was indeed a worthy foe.

That was when the fire engulfed the man, and he let out a terrible scream that brought Knox's hands over his ears. The fire continued, unrelenting and as hot as any of the lava they'd encountered so far. Finally, the screaming cut off, and Tress stepped forward, a wiry smile on her face.

"Next," she said casually.

The next opponent was a muscle-bound man with fire burning at the top of his horned head and had eyes of bright blue. He didn't announce himself or say a word; he just ran into the area and began to shoot balls of fire. Knox batted them away one by one with his axe as he prepared to face off against the huge fighter.

Clearing the distance between them with the help of an Ethereal Step, Knox appeared before the large fighter and struck down with his axe. The blow was enough to stagger the horned demon back and put a line across his chest where the attack had landed. But he appeared no weaker for the attack and threw more fire, this time a stream of it, right at Knox's face.

A halo of power surged around Knox, and the fire suddenly split around him. Zhul stepped forward, chanting softly under his breath.

Next came Tress, water spilling forth from her as she attempted to bisect the mighty demon. However, he burned so hot that the water turned to steam before it could reach it. Suddenly Terris appeared behind it and cut at its horns, cutting one free and slipping back into shadow before it could respond.

The shadows seemed to swirl around the demon, and suddenly, a shower of daggers appeared all around it, slashing forward and impaling it. This was enough that the demon fell to its knees in pain and Knox burst forward out of the protective bubble to deal the final blow. He cut its head clean off, and the intense heat faded.

This continued, each foe harder than the next for what felt like an eternity until finally the announcer called out above the din of battle that they'd be facing the final champion.

Out walked a man in iron armor, simply dressed, holding a sword that radiated darkness. He had a gentle look upon his face, like he couldn't possibly be a demon or anything so foul.

Then, while Knox was checking him out, he looked up, and they met eye to eye. There was something terrible about his eyes, something so horrible that it made Knox take a step backward, though he knew not what it was.

Then he felt the power emanating off this foe and nearly took another step backward.

"Careful," Knox said. "He is easily twice as strong as anything we've faced so far."

"What?" Tress said, unconvinced. "He seems so fragile."

"Looks can be deceiving," the man said, his voice ringing out clear even from the great distance between them. "I am Lucy, the final demon you will face today."

"Well, Lucy," Tress said, still not intimidated by the slight of build man, "give us your best shot."

"Very well," Lucy said, inclining his head and disappearing.

He reappeared right in front of Tress, his black sword already firmly placed into her gut as he twisted it, causing Tress to scream in pain.

That was more than speed, Knox realized, that was tele-portation.

"Tress!" Terris screamed as he plunged his daggers into the back of the man named Lucy. Before his blow could strike home, Lucy teleported back away, his sword dripping with Tress's blood.

"Oh dear," Lucy said, his voice clear as ever. "You bleed far too easily if you expect to beat me."

By the time he finished his words, Tress was already healed and standing tall, but the battle was on.

Knox used Ethereal Step to appear before Lucy, axe ready to strike, but Lucy merely blinked to the side as the blow came down and stabbed Knox in his gut, shattering his mystical armor and cutting through the physical armor like butter.

"Bad call," Knox said, spitting blood and casting Luminous Surge right in the demon's face. It worked, he couldn't blink away fast enough and took the blow right in the face.

As Lucy stumbled back, releasing his grip on the sword, Knox activated Dimensional Shift, leaving the sword behind as he switched places with Lucy. Turning Knox saw that the sword hadn't appeared in his gut, but it had been a nice try. Instead, Lucy picked up his sword just as fire rained down from above, and vines reached up to restrain him.

But Lucy proved to be too fast, blinking away and appearing before Zhul.

"You are the healer. I can't have you helping them; it will drag this on," Lucy said, but Zhul wasn't waiting for him to finish his monologue. He lashed out with vines and grabbed hold of the demon.

Knox ran to intercept the demon, axe ready, but he decided at the last second to begin casting Radiant Glyph instead, multiplying his next attack. Lucy struggled to free himself, his teleport seemingly not working to free him from the trap.

"Get clear," Knox yelled as he began to cast Luminous Surge.

The power built up and hit his runic formations, filling them to the brim with power and multiplying it. The wave of energy that was released could destroy city walls, but it was centered on a single target.

Lucy took the attack face first but could not move against it, block or otherwise. But instead of feeling the power inside of him diminish and die, it seemed to bolster and reach new heights.

"I am not some second-rate demon that you can slay with such tricks," Came Lucy's voice from inside the maelstrom of dust and debris.

"I'm not strong enough," Knox muttered under his breath as a wave of something hit him, seemingly overwhelming his mind. "I'm too weak to stand against something so strong. I can't win."

All around him, he heard the others muttering similar cries of defeat, and it struck a chord with him. Suddenly he stopped holding back, something inside of him burst free and he felt himself grow, his skin turn golden. His mind was no longer under the attack from this minor demon and with a wave of his hand he released the magical hold it had on the others as well.

"To death," Knox shouted the words. "We refuse to submit to your rein, prince of demons. Remove yourself from our presence or fall like so many of your brethren have today."

Lucy appeared out of the dust and he looked like he'd been beaten to an inch of his life. Blood poured down his face in numerous cuts; his clothing, so delicate and silk-like, was torn and ruined. Even his sword didn't seem as dark and foreboding as it had once been.

"You haven't beaten me yet, you second rate Titan," Lucy said, scorn in his voice. "I've got power to spare still and I will call upon it all to bring you down."

Knox appeared before him, his spells activating almost without thought. He placed his hand on Lucy's head just as Lucy slashed and stabbed into his golden flesh, unable to penetrate it.

"Luminous Surge," Knox said as he activated the spell.

Power flowed out of him in waves as he used his signature spell, completely obliterating Lucy's head in one final attack.

Knox was sure the dungeon was finished now, but he felt something else while embracing his power so fully. It was another presence of immense power, almost as if he could feel the personality or being that was the dungeon. He reached out to it and felt it as it began to create loot for them, pulling upon ancient unknowable power reserves to do so.

Then, just as fast as he'd sensed it, the power faded and was gone. Before them lay four chests of glimmering orange and gold.

Knox began the process of pushing back his power, and eventually, he felt himself shrink to a manageable height and size. All the while, his teammates were silent, but Knox didn't mind. He had loot to get after all, and something told him it would be a good one.

Inside the chest on the far right, Knox found a curious item. It looked like a simple ring, but Knox peered into it and determined what it did.

This ring could take and store spells, up to five of them, but if you used the same spell it would magnify the output by that many times. For him, it meant he could store five powerfully enhanced Luminous Surges and release them all at once with enough force to burn away a city. Just another tool that he knew he'd find useful in his fight against the darkness.

He paid only mild attention to what the others got in their chest: pieces of armor, a weapon, and a staff. Each would be a powerful artifact that would do mighty tasks when called upon, but Knox was happy with his rather simple yet sturdy piece of loot.

CHAPTER 18
RETURN

"Are we going to talk about how you grew super big and turned golden?" Tress asked as they walked free of the dungeon and prepared for their return trip back to Luminar.

"Yeah," Terris said, looking at Knox with wide eyes. "Is that a technique you can teach me or does it just happen when you get strong enough?"

"I am also interested in knowing how you did that," Zhul said, his childish features making him look like an eager schoolboy.

"It isn't anything any of you will need to worry about," Knox said. "It's because I am a Titan that I am going through these changes."

They all seemed satisfied by this answer and soon they were on the road again, running at incredible speeds toward their destination. What would have been a trip that would take weeks, would be finished within one.

By the time they reached the pass that led into the area around Knox's home, they came upon a familiar group and slowed to meet them.

"I told you we'd catch up," Knox said, his eyes ran over the group and after seeing that all were present, he relaxed a bit.

"Was it worth it?" his mother asked, her expression as stern and worried as it had been when he'd left.

"Yes," Knox said simply. He'd grown a good bit from all the essence, his normal body even reaching the A Ranks finally, meaning he was at least over level 50 now. With the help of his axe, he'd really sucked away a record breaking amount of essence.

"You feeling alright?" Dernal asked, but Knox just shot him a look, not fully having forgiven him yet for the betrayal he'd felt.

"He's fine," Scarlet said, also shooting a glare toward Dernal.

"Alrighty then," John said, smiling wide enough that Knox thought he might split his lips. "Shall we finish this little journey and get back, I'm ready for a hot bath."

"Keep up as best you can," Knox said, jogging forward and weaving through the wagons and groups of people that were trying to make it through the pass before the snowfall started once more.

They made good time, but Knox knew he'd have to slow down a measure soon, as he was pushing the non-A-Rankers to their limits of speed and endurance. He hadn't even slept since he'd unlocked his new maxed-out attributes, but he felt that perhaps he would need to soon if he wanted to keep himself in tip-top shape.

They passed through where Keenlen's Vale had been and his mother bid them to stop so she could visit the remains of the home Knox had grown up in.

As it had been before, the house was one of only a few standing, but amazingly, it all looked as if nothing had changed. Perhaps someday soon, people could come back here and live if they wanted.

"I worked so hard to reinforce this house, making it as sturdy as possible. I wanted a home that would stand for a hundred years if it meant it would keep you safe," Scarlet said.

They stood alone inside the abandoned living room of the home, just Scarlet and Knox.

"It had withstood the rampaging of an A Ranked monster, so

I'd say you did pretty well," Knox said, sitting down in his father's old favorite chair. "I began to see the runes around ten years ago, and I became obsessed with understanding them. I thought that perhaps if I could understand the runes, I might get some insight into the person who put them there."

Knox turned to regard his mother and she averted her eyes as if ashamed.

"I am as much to blame for you wanting this life as Dernal or Askar," she finally said, shaking her head. "I feel like I owe them both an apology."

"Just promise me," Knox said, walking over and meeting eyes with his mother, "no more secrets."

"I'm an open book," Scarlet said, reaching out and embracing her son.

With their visit concluded, they traveled through the forest and into the Shadowfall Swamp—the transition between which had become harder and harder to tell as trees grew normal and abundant in the swamp now, hiding much of its old features. Traveling through the woods, they arrived at Luminar after only a day of travel through the swamps.

Leo met them by the gate and went straight to Knox.

"Ramses needs to speak with you immediately," Leo said, and by the look on his face it appeared to be urgent.

"Lead the way," Knox said, leaving the others to show the newcomers around Luminar.

The city bustled with activity, and the noonday sun overhead was unimpeded by clouds or overcast of any kind. They reached a small hut and went inside to find Ramses in bed, looking worse than Knox had ever seen him.

"I need to return," Ramses said immediately. "Being away from my Titan Engine after expelling so much power has left me weaker than I anticipated."

A mix of emotions ran through Knox suddenly. He'd meant for Ramses to fight at his side against the darkness, but how could he do that if he were laid up in bed?

"I've unlocked much of my potential as a Titan," Knox said, showing his arm to Ramses. "Perhaps I could open a portal back for you?"

"You need a tether," Ramses said, each word seemed difficult for him to say. "I could do it if I had power enough, but I'm much too weak."

"Then how do we get you back?" Knox asked; certainly, the Titan Born had an idea or two.

He sat up suddenly and sounded more animated than before. "We travel via boat," Ramses said. "I've already sent several squads of your golems to fix up a ship, and with those pirate golems you have teaching them how to man a ship, we've got a crew. Will you sail with me and return me to my seat of power?"

"You need me to go?" Knox asked, confused. "Surely you can make it back on your own?"

"If you go, we can finally connect our Titan Engines, and our power will be bolstered. If you do this for me, I will stand with you against the Dark Titan," Ramses said, a smile appearing on his face.

Knox didn't know Ramses all that well, but something didn't seem right to him. "How is it that me going to your Titan Engine will speed the spread of my own to yours? I thought it was simply a matter of time before it reached yours after the changes you made?"

"True, but your presence will do what mine has done, hasten the spread, and sooner than you can expect, we will be true Titans," Ramses said.

Leo had already left, so Knox felt safe doing what he was about to do. He released his hold on his power and let himself take the form of his true self.

"Goodness," Ramses said. "You've somehow progressed further than me in such a short time? And I see you have freed yourself of your restraining bands as well."

"I have," Knox said. "But I'm not convinced that you need me at your complex to be able to achieve your goals. Surely, if you return alone and with the help of my golems, you can ensure our two Titan Engines will merge their spread?"

"I need you," Ramses said, emphasizing the words. "It is a matter of life and death. I've pushed myself too hard and if I cannot return and siphon a portion of your power off, I will die."

Knox didn't know what to think about what he'd just heard and he stared at the man for a long moment before responding. "You need to take power from me?" Knox asked.

"I'm sorry, I wasn't trying to hide it, I just am not recovering and I'm certain now it is because I pushed myself too hard too fast while out of the influence of my Titan Engine. So it stands to reason that if we are to face off against the Dark Titan, we will want our System to engage with hers as well. We can't do that until we are combined and powerful enough to force that connection."

Knox listened to Ramses speak and wished he knew more about how the Titan Engines operated. "I'll consider it, but if I'm being honest, I meant to go take the fight to the Dark Titan immediately. Her sickness is spreading, and I don't know how long we have before she grows too strong for us to handle."

"Time is never going to be our friend, but if we work together and with your new power, we will succeed," Ramses said.

Knox pinched the bridge of his nose and remembered the words Echo had said. Together perhaps they'd be able to overcome the threat after all, with that idea in his head, Knox nodded.

"Fine," Knox said. "Prepare the ship, we will leave as soon as we are able."

CHAPTER 19
FAREWELL

KNOX DIDN'T MAKE a point of spreading his plans to everyone else, but one by one he was approached with requests to go with him on the journey through the ocean to some distant island. Dernal came first, a conversation that Knox had been avoiding for several weeks now, coming to a head as he sat next to him in the eating room.

"Hhrrmm," Dernal said, starting off the conversation much as he did in the past.

"I'm not interested in talking to you right now," Knox said. He'd tried to keep himself distant from Dernal considering what he'd done to betray his trust, but he could tell Dernal was going to be persistent about it this time.

"I did what I felt was right," Dernal said. "I won't be apologizing for it, but you need me along on this journey through the endless waters."

"Why?" Knox asked. He meant to address both of his comments, but he only answered the second.

"Because I have experience navigating on the water, no one else here has spent as much time at sea as I have," Dernal said. This surprised Knox, but he realized he knew very little about Dernal's past. "And you'll want to take Leo. He knows much about the folk you will find out there, perhaps even avoid a confrontation with his people."

"Why didn't you just tell me? You went so far as to help me become an Adventurer; why not tell me? And don't give me that oath crap; obviously, there are ways around that. Otherwise, you'd never have helped me become an Adventurer in the first place," Knox said, his frustrations rising with each word spoken.

"I've told you already, I did as much as I felt comfortable doing. It just wasn't my place," Dernal said.

"If you can truly navigate, then I'll consider bringing you, but Leo isn't needed. I am a match for anything we might face out there, and we will make it to our destination, one way or another," Knox said.

He wanted to put as few people at risk as possible, which meant he wasn't planning on taking the entire crew of regulars. In fact, he'd man the ship with golems and Ramses alone if he could, but he felt like he needed at least two or three of his strongest to come with him, just in case battle were to happen.

"That is all I ask," Dernal said, standing and leaving Knox alone with his thoughts.

His mother found him next, followed by Terrim, then all of the rest of his friends, and surprisingly enough, even Askar—though he only said that if Scarlet was going, so would he. They'd apparently begun the process of forgiveness with each other, though Knox hadn't the slightest idea how it was going, only that he saw them together quite a bit.

In the end, the conversation with Beth and what followed stuck in his head the most.

"I've missed you," Beth said, catching him just as he was about to leave his private quarters. It was nighttime, and he was just popping out to check on Ramses. He'd been giving him small doses of power from his own core, a process that was extremely uncomfortable, but he'd kept his essence level with the help of monster cores. Something about getting power straight from another Titan seemed to help Ramses more than pure essence.

"I'm about to check on Ramses, so if this is your plea to join me at sea, can it wait till tomorrow?" Knox asked, a bit more frustrated sounding than he meant to sound.

"I've missed you," Beth repeated, pushing him back into his private quarters.

The room was sparsely decorated, only the essentials interested Knox as he spent very little time when not studying, inside his room. The glow of a lamp brightened the room just enough for Knox to navigate it while looking over his shoulder and walking backward to avoid having Beth run him over.

"I've missed you too," Knox admitted. "But like I said..."

He never got a chance to finish his sentence, she pressed herself against him and kissed him. They locked together and shared a passionate minute of kissing, until Knox had to take a breath and pushed her back gently.

"I've missed that," Beth said, smirking. "Tell me why we haven't been doing that more and why didn't you take me with you when you left?"

"Because I was stupid?" Knox asked, wanting nothing more than to melt back into her touch. "Let's do that thing where we kiss and make up."

"Let's," Beth said, melting back into Knox's arms as they began to passionately kiss once more. Gone were the fears and inhibitions he'd felt before, so long had it been since he'd felt Beth's embrace. Gone were the feelings of guilt over lost loved ones. He only felt the fiery passion for Beth and having her near.

She hadn't asked but he was considering bringing her along now if for no other reason than he didn't want to think about not having her around. He lost himself in the passion and forgot all about checking on Ramses as they took their kissing to the bedroom.

Sometime later, both of them lying naked beside each other, their conversation continued.

"It has been too long," Beth said, yawning. "Don't you go leaving me now and never coming back, got it?"

"I'll always return," Knox promised her. "I've got to, for the fate of the world rests on my shoulders."

"Sounds like a heavy weight," Beth said, the sincerity in her voice catching Knox off guard.

"It is," Knox said. "Sometimes when I think no one is watching I feel like I might sag and fall from the weight. I know it isn't solely my responsibility. In fact, it is because of that, that I've chosen to help Ramses so he can help me. But damnit, it feels like it's only me standing before the darkness that threatens to take away all I've gained over these several months."

"I met your mother," Beth said, the suddenness of the change of topic throwing Knox for another loop. "She seems nice, if a bit stern. She talked to me about you, asked questions and refused to leave until she heard what she wanted."

"Oh," Knox said, imagining the two of them going at it in a verbal joust. "I hope she didn't get too mean with you. She's being a tad overprotective; you should have heard her when I told her she couldn't go with me on the ship. I'm half expecting her and a dozen others to try and sneak aboard when I'm not looking."

"Oh, we definitely planned that out, but then I reminded them of your odd sense that cues you in on people, but your mother didn't seem concerned by it. I legit think she is going to go whether you like it or not," Beth said, sitting up as she spoke.

Knox had trouble concentrating for a moment as he took in her exposed chest, but he regained focus and nodded along as she spoke. She swung her legs off the bed and began to dress as Knox considered her words.

"If she does, are you going to join her?" Knox asked. "It might be a pleasant surprise if you did, though I can't give you permission to, because it's far too dangerous." Knox spoke with a teasing tone, but he was pretty serious about it. The trip was going to be dangerous and take who knows how long. Despite that, Ramses was sick and though he'd spoken with Dernal about how to get there, they'd be completely relying on a sick man to ensure they didn't get lost.

"I'll try," Beth said, a hint of serious teasing in her voice. "But first, I have to convince your mother that I'm worth taking. I've leveled up a good bit while you were gone, but I'm still a good month or two from entering the B Ranks. And by the way your mother is acting since becoming part of the Titan System, she'll be hitting the A Ranks any day now."

"Right," Knox said, thinking back to how all of the higher rankers had reacted when suddenly their taint was pulled from them, and they had to pick paths from the Titan System.

Zhul had almost immediately left after his training with Gowlen, he came back later clearly into the S Ranks. He must have been so close before, that killing only a handful of monsters set him over the edge. Meanwhile, Tress and Terris were off searching for the final few A Ranked Monsters in the area, doing a service for the city and gaining precious essence for themselves, while getting a chance to try out their new abilities and spells.

In all, Knox was surprised by none of their choices when it came to the paths they chose. Though, despite the paths, Knox was amazed at how proficient they were at calling on their old skills just as easily as their path skills. It took practice and lots of failure to do so, Knox knew by experience, but they'd done it.

The rest of the night with Beth was a blur of meaningless conversation where they talked about everything and anything, but Knox enjoyed every moment of it. He'd begun to think that Beth and him were not to be, but now he knew with certainty that he cared for her more than he'd realized before. Not only did he love her as a friend, now he was beginning to realize that he loved her romantically as well.

CHAPTER 20
LIFE ON A SHIP

THE SHIP WAS a mighty affair with several decks filled with supplies and golems. Each golem worked with the practiced ease of a weathered seaman but without the need to feed or rest. This was to say, they were set to leave within the week, and Knox was eager to complete the journey.

Knox had just finished getting Ramses settled into the captain's quarters, the only room with a proper bed, when he sensed several people approaching under some type of veil. It was strong, and if he hadn't been expecting it, he might have missed it, but as it were, he sensed his mother's approach.

He'd allowed for Ramses, Dernal, Tress, Terris, and Zhul to come along, but no one else. Even getting the three previously A Ranked Adventurers to come had been harder than he'd expected. They clearly wanted to do as he commanded, almost in a weird way, but none of them wanted to leave the chance to collect essence. Only when he promised that they'd likely encounter sea monsters and the like, did he get them to agree.

Knox knew nothing about boats or ships, but he'd heard Dernal speak about Port and Starboard, as well as Stern, but the meanings hadn't sunk in yet. So, he went to the front of the ship and called down to the space around the veil.

"I can see right through that veil of yours," Knox said. Then, with a wave of his hand, he disturbed the makings of the spell. Touching the threads of magic behind it all was much easier than he thought it would be.

The area wavered, and several people stood looking surprised.

Terrim, Murdoch, Henry, Leo, and John stood looking sheepish for being discovered. They all looked at John, who shrugged and said, "I told you it wouldn't work."

Knox was surprised not to find Beth or his mother, but he let it go after going down to bid them farewell once more. Terrim had words to say, but Knox took them for what they were; a friend worried about another friend and didn't hold them against him. He was a good man and a better friend. Part of the reason why Knox didn't want to have him along was because of that very fact.

It was going to be dangerous at sea for reasons that Knox didn't think they were really considering. Sea monsters would be a unique challenge for anyone, but the threat of being pulled under the water to the dark depths was one that weighed heavy on his mind. He wouldn't lose any of his friends to the water, he refused to, so bidding them farewell the golems began the work to get them out to sea.

Constructing a ship from the remains of a mostly burnt out one hadn't been easy, but the golems were nothing if not efficient. Going up to the top deck, he found the three pirate golems standing and peering out toward the sea.

"You three ready to make sure we don't make any mistakes," Knox said, he'd joked with them that they were truly the only real sailors they had, but it was true.

"I'm ready to have the wind in my hair again," Borris said, he had no hair, but Knox didn't mention it to him.

"I believe we've instructed the other golems well enough to get us going, but I'd like permission to be the one calling the shots, navigation is one thing, but we will want to avoid the major trade lanes as well if we want to stay clear of other pirates," Edgar said, never taking his eyes off the horizon as he spoke.

Vlad stayed quiet, his eyes on the ship and not the water before them. Then he surprised Knox by speaking in a low, almost whisper. "How well do you think we can float with our new bodies? You better hope we don't lose too many golems in a bad storm."

"Can't we set up harnesses to keep them attached, it should be more than—," Edgar cut Knox off mid-sentence.

"We've seen to it already, but nothing is foolproof at sea," Edgar said. "We will do as best we can, and Vlad knows it."

The idea of one of them, basically immortal, sinking to the depths was something that gave him pause.

"I'll do my best to ensure that doesn't happen, but if you aren't up for the risk, please stay behind. We will manage one way or another," Knox said, not wanting anyone to come that wasn't fully prepared for the risks they might encounter.

In response, they all turned to look at him and laughed.

Edgar responded for them. "We lived lives as pirates, death was always right around the corner from either our own kin or the many other pirates and nasty beasts out at sea. The idea of immortality at the bottom of the sea isn't something that scares us."

"Good," Knox said, suddenly distracted as he thought he felt something with his sense, but when he focused down, it was gone. Odd. "Make ready to set sail and pull anchor."

With that, Knox left to check on the supplies, they'd brought an overabundance, despite Dernal's assurances that the trip would take no longer than two months. There were only six mouths to feed, but Knox wanted to be prepared for anything.

It wasn't until they were a week out into the trip that Knox felt the feeling again with his sense, this time more persistent. He followed it to the lower decks and this time he didn't lose it. Reaching out with his new ability to touch the weaves of magic all around them, he disturbed the spell. This time it took a great effort that had him nearly panting for breath before he truly got the spell to unweave.

Standing before him with a sheepish look on her face, was his mother and beside her stood Beth.

"How is it possible that I couldn't detect you?" Knox asked, more dumbfounded than upset at finding them.

"I've got more than a few tricks up my sleeve that you can't account for, Mr. Titan Born," Scarlet said, a sly smile on her face. She was obviously proud of herself, but why had she brought Beth? It didn't add up.

"Why did you both feel the need to come?" Knox asked, pinching the bridge of his nose. "I mean, you know it's going to be dangerous, and I can't focus on keeping you safe and keeping this ship from being torn apart."

"You don't need to protect us," Scarlet said, Beth nodded eagerly beside her. She was in full combat gear, bow at her side.

"Yeah," Beth said. "We are strong independent women who are here to protect you, not the other way around."

Knox rolled his eyes at Beth's obviously sarcastic words, but he had to admit, he was happy to see both of them for different reasons.

"Fine," Knox said. "But you should know we don't have any decent beds, just hammocks that aren't as comfortable as they look at first glance."

"We'll manage," Scarlet said, sounding very proud of herself. "If nothing else my ability to hide from you proves that I'm worth keeping around in a conflict. Imagine what I could do if I truly wanted to cause some damage."

"You picked the same path as me," Knox said, rolling his eyes. "I know exactly what you are capable of."

"Yet you didn't see through my veil," Scarlet said, still smiling wide.

"You're right," Knox said, focusing his sense around her until he found what he was looking for. "You have an artifact that helped you, I can sense it in your pocket. How much longer was it going to work before it broke?"

Her smile faded and she rolled her eyes right back at Knox. "You take all the fun out of it. I had another day or two before it failed completely. Stop teasing us and show us to the baths, we are running short on supplies and your girlfriend eats more than I accounted for."

Knox blushed a little at that, but he locked eyes with Beth, who just shrugged. *Fine*, Knox thought, *she could call herself my girlfriend*, he didn't have any issue with that, but man he wished they'd have not snuck onto the ship.

"I love you both, so please be careful. I sense something massive coming for us about a day's journey away if it keeps course. Ramses says there are all types of sea monsters in the direction we are going, but he dealt with them before so I should be a decent match for whatever we encounter," Knox said, by way of catching them up on the situation aboard.

"Oh, you finally found them," Tress said, appearing behind Knox and surprising him.

"You knew?" Knox asked, turning.

"I helped," Tress said brightly. "Can I have my amulet back now?"

"Sure thing," Scarlet said, handing back a golden amulet with a blue gem set into it.

Knox leveled a stare at Tress but said nothing.

Several days went by, a wind produced by Tress had given them a bit more speed and kept them away from the large threat that lurked in the water, but it was slowly gaining on them and they were at the top speed that the ship could handle. Soon battle would be upon them and Knox found himself wanting the chance to release some of the building tension he'd been feeling over the past week.

"When the fight starts, I want you both below deck and ready to help if you are called upon, but not until then," Knox said, Scarlet and Beth both nodded but he couldn't help but think that they had their own plans.

Over the last few days, he'd noticed that they spoke a lot and while Knox was happy to see it, he also wondered at what they had to talk about so much. Sure, Scarlet looked young still, but there was enough of an age gap that he figured they'd have less to talk about, but it seemed to be quite the opposite.

"We understand," Scarlet said when Knox didn't stop staring at them. He cared so much for both of them and yet they had placed themselves in danger because they also cared about him. "We do, we promise to only get involved when we are called upon." Scarlet added when Knox didn't respond.

"Fine, be safe, I'm going up," Knox said, then turning back he continued. "If for whatever reason the monster compromises the hull, get to Ramses and get to a lifeboat. I'll keep you safe as much as possible."

"I've had a hand in reinforcing the hull, it'll take quite a monster to get past it," Scarlet said.

Knox nodded, he believed her, as her runic formations had been key to keeping his old house in a single piece. It would take a powerful monster to take out their hull, or perhaps backlash from his own spells and abilities to do so. Either way he'd instructed the rest of the team to be careful when slinging spells as they only had the one ship.

The sea air filled his lungs as he took in a deep breath. It was a wonderful feeling, this out in the open sea. He'd found his sea legs early on, adjusting to the constant motion, however Terris had not. Standing over to his left and retching over the side of the ship, Knox realized he'd be little help in the upcoming fight.

"Do you want to go below deck and protect our guests?" Knox asked, but Terris just shot him a look, his face practically green from the motion sickness.

A sudden spray of water and a surge of power caught Knox's attention. He raised his hands and cast Mystic Veil just in time to lessen the damage from a powerful beam of water aimed at the mast. Then from out of the water several dozen tentacles began to rise. Whatever monster they'd been running from, it had caught up.

"Attack!" The cry went up from Edgar and Tress at the same time.

Knox watched as Edgar let loose a torrent of fire that didn't do so much as singe the tentacle closest to him. Next Tress unleashed a bar of fire that bisected a tentacle, then with a raised fist she called down Lighting on several others from a seemingly clear sky.

But she wasn't finished, using her combination of newly learned spells and the techniques she already mastered, she unleashed a bolt of molten lava, burning away yet another tentacle.

In the meantime, Zhul did something that Knox had not seen from him before, sending out an Arcane Pulse, he followed it up by transforming himself into a large fish like creature and diving into the water. Knox knew that he'd taken the Mystic Path with a specialization on Druidic magic, but this was a sight to behold.

Terris threw up again and rolled to the ground as the ship began to tilt under the pull of so many massive tentacles.

It was time for Knox to get involved and he knew just what to do. Using his Void Grasp, he summoned tendrils from the void of space to begin immobilizing and draining the tentacles of their power. Next, he cast Lustrous Chains, further tying up the tentacles and making them an easy target for his next spell.

With a cluster of four tentacles nearby, he cast Luminous Surge at them and literally blew them apart. This monster, by the feeling of his sense, was at least B Ranked, but it was so large that it was fighting above its weight class.

Zhul would do what he could to whatever lay beneath, Knox was certain the man-child was up to the task, they just had to keep the ship from sinking into the depths of the ocean in the meanwhile. Knox took in another salty breath and felt the wind on his skin as he jumped into the air, axe ready.

He cleaved through them all with ease and Ethereal Stepped back to the deck, where he found Terris finally attacking a tentacle to his left. He stabbed it and something black began to spread over the tentacle until it fell back into the water.

This wasn't going so bad after all, Knox thought, just as things turned for the worse.

A new set of tentacles rose up, breaking his chains and destroying his void tendrils. These new tentacles were darker purple than the rest and power vibrated off them in waves. That is when Knox made the realization of what he was feeling. It was like each of the tentacles were a monster of their own and each of them were B Ranked.

They weren't fighting a single sea monster, but a grouping of them attached to one base monster. Lightning struck Knox in the chest suddenly and for a single moment he thought perhaps Tress had missed and hit him, but no the attack had come from a tentacle. Then all hell broke loose as each of the half dozen new tentacles began to unleash magical attacks.

Fire, water, lightning, even rocks, began to rain down on the deck, destroying handrails and other non-runic reinforced items. They had to move fast if they were going to keep the ship in a single piece.

Knox rushed forward, cutting down with his axe as all around him his teammates sprang into action, even Dernal began to cast spells to repel the tentacles.

One down, then another, and then four more would appear,

Knox needed to speed along this monster's death and he knew one sure way to do that. Running to the side of the ship he leapt off, sliding down a massive tentacle as he went in search of the main body.

The first thing he saw was Zhul as a massive fish creature with sharp teeth, biting into a humongous bulk of a creature below. Whatever he was doing, it just wasn't enough damage fast enough. Knox began to trace runic formations in the air, but a stray tentacle knocked him aside and he decided to use his ring instead.

Raising his hand, he unleashed the five Luminous Surges he'd stored within it and watched as the magic ignited the very water around him. The wall of light that shot out burned with such an intensity that even Knox felt himself begin to be damaged by it, if only barely.

Zhul did the smart thing and bolted out of the way just as Knox's attack smashed into the sea monster, cleaving it into two and blowing tentacles all over. The water went dark suddenly as the sea monster died, releasing a dark substance that must be its blood, into the water.

Knox looked for the surface, but he was momentarily turned around and didn't know which way to swim as he sank ever deeper from his heavy armor. Activating Solar Wings, he began to move in a direction with speed, but the water seemed to grow colder, and a pressure closed in around him, he must be going deeper he realized.

Suddenly, something grabbed him in its mouth and Knox nearly lost hold of his axe. Swinging it about, he was ready to cut into the monster when he recognized the fish Zhul had turned into only minutes ago. He let the fish take him, raising him higher and higher in the water until they broke the surface and splashed onto the deck.

Pain in Knox's head and a building pressure had him on his knees. Something about moving so fast from down below to the surface really made him hurt. Zhul was over him chanting the words of a healing spell before Dernal could make it across the deck. The pain eased and he felt the pressure in his head normalize.

"That was a close one," Knox said, but suddenly lightning smashed nearby him and he realized some of the tentacles were still attacking. But before he could get up, Tress put down the last magical one and the golems, Edgar, Borris, and Vlad, worked together to push off the rest, not even bothering to attack.

"Damn Krakens," Edgar said, walking over to see Knox. "They are the worst that you can encounter out here and of course we find ourselves a mighty powerful one at that. Should be smooth sailing from here on out."

"Don't ever say that," Borris said, drawing out the last word. "You know that's a heap of bad luck."

"He's not wrong," Vlad said, nodding sagely.

And just like that they'd dealt with their first sea monster attack, but it was far from their last.

The next few weeks involved several shark attacks, a dozen or so sirens, and various other monsters all hell bent on taking down their ship.

CHAPTER 21
PIRATES

Those were all manageable to a point, but their biggest challenge came when they encountered a literal fleet of ships, some two dozen of them all bigger than their own.

It all started in the early hours of the morning, as Knox was talking to Dernal who'd been speaking to Ramses about how they should be close already.

"According to Ramses, we ought to have gotten there already or at least be within spitting distance," Dernal said. "But as far as I can tell, there is nothing out here worth seeing. Can you sense anything?"

"No," Knox answered. He'd been trying to spread his sense as wide as possible, but besides the abundance of life out in the water, he sensed nothing else yet. "I'll keep trying, but Ramses has a better sense of his Titan Engine, he should be able to feel it from a great distance. Even now I could tell you which direction to go if you wanted to head home to my Titan Engine."

"Perhaps we ought to bring him up here and see if the sea air will put some strength in him," Dernal said, his eyes on the horizon.

"Couldn't hurt," Knox said, turning to go get the Ramses.

"I'll be careful with him." Knox assured Dernal when he shot him a look that seemed to say as much.

The ship swayed and the water sprayed over the edge as dozens of golems went to work keeping them going a mostly straight path. They'd been relying mostly on artificial wind from Tress, but they allowed her plenty of breaks where they were forced to submit to the direction of the wind.

The captain's quarters were a lavish affair with fine wood-working and even a few tapestries. This room was one of the few that hadn't gone up in flames, due to a series of runic formations surrounding it that Scarlet had discovered later. She admired the work but claimed she, of course, could do better.

Knox didn't even bother knocking, figuring Ramses was asleep as he was most of the time. Sure enough, as he entered the older man snored in the large poster bed with its fine sheets and warm blanket. He'd opened a window, letting in the occasional spray of water and cool air.

"Ramses," Knox said, nudging him with his hand. "Time to get up and make sure we are on the right path."

Ramses stirred and then sat bolt right up. "What's that now?" He asked.

"Time to go topside and give us some directions," Knox said. "You should be feeling better by now, we are well within the range of your Titan Engine. I actually felt when we left mine, though I don't feel nearly as diminished as you, I am noticing a slowing down of my power."

"Just don't overtax yourself doing a massive teleportation spell and you ought to be alright," Ramses said, swinging his legs over the side of the bed and slipping on a pair of shoes. He wore a rope, and his shoes were no more than slippers, but he hobbled on after Knox as he went for the door.

Thinking better of it, Knox turned back and lent him an arm, but to his astonishment, Ramses declined and stood all the taller for it.

"I'm feeling more refreshed, now that you mention it,"

Ramses said. "My power is indeed returning, but I also sense something foreign at my seat of power, oh dear they've returned. I hadn't noticed until you woke me, but we are close, maybe a day's journey from the Titan Engine. Hopefully we aren't too late."

"Too late?" Knox asked, and Ramses averted his eyes. "What aren't you telling me?"

Ramses looked at the floor and let out a sigh of frustration. "I suppose it's about time I tell you the full truth."

"You better," Knox said, rounding on the older man with fire in his eyes. "I've gone way out on a limb for you to be keeping secrets."

"I left to find you for more than the reasons I've said before. I'm powerful, or at least I was, but part of what diminished my power the most was a certain conflict I was having with a group of pirates and their S Ranked Captain. He didn't like the System Spreading over his waters and he came for me. I put up defenses and barred his entry to my island, but it cost me a great deal of power. So I locked down the Titan Engine, putting all power into defensive enchantments and fled to find help."

"I'm no stranger to dealing with Pirates, so why didn't you just tell me all this?" Knox asked, his mind swirling with thoughts of what he'd need to do now. Would he have changed the layout of who he'd brought with him if he'd known? Perhaps, but he did have the strongest adventures with him now, so that would have to do.

"I was too afraid to admit the truth," Ramses said, putting his face in his hands and making a show of being distraught. "I'm a terrible person, sure, but now that we are nearly there and my power is returning, we can defeat the scaly bastard together."

"Scaly?" Knox asked, confused by the descriptor Ramses had chosen to use.

"Oh yeah, he is some kind of dragon-humanoid hybrid looking fellow, he even breathes fire and all that. Extremely unique combination if I must say so myself. When I first encountered him, I propositioned him for a study and he did not like that. From what I can feel right now, they've broken the island defenses and are close to making it into the complex, but not so close that we won't have time to deal with them."

"Follow me and let's get moving in the right direction," Knox said, shaking his head at the turn of events. He'd need to tell everyone and get them ready for a fight. An S Ranked Pirate would be no push over, even for his new powers, but he was confident that he had a team powerful enough to deal with him.

"So that's pretty much it," Knox said. "We are heading into a massive encampment of pirates, same dance as before." Knox looked to Beth and Dernal as he said that part, seeing as they were the only ones there to have actually dealt with pirates to the extent he had.

"How many do you think and how strong are we talking in general?" Tress asked, she was in full business mode now.

"The captain is said to be S Ranked and some kind of dragon monster humanoid, so expect a surprise or two from him," Knox said. "Speaking to the rest, we are in range enough for my sense to wash over them, but they are so varied that I can't pinpoint a range really. I'd say on average we are looking at B Rankers and a few A Rankers."

Suddenly Knox wished he'd brought Aetex along, he was also technically in the A Ranker range, but he'd been adamant about staying behind to help protect his people, something Knox hadn't argued hard against. Still, he'd have felt better having the strong man at his side with his confident speech and one-liners of how they'd defeat the enemy with ease.

"To Death then," Beth said, locking eyes with Knox.

"To death," Knox repeated. "But I doubt it will come to that, we are strong enough that between Tress and myself, we will lay waste to most of their forces at a distance. I've been working on an old fire throwing technique mixed with my Radiant Glyph and I think I can pretty much hit them from a mile away with it."

This would be helpful, Knox thought, as he was limited in his range of spells. But under the guidance of Tress, he'd been experimenting using his older techniques in new ways that he'd learned from Gowlen. He could now summon a giant ball of fire and launch it a great distance, something he'd never been able to do before. He still needed a fire source, but Tress was happy to summon forth flame for him to use.

That mixed with his ability to magnify his spells, meant he could call forth a mighty powerful bit of fire. He'd already made sure to renew his buffs and fill his ring back up with Luminous Surges, so he was as ready as he'd ever be.

"We are only a few miles away and when the combat starts, it is going to be pretty crazy until it's over," Knox said. "I suspect many of them will flee and surrender after a point, but don't allow ourselves to get surrounded. We will bring the ship in close after I've laid waste to as many as possible, but remember, our lives are precious so don't be a hero if you can help it. Fight alongside us, do not plow on ahead."

"Be sure to take your own advice," Beth said, her eyebrows raised teasingly.

"I will," Knox said, hoping to reassure her but then realizing something he added. "Eventually Terris, Zhul, and I will need to go seek out this captain, but I'm wanting Tress and Ramses to stay behind as a backup plan should we fail or need to retreat."

"Are you sure I won't be more suited to the front lines?" Ramses asked, his color had all but returned and he walked with the grace of a much younger man. "My powers are returning at an alarming rate, and I will need to secure the Titan Engine at some point."

"Not until I've dealt with this captain," Knox said. "You are needed as a barrier and protection for the rest of the crew. Do not abandon your post, do you understand?"

"I do," Ramses said, though it sounded as if he didn't, but Knox let the issue drop. He would do what was needed when the time came, though he'd lied he'd shown himself to be mostly trustworthy in other regards.

"Everyone, get into positions," Knox said. "It is time to bring the heat."

In the distance was a small island surrounded by ships, so many in fact that Knox doubted they'd all be able to make land and unload their people. That made things all the easier for him, as he planned on forcing them into the water here in a few seconds. Knox finished his Radiant Glyph, it was ready to amplify some magic. Tress created some fire and Knox drew from it, creating a massive fireball that formed over his head.

He aimed the fireball, positioned it to be multiplied and let it loose. It grew suddenly to an enormous size as it flew overhead toward the array of ships. It grew so large that it was the size of one of the biggest ships their fleet had, making Knox smile as sweat poured down his face. He'd stayed connected to the spell and would break it apart in a moment, but he had to hold on just a little longer.

Barriers of blue and all sorts of other colors began to spring into being around the ships, but Knox ignored them. He was confident that his attack would shatter any such barriers. Beside him, Tress was calling down lightning from a great distance and breaking barriers with one hit.

His attack finally made it overhead and Knox flexed his magical muscle, shattering the construct and raining molten fire down on the ships like hundreds of fireball spells that an Elementalist might cast.

Taking a deep breath, Knox prepared the next volley, Tress lit some fire for him, and he did the rest, launching a slightly smaller one that expanded the moment it hit the area with his radiant glyph. Once more he rained fire down, shattering barriers and igniting ships aflame.

"Just a few more and we will go in closer," Knox said, panting now from the exertion it was taking to do the technique.

He reapplied his runic formations and began to build up the fire for another attack when suddenly fire of the deepest blue appeared from the lead ship, it wasn't on fire yet and it had moved to position itself toward them.

"Tress, Zhul, throw up barriers," Knox commanded, and they stopped mid cast to do just that.

A green hue barrier, feeling as solid as steel appeared, then a blue one over that. These were old techniques that each of them had used so often that it might as well be second nature, however they'd mastered how to add them to their list of spells within the new system already. Knox was thankful of such feats of learning, because the blue fire shattered his Mystic Veil and Prism Ward on contact, he'd hastily put up both a moment before contact.

Next went Tress's barrier, it held for longer and it was meant to take much more of a beating than Knox's. His were more meant to slow the incoming damage, not block it altogether, so he wasn't surprised when they failed after slowing the intense attack. After a long second, Tress's barrier failed, but Zhul's held strong against the S Ranked fire, a testament to his power.

The fire dissipated and Knox reapplied his two spells, Mystic Veil and Prism Ward. Tress chanted and a moment later, though it obviously took a measure of her strength, she had the barrier back up. Just in time too, as another wave of blue fire smashed into it, doing much the same it had before, except this time it cracked Zhul's barrier, before fluttering out of power.

"Full sails ahead, we need to confront that Captain before he burns the ship to cinders," Knox shouted, and the golems went to work getting them on a direct course for the vessel.

The wind whipped his hair and the salty water sprayed all

around him as he stood at the front of the ship, ready for anything. But no more fire came, he might be limited in what he could do with it, or he was just plain tired after using such a powerful attack.

Gust by gust the ship moved forward at an incredible speed. At the last possible moment, Knox called for the ship to stop, and they began to turn, putting themselves in line with the other ship.

"Throw anchor and prepare to board the enemy ship!" Knox called out; the golems moved fast to listen to his commands. They were close enough to the island that the ocean bed beneath them probably wouldn't be so far away.

All around them ships burned, but the lead ship was in perfect condition and Knox could sense powerful runic formations keeping it intact and fire free. If he had time to study them, he would, but he exchanged a look with his mother to find that she was already taking notes. She too was as curious as he was when it came to new formations or ways to use runes.

"I'll be standing by," Ramses said, power growing around him and his skin seeming to turn a metallic blue color as he gathered his power.

This wasn't exactly how he planned on confronting the Pirate Captain, but a plan was only as good as it was flexible, so he signaled for Ramses to fall in line with them. "We are close enough to ensure the safety of our ship, come with us," Knox said, and Ramses nodded. With a wave of his hand a solid disc of metal appeared, and he stepped up onto it.

"Stand close," Ramses said, each of them getting on and huddling together. "Oh, and Tress take care of those pirates trying to rope on over."

Knox looked and sure enough a dozen or more pirates were swinging over to the ship. Knox blasted a couple with his Luminous Surge, but most were taken out by a mighty gust of wind from Tress. That'll have to do for now, Knox thought as they landed on the black wood deck of the ship.

It was constructed in a way to look like it was a dragon, a full-on dragon's maw at the front of the ship and an outline of wings folded in on the side of the boat. The fire had come from the dragon's maw, Knox realized, and he headed that way with his party in tow.

None of the pirates they met were above B Rank and they were either cut down or surrendered as their comrades were cut down beside them. The fiery of battle notwithstanding, the fight to take over the ship was going on without a hitch, until they reached the far end of the ship, and the true power of this vessel showed its head.

Man or beast, Knox couldn't really tell, but this thing that looked like a dragon crossed with a giant, stood a staggering ten feet tall, had clawed hands, a massive maw and glowing blue eyes with snake-like slits. He'd fought a dragon before and they were no easy foes, but this man had the cunning of a dragon mixed with the ruthlessness of a human.

Knox took all this in as he watched the blue fire begin to build in his maw.

"Barriers up!" Knox called, releasing his hold on his power and going full ten-foot Titan. He cast his spells with an ease that he could never before, infusing them with power beyond his former capabilities. These new barriers he cast wouldn't just slow the magic, it should stop them. And good thing too, because at this range and with Tress and Zhul struggling to get their barriers up, his were the only thing that protected them for a frightening two seconds.

The heat in those seconds was intense enough to draw sweat on his brow and bring the others to their knees, all but Ramses, who looked cool as ever. He was chanting, Knox realized, and as the newest barriers sprung up the heat left. Ramses finished his spell and a single arrow appeared made of water, it zipped out and struck the captain in the arm, piercing his thick hide.

"How dare you return, coward," roared the gravelly voice.

"I've brought friends this time," Ramses spat back.

All around them was blackened wood, but somehow it hadn't

charred or given way despite the intense blue flames. Knox didn't wait for the monologue to continue; he raised a hand and unleashed a Luminous Surge.

It blew the captain backward and a single drop of blood rolled from his nose.

"Powerful foes indeed, but have you forgotten what I can do?" Roared the Pirate Captain. He lifted his hand and on it he had three rings, each one with intense magical auras.

"Barriers now!" Ramses cried, and we all reacted at the same time, putting up our barriers, Ramses included. Despite this the world shook and shattered from some unseen force and they were all thrown back halfway across the deck.

"Forgot to mention that?" Knox asked, his voice seeming to vibrate a bit more than he was used to. "Time to end him. Keep him busy while I set my next attack up."

"Will do," Ramses said, he was bleeding from his nose now and Knox realized that he was as well. Whatever that blast had been it left him rocked and weak feeling, almost drained in some ways.

Knox worked steadily and deliberately as his little force rushed the S Ranked Pirate Captain. Though to call him only S Ranked would be wrong, Knox was feeling far more power from him than he felt from Zhul or Ramses—the two S Rankers he had on his side—at this point.

The world shook as they attacked, each of them letting loose all they had and failing to draw more blood. All the while, attack after attack came hurdling for Knox and he had to cut his spells off early to reposition himself. But finally, as he moved closer, he got his multiplying spell in place and he leveled his five times Luminous Surge at the Captain, ready to end the fight.

"Get clear," he shouted as he raised his hand.

They did so and Knox released a blast of light so bright and powerful that it burnt away some of his skin and blew back his friends right off the side of the deck. It hit with the force of a true

Titan, being magnified as it was, and the dragon pirate stood no chance.

Broken and bloody he fell to the ground, somehow still alive, but not in fighting shape any longer.

Knox walked up close with his axe ready. "Do you submit?" He asked with his Titan enhanced voice.

"Never. And be warned, my people will come for vengeance, and you will die that day," coughed the pirate and Knox raised his axe, swinging down with all his might. The blade of the axe shattered against the dragonhide skin, but despite that a jagged edge finally pierced through, opening the back of his neck and damaging its spine.

It fell to the ground along with Knox's axe, in two pieces.

CHAPTER 22
TITAN ENGINE'S COMBINED

IT WAS a great loss to have broken his weapon, but it wasn't equipped to fight against another Titan, or even an S Ranker, so he didn't mourn the loss too much. His friends made it back onboard as pirates surrendered en masse.

"Take your people and go," Knox commanded one of the pirates that came near.

Ramses interjected himself between Knox and spoke. "Unless you'd prefer to fight under my banner?"

Ramses offered them sanctuary in his city if they chose to follow him instead of their slain pirate captain. A surprising number of them signed on with him, but Knox was wary of them, and he kept a close eye on the three hundred or so that joined forces with Ramses.

By the time they'd sorted out all the pirates and moved their ship into a position to join Ramses on the island, things were all sorted out.

"Now what?" Knox asked, looking to Ramses for the next phase of his plan.

"Next," Ramses said, "give me time to work on the Titan Engine."

Knox nodded and let him go off into the jungle, following behind with his own crew, save for Terris and Tress you remained to guard the ship.

Where Knox's complex had been fashioned after advanced technology and lots of cogs, this new complex looked as if it were built under the sea. Corral buildings grew straight out of the ground, mixed with various shells being used in the design of everything from handles to protective shielding. In all it was very water themed, with many fountains and sources of water all over, despite rising out of the ground some twenty paces high.

"I like yours better," Beth said, as she looked over the city her mouth opened in amazement.

"Same," Scarlet said, nodding sagely.

"It's alright if you like this one better," Knox said, sighing. "There is a certain soothing aesthetic to it."

Knox had returned to his previous size and limits but he felt a strain around his arm when he did so. Looking down at the focusing band he wondered at the limits it might have, if any, or perhaps he was just worried about nothing. His mother, ever observant, nudged him.

"What you did was necessary," she said, likely thinking he was worried about having to take another life, when the opposite was really true. He didn't want to leave any enemies alive that could harm them, so much so that he'd considered wiping out a legion of pirates.

"He said his people would come for vengeance," Knox said, looking at his mother. "I don't think he meant the other pirates; they were all too eager to abandon him. I hope we haven't stumbled into yet another threat."

"If we have," Beth answered before Scarlet had a chance, "then you will deal with it like you've been doing. You are strong, the most powerful person I know. And most importantly of all, you have us."

"Indeed," Dernal said, and Knox looked at him for the first time in a while without any anger building up in him.

"You're all good friends," Knox said, glad to be surrounded by such supportive people who would walk into death's literal door for him. He'd always had good friends, but to see them tested and their friendships remain strong after all this time, he was truly blessed by them.

"I need you," Ramses said, his voice appearing from a bubble that appeared out of seemingly nowhere. "Come here now."

Despite the lack of urgency, he sounded almost bored, Knox hurried to find him in the lower depths of his complex. The layout was familiar, only the design being different. So, he found him within the span of ten minutes laboring over an exact replica of his own Titan Engine.

"What can I-" Knox began to ask but Ramses interrupted him.

"Infuse some power into the Titan Engine and wait for me to guide it," Ramses said in a rush.

Knox wanted to ask why and to tell Ramses he still didn't trust him much further than he could throw him, but that fell apart when he realized he could probably throw him quite far now and he had little trust for the man. But Knox was Knox, and he went out on a limb to trust the man one last time.

He walked forward, setting his hand on the Titan Engine and peered into the weaves of magic, transferring a small portion of himself into it.

He felt it tug for more and he let it take what it needed, something was happening that he felt needed to and he didn't want to stand in the way of it.

Tendrils of power swam around him as suddenly he felt himself receiving power as well, a back-and-forth shared connection was forming between the Titan of Light and the Titan of Water. Then as sudden as it had started, it ended, leaving Knox breathing hard and slightly confused at the new feelings he was having.

It was as if he were in his own domain. He felt his power

surge, and no longer was he losing power from being outside of his realm of influence.

"We did it," Ramses said, even more out of breath than Knox. "Our Titan Engines have merged purposes, for better or worse, we are connected now."

"How long until we can return and hunt the Dark Titan?" Knox asked, a feeling of energy buzzing through him and calling him to action.

"I think a month should give me enough time to recover, then a month's recovery after teleporting, so two months?" Ramses said, but Knox just groaned.

"And if we work together to open the portal between our two locations?" Knox asked.

"Two weeks both ways, but I could be wrong about recovery," Ramses said. "Now that we are connected it shouldn't be as hard to open the ways between."

"Why don't we try now, I feel energized," Knox said. He truly did feel more energized than he could ever remember being in that moment.

"It'll pass, we just did something incredible, but it had a cost. Whether you can feel it or not, you are weakened and will remain so for at least a week or two," Ramses said, but Knox shook his head.

"You don't feel what I feel," Knox said, then as he let himself really feel what was going on around him, he noticed the focusing lens or Aurorapex around his arm had grown warm in a way he hadn't noticed before.

Reaching out he touched it and was surprised when it came back hot to the touch.

"Ah I see," Ramses said, noticing what Knox had done. "I believe that artifact is somehow lending you power as well as stabilizing you so that you can more fully approach the reaches of being a Titan. The heat is a sign that it is reaching the limits of its power. Allow yourself to feel weak and take the stress off it before you break it. You won't want to go back to wearing your restraining rings again, would you." Ramses showed his own rings, each one a swirling vortex of power under Knox's new sight.

"I understand," Knox said, at least he was pretty sure he understood, but how to stop himself from being empowered by it.

Closing his eyes he focused on the strands of magic surrounding the artifact and his intentions. With the mix of those two in his mind, he saw a way to alter the effects, if only slightly, so reaching out with his mind he did so. It wasn't an easy process or one that took a small amount of time. In fact, he was at it for hours, his eyes scrunched in concentration as he worked, but time had no meaning to him when he was in the zone of focus.

With his touch came understanding of the focusing lens, how it took the latent power that Knox had inside of him and focused it in ways that weren't harmful to his body, but Knox had already slowed that process as well because he was so eager to remain looking the same. He saw that unless he gave way to his true form, he'd be putting more undo stress on an artifact that didn't have an unending lifespan.

He was sad to see that if his calculations were correct, and his mind was operating at a whole new level as he concentrated so they were correct, he had a matter of years to use the Aurorapex before it wore out. He had years to discover a way to reach the godlike level that this device allowed his attributes to operate at.

Doing what he could, which included allowing himself to grow a touch taller and a slight golden hue to his skin, he added some time. Next, he turned off the power influx ability that was keeping him operating at full bore when what he truly needed was rest. He believed Ramses now about the time it would take to rest and recuperate, but that didn't mean he would do nothing.

"Have you discovered the dungeon or labyrinth in your complex yet?" Knox asked, a sly smile crossing his lips. "Because your complex is surprisingly the exact same layout as mine and I bet you have at least one of them down there."

"The lower corridors have been flooded since I arrived, only after lifting half the city did some of them drain, but I found no dungeon or labyrinth as you called it, just vaults and workrooms."

"I've got a breathing stone that says we can explore even in the waterlogged areas," Knox said, smiling wide at Ramses as he thought of the adventure they could have in two weeks.

CHAPTER 23
UNDERWATER SEARCH

"I LIKE YOUR NEW LOOK," Beth said as they lay in a bed made of coral and some type of soft sponge for the mattress. The blankets were normal enough, having been brought over from Knox's own complex.

"Thanks," Knox said, answering seriously to her teasing words. She was referring to his golden hued skin and he couldn't help but wonder if the others saw him as strange for the changes. "At least I'm not ten feet tall and full-on golden."

"I could live with that," Beth said, laughing. "You did get a bit bigger though, I can tell."

Now it was Knox's turn to blush. He'd allowed his entire body to grow about one tenth the size that it had been, alleviating the smallest amount of strain on the Aurorapex, but he hadn't considered other aspects of his life and how they'd change. Beth didn't seem to mind it though, so he didn't think any further about it.

"You ready to go searching for that dungeon today?" Knox asked, fishing a small shell from his trousers and handing it over to her.

These were small enough that they fit under the tongue with no real issues, the edges having been sanded to a smooth finish.

With Scarlet's help he'd improved the effects of the runic forma-tion and even added a way of communicating over short distances, though this required a second paired shell in the ear.

The new breathing shell not only provided air magic into your mouth, but it created a small shell of protection around your head that would also be filled with air, making speaking possible. It was a clever use of runic formations that Knox wished he'd thought about in the past.

They finished getting dressed before Beth answered.

"So, you are sure there is no labyrinth?" She asked. "It would be nice to have another influx of power for all of us."

"I think it was unique to my complex," Knox said, sighing.

They'd been searching first for the labyrinth but where it ought to be they found only another vault system with work rooms and more treasure, like a lot of treasure. Ramses was hard at work using Knox's golems to create a pump system to move the water out of the area but the work was slower due to lack of resources that the labyrinth would have normally provided. Instead, they were forced to venture out to sea and find deposits of iron deep in the water.

Surprisingly enough they had been finding plenty of metal, but mostly scrap from sunken ships and that metal took time to process, since it had to be cleaned and sorted instead of melted straight down. Something to do with melting down metal that had existing runic formations on it causing untold damage to the furnace.

But one thing that Knox was sure would be in the right place was the dungeon, he just had to find where exactly his decided to be. Dungeons were different as they were more naturally occur-ring, but that didn't mean he wouldn't have one here, only that they'd have to search a bit more to find the location.

"It's a shame," Beth said. "There were so many resources inside the labyrinth, that you'd think it was a natural part of these places."

"We can keep any eye out, perhaps there is a labyrinth, but it might not be filled with monsters like ours was, but perhaps only a place with resources to be harvested," Knox admitted.

He was more interested in the potential dungeon though, a week had gone by, and he'd only killed weak sea monsters and the occasional water goblin that appeared on the shore—no idea what they were actually called but they had the look of a goblin but with blue flesh, gills, and webbed hands and feet.

"There is no telling what kind of loot we will find inside," Beth said, rubbing her hands together much in the way Knox did mentally when thinking about loot.

"It's likely a weaker dungeon, like ours, but it will be fun to clear out regardless," Knox said as they finished dressing and headed for the door.

They'd made it a point to each have their own huts to sleep in, but Beth hadn't been back to hers in days and Knox was kind of warming up to the idea of sharing one with her.

"I need to run by my place and change this shirt," Beth said, reaching over and kissing him on the cheek. "I've reached the limit on re-wearing clothing."

Knox was about to say that he hadn't noticed any stench but thought better of it and instead kissed her back while holding his tongue.

He went looking for his mother next, he wanted to do a final check on the three shells he'd made without her help to ensure he'd gotten it right and he just wanted to talk with her as he'd had little time in the last two days to do so.

The island air was intoxicating with its freshness and salty smells. They ate much of the local fruits, each one so sweet and tender, though the seeds were plenty big. Knox had a standing order to collect the seeds of his favorite fruits to try and grow back home and so far, his collection was vast with at least six different kinds.

Instead of the cobblestone ground and solid hard packed dirt that Lumisar had, this little city, which Ramses hadn't named yet, was mostly sand. So much sand in fact that Knox was constantly pouring it out of his boots and finding it in all the most unfortunate places.

Then there was the sun, it seemed like this part of the world was in summer, because it was warm constantly, except for the occasional cool breeze. But the heat was manageable even for the weakest among them, with the sea air doing a lot to make it so.

He encountered Dernal as he walked toward his mother's hut, and he waved in greeting.

"Hhrmm," Dernal offered in response. They met eyes and Knox smiled. Dernal had been a good friend for so long that he couldn't see himself holding a grudge any longer.

He didn't stop to tell him as much, but instead tilted his head and let him go about his business. His relationship with Dernal had always been one of mentor and mentee, one that Knox cherished. What more he might have to teach him, Knox didn't know, but he was open to hearing from him once again. He found himself glad to have brought such a stalwart companion along with him.

Now that they'd arrived and most of the danger seemed to have passed—pirates that Ramses had adopted continued to be a near constant possible threat, but they'd remained on their ships with promise to return when the trade routes weren't as busy—Knox wished he'd brought more of his friends along to challenge the dungeon they were hoping to find. Where or not they would, Knox couldn't care less, but it meant the island was relatively safe.

He found his mother just as she was leaving her hut, wearing nothing but a tunic and loose pants, gone were her heavy flowing robes that she almost always wore.

"Change of attire?" Knox asked, figuring the heat likely had something to do with that change.

"Between the heat and some modifications, I'm doing to my battle robes, I thought it was prudent," Scarlet said. "Any luck finding what you've been looking for, the dungeon and labyrinth?"

"Not yet," Knox said, pulling out the shells he wanted her to inspect he handed them over. "Can you check these out and make sure I got it right?"

"Sure thing," Scarlet said, turning and waving Knox after her into her hut. The interior couldn't be more different from Knox's currently well-kept and clean layout. Where he had items put away and in order, she had her stuff sprawled out everywhere.

Her robes were inside out on her bed, strands of white stitching covering different parts glowed with runic formations. Various items filled the two tables she had added to the room, from shells to notebooks to inscribing implements.

"I told you we discovered the workrooms, right?" Knox asked, but Scarlet just laughed.

"The chaos of my personal space helps me think," she said, pushing items around to give her space enough to sit at one of the tables and look over the shells with a magnifying glass that was heavily covered in runic formations itself.

"Well," Knox asked after several long seconds. "Did I do it right?"

"It isn't perfect," Scarlet admitted, but then she smiled wider. "But it will do just fine. You are such a quick study!"

"Must be something I learned from my mother," Knox said, grinning at her.

"Tell me again," Scarlet said, brushing a hand on his exposed arm. "This transformation you go through, it is only physical right? I'm not going to lose my son just because he's becoming a Titan, right?"

With a quick thought Knox released his hold on his magic and let himself transform. His skin took on a more golden hue until it shined as much as polished gold, then he grew several feet until he stood a massive ten feet tall, barely missing the roof of the hut's twelve paces tall ceiling.

"I am and I always will be, Knox," he said, his voice taking the slightly deeper reverberating tone that it took when he transformed. Then gripping the power again, he settled into the medium state he'd prepared for himself, with slightly golden skin and a height that put him just under Terrim. "See, I'm fine."

"The magic required to transform you back and forth is just unfathomable," Scarlet said, her eyes going to the Aurorapex on his exposed arm.

"You can study it," Knox said for what felt like the hundredth time. "I just can't take it off."

"Sit and let me have a look," Scarlet said, this was the first time she'd had him do so, but Knox didn't hesitate to follow her orders. "The magic is so complex; I can barely understand or even see some of the runic formations. It's like they are something deeper than the form of magical script we have access to."

Knox was surprised she could see any formations at all, when he'd first looked, he'd seen nothing but power. Turning his new enhanced gaze on the Aurorapex he still saw nothing but raw and powerful magic. Then gazing deeper, he saw a structure to it, his eyes looking into the very formation of the magic itself. Perhaps you could call some of the forms runes, but they seemed to be much more than that and not something Knox felt comfortable messing around with.

Scarlet took notes and kept raising her eye piece up to inspect it. "Do you mind if I look through that," Knox asked, wondering how powerful it must be to see actual runes when his sense could not.

"It's a magnifying glass," Scarlet said, handing it over.

"It's powerful," Knox said, grabbing hold of it and raising it to his eye.

"It magnifies your natural ability to sense magical energies, so whatever you can already do is simply magnified," she said.

When Knox looked through it he saw dozens and dozens of the tiniest most complex runes he'd ever encountered. There were combinations that, as he looked closer, he saw they were different layers of runes just written atop each other somehow. But the worst part about it was the lack of understanding that came as he looked at them. Some of these runes were formations and curves he'd never even seen before, and he'd seen a ton at this point.

It was like whoever made the item on his arm had used a more advanced set of runes to do things Knox could only begin to imagine. This was power that he needed, but he would have to be careful. Even a single rune could hold great power and potential if they got into the wrong hands.

"Give me a fresh page," Knox said, pulling his notebook from behind him and handing it over. He didn't want to look away for fear that it might all disappear.

He began to record as much as he could, focusing on the ones he'd never seen or had any idea about, only making notations of the formations as he was more concerned about the individual runes that were being shown right now. Minutes sped past and Knox kept filling up the page, only looking away for moments at a time. When he finished, he'd filled a dozen pages and wasn't halfway from being finished.

"I need one of these," Knox said, hefting the lens.

"It was a dungeon drop and I've never been able to replicate it," Scarlet said, taking it back and holding it close to her chest. "You are welcome to use it, did you really see all these formations and runes from using it? I saw only a couple myself; your magical sight must be off the charts."

"It's a perk of sorts I get from being a Titan, it's called Unbound Sight," Knox said, looking longingly at the eye lens that Scarlet kept close to her chest. "I should get going, but do you mind going over these runes and seeing what you can figure out?"

Scarlet brightened and snatched the notebook from Knox's outstretched hand. "Of course I can," she said, her eagerness giving Knox only a moment of pause before he walked out in search of Beth and with his three newly checked shell contraptions.

The water was oddly warm as always, but Knox didn't let it get his mood down. He was living his best life in a tropical paradise and was currently diving deep into a pool of water with a woman he was beginning to think he loved; what more could he ask for?

Well, he could think of many things that he could ask for, the least of which being that he was home with all his friends, but Aetex would protect them if they needed protection. He could also wish that the Dark Titan wasn't going to be an issue, but he knew that his greatest battle awaited him, and it would be coming soon.

All of those thoughts went away as water covered his face, yet his head remained dry.

"Can you hear me?" Knox asked, his words seemed to echo slightly in his own ears as he spoke.

After a momentary pause a response sounded in his left ear where the shell lay. "I can hear you loud and clear," Beth said, her voice also sounding through the shell as clear as a newly rung bell.

"Let's explore down to the left this time," Knox said. They'd taken the corridor down to the right and explored it quite a bit, but nothing had come of it. This time they'd be taking the left corridor, and he was hopeful that they'd find what they were looking for. The water level had dropped a good foot or two as the pumps worked to get the sea water back into the sea, but for now they had their magical shells.

"I'll beat you to the end," Beth said teasingly as she shot forward, swimming slightly faster than Knox, though he didn't want to tell her that he let her go faster than him on purpose. His new powerful legs and muscles in general would allow him to really move if he wanted.

They raced to the end, careful to keep a lookout for any

threats, though they'd not encountered any thus far in their explorations.

Light was provided by bright pearls that glowed with a white light of eerie potential. Shadows cast in the water seemed to stretch out longer than they ought to, and everything had a sense of odd wonder and mysticism down here. However, despite the feelings he had, nothing spooky came out to attack them while they searched.

Workrooms, more vaults, and various other rooms with meanings that Knox didn't know as he'd not even explored his own depths this much at Luminar, filled their vision. It was right around the time they were about to give up for the day, hours into looking and their skin was turning mushy even for Knox, when they encountered a wide door sealed off by a series of activation runes.

Knox put his hand on it and immediately the door gave way, sucking them into it as the door behind wasn't filled with water. Once inside the door closed behind them and the water drained away into the floor. They stood in a room no more than ten paces across in every direction and spherical in design. In the middle was what they'd been looking for, a Dungeon Spire.

CHAPTER 24
NOT A WATER DUNGEON

"Should we take a look?" Knox asked, but Beth just shook her head.

"How are we getting out of here?" she asked, eying the door. "With the water flooding in we are basically trapped."

Knox considered her words and looked at the runic formations on the wall. Several had been damaged, but they were still recognizable to him. It only took him roughly ten minutes to work out what the broken ones were meant to do and how to replicate it with his own Radiant Glyph spell.

"The door is meant to hold back water, even when open," Knox said. "But I think I can craft a runic formation to hold back the water long enough for us to get in and the door to close. But it will be tight time wise."

"Or," Beth said, looking at the large draining holes all around the room. "We open it up and let the excess water drain into here until we've solved the water issue."

"That is," Knox began to say, then really thought about it, "genius! We can solve the water issue and we found the dungeon. Two for one! I just need to work out how to keep the door open and not automatically shutting behind us."

It turned out the answer to that final little riddle was easy, he just had to keep a continuous contact with the door and it stayed open while an immense amount of water entered and filled the room. But just as before, the water drained, if a bit slower than Knox would have cared for, but it did drain. So, after a time, they were an hour into it and still no end in sight, it would drain completely.

After what felt like a small century worth of time, the last of the water from this level drained into the room and Knox spit out the water breathing shell. Beth did the same and handed it back to Knox, who didn't take it.

"Keep it for now," Knox said. "This dungeon will most likely have water rooms or be water themed. Let's grab Dernal and Zhul then check out the dungeon."

Having two powerful healers, one an S Ranker, would mean that they could at least check the dungeon out without much care before trying for a full clear.

They left the room and noticed a staircase leading down was still filled with water. Oh well, Knox thought, they'd at least sped along the draining of much of the complex, if not the entire thing. He did start to notice areas that were overgrown with some type of sea growth, all rocky and spiky, that might have been drains built into the sides of the walls.

Reaching down he broke off the growth and sure enough, there was a drain set into the side of the hallway. Had he noticed this before he was sure he might have been able to save them a bunch of effort. He'd share his findings with Ramses and get the golems clearing out the drains deeper into the complex. With all of them clear Knox was sure the complex would do its normal functions of keeping water clear.

It didn't take them long to get Dernal and Zhul down here, Terris came as well, leaving Tress to guard the ship by herself and Knox couldn't have done anything to stop the man, he was so eager to do something that at the very mention of a dungeon being found had him appearing from a far-off distance.

"So here is the plan," Knox said, then he laid out the plan.

They go in and then search the first path, if the mobs are strong enough, they clear it out, if they are super weak, then they move to the final path and collect whatever loot they can for weaker members of the city.

"And if it's a secret hidden S Ranked dungeon?" Terris asked, eyeing Beth and Dernal with a slant in his eyes that seemed to say, 'what about these weaker people?'.

"They'll be fine, we can always back out if the first path is stronger than I suspect," Knox said. He didn't know exactly how it all worked, but something told him he wasn't going to find some super rare S Ranked dungeon in the middle of nowhere.

As best as he'd learned, dungeons grew stronger by use, as counter intuitive as it might seem. The more use the dungeon got, the more power it would use to create stronger mobs to help deal with invaders, which also resulted in additional stronger loot and essence gains. Something out here untouched for countless years would be weak, similar to his own dungeon.

So, when they stepped up to the Dungeon Spire and entered into the familiar cave-like structure, Knox didn't expect to find what he found, signs of life inside the dungeon.

Or at the very least, signs that somehow someone had been here recently. Knox had never, not once, ever seen the remnants of other Adventurers inside of a dungeon before, but here before them lay three skeletons in various decayed armor and the signs of a camp.

"Something isn't right with this dungeon," Zhul said, kneeling down and examining the skeletons. "From what I understand, which is from years of experience, each time someone enters a dungeon, a new layer is added, and the past ones are destroyed. That is why you can't leave a dungeon and come back later to finish it. This is unprecedented."

"There are only two pathways," Terris said, jogging back from where he'd gone forward to check out the dungeon paths. "This is a higher-level dungeon for sure and a powerful one to have so few paths."

"I suggest a tactical retreat and refit of the party," Zhul said, looking at Beth and Dernal much as Terris had.

"I don't know," Knox said, still unconvinced that any of this was really an issue. "Why don't we check out the first path and just see what we are dealing with. I'll even call forward all my power to make sure we are safe."

"In that case," Zhul said. "I suggest you and I go, leave Terris to guard the two others. Something killed these three while they slept, otherwise why would they be lying so?"

"I'm not staying behind," Beth began to say but Knox caught her eye.

"This is serious Beth, just let me look ahead and see what we are dealing with, then I promise if it is something you can handle, I will bring you to fight," Knox said, really pushing in his tone the seriousness of the situation.

"I vote we retreat as well," Dernal said, even going so far as to walk up to the Dungeon Spire and place his hand on it.

Knox moved forward with speed to remove his hand before he could retreat alone, but it was for not, Dernal stayed right where he was and the runes on the Dungeon Spire flashed red.

"Oh shit," Knox said, sensing the magic surrounding the spire and feeling a portion of its intentions in that moment. "It won't let us leave until we've defeated it. I don't think this is going to be an easy dungeon after all. I can sense an ancient presence that weighs down on even my power. We might actually be in an S Ranked Dungeon."

"The plan remains sound," Zhul said. "First we go check the first path, then we decide how to proceed."

"We will be safer together," Dernal said, surprising Knox. "Everyone, get your stuff and set up camp."

Zhul and Terris looked to Knox, Beth looked back and forth between Dernal and Knox, but no one moved.

"He might be right. Let's stay together for now, the first path is always the weakest, so it'll be good for them to get some essence from it while they can. However, when it gets harder, you will be staying behind. I don't think these people were killed in their sleep, I think that it is more likely they couldn't defeat the dungeon and decided that waiting out the dungeon was better than death. Either way this dungeon is strange, so be alert."

They moved quickly, clearing out the old camp and remains to the side, and putting up their own gear. After only minutes the camp was prepared and they ventured toward the first dungeon path. Walking through it, Knox assumed he'd be assaulted by some water creatures so imagine his surprise when instead of a straightforward tunnel leading forward, they found themselves in a wasteland of hot air and sand.

Looking all around, he counted out his party members, all present. "This is a themed dungeon path," Knox said, his chest clenching a bit. "I've never heard of one on the first path, what does this even mean?"

"I don't know," Zhul said. "This dungeon is older than any I think I've ever faced. It acts in ways that I've only ever heard in the darkness rumors of times lost."

A man signaled them from a distant dune, his clothing odd for such a hot place. He was covered from head to toe in cloth, it must have been terribly hot for him. Meanwhile, the rest of them wore armor and had much of their skin exposed to the sun, which was quickly beginning to burn them from even the short exposure.

Knox allowed himself to shift to his ten-foot self and it lessened the heat's effects on him, though he glimmered and shone like the sun itself with the amount of heat bouncing off him. With a quick adjustment, he was able to dull his surface, making his golden skin a muddy yellow color instead, still metallic just dull.

The man approached fast over the period of a few minutes and each of them were sweating profusely by that time.

"Well met, champions!" Came the voice with an accent Knox had never encountered before. "Please, you must escape the sun with me, or death will soon be your partner. The hunt begins tonight when the suns rest over the horizon.

Knox spared a glance upward and indeed there were two suns, each blazing balls of heat, one blue and one yellow. That explained some of the heat. That, and the yellow sun was huge in the sky, taking up a quarter of the sky as it currently sat.

They followed the man over another dune of sand and blessedly into a large tent set among a small oasis in the desert, with trees and even some water. These trees were very different from any Knox had encountered, with long branchless trunks and huge leaves that gave shade on the top. Some types of fruit grew at the top, purple and orange by the looks of it, again nothing Knox had encountered before.

If nothing else, this dungeon was proving an exciting adventure into the unknown. Knox shrunk himself down to enter the tent and in doing so drew the gaze of the man who'd led them here.

"My name is Izel," the man said once everyone had come in. "It is not often that Titan's walk among us, but you are welcome here. Rest and feast while we wait out the heat."

With that, women in far less clothing than Izel came to deliver platters of food and drink. They learned that these were his daughters and that he had sixteen of them, many of them twins. Knox kept his eyes averted as best he could, finding Beth's own gaze on him more than once, he was sure could get himself in trouble if he wasn't careful.

But that worry was nothing against what lay ahead. Izel had spoken of a hunt, but he'd disappeared shortly after entering the tent, saying he would return later to tell them of the great hunt.

It was well into the hours of the day when he finally returned, and he wasn't alone. A half dozen armored figures were with him, but they didn't draw weapons, instead they found pillows and sat around with Knox's group.

"Now that all the hunters have arrived, I will tell you of what beast you will be hunting tonight," Izel said, rubbing his hands together. "The mighty sandworm!"

A chorus of oooh's and aww's followed but then Izel looked back down at the tablet he'd been holding and cleared his throat.

"Oh, my mistake, that was last month, this month you are facing off against a Sand Dragon, twice as deadly and far easier to find," Izel said.

"Sand Dragon, you say?" Zhul said. "I've encountered such a beast before, they are not easy to kill but they are weak to water magic."

"Indeed, they are, but do not underestimate the great dragon, for she has taken many hunters' lives in the past," Izel said, looking thoughtful as he spoke.

With that the other hunters began to get up and file out of the tent. The interior of the tent was filled with light from glowing rocks hung all around the tops, so Knox hadn't noticed when the sun had gone down. Only when the tent flaps opened did he realize, yet the heat was still present, if perhaps a little less intense.

"Let's go," Knox said, looking at his team and wondering how they'd be finding a dragon in the middle of the night in a vast desert of hot sand.

The group followed him out and Knox made it a point to follow the other hunters, each of them making for a straight line out into the sands.

"We will follow them for now, but if I sense anything we can check it out," Knox said, his reliance on his sense would be his best tool when tracking something, he knew.

"Tell me what you can about the sand dragons," Knox asked Zhul.

"They are different from most you are likely to encounter, more serpentine and no visible wings. They've got four legs, but they tuck into the body and allow the dragon to snake its way through sand like an eel in the water. But the worst part about them is their breath attack. It spits sand at such a high speed that it will take the flesh right off the bone."

"I sense so much life out here, powerful monsters but I can't pinpoint which would be the sand dragon," Knox said in response.

They traveled into the hot night air for several hours before the team in front of them split into two distinct groups, each going their own way.

"What now?" Knox asked.

"Let's go our own way and see what happens," Beth suggested.

"Follow one of the groups, they obviously know what they are doing where we do not," Dernal said.

"I think we ought to just give up and let one of them win," Terris said. "The way these themed dungeons work, you can fail sometimes and still finish the scenario. We might not get any loot, but it would be safer."

It was while they discussed that Knox felt something strong approaching their location. AS it turned out the two other groups were merely getting into position and hadn't gone very far after all. They began to shout and lay out traps all around, from spikes to runic tablets that would explode with powerful magic.

"Get ready," Knox said. "The dragon is coming."

No sooner were the words out of his mouth than the dragon appeared. It was more snake than dragon, Knox thought, but it had a narrow open maw, like the face of a wolf, but covered in scales the color of sand. Spikes protrude out in a backward direction, each of them seeming to twitch and move under the light of the moon. Only about twenty paces worth of the dragon was out of the ground, the rest of its body hidden beneath the sea of sand.

Knox wasted no time in filling the area with light by casting Luminous Surge, then wishing he had a proper weapon, he lifted scarlet the axe in a defensive position, not sure what he could do with it.

Beth let off arrow after arrow, but the dragon might as well have not felt either attack, as it panned its head around to see the little figures surrounding it. With impossible speed it struck, taking one of the members of the other party into its maw. The man shrieked and screamed, but his cries for help were short lived.

However, this did trigger a binding trap from the same party, and blue shining chains covered the dragon, pulling it toward the ground as it struggled against them. Figuring these guys had the right idea, Knox cast Lustrous Chains followed quickly by Void Grasps. Zhul followed suit and soon vines appeared to drag the dragon lower.

Arrows flew, enhanced by the elements, Terris struck out with powerful waves of dark energy, Dernal shot bolts of light and Knox prepared a multiplied attack. Using his Radiant Glyph spell he constructed a powerful array of multiplying force runic formations, much as he was getting used to doing when facing an impossible foe. Next, he readied to release the five store spells, but first he released his hold on his power and released the spells with the full force of his might.

The attack lit up the area like it was noonday, striking the dragon with terrible power. It shrieked and screamed, but the results were inevitable. The dragon went silent only moments later, falling dead on the hot sand.

Immediately the two other parties ran forward, eager to do something, perhaps harvest the monster core. The ground rumbled and shook suddenly, Knox looked at his party members, but they were as confused as he was.

Then Knox noticed that the other two hunting parties were throwing down more and more traps, literally covering the body with them.

Then he felt it, a deep terrible power rising from the ground right beneath them. Whatever was coming was easily twice as strong as what they'd just faced. Surely one sand dragon was enough, but then he felt the one approaching and realized something.

"We just killed a baby sand dragon, its mother is on its way," Knox called, the sense he had for the two was unmistakable now.

They were about to be in the fight of their lives, and he'd just blown through his most powerful spell combination.

"Cover me while I reload the ring," Knox said, beginning the cast of the first one while focusing on the ring. It took several minutes to cast each spell in a way that the ring would take it, but he didn't have that kind of time.

The first spell locked into place just as the mighty Sand Dragon appeared, looking the same as its child but four times its size and eyes that glowed with golden power like the sun.

Waves of intense power rolled off this new monster, even as dozens of traps attempted to tie it down and blow it up. Not a one seemed able to do much more than annoy the monster as it drew in a breath. Knox watched as it happened, helpless to do anything but reapply spells to his ring as people fought for their lives.

It released the breath it was taking and the hunters on the left were obliterated by a spray of sand that didn't even leave bones or armor behind, so powerful was the concentrated blast. Knox saw that it was beginning to take in another breath, its focus on his friends this time as they threw all they had at it.

Must work faster, Knox screamed internally as he locked in the third spell. But it was no use, the dragon was about to release its breath and he needed to cast a barrier and wards. He released his next Luminous Surge mid casting in favor of laying out a Mystic Armor on himself, then rushing forward he flooded his body with power, growing in size temporarily, everyone on him seeming to adjust and grow with him.

When he stood a mighty twenty paces tall, he locked eyes with the Dragon and roared. This got the thing's attention just as it released its attack into Knox's face.

Knox punched right through the attack, deflecting much of it, but still he felt his armor give way under the powerful blast of sand, shattering into millions of particles of light. But Knox wasn't done, he cast Solar Wings and lit up the area as he slammed his foot down, creating a shattering of light to appear on the ground.

His fist connected with the dragon's face, and it reeled backwards from his impossible strength. Then Knox jumped on it and began to choke it out.

Chains, vines, and more wrapped around him and the dragon as it struggled to dislodged Knox. It had several paces of length and girth on him, but he held fast squeezing with every bit of strength his attributes lent him.

"Not today," Knox screamed into the dragon's face as it began to take in more air and sand to prepare for another attack. He reached around its head and grabbed at the top, pulling with all his might. When his strength proved not enough to rip the dragon's head off, Knox roared in frustration and peered into the fragments of magic all around him.

Something was empowering this dragon to be a threat far beyond anything they should be facing in this dungeon, and he sensed it looming over and watching the challenge. With a single thought, he cut off the presence from being able to watch and suddenly the dragon shrunk several paces, not super noticeable in the heat of battle, but its power became that of a true S ranked foe.

Now, pulling as he was, the dragon's head began to pop and scream as bone, sinew, and muscles tore apart. Within a moment and as Knox allowed himself to return to this ten-foot height of golden majesty, the dragon died.

"Dragons and Titans, oh my," Izel said, appearing out of nowhere in a puff of purple light. "You blocked my little trick, but don't think my final play will be so easily thwarted. You, Sir Titan, will not be able to fight what you can't see."

And with that Izel snapped his fingers and a pain slammed into Knox, like a flash of light in his sense that prevented him from focusing on it. His normal sight was fine, but suddenly the world seemed quiet, and Knox couldn't track anything with his special sense.

"You can't do that," Knox said, letting his body shrink under his suppression to appear more human once more.

"When you are as old as me, you do what you please," Izel said, laughing wickedly as he disappeared, then a doorway appeared before them, a dungeon door.

"You alright?" Beth asked, she had blood coming out her ears and looked like she'd had the fight of her life.

"I'll live," Knox said. "I can feel the effects receding from whatever he did to blind my sense, so let's just go back to camp and wait it out, otherwise I'll be at a huge disadvantage."

No chest appeared and Knox realized that there would be no loot from this dungeon, at least not during this phase of it. They agreed and walked through the dungeon door only to find themselves in a thick forest with trees as wide as Knox was tall when he'd gone full Titan.

"I don't think waiting will be an option," Zhul said. "I sense incoming, make yourselves ready."

Knox watched with his eyes and listened with his ears as several targets approached. He had no idea their power, but he guessed that they'd be close to unstoppable if the dungeon had its way. The first of the targets approached, a man in wooden armor with green skin and hair made of leaves and vines.

Then another and another, until they were surrounded by a host of such creatures, each with weapons from bows to clubs.

"To death," Knox whispered as he pulled free his axe and readied himself for the upcoming battle.

"To death," Came the cry from all present and Knox felt a sense of pride growing within him to be surrounded by such loyal friends.

Meeting eyes with Beth, Knox nodded at her. He'd do all he

could to keep her safe above all the others, she was plenty strong herself and he knew she wouldn't want the special treatment, but he had to keep her safe. He loved her after all.

Turning to her he almost said it, but he held his tongue, now wasn't the time.

"There need not be any fighting," came a familiar voice, Izel the dungeon speaker. "Come and hear my proposal and be on your way with your loot. This will be the easiest dungeon challenge you've ever faced."

Knox was immediately on guard against a possible attack, but when none came, he called up to the man standing above them on the high branches. "Tell us then," Knox said. "What challenge do you propose?"

In a puff of purple smoke Izel appeared before Knox and leaned forward. "Whomever you love the most of those present, must stay with me. They will be cared for and if you ever wish to exchange them for one you love more dearly, I will accept that change. However, no amount of violence will dissuade me or free them. It would take the true talents of a Titan to do that and you my friend, are not powerful enough, not yet at least."

"No deal," Knox said, without a second thought. "Allow us to leave, we will not participate in your games."

"There is no leaving," Izel said, smirking wider than should be possible. "Submit or fight my unending horde and all shall die. Or perhaps you'd like to think on it as the last group did. They waited to their very deaths, unable to defeat my horde or leave their loved one behind."

"You are a dungeon inside of a Titan Complex," Knox said, his words filled with disbelief. "How is it that you are so evil?"

"I am not evil," Izel said, seeming taken back. "I am merely lonely."

"We will not give one of our own, so bring the pain because we will defeat anything you can throw at us," Knox said, venom in his words.

"So be it," Izel said. "Kill them but leave the girl, she will be staying with me. He obviously cares for her a great deal."

Knox looked to Beth, but he couldn't make out the expression on her face. Somewhere between shocked and horrified was probably the best guess he could give it. There was no way that he would allow her to be taken by some psychotic dungeon that claimed to be lonely. There had to be another way and he'd find it!

The first wave of wood wearing armored men came and Knox met it with the fullness of his power, striking down one with his bare hands and casting Luminous Surge on another, while keeping his back to Beth. They wouldn't take her; nothing would stop him from protecting the ones he loved.

Dodging low, his team formed up around him in a semi-circle with Beth behind them. Each of them fought like lions but their enemies were fighting with the strength of dragons. Knox didn't need his sense to know that each of these fighters were S Ranked. Dernal took a hit and went down, but Zhul brought him up, he was chanting heals full time now as Terris fought for his life alongside Knox.

Beth appeared at Knox's side, bow ready and striking out at one of the incoming attackers. Knox noticed that the man dodged and turned away a strike meant for him to avoid hitting Beth.

"They won't harm you, use that," Knox said to her, and Beth smiled. She rushed forward, putting herself in the way of an attack that would have taken Terris full in the back. The attack faltered and failed, lights of green flashing away in an instant. But it still wasn't going to be enough, there were too many of them.

Dernal was no longer moving and Zhul had stopped throwing heals on him, but without Knox's sense he couldn't tell if he was dead or not. Still, he fought on, his body glimmering light from so many cuts on his metallic skin, but he refused to be undone by these enemies. Terris fell next, unmoving as Zhul pulled his body beside Dernal's and cast a globe around them both of green light.

"I've done what I can to stabilize them, but they are injured beyond what I can heal unless you can buy me a few seconds," Zhul said, turning aside attack after attack as he spoke.

"I'll try," Knox said, his words barely registering above the din of battle.

He fought like a true Titan, destroying foe after foe with a single blow, his ring released its charge, and he obliterated three at once, but still a dozen more appeared, joining the fight. It was impossible, he couldn't save her, this was the end.

Knox couldn't believe his own internal voice, how could he give up so easily, no! He focused on his sense, still it was like staring into the sun, but he did it anyway.

"I am Knox!" He screamed. "The Titan of Light. You shall not defeat me!"

And suddenly with all his will bent to the task he could feel a measure of what was around him. More and more were coming, being created out of thin air, just out of sight and the one doing it, he could sense Izel some distance away. Even with his sense somewhat returned, he was still fighting on his back foot.

He killed as many as possible, a literal pile of bodies forming as he stepped further back and killed some more. Wait, where had Beth gone in all the trouble? Shit, someone had her about ten paces away, dragging her toward Izel.

Knox used Ethereal Step and decapitated the man with a chop of scarlet. He let his own aura form around the axe, reinforcing it and making it a weapon worthy of a god.

"Zhul is down!" Beth screamed and Knox turned just in time to see him take a spear to the gut as he lay on the ground. Several more followed but Knox was helpless to do a thing. If he left to help, he'd be leaving Beth to her fate.

"I can't save them all," Knox said, looking down at Beth and wishing he'd never brought her along. How stupid had he been to do such a thing.

"I can," Beth said. "You have to let me go." Tears poured down her face, but she'd never looked stronger than in that moment.

"You don't mean it," Knox said, his voice trembling. "I can't. Beth, I love you. I can't leave you."

"I love you too," Beth said, a sly smile on her face. "Don't forget me. You can return and beat this jerk later. I'll be safe, he's just lonely right?"

"No," Knox whispered, but he felt the life leaving his three friends and he turned blasting away an attempt to end them with his Luminous Surge.

"It's my choice," Beth said, then turning she yelled out into the void. "Stop the fight, I'll stay! But you must release my friends and heal them immediately."

"Deal," Izel said, appearing in a puff of purple smoke. Then looking at Knox, who still fumed with rage and refused to let go of Beth's hand, he said, "I expect you to return, Titan of Light. When you do, you shall be the end of me, and I will finally be able to rest. Until then, you have my word as a dungeon that I will not only keep your loved one close, but I shall train her in ways she can only imagine. She will return to your side, a mighty champion fit to stand beside a Titan."

Knox felt the world crumbling around him as he screamed and fought to strike down Izel. But a force held him back, hands pulled him toward a door. "No!" Knox screamed one final time as he was forced through a door and found himself in the dungeon room outside the second themed door.

He tried to reenter, but the doorway was just stone now, unaccepting of other Adventurers. He hardly noticed when the others appeared, beaten and battered but alive.

Nothing mattered to him anymore as he leaned against the door, tears pouring down his face and blood covering his pounding fist. He reached into the very fabric of magic with his Titan connection, willing a way through the door, but no matter what he tried, it did nothing. Something about the domain of the dungeon was limiting his control and he knew of no way around it.

For all his power and might, he'd failed in the worst possible way. He'd told her he'd never leave her behind again, and he'd broken that promise.

"I'm so sorry," Knox whispered as he slammed his head against the door. The metallic skin did not crack, but he wanted nothing more than to put himself to sleep or enter a void where emotions weren't assaulting him from every angle.

"There's loot," Terris said, sounding surprised.

Numbly Knox turned to see five chests of a clear material that could have been glass for all he could tell. He wanted to shatter the gifts of the dungeon, not take a single thing from it, but a part of him called that plan stupid. He needed all he could from this dungeon so he could come back and unmake it after defeating the Dark Titan.

This was no longer a task that he needed to do, it was a quest that he could not fail at, lest he leave his love to live out her days with a dungeon that could be doing who knows what to her.

Knox stood, moving robotically and opened the first chest. He pulled out a bow that thrummed with power, but it faded from his grasp a moment later.

"Sorry," Came Izel's voice echoing through the chamber. "That is for my pupil. The next chest if for you."

Knox didn't even turn to see if the dungeon speaker had appeared, he simply walked to the next chest and opened it. Inside he pulled piece after piece of golden armor. Without thought he ripped the remnants of his current armor off and put on his new armor. His sense told him what to expect from the armor, defense unparalleled, a sphere-like barrier that he could call upon in a time of need, and an amplifying effect that would multiply his attributes by a tenth of their overall potential.

It was a legendary set of armor, and it would help him defeat the Dark Titan, this he knew. But the cost weighed heavily on him, and it was as if his body worked without his commands. He lifted each of the other chests, revealing items for the remaining three Adventurers.

A crown of vines for Zhul that would increase the power of

his transformations and give him access to ancient forms of lizard-like beasts large and terrible. Armor as dark as the night itself for Terris, that when he put it on, he realized he could jump to points all over the room, shadow or not. And for Dernal, a mace that shimmered with celestial light. With it Dernal gained access to his summoning of his Celestial Guardian once more, enabling him to call upon one rank higher than he ought to be able to do.

In all it was loot that rivaled anything they could hope to get elsewhere, the quality and power that each item held was truly S ranked quality, yet still Knox could feel nothing but regret having challenged the dungeon that he assumed would be the easiest one thus far. How ancient and terrible this dungeon must have been to be able to do all of this, perhaps even stronger than the S ranked monsters they'd faced.

"It's time to go now," Dernal said, resting a hand on his shoulder. "She'll be safe, just focus on what you need to do."

Knox looked at Dernal with tear filled eyes, though none fell free from his eyes. "I'm going to destroy this dungeon," he said, placing his hand on the Dungeon Spire after Terris and Zhul finished packing up. "Mark my words, dungeon!" Knox yelled the words as loud as he could. "When I return, I will unmake you!"

CHAPTER 25
PAIN

Knox immediately went looking for Ramses upon returning with a plan already forming in his head. He'd take the combined might of their power then he'd cast out the dungeon, destroying it and freeing Beth.

He found Ramses resting in his chambers, the room much bigger than it needed to be and decorated with some very curious artifacts. Knox ignored them all and went straight to the bed, shaking the man awake.

"W-what is it?" Ramses said, startled awake.

"Get up, we have work to do," Knox said. "The dungeon inside your complex is not only self-aware but took Beth as a prisoner. I need your help to defeat it and somehow cast it out."

"Give me a moment to come awake," Ramses demanded. "Now you say the dungeon is self-aware? Has it begun to not reset and limit its paths inside then?"

"You've heard of this happening before?" Knox asked, a bit astonished.

"I have, we had records on dungeons going back hundreds of years, but never did I think to verify the truth of such wild claims. It took an army of Adventurers to take down the last dungeon that behaved in such a manner, surely you don't think the two of us will be enough?"

"Why not?" Knox asked, stubbornly ignoring the truth that Ramses was trying to lay out.

"Because, my dear boy, if you with all your power wasn't enough, I don't think my presence will bring more than a bit more knowledge to the table. Unless of course you think I've some unlocked power that I am not showing you, which I can tell you now, I do not. I'm not one to hide power when I have it to show off."

"So, you won't help?" Knox asked, feeling his anger building.

"It isn't a matter of will or won't," Ramses said. "It is a matter of can or can't. I can't help you now, but in the future when we've both grown stronger, we will be able to free your friend, if she lives long enough."

"She'll survive," Knox said knowingly. "She is as tough as iron and as resilient as anything I've ever seen. If anyone can survive inside the dungeon, it's her."

"Tell me everything you know about dungeons and how to kill them," Knox said, his temper cooling as a new plan began to form in his head.

Knox ignored the calls from his mother asking him if he were alright, instead heading straight back into the depths of the complex to confront the dungeon with the new information he'd learned. According to Ramses dungeons had hearts or cores that you could find if you knew how to look. These cores once destroyed would be like ripping the heart of a humanoid. It would kill it near instantly.

The biggest drawback being that those that killed dungeons often died themselves as they got stuck in a dimensional space unfit to sustain life. Few have escaped but Knox didn't care about that right now, he'd kill this dungeon and figure out a way to escape with Beth. He had the limited ability to teleport, if he leaned in on that and focused on a place, he was certain he could do more long-range teleportation, though he'd not yet tested it.

Reaching the dungeon spire he placed his hand on it and waited for the transfer to come. Instead, the runes glowed red, and nothing happened. He pressed his hand harder, and the surface began to grow hot to the touch. After a few minutes it was so hot that he had to remove his hand or suffer more burns.

"Let me in damnit!" Knox screamed the words at the dungeon spire, but no response came.

"Let me in," he said, his voice going low and his grief threatening to overcome him. "Let me in, let me in, let me in," he repeatedly whispered as he slammed his fist against the hot surface of the dungeon spire.

But no response came and eventually the spire grew cold once more. No matter how many times he touched it, the dungeon refused him entrance. He stayed there for the better part of a day, trying over and over again, before he finally resigned himself to his fate and the fate that Beth would have to wait.

"I've long suspected dungeons to have a mind of their own," Scarlet was saying as Knox lay in his bed, unwilling to get out just yet as she stroked his hair gently. "But to imagine them taking a hostage and acting so unfairly, it is unimaginable."

"And yet here we are," Knox said, finally sitting up and acknowledging his mother's presence. She'd been here for the better part of an hour talking to him, but he'd just been staring off into nothing while his mind worked over and over how he'd failed Beth.

"Welcome back, my son," she said, a kind smile appearing on her face. "Are you finally ready to do what needs to be done?"

"What's that?" Knox asked, swinging his legs over and flexing his stiff muscles as he moved into an exaggerated stretch and yawn.

"Get stronger by any means necessary," Scarlet said. "There are monsters out in the sea that are strong enough to give you a decent payoff in essence. Take the ship out and do some hunting. It'll help clear your head, then when you get back you can help me fashion a better axe for you. The facilities are good here, but we might want to wait for the actual crafting when we return to your facility as you have better metals on hand."

"Not a bad idea," Knox said. He could definitely go for some killing right now and if that meant he also grew stronger, all the better for it. "I'll take the boat out and go hunting, tell the others I'll return by the end of the week."

That was when they planned on returning and Knox needed to return as much as he needed to hunt. He owed his friends an explanation of what happened to Beth, and he was eager to get it over with, painful as it might be.

"Thank you for being here," Knox said, looking up at his mother. "I'm glad to have you at my side."

"And I'm happy to see you smiling again," Scarlet said.

Knox frowned, not realizing he had smiled. It wasn't that he didn't want to be happy or anything like that, he just felt empty inside so smiling felt like he was lying to himself. He had to remind himself that he hadn't lost her yet and that if he wanted to ever save her, he needed to grow stronger.

"I'm off to kill some monsters," Knox said, then standing he began the process of putting on his new armor.

Over the next few days Knox immersed himself in the hunting and killing of sea monsters. He gained much essence and harvested cores the size of his head, all the while keeping his body the ten-foot metallic version of himself. It was easier that way, almost as if some of his emotional range was dampened while in the state.

After the fifth day he was even able to enjoy the hunt once more, somewhat forgetting that he needed to return soon he went ever further out into the sea. Twice he happened upon pirates that weren't loyal to the banner of Ramses and both times he left them in a watery grave. He was no longer collecting souls either, as his army of golems back home had reached a peak that he didn't feel he needed to add more to just yet.

Though he tried and mostly succeeded in pushing out his worry and fear of failure over Beth, there was a certain part of him that nagged at his mind that he could be doing more. What more he could do wasn't exactly spelled out for him, but he searched deeper and further than he probably ought to when he finally came across a being that was strong enough to give him pause.

Knox, the golden Titan of Light, stood resolutely on the deck of his ship, his eyes ablaze with the fiery determination that had become his signature. The sea churned violently around him, whipped into a frenzy by the presence of the colossal sea dragon lurking beneath the surface. Its skin, a mosaic of translucent scales, shimmered like a mirage, giving the beast an almost ethereal quality. Yet the destruction it wrought was anything but mythical; its scalding breath turned patches of the ocean into boiling cauldrons, unleashing storms that could rend ships to splinters.

This dragon was more than a mere adversary to Knox; it was a treasure trove of resources. From its bones and scales, he would forge weapons and armor of unparalleled strength, equipping his comrades for the battles ahead. He had already amassed an array of materials from other formidable creatures, but this sea dragon was the ultimate prize.

With a determined grit, Knox swung his ship into the eye of the storm, steering it straight toward the heart of danger. Then, without a moment's hesitation, he dove into the roiling waters. The ocean, dark and unwelcoming, tried to swallow him whole, but Knox shone like a beacon of defiance. His golden aura pierced the murky depths, casting a radiant light that sliced through the darkness.

As he descended, Knox's strategy was clear: he would rely not on magic but on his own physical prowess. In his quest, he had pushed his body to limits unknown, honing his strength and agility. Each battle was an opportunity to test himself, to tread new paths of physical endurance and martial skill.

The sea dragon, sensing Knox's approach, let out a thunderous roar that shook the very foundation of the sea. It moved with a grace that belied its monstrous size, its body undulating through the water with lethal elegance. As Knox neared, it snapped its jaws, each tooth as large as a sword, capable of shearing through metal and flesh with equal ease.

But Knox was undeterred. He maneuvered through the water with surprising agility for one of his size, each stroke bringing him closer to the leviathan. His every movement was a dance of light, his body leaving trails of luminescence in the water, painting a picture of his fearless advance.

The dragon lunged, its maw agape, ready to engulf Knox in a tomb of teeth and darkness. But Knox, ever the warrior, met its charge head-on. He ducked beneath its jaw, narrowly avoiding its razor-sharp teeth, and positioned himself along its underbelly. There, he found his target: the softer scales that provided a chink in the dragon's otherwise impenetrable armor.

With the precision of a master blacksmith, Knox struck. His fists, reinforced by the power of his unyielding spirit, became weapons of their own. He pounded against the dragon's scales with relentless force, each blow a testament to his extraordinary might. The sea dragon thrashed wildly, trying to dislodge the golden Titan clinging to its belly, but Knox held firm.

The battle raged on, a tempest of fists and fury beneath the waves. Knox, his strength never faltering, continued his onslaught, driven by a purpose that transcended the fight itself. This was more than a battle for resources; it was a test of wills, a clash of titans in the truest sense.

Finally, with a mighty roar that resonated through the water, the sea dragon succumbed to Knox's indomitable spirit. It floated, defeated and lifeless, as Knox emerged victorious, his golden aura now a halo of triumph.

As he surfaced, Knox felt a numbness fall over him. He'd done it, but he still had work to do. Going back down, but with ropes, he tied up and locked into place the great beast. The scales were powerful enough that he needn't worry about predators getting through them easily, but still he hurried the process back to shore.

When the dragon was finally beached, he began the grizzly work of ripping into its flesh and harvesting its materials.

CHAPTER 26
CREATION AND GIFTS

AFTER HE FINISHED HARVESTING all the supplies, including enough meat to feed his people for some time, he spoke with Ramses, taking lessons about teleportation and how he could help with it. By the end of the third day of his return, he was ready to help.

Ramses stood in the main room where his command chair lay and behind it the portal. Ramses simply reached out and touched it, while Knox did the same. Lending a portion of his power to the task, Knox barely noticed as the portal flickered to life and the process was finished.

"So much easier with two of us and within the connected system. It didn't even take that much out of me," Ramses said in surprise. "I'd say, maybe a day or two of rest and we will be ready to go hunt that Dark Titan of yours."

"Good," Knox said, as he stepped forward and through the portal.

He appeared before a perplexed-looking Mic, surrounded by golems ready to unleash power.

"Stand at ease," Knox commanded, and they lowered their weapons and hands.

"Welcome back," Mic said. "I've got so much to fill you in

about, but first, you'll be happy to know that we defeated a small army of Adventurers while you were gone."

Knox groaned and listened as Mic broke down what had happened while he was gone, sparing no detail it would seem.

According to him all had been mostly peaceful, until an army of two hundred Adventurers appeared demanding the city be vacated and given to their control. Aetex had spoken with them and then punched out their top official, kicking off a short and brutal war. They'd lost lives on both sides, but the Adventurers, all C Rank and above, retreated. Aetex was currently out patrolling to ensure they didn't return.

"Then it's dealt with?" Knox asked. "Good, I've got work to do and I wish to not be disturbed unless it's truly an emergency."

With that Knox went deeper into the complex and found a workshop where he could begin to do what Scarlet had suggested, working on a new weapon, one worthy of an S Ranked Adventurer at least.

Scarlet had worked hard on replicating the effects of the previous axe, which stole a larger portion of base essence from the ones Knox killed with it or really anything near it. So far, she'd come close to replicating much of it, but not anywhere near the percentage that his previous axe could pull in. She told him she was worried about the metal being able to execute the functions and still remain intact.

It would take a powerful metal to do what she wanted and Knox, thanks to Zhul, had a lead on something called Runeth, an extremely dense and powerful metal that conducted essence much better than any other, yet if not reinforced by runes it was susceptible to breaks and cracks. While Zhul left to talk with his contacts —he said he'd return within a week or less with the metal if he could get it, taking parts of the dragon as payment—Knox began work on prototypes.

He forged using the most powerful metals he had access to and used his mother's axe design as well as the runic formations she'd provided to make them. He made small changes, like adding a spike on one side but otherwise this axe would be as ready to cut trees as it was to cut necks. He planned on giving the axes to Askar, Terrim, and any of the other prior woodworkers that wanted one.

The job functions that everyone filled was an interesting side thought for Knox. They still needed woodcutters and all the other odds and ends professions to keep things running, so even Askar had taken to clearing trees on occasion, when the golems had other duties to attend to. Then there was the maintenance golems and their constant upkeep of the complex.

Knox had made a deal with Ramses to allow for all the golems at his complex to remain and help with its defense and development, under the guidance of Edgar, Borris, and Vlad. It was not really a risk, since they had to obey Knox's command, but Knox had left the command pretty loose to allow them to be flexible. Just a general, don't start being pirates again and maintain the safety and health of the complex as best as you can type of orders.

Ramses said that as their Titan Engines grew the connection would become more permanent, making it possible for the portal to activate on Titan Engine power alone. To that end Knox had provided him with many of the Cores he'd collected of the super powerful monsters, while keeping a few to experiment with himself, as well as sucking in a few for their raw essence, like the sea dragons.

He was reaching new heights of his power, and soon he'd be as ready as he possibly could be to try and take on the ancient Dark Titan. A part of him wondered if he could have saved Echo and stored his considerable mind to access later, but that time was said and done. He had Mic, who despite his memory loss, Knox was sure now that he'd worked for the prior Titan that he'd met, the echo. He'd not really had a chance to ask him detailed questions about it and likely wouldn't for some time as it wasn't a priority for him right now.

Focusing up his thoughts he got back to work, pouring the metal into the cast he'd made for the axe head. Then as it cooled, he began inscribing using the most advanced tools he had, adding layer after layer of runic formations his mother and he had worked on. It was a laborious project that took time and he had to do it in a short amount of time as the metal cooled for the first set of runic formations.

When the metal finally cooled, Knox could target other locations and begin to focus on the more complex formations that would literally weaken the metal as he went. However, he'd also strengthened it with his first batch of Runic formations, so it should be a wash if his and his mother's calculations were correct.

Hours later he'd failed on his first attempt, the axe head split down the middle and he was back to the drawing board. For this he'd brought his mother down and they rebalanced what would and wouldn't work. Although he knew you could rarely expect the first prototype to work, he'd really hoped it would be more successful.

After deciding that it was the type of metal being used, they adjusted the intake of essence formations and redoubled the fortifications with the new available space on it. This would be an adjustment that would only need to be done on the weaker metal, the Runeth metal should theoretically be able to withstand the stresses.

Knox went back to work on the metal, his mother leaving him to do the more laborious parts of it in peace. There was a certain amount of pride and fulfillment he got from doing this work and he even sent away the golem that kept coming to check up on him and asking if he required assistance.

There was one part that he hoped to get help from, at least on these prototypes, but it required help from a Necromancer that was walking the Soulbinder Path. He hoped to use some of their captured souls to give the axe increased durability and power. Knox had reached out to Frederick, and he was going to send down the most powerful Soulbinder they had when he returned from a hunt he'd been on.

It just so happened that the man returned just as Knox

successfully finished the first prototype, the fixes they made causing the axe not to crack or break, though it had been close.

"You called fer me?" the man asked, Knox struggled to remember his name and it came to him just as he turned to regard him.

Corey the Soulbinder Necromancer, his last name eluded Knox's memory, but the middle-aged man had been a crafter of sorts, working on various tasks that Mr. Tome didn't bother with or were too busy to deal with. That made Knox think of Mr. Tome, and he decided he'd go visit him and see about crafting a new boomstick, his own had been adjusted over and over again but with the new metal he was getting he hoped to have enough to create a more elegant version of it with multiple shots.

But that was for another time, right now Knox looked at the middle-aged man with his short greying hair and several scars on his face, he looked like a rough and tough man and Knox had no doubt he was. He'd achieved what others had only dreamed of in such a short period of time, reaching into the B Ranks at level 42 if Frederick was to be believed.

"How do you level so fast?" Knox asked, eying Corey and wondering if he had some secret to it.

"I forged a soul-infused weapon that sucks in essence, made my trip upward much easier," Corey said, then spitting on the ground he added. "Too bad the damn thing won't shut up. Used the soul of a pirate and it just wants to go on and on about how adventurous it used to be and how I've messed up its existence. Most unruly spirit I've dealt with so far."

Corey held up a sword that gleamed with power and Knox sense could feel something residing inside of it, like an extra layer of odd ethereal enchantments giving the blade additional powers.

"That is why I asked you here," Knox said, grinning down at the blade. "Can you enhance my weapons with spirits to give it a similar effect and durability?"

"Not that one," he said, motioning to the cooling axe head. "I need to infuse the spirit when the metal is red hot and it cools rapidly during the process, so adding runes becomes difficult at best, impossible at worst."

"But you can do it," Knox said, deciding this axe head would go to Askar as he picked it up and added a shaft to it, polished dark wood that he'd reinforced to be nearly as durable as steel.

"I can," Corey said. "You've got any of those stones you store spirits in, they are handy to capture spirits in. I've got a few but you will want to capture one of those spirits you've got around you, I see a dragon, and several other monsters trying to torment you."

As Corey spoke his eyes went a hazy white as if he were peering into a realm that only he could see. This was another of the times that Knox kind of wished he'd picked Necromancer as his ordinary path and not the Mystic. But as far as he knew he couldn't—not yet at least—access an additional path. But he was hopeful that with him rising higher and higher into the levels available to him that he'd get access at some point, then he'd definitely take Necromancer, or perhaps Warrior, okay he wasn't really sure.

"You can capture souls after they've been dead this long?" Knox asked, surprised at this.

"Only the remnant of powerful spirits like these, though they fade with time, but yeah, necromancers can harness even them," Corey said.

"Follow me and I'll get you the best Soulstones we have," Knox said, leaving the room and raiding the supply of Soulstones a few doors down. Mic had instructed several people how to make them and the quality had been improving steadily, but they were not as good as the originals yet, and those were the ones Knox found, tucked away where only he could find.

With the Soulstones in place, Corey went to a sitting position and began to chant, one by one the stones were filled to bursting with energy.

"Save the sea dragon for a weapon I'll be making later, use the weaker ones first," Knox instructed Corey and he nodded.

Their first attempt ended badly, or at least it ended with Knox having only finished a quarter of the runic formations he needed to do to reinforce the metal, yet when he went to do the other part to allow for essence absorption, the metal didn't crack or shatter. Something about the spirit gave it power to reinforce it.

Picking up the weapon Knox nearly dropped it a moment later as something brushed up against his mind. It wasn't as Corey had said, a voice complaining, but a more feral urge to act and attack. The voice was that of a monster and it did not hold the intelligence to speak on its own.

After a minute of holding it, Knox swung it around after attaching a handle, testing the weight. It had a good weight to it if a touch heavier than Scarlet. This would be a weapon for Terrim, he'd love it, Knox was sure.

They continued working, making six prototypes before they had only the three remaining powerful souls to use. Knox wanted to keep them for making his final weapon. Corey told him he had unlocked from his tree an ability that he could use only sparingly that allowed for multiple souls to be infused, but it had a high risk of failure. And even if you did everything right, the strongest soul would consume the others and be that much more powerful for it in the end.

He warned that he could create a weapon that would refuse to fight if it wished and there would be nothing, he could do about it. Knox was willing to chance it and instructed him to collect all the souls he could fit into a weapon in the meanwhile. Knox himself made it a point to keep a few Soulstones with him, just in case, then he went out to find Terrim and the others, ready to give out some weapons.

He had only axes, but anyone willing to use his design would be getting a powerful boost in their ability to level, so much so that Knox instructed Corey to make as many spirit-infused weapons as possible—though he later learned he didn't have to as he was already doing it.

Knox found Terrim with Danielle and his face fell the moment he saw Knox, pulling him into a hug.

"I'm so sorry, man," Terrim said, his voice filled with compassion. "Just tell me when and I'm at your side to get her back."

This stopped Knox short, obviously word would get out before he had a chance to tell everyone, but the offer brought tears to Knox's eyes, despite trying to hide it.

"I know I'm not much help," Danielle said, her voice sweet as honey. "But tell me what I can do to help, and I'll do it."

"Right now," Knox said, clearing his throat before continuing. "Just being yourselves is enough. Once I've brought down the Dark Titan, I'm coming for that dungeon and nothing, not even Gowlen himself will stand in my way."

Terrim met Knox's eyes and nodded. He was the best of friends, ready to dive into battle and die at his side no matter the situation. "To death," Terrim said, slapping Knox on the shoulders. Despite their strength difference now, Knox let himself fall to the side a bit as he would have before his changes.

"To death," Knox said when he'd recovered from the mock blow. "I come bringing gifts to help you keep your promise. This is your new axe; it'll increase the flow of essence you can collect and enable you to level all the faster for it."

Knox held out the blade, the process of adding a spirit had given the metal a dark color with a purple hue. Runes were visible all around the axe, including the shaft, but they would not fade with time, as even they were reinforced without. A grip had been tied to the bottom and a loop of leather to hand the axe had been added as well.

"We chopping trees?" Terrim asked, giving the axe a few test swings. Then, suddenly his eyes went wide, and he dropped the axe. "What the hell? It, uh, spoke to me but not really with words."

"Pick it up," Knox said, gesturing to the ground with a grin. "It won't bite. It has been infused with the soul of a monster I killed. I don't know specifically what extra capabilities it has yet, the identifying device didn't even say anything other than the extra essence draw, but it is a special weapon, that much is sure."

Terrim carefully picked it up from where it had fallen and looked at his friend with a critical eye. "Giving me haunted weapons now? This is some new level of bullshit."

"You'll get used to it," Knox said. "What are you going to name it?"

Knox was a big proponent of naming weapons, especially ones with spirits attached.

Terrim looked at it, a look of disturbed silence on his face as he mentally wrestled with the promptings that were being fed into his head. "Bane," he finally said, swinging the axe around a few more times. "Because this thing is the bane of my sanity and if I go crazy, I'm coming for you first."

Knox raised his hands in mock surrender and smiled wide. "Understood," he said, then he bid his friend and his girlfriend farewell, looking for Askar.

He'd get the non-spirit enchanted weapon because Knox didn't want him tempted by monstrous spirits. He could trust Terrim to remain strong and hopefully he'd find some other mentally strong candidates willing to wield them, but not everyone could be trusted to resist temptations. He would have to speak to Corey about using weaker spirits that weren't as tempting for most of the weapons, as they'd still give the absorbing bonus, Knox was pretty sure.

He found Askar alone eating some food in the giant mess hall that had evolved since he'd last visited. Four separate sections were appearing, one for drink, and three for food, each area serving different food. Knox was pleasantly surprised to find Askar not at the section dedicated to drinks.

"Son," Askar said as Knox approached.

"Father," Knox said in return. That little interaction was enough to let Knox know that Askar was doing much better than he'd been doing in the past. There were many names or lack of names he could have used, but son wasn't among the ones that Knox feared to hear.

"I wanted to talk to you about Scarlet," Knox said and Askar turned his head away to take a deliberate bite from his food. Finishing it, he looked back up to Knox and spoke.

"What about her?" Askar asked. "Is she off to go onto another adventure where I get left out?"

"Sorry, that was my fault actually," Knox said, feeling as if he could understand the pain of separation more keenly now than before. If his love was anything like what he felt for Beth, then it was akin to having your chest ripped open. And Knox should know, he's had that nearly happen on occasion.

"She always has a choice," Askar said, his eyes drifting to the drinking area of the eatery.

"She's back now and I just wanted to see how the two of you were doing?" Knox asked, he'd been curious about the times he'd seen them together and wanted to know if they were back together or not.

Askar sighed and shifted in his seat before continuing. "It's complicated, but whatever we decide, just know we aren't making the decisions because of you," Askar said then seemed to consider his words he added, "that sounds a bit harsh, but it wasn't meant to be. I'm not good at this being a father thing, but I did want you to know that your mother and I are... well... we're proud of you."

This caught Knox completely off guard and left him sputtering to figure out his next words. "I, well—uhm—yeah, it was nice talking with you father. I've got a gift for you before I leave, I should leave and uhm, see to something."

Knox held out the axe and Askar examined it.

"You know I'm a fair decent hand using a sword, got any of those hidden under your gawdy cloak?" Askar asked, and Knox relaxed, this was the father he was used to dealing with, overcritical and judgmental.

"I don't," Knox said, nearly taking the axe back before Askar could grab it. "But I put a good amount of work into this weapon. You'll be one of only a few with a powerfully enchanted weapon like it, for now at least."

"I'll take it," Askar said as if it were a burden to do so. He stood from where he sat and gave it a few test swings, before nodding sagely that it was balanced well and would be useful.

Knox understood the look keenly because it was one that he'd used many a times before. Seeing that his father was as happy as he was likely to be and wanting to leave on a fairly good note, Knox departed with a simple head nod, one that Askar barely returned.

"I'll win her back you know," Askar called after Knox, but Knox pretended not to hear. He wasn't sure he wanted to get into the middle of his parents' love lives after all.

Murdoch was just coming out of a meeting when Knox found him. He'd been working on a weapon for him, but it had taken him time to figure out the balance between the blade and getting it infused with a powerful B Rank spirit he'd gone out and collected, a task becoming all the harder as the final stronger beasts were driven out of the swamps.

Those that had come from the Adventurer's Guild had been mostly helpful with those tasks. Knox was surprised to learn they hadn't abandoned them when the small army of Adventurer's Guild members had arrived, but he had an idea that that group was sent from Silas and not through official channels. He might be a problem in the future, but for now Aetex was more than able to deal with the issue. He'd need to find Aetex soon and have some words with him about the upcoming adventure.

"Come to me to ease your burdens under the mighty weight of a drink, have you?" Murdoch said; his response to Knox standing outside the meeting hall was a classic Murdoch response.

"You heard, I take it?" Knox said, unable to go over the story one more time as it might just kill him inside.

"I did and I am ready to return by your side and slay that awful dungeon that would dare split up our mighty party," Murdoch said, being a touch more over the top than usual.

"Are you drinking on the job again?" Knox asked in a hushed whisper. Despite the fact that a few elderly gentlemen leaving the meeting looked their way, System enhanced hearing being what it was these days, it seemed like everyone was operating at tip top shape.

"No," Murdoch said, then giving him a very sly smile that said that was indeed what was happening. He even pulled out a silver flask and took a sip while they walked.

"I'm needing to speak with you, are you in a decent enough condition for me to do so?" Knox asked.

Murdoch straightened and made it a point of looking sober and boring. "I'm ready," he declared.

Sighing but not wanting to waste any more time, Knox launched into it.

"I'm wanting to take as big as an army with me into the city below, Sintra tells me we will have to deal with armies before we get a chance to deal with the Dark Titan and I just wanted to know our numbers and if you'll be able to come and fight at my side," Knox explained.

Murdoch seemed to legitimately sober up upon hearing Knox words, tucking his flash away he looked up with his eyes for a few moments before saying.

"Are we counting golems among the ranks of the army?" Murdoch asked, counting off on his fingers now.

"Yes, we will want to leave a force behind, perhaps a hundred, but besides Aetex, everyone with a decent power level will be coming with us to fight," Knox said, letting Murdoch in on part of the plan he had to keep the complex safe.

"Then we can field close to nine hundred, golems and the dark elves included," Murdoch said, any trace of his drunkenness gone.

"Dark elves?" Knox asked, not hearing this term used for them yet, but it made sense.

"That's what everyone has been calling them, they don't seem to mind it," Murdoch assured him.

Knox was surprised at the number, but at the same time he wondered if it would be enough. He knew little about armies, but these people would have been a part of the system for some time and likely sporting power equal to if not greater than what most of Knox's troops could field. And besides all that there was the lack of military training, each of his people worked well in small squads or groups, not in large scale combat.

"Have the necromancers learned how to raise more undead for longer periods of time, like Captain Dread had been doing?" Knox asked, not fully expecting Murdoch to have an answer, so a look of surprise covered his face when he got one.

"Frederick is the best at it, but the most they can manage is about ten or twenty on average, but for a shorter period of time. Though by recasting and focusing all their mana into it, Frederick has maintained as many as fifty monsters so far. We've actually got a cold storage set up to keep the corpses of monsters and a few hundred pirates, thanks to Mic's discovery of the room. All sorts of neat discoveries have happened since you left. Did you know there is a craft room deep down that seems to have been made to construct giant golems that allow you to sit within them?"

"I didn't," Knox admitted, but he couldn't be bothered with getting sidetracked now. "Let's circle back to that, how many undead can we field altogether would you guess?"

"At least a hundred and fifty," Murdoch answered immediately as if he knew Knox would be asking that question next.

"Good, now tell me more about those large golems," Knox

said, the allure of such constructs being too hard for him to ignore.

Murdoch went on and on about them and how Mic said the constructs were impractical because the power usage would require someone inside of them funneling massive amounts of mana through them as well as having several monster cores to feed it power to limbs and weapons. Apparently, it had a projection weapon that shot out concentrated beams of mana powerful enough to cut a man in half.

Murdoch said Mic was against putting any resources into building a complete one, despite admitting that one was nearly complete in the factory that was apparently the size of three dinner halls and just as tall. Knox made a mental note to check out this new factory that had been discovered, but he trusted Mic. If they didn't have the resources for it yet, then the giant golem that one could ride inside would have to wait.

Bidding Murdoch farewell, Knox went out to speak with Frederick some more. He needed to secure the promise from all the necromancers that they'd come to battle with him, since Frederick had been pretty standoffish about battle in general it was important to Knox that he secure a promise.

It turned out to be easier than he'd thought, the moment he mentioned it Frederick practically begged to be a part of the newest expedition leaving the complex. He said he'd been speaking with many of Sintra's people and a fair few were necromancers. He wanted to learn from them and gain their trust, so he was all in on going to help free their kingdom.

Next, he went to find Leo, John or Dernal, expecting to find them individually; he was surprised to find them all in a larger meeting room that had no designated use as far as he knew. They'd used the table to fill it with maps and other items.

"What's this?" Knox asked, and Dernal turned to him, clearly surprised to have seen him appearing.

John spoke up first, covering one of the maps with his hand and looking to each of his companions before speaking.

"We were just looking over some maps of the area and updating them. Since the fall of the Shadowfall Swamp and it not being a swamp anymore we were playing with ideas of new names, perhaps you can help," John said, but it was clear he was hiding something.

"Call it what you will," Knox said. "I was just coming to get your commitment to travel down into the depths of the ground to fight against the Dark Titan."

"About that," Leo said, looking downturned. "We are Adventurers Knox. We love a good Adventurer as much as the next person, but with the recent attack by the Adventurer's Guild, we feel like there might be some work to do here up on the surface that we are uniquely qualified to do."

"We've spoken with the Dawnbringer, and she's agreed to support us with a plea to the king to avoid any further attacks and perhaps even have them welcome the System with open arms. It is an inevitability that the system will come to them, so we should try and prepare them," John said, looking to Dernal for support the short stout man just grunted his usual, "Hhrmm."

"You won't be going with me to face the Dark Titan?" Knox asked Dernal specifically, narrowing his gaze to him and feeling a touch of further betrayal.

"You want me by your side?" Dernal asked, his terse tone indicating that he didn't think so.

Knox thought it over before responding. Surely, they did have an important mission to accomplish, but Dernal had been with him through thick and thin, through it all, could he finish the last part of his epic journey without the man by his side? No, he decided, he couldn't imagine taking on the Dark Titan without the aid of his closest mentor.

"I do," Knox said confidently. "I can understand that you both cannot go, along with Eleanor and a few of her closest followers, but this really is an all-hands-on deck situation." Knox used a bit of the lingo that Edgar had repeatedly used while they were on the ship. It had a nice ring to it, and he'd found himself adopting it without realizing.

"Then I will stand by your side," Dernal said, not a moment's hesitation in his words.

"What of our quest?" Leo asked. "It would be much easier with your contacts on our side."

"I'll leave you with a letter of writ, it'll be enough for most of my contacts," Dernal said, never leaving his eyes off Knox and a small smile growing on his face beneath his mess of a beard.

"I look forward to the success of your quest," Knox said, going forward and hugging each of the group, Leo and John. They'd grown rather close over the months, each one acting as a mentor in different ways to him. Leo was wise and powerful, John, less so but still knowledgeable about certain aspects of life. To think this might be the last time he saw them, depending on when they were set to leave and if he succeeded in his mission, he had something he needed to tell Leo.

"If we all fall in battle against the Dark Titan," Knox said, looking right at Leo. "I want you to take up the mantle of Titan of Light and do what you can to stem the spread of darkness."

It wasn't a sudden decision; it was one he'd considered for some time. There were others he felt might be more qualified, but they were set to go with him into the depths and if they failed, Knox had a feeling none would return.

"I don't know what to say to that," Leo said, stepping forward and pulling him into another hug. "Except that you will not fail, so I needn't worry. Be strong Knox, Titan of Light, for you are the greatest among us, in mind, body, and spirit."

With that Knox finished his goodbyes and left them to their planning, Eleanor joined them shortly after Knox left, but he had little to say to her, other than wish her good luck and safe journeys.

CHAPTER 27
DEPARTURE

Zhul returned with the Runeth metal and Knox crafted his ultimate weapon using the spirit of the dragon. It was a hard and laborious project, but one that was satisfying in the end. He touched the axe after its creation but felt no spiritual pull or emotion from it as he had expected. The metal gave off an iridescent look but in all didn't look too far off from steel.

The preparations were taking days longer than Knox expected and Aetex returned at the end of the final day of those preparations, so Knox took him aside to speak with him privately.

They stood in his personal quarters, most of his items had been packed so it was a sparse room with several sets of Beth's closes folded and put aside as well as a few of her personal items that had slowly migrated over to his quarters.

"I need you to stay behind," Knox said, getting straight to the point.

Aetex's eyes went wide, and he mouthed a few words before finally forming a coherent sentence.

"I'm meant to go with you," he finally said. "My mission was to keep you safe, and I can't do that if I stay behind."

"I need someone powerful enough to protect Luminar while I'm away. There is no one else that I trust for this task that can wield as much power as you can," Knox explained, sitting on his bed beside the massive man, his head almost touching the ceiling of his quarters.

Aetex sighed and sat as well. "I'm sorry Knox, but I have to insist," Aetex began to say but Knox held up a hand.

"In combat between us, if we were to fight now, who would win?" Knox asked, for the effect he allowed himself to grow and turn golden. He was a few heads taller than Aetex in that form, a change Aetex definitely noticed.

"You have grown much since my arrival, but this Dark Titan isn't the final or most powerful threat you will face," Aetex said, his hands waving about as he spoke.

"Who would win?" Knox insisted on asking again.

"You would, young warrior," Aetex said, and Knox allowed himself to shrink back, his clothing and anything on his person changing proportionally as he did so. It was amazing that his shirt, axe, and other items could change so easily but it was such a mundane thing he'd barely given it a thought.

"Then you've done your job, you've kept me safe long enough to surpass you," Knox said, he'd thought through his plan to get Aetex to stay and he knew he was getting through to him.

"I suppose, but Mah'kus has a greater plan for you, I am meant to-," Aetex said, but Knox stopped his words with a hand.

"And when I finish off this Dark Titan, I will return to deal with the return of Gowlen. I'm not ignorant of the greater threats, Aetex. In fact, this is just one step of many that I'll need to take, I know this, and I'm prepared for the long journey ahead. But on this step, I need you to support me by protecting Luminar. Can you do that for me?" Knox asked.

After a long pause, Aetex answered.

"I can."

"Good," Knox said, putting his hand on the large man's shoulder. "Once the Dark Titan has fallen, I will find and unite all the Titans. Only then will we be able to face off against the threat that is the Titan Gowlen."

"When that time comes, I will be at your side," Aetex said, his voice booming with his usual confidence.

"To death?" Knox asked, repeating the phrase that Aetex hadn't much liked, but his other friends had rallied behind.

"To death," Aetex proclaimed with more enthusiasm than Knox expected.

Knox came to the meeting with Sintra with apprehension in his steps, this would be the final meeting before they left, and he hoped to the Titans above that he'd made the right decisions so far. He wasn't the sole person making all the decisions, but his words were being treated as law and few, if any, were openly opposing the idea.

"I've one matter that I must speak with you about that bears repeating," Sintra said as Knox entered and took a seat around the table. She had no one else around this time, making it a personal meeting between the two of them.

The room was lit by lamplight, and it cast eerie shadows about the room from where it hung to the side. The tables and chairs were stained dark, but sturdy, probably Mr. Tomes work.

"Which is?" Knox asked, giving her his full attention. She'd gone over troop deployments and ways they could bypass much of the defenses, while also going over the monsters they might encounter on the way, but her information was sorely lacking about the Dark Titan and her capabilities. Most of what she had to say revolved around a powerful artifact she claimed the Dark Titan used to gather most of her enormous power.

"The great Siphoning Gem, my people have many names for it, but your tongue cannot speak them well. If we are to defeat her, you must first find a way to disable or destroy it. I believe that with it gone, much of her power will flee her and it will be a symbol to my people that her reign has ended, which would rally them to my side once more," Sintra said, bringing up once again this gem she'd spoken of many times in the last few days.

"And you know where to find it?" Knox asked, parroting questions he'd already asked her.

"All who visit our mighty city know where it lies, it floats above the seat of my power, the castle, in plain view of all so that they might be reminded of the power she holds over us," Sintra said.

"Let's say I break it, then I can count on your army to fight alongside us against her?" Knox asked, turning the topic toward the battle he was most anticipating.

"None will be able to stand at your side when you trade blows with her, none perhaps except for Ramses the other Titan," Sintra said simply.

"She's that strong?" Knox asked, feeling more than a little apprehension toward the upcoming fight.

"Her strength, even if you diminish it, will be vast. She has ruled quietly over our people for many generations and our lifespans are long. It was my great grandfather that first welcomed the witch into our courts, and he died for his foolishness. Great power corrupts and over time her ways darkened beyond the help of our people and to the detriment of our society."

"But she wasn't always like that, when did she start to change?" Knox asked, eager to understand what had changed to make this Titan such a threat.

"It is impossible to say, our records are diminished or destroyed by her, but the eldest among us tends to agree that the purple stone that she found was the start of her downfall. Her oppression spread forth and took all of the kingdom under her control and eventually she spoke of conquering the surface world as well—when she could still speak as we do now," Sintra said.

Knox wanted to know what truly changed her, was it the aspect of darkness that her Titan powers gave her or perhaps something else? Was it the pure nature of power to eventually corrupt its user when no one could no longer stand against you. Was Knox doomed to one day betray the world because his accumulation of power became too much? So many questions warred for space within his head that he stayed silent, unable to voice a singular one for some time.

When finally, he decided on a question, it was a simple one. "Why can't she speak?" Knox asked, saving the other more personal questions for himself and his own musings.

"Her flesh began to wither and decay soon after taking possession of the great gem, she is no more than withered bones of the darkest night, her form covered by a cloak of darkness itself," Sintra said. "It was once said that she shone like a light in the darkness, they spoke of her much as you can appear now, metallic and glorious. But whatever she once was, she doesn't possess that ability any longer."

This was news to Knox, some little tidbit that he hadn't pulled free from her before. If she could no longer present herself as a metallic being, one of the Titan's most singular traits, then perhaps she wasn't even a Titan any longer? Perhaps she'd become something else entirely and that might work to his very advantage.

They finished up their discussion of more mundane things, going over travel plans and such, before Knox bid her goodbye. He left and immediately went out to find Mr. Tome, who he hadn't spoken with in some time since returning. He had plans for his boomstick that involved releasing energy similar to the large golem designs Murdoch had spoken of, but that involved getting Mr. Tome involved before they left.

He could take much of what he needed with him to work along the way, but he wasn't even sure if Mr. Tome was among those going yet, as he knew several had opted to stay behind, for either defensive reasons or personal reasons of their own, which he had decided to respect, not wanting to force anyone to do the impossible task he was asking them. It would come down to grit and a desire to really do their absolute best, and that wasn't likely to be forced out of someone.

He found Mr. Tome in a workshop below ground, working away as he always seemed to be. The older short man had constructed a series of stools to help him get to all the higher benches, as they were built into the room and not easily adjusted.

"Come back later if you want that door fixed Johnson, I told you I couldn't get to it before I have to leave," Mr. Tome said without turning to see who had entered.

"So, you are going with us?" Knox asked, and Mr. Tome turned with a wide smile on his face.

"There will be work to be done, so I will be going along, yes, but not for fighting. I'll leave that to the younger generations," Mr. Tome said, despite his words Knox knew that he was in a party himself and had proven time and time again that he was a threat to any monsters or pirates that stood in his way. His inventions had been getting stronger and stranger the longer he worked down here.

Looking at him now, Knox could sense at least three new gadgets on him that he couldn't identify. This was Mr. Tome though; he was a man of inventions and creation. He wanted nothing more than to be left alone for the rest of his life to create and discover, it was part of what drew Knox to him as a child. His passion matched Knox's and in practice he proved that being out in the middle of nowhere didn't mean you couldn't discover and learn.

"I've a project that I need you to help me with before we go," Knox said, then he went on to give the short version of the large golem and its energy-based weapon that used monster cores as fuel.

"With how much mana you've got, I bet we could get it to work both ways," Mr. Tome said, discarding the project he'd been working on. "The size will be an issue, you sure you don't want the entire thing shrunk down, made into a battle armor of some kind?"

"I think if we focus on the most powerful weapon it has, the repeatable energy boomstick, it'll be enough to give me an edge,"

Knox assured him, though the idea of wearing a suit of armor that made him even bigger than he could get as a Titan, did intrigue him, but he reminded himself that if he could defeat this Dark Titan, he would have all the time he needed to explore such options.

"Indeed, let's go take a look," Mr. Tome said. True to his character, Mr. Tome was ready to drop everything for a chance to learn something new or tinker with a new toy.

They traveled down deep, much deeper than Knox had before until they finally reached the workshop. It was a massive affair where everything, down to the tools that needed to be used, were all sized for something closer to Knox's full size or perhaps even bigger. Several pieces of this impossibly large golem were spread out here and there, massive chunks of armor and even a few weapons, a sword, a shield, and then the arm cannon they were there to find.

Knox let his body shift and grow, Mr. Tome adjusting his spectacles as he did so, but saying nothing until he'd fully shifted.

"You truly are growing up my boy," Mr. Tome said jokingly.

A thought suddenly occurred to Knox as he grew to the height to better fit the large assembly machines and the massive cannon-like boomstick that was attached to an arm that made even his look miniature in comparison. Could he shrink items, even a bit if he were to hold them as he transformed? He decided that a quick series of tests were in order.

"I'm going to try something, a test of sorts, to see if I can permanently shrink things by adjusting my size, and releasing an item, then adjusting my size again," Knox said.

Mr. Tome nodded but said nothing.

Knox went over to a large piece of metal and grabbed hold of it, then he repressed his Titan form, shrinking himself along with the item in his hand. Next, he set it aside and prepared to change again, but only seconds after releasing it, the item grew back to its normal size.

Well shoot.

There went that idea, Knox thought, sharing a look with Mr. Tome.

"Seems like they retain their shape after a time," Mr. Tome said. "Perhaps there is a trick to it. Keep working on it and see if you can force a state change of the item while maintaining your own shape."

Knox could see what angle Mr. Tome was coming from, but he doubted instantly that he could do it. When he grew and shrunk, he was forcing and suppressing himself, his very being, and his body just reacted without thought. To separate the process into pieces just wasn't something he felt capable of doing right now.

But he tried, holding the rod he tried to imagine it shrinking to its smaller size, from several paces long to only a pace or two. But it was like staring at the wall and watching paint dry, it was boring and nothing really happened. But he continued to try different ways, even shrinking and enlarging himself a few times to test how long it took the rod to shrink.

After nearly an hour of messing around he pushed the idea from his mind and looked at Mr. Tome. "It won't work, I'm just not in control of the changes like you might think. It happens because of me doing something else, not because I choose to be bigger or smaller."

"I bet there is a trick to it, keep trying on your own time. I think I've worked out a thing or two about this boomstick," Mr. Tome said. He'd found his way atop the large flat table where the gun was set and had been working on it for some time. "A lot of this has to do with rune work, more your area of expertise, but the design is something I can replicate on a smaller scale, I'm sure of it."

With that, they went to work, Mr. Tome taking notes and Knox doing the same but mostly focusing on the runework involved. It was surprisingly simple, more of a transfer of power that went through some magnifying lens that took the raw energy and focused it to the point of a needle. Mr. Tome would have to handle the glass work, but Knox could do the rest.

They informed Sintra that there would be a small delay and spent the next two days straight working on the project, hand in hand until Mr. Tome had produced, with Knox's help, a smaller handheld version of the device. On its first test, Knox cut a tree in half with it and depleted the monster core in a single blast. But after some tweaking he was able to power it with his mana and get a dozen shots off before his own mana was depleted.

Finally, the time came, and the literal army of people departed, leaving only a few dozen behind with a hundred golems, Mic, and Aetex. Following Sintra into the massive ground crack that still hadn't closed up, they quickly found themselves in a dark massive tunnel that curved downward. These were artificially made by Sintra on their way up using Elementalist powers, so they were sturdy and not prone to failure.

They lit the way with magical light balls that Knox had designed some time ago, as torches would bring too much smoke in such a closed space. They traveled with five people shoulder to shoulder, so they snaked a good distance back before everyone made it underground. Knox was at the head with Sintra, and his party, which included Dernal, Terrim, Murdoch, and a few others.

As the spear of the group, they'd scout ahead and look for threats, such as the spiders that Aetex had once encountered. It was that same type of spider that attacked them later on the third day of travels. It started with just a few spiders, some as big as a man, but most not. It wasn't until they killed all these off that a massive spider the size of the tunnel appeared, blocking their way.

"Stand back and let us handle it," Murdoch said. "We need the essence more than you do."

Knox just shrugged, feeling out toward the spider with his sense and finding it to be a suitable match for the rest of his group, he sat back and watched the fight play out.

The fight started with Terrim rushing forward, shield raised, with Murdoch and Frederick at his heels. Terrim slammed into a leg, cutting down with his enhanced axe and drawing a line of gore. Murdoch appeared a moment later, slashing with his weapon and leaving several lines. He had no specific offensive abilities other than his voice, but he remained an expert fencer.

Frederick on the other hand had an abundance of abilities and activated one immediately. Throwing a green bolt of withering energy at the spider's head, followed by spectral chains reaching up to gather around its legs, slowing it considerably. The spider broke one of the chains and was about to slam down on Terrim when Murdoch proved his class wasn't just good for diplomatic reasons.

He shouted out a command that even Knox felt, a command to stop and the spider listened, halting in place as Terrim slammed forward taking a leg off about seven paces above the ground. It spewed forth green ichor as it wobbled back and forth. Suddenly Murdoch moved and began to climb, moving with a speed that surprised Knox.

Before long, with Terrim and Frederick fighting off sprays of webbing and strikes of spider legs, Murdoch reached the top, the spider unable to pull him down with its massive legs.

Knox wanted so badly to help his friends, but at the same time he knew the importance of letting them have a win by themselves, so he stayed his hand even when Murdoch nearly fell off from a height that could be back breaking. But instead of falling, he slashed downward and caught himself. The spider cried out in pain and slammed itself against the tunnel wall, shaking the ground and once again making Knox want to step in before the tunnel collapsed.

But, biting his lip and hoping it wasn't a mistake, Knox withheld his help as Murdoch spoke another command to the spider and it stiffened. All the while Frederick and Terrim beat it down, with Henry standing behind them throwing out heals as needed. Knox shared a look with Dernal, who just shrugged, even though he was capable enough to take out the spider with how fast he'd risen, but he knew the importance of letting them have a win as well.

So, the fight continued on for another several dozen seconds, though it felt like excruciating minutes. Back and forth, the battle went, with Murdoch nearly falling to his death more times than Knox cared to count. Until finally, he came around the side, holding tight to hair-like protrusions on the spider's massive head, and stabbing it right in the face.

Several more smaller spiders suddenly appeared from behind the larger one. Though the larger spider was slowing and likely close to death, Murdoch had to escape back or be overwhelmed. Or at least that is what Knox thought. Instead, he held out a hand and spoke to the closest ones, turning them against the other spiders.

The battle ended with Terrim taking the final of the legs down to a stub and cleaving hard into its center as the spider lowered itself. Murdoch dismounted after killing his opponents, two spiders landing beside him, ready to continue to fight at his side. With a swish and flick, Murdoch put them down as well.

The fight ended and Knox finally took a breath. His friends were far more capable than he'd thought of giving them credit for and he was glad he hadn't one-shot the spider, as he knew he could have.

CHAPTER 28
WELL TRAVELED

THEY MADE camp in the shell of a city that Sintra said used to be booming with people even when they'd passed through it months before. However, it was a ghost town now, not a single person could be found, though many corpses lay rotting in the streets and in their homes. They cleared out a section of houses and made camp for the night, Knox insisted that they shouldn't stay more than a night here as the place gave him the creeps.

It was during the night that the trouble started, first with one of the scouts not reporting back, then with screaming in the distance.

"I'm going out to see if I can help them," Knox said, Terrim nodded and started to gather his things as well. "I can do it alone," Knox added, but already his party was gearing up, Dernal included.

"You can do anything alone, but that doesn't mean you have to," Dernal said, pulling his belt tight and adjusting his weapon.

The night, if it was truly nighttime, was dark and foreboding in the underground. What little light they had cast long shadows and every few feet Knox could have sworn he saw something moving within them. But when they'd check they found nothing, so they continued onward and forward. There was a scent in the air, something stronger than even the scent of death and decay, but Knox couldn't place it.

There was a bitterness to it that reminded him of something in the past, and he only realized what it was when they came up to a figure standing in the dark, with long black hair and a sickle held out to one side. The dark child stood over the corpse of the scout they'd sent out, blood dripping from her weapon.

She turned her head ever so slightly to indicate that she saw them and began to laugh. It started as a low chuckle, then evolved to a manic laugh that sent ripples of emotion through Knox.

Readying his Luminous Surge spell, he growled in response to seeing this figure once more. For one thing, it meant the Dark Titan was on to them and knew they were coming. For another, he'd thought himself rid of her.

Figures rose out of the dark all around them, each with a hazy black shadow around them and the laughter reached a fever pitch before cutting off completely as she turned to face them.

"You will die here," she whispered in words so low that Knox barely heard them. "And when you fall, you will rise again, but under the dark ladies power."

In response Knox released his spell and it smashed through the darkness like a beacon of light, pushing back the many dark risen entities and obliterating the dark child. She screamed in agony, but as she had a tendency to do, she disappeared before Knox could be sure he got her.

"We need to get back to the group, these risen dark fiends are going to be an issue," Knox said, recasting his spell behind them and clearing a path. His spell was so powerful that those corpses infected with the dark ooze fell to pieces at his command, but he could only cast so fast and literally hundreds were rising all around them.

Turning as swiftly as he could just as two grabbed ahold of Terrim, Knox cut him free with a simple flick of his axe. He felt the spiritual pull take in the power they had, and he felt sick for it. It was while using his axe against the dark ooze that he felt the first stirrings of the dragon he'd trapped within it. A hunger for destruction and a pull for power.

Knox began to use only his axe, listening to the drawing of the axe to guide his movements. He was a killing machine, but even so they would be overwhelmed soon.

Just as hordes more appeared around them, three figures appeared cutting through the mass as easily as Knox had been moments before. Tress, Terris, and Zhul looked almost bored as they cut through the throngs of animated dead.

"We've decided it is time to move on," Tress said, smiling. "The caravan is already prepping, and we've got a long way to go if we are going to get them out in one piece. Care to help?"

"Gladly," Knox said, his party having never stopped fighting back the encroaching horde. Knox ignored the call of the axe for a moment and began to throw down his multiplier spell with Radiant Glyph. When he was finished, the trio giving him all the room and time he required, he unleashed a powerful Luminous Surge that parted the sea of undead for nearly a mile.

"I can cast this over the entire caravan from behind," Knox said, the effort of the battle hadn't even begun to tire him out yet, but his heartbeat furiously in his chest and his palms grew sweaty. To alleviate the feelings, he allowed his body to morph into its true form, rising several heads above all but Terrim and allowing his skin to turn the sheen of gold.

It was enough to calm his body and push out the darkness that he hadn't realized had been trying to take root. He sighed from the feeling of power that washed over him, so relaxed he felt that it startled him when a voice sounded in his head.

"Feed me more of those delicious ones," it said, a hunger in its voice that Knox recognized.

"So, you do have a voice?" Knox asked inside of his own head, figuring the dragon soul he'd captured could hear him.

He was right, it responded almost immediately. *"I hunger for more, go and fight!"*

"Alright," Knox said aloud, rushing forward and signaling for his group to follow. He cut down as many with his axe as he did with his spells, but in time they made it to the main body of the caravan. They were fighting for their lives, and Knox could see that some had already fallen.

Casting Luminous Surge on them, he healed many and destroyed the root of darkness in twice as many more.

The night was long and hard, but they made it out of the city after several hours of fighting. Knox was just beginning to feel the pull of exhaustion from the constant spell casting and fighting when they made camp several miles outside the city.

"You three keep watch if you can," Knox ordered Tress, Terris, and Zhul. "With as strong as you are you should be able to resist the dark ooze if you get infected. Come to me if you feel strange so I can purge you of it."

With that task assigned, he got a count of the dead, they'd lost sixty-five souls already, five of those were golems ripped apart beyond repair. Knox recognized several of the names and made it a point to visit the left-over party members, offering thanks for their sacrifice. It took much of the night before he finally sat at a fire with his friends, ready to relax.

He didn't need sleep just yet, he wouldn't for several days at least, and only if he kept up the laborious pace that he'd been doing all day, which was unlikely given the threats they'd faced on the open road.

"We almost lost old Henry," Terrim was saying, gesturing to a man asleep on a bed roll some dozen paces off. "This quest of yours is going to see one of us dead, isn't it?"

Knox couldn't tell the state of Terrim's emotions at that moment, but his voice was flat and not filled with humor as it normally would be.

"Perhaps," Knox said, looking the man right in the eyes.

"To death," Terrim said, a hint of pride in his voice.

"To death," echoed the rest of the group along with Knox.

"I'll fight to keep each of you alive, even if it costs me my life," Knox said. He felt as if he needed to reassure his friends that he wouldn't abandon them, but each of them looked at him with looks that told him the words weren't necessary.

"And we will gladly die to see that this quest of yours is accomplished," Dernal said, surprising Knox with his words.

"Not that we necessarily want to die," Murdoch added. "But I'm with old Dern here, we know how important it is that this Dark Titan falls. So, if that means we die to get the job done, then damnit you all better say nice things about me at my funeral. Oh, and I want a statue made up where I look heroic and perhaps tell tales to the ladies of how if not for my noble sacrifice all would have been lost."

"I do not fear death," Frederick said, breaking his normal silence in matters. "But if you all fall, I will seek to add your spirits to my horde, and you will fight on after death."

"Your horde?" Knox asked, he was unsure how many spirits Frederick could call on now, but it had started just with his family.

"With all those who have died, a tenth of them lingers and I add them to my family," Frederick said, gesturing around himself.

Knox's sense could almost feel something around Frederick, but it was hard to place and so different from any other powers he'd felt that he couldn't be certain it was anything at all. Such were the mysteries of the spirit realm that existed alongside our own physical realm.

"Can you manifest any of the spirits, is Sarah with you?" Knox asked, suddenly feeling empty inside.

"I can," Frederick said and with a wave of his hand his father appeared sitting beside him. He waved up at Knox. "Unfortunately, Sarah did not linger after death, she went on to wherever it is that spirits go after death."

The pit in Knox's stomach grew and he didn't know how he felt about it. Sure, it was nice to know that her spirit had moved on, but what did that even mean? Was there an afterlife like some thought or did that just mean her spirit wasn't strong enough to hold on and she went the way of all energy, dispersing out into the world. It pained Knox to think that she was gone forever, but it pained him even more when he thought about Beth and how she might die while he struggled to get strong enough to free her.

They had a long journey ahead of them, several weeks at least, and many cities like the one before them to pass through. They'd expected military response to such a large group traveling, Sintra even had contacts that she thought would be joining them, but each city they traveled through was a deadzone of activity and filled with risen dark ones.

They fought long and hard, the weeks turning to a month, then two as they moved every deeper into the dark underground. It was with great relief and much anticipation that Sintra said they neared the final city, her capital and former seat of power.

Knox gathered all of his most trusted allies together for a final meeting where they discussed his plan. He would go forth and destroy the gem by himself, as a solo mission would attract less attention. No one liked the plan, but many, like Zhul, thought that there was a wisdom in it, however even he thought that two could go and be just as sneaky.

He gently reminded them all that he was several stages ahead of them in every way, and that no one, not even a combined Tress and Terris, could keep up with him at full run, not to mention that he could teleport great distances.

Then of course Ramses spoke up and Knox quieted.

"As much as it pains me to say, the power required to strike down that gem might be too much for even you," he said. "You will take me, as that is why I've come, and together we can strike it down and then face off against the Dark Titan herself."

Knox nodded, convinced that maybe he did need one person to help him. Ramses had shown to possess a mighty power himself, even his skin tone and size had increased along the way as he grew stronger. He wasn't quite to the point where Knox was, in fact pretty far from it, but he had access to higher level spells that Knox didn't, seeing as Knox was only powerful in attributes and not level yet.

Knox had learned a few new tricks as he filled out his traits and talent tree, but it turned out to be a mostly useless ability since he possessed the Aurorapex. The new ability or spell he'd gotten was called Dawn's Ascendance. It allowed him to channel the peak might of the Titan of Light, transforming into a being of Radiant Metallic skin with enhanced attributes for a time.

However, the two times he'd used it, he felt very little difference than when he wasn't repressing himself. However, he had unlocked several talent free points and gained access to many strengthening talents. One offensive one that he was keeping in his back pocket was the peak talent for the Luminous Vanguard tree, Radiant Judgement.

Radiant Judgement allowed him to harness the full might of the power of light to judge a specific target and bypass all defensive magic for a short window of time. He planned on using this new talent to take down the Dark Titan when the time came, but it was unpracticed and new to him, the knowledge being provided as with all talents.

All of which to say that Knox felt comfortable in his own power to get the job done, but happy to have Ramses at his side when the actual battle came upon them. With the meeting done, Ramses and Knox prepared for their secret mission into the city and to the palace to deal with the dark gem that gave the Dark Titan so much of her power, or so they hoped.

CHAPTER 29
COVERT OPERATION

Knox and Ramses listened for the tenth time, or at least it felt that way, about how best to navigate the city and get to the castle. Sintra told them of underground passageways, secret ways here and there. Knox took many notes, but he was more interested in the city in general. So far it was the busiest place they'd encountered; the streets bustled with activity and if not for a secret path that took them to a hidden cave within the outskirts of the city, Knox feared they wouldn't be able to keep his people hidden for long.

It was odd to him that they'd not needed the large fighting force just yet, but the quest wasn't over yet and the time might come when a fighting force was needed. He hoped it wouldn't, but only because his sense told him literally thousands of people live below and if only a quarter of them could fight, they'd still be outnumbered.

"Remember, stay under a cloak and hood and you'll be fine even in public," Sintra was saying, reminding them once more that her people valued their privacy so random checks were not common.

Knox changed out his bright golden cloak for a dark black and purple one from one of Sintra's people, Ramses doing the same.

With the hoods up and the natural darkness that filled the underground, they were easy to hide. Even Sintra approved after seeing them and they left to sneak into the city through a special passageway that Sintra had shown them.

All the while they kept quiet and moved with stealth, while trying their best to remain inconspicuous. They made it into the street level, a thriving city bustling around them and headed for the castle on their planned route. The castle could be seen in the distance as a great silhouette with a massive glowing purple gem above it. The purple light provided most of the light that filled the city and Knox wondered how dark it would become without it.

All was going well until they neared the passage Sintra had told them to use, guards in purple armor stood outside the house and the area was cleared of people. So much so that Knox turned aside before their trajectory was recognized.

"What do we do?" Ramses asked, a bit louder than Knox would have liked.

"This is the only way into the castle," Knox said. "We have to get in but let's lurk around a bit and see when they do a guard change."

So, they did just that, walking in a slow circle from block to block, but staying far enough away not to gather attention. Sintra had given them the location of a few of her contacts in the city as well, but Knox wasn't ready to abandon his plan so easily, so they continued to wait for the guard change. It happened some two hours later, Knox and Ramses sat at a diner of sorts where they had been sitting outside, no wait staff had come to bother them, Sintra's people truly valued their privacy it would seem.

They waited even longer, going from place to place while Knox watched the new guards with his sense. Some twelve hours later, the bustle of the city never seemed to ebb or flow more or less than it did when they'd arrived, the guard shift changed again.

"There we have it," Knox said. "Let's move now and we should have twelve hours before the next guards come and notice anything wrong."

Ramses nodded and they headed for the two guardsmen. With a wave of his hand, both clutched at their throats and Knox took one on the arm and through the door. He sensed no one within and so they weren't surprised to find it empty. They'd moved fast enough that they might not have been seen and thanks to Ramses' ability to cut off the sound coming from their throats, they'd made little noise before Knox could knock them out.

He stripped them of armor and weapons, tying them up and gagging them with the little supplies they'd brought. He was trying to avoid killing too many of Sintra's people if he could help it, but he wouldn't hesitate in the heat of battle. Ramses chanted over them and informed Knox that they wouldn't awake for at least a day if not longer.

The house they found themselves in was small, only two bedrooms and they found the tunnel leading into the palace where Sintra said it would be, under a carpet in the cooling cellar. It appeared untouched and Knox thought for sure that though the house might have been located, they hadn't known about the way in, or so he hoped.

It worked in a way that allowed them to close it behind themselves without leaving a trace of what they'd been up to, the carpet literally attached to the door as it was.

The tunnel was narrow, and Knox realized that without his suppression of his Titan form, he'd be hard pressed to get through it even at a hunch. Ramses was a tall man and had to hunch a little as it were, but they managed it, moving at a swift pace and hoping that the other end wouldn't be guarded.

It was supposed to lead out into a palace cellar where food would be kept cool. Moving at a decent pace, it still took them several hours of walking through the winding pathways to reach their destination.

When finally, they reached the end, it took them a moment in the dark of the tunnel and the dim light from Knox's light contraption, to even notice the narrow tunnel leading up with handholds added into the stone. Knox barely fit up this upward climb and with the sides pressing in all around him he felt more than a little pressed in.

Ramses' lighter weight and skinnier self, fit much better than Knox with his armor and cloak, so much so that Ramses complained a few times that Knox was setting a very slow pace, and he should pick it up. Knox ignored the verbal jabs and kept going, focusing on moving.

Finally, they reached a wooden trapdoor set into the stone and Knox reached out with his sense, finding the way ahead empty of anyone. He pushed upward on the door, but it held fast. Increasing the strength he put into it, he got it to move, but not before making something above crash down noisily.

He pushed as hard as possible and got free, making more noise, but Knox sensed no one for dozens of paces so he hoped they hadn't heard. Someone had placed crates of mushrooms atop the exit, but no guards awaited them at this end, which meant that Knox had been right. They'd suspected something to do with the house but not that it was an entrance to the keep.

Now came the difficult part, they were to stick to passageways meant for servants, and Sintra insisted that anyone they come across should be killed, as no one serving in the castle directly under the Dark Titan could be trusted. Knox didn't like this plan, but he wasn't going to fail his people because of it. So, as they moved through the passageways leading up and up, he wished hard that none would cross their path.

In an odd turn of events, his wish came true, and they were nearly at the top before he sensed anyone that might be crossing their path. He waited, and sure enough, they went another way, avoiding them. It was almost as if they could tell where they were and purposefully avoided them. But Knox knew if that were the case, they'd be found out already.

The guard change wasn't meant to happen for another eight hours, so they had time and if they hurried, they might make it out before the change even happened. Though based on the massive gem over the castle they'd seen from a distance, the people would notice when it ceased to be there. The missing light alone would be enough to cause some Chaos, but Knox was counting on that.

When finally, they reached the upper floors they had to risk going out into the area proper, a main staircase was required to reach the rooftops and the area bustled with activity. Sintra had no easy plan or path forward from here, short of 'fight your way through'.

As it turned out it wasn't going to be as bad as Knox thought, all but a single figure cleared out of the room as they neared, but it was the power this individual had that gave Knox pause. He was clearly an S Rank or above based on his aura.

"I think we've been had," Knox said. "They know we are coming, and we have a single powerful foe waiting for us."

"Can we handle him?" Ramses asked. "Surely it isn't the Dark Titan?"

"No, I haven't sensed anything that powerful yet, but this person will be a difficult challenge to deal with quietly, but I've no doubt we are a match for them," Knox said, taking a deep breath and walking out into the opening with Ramses trailing behind him.

Before them stood a massive dark-armored figure that stood nearly as tall as Knox when he stopped suppressing himself. The armor glowed with deadly potential and complex runic formations. Knox was glad that his own armor was as advanced as it was, or this guy might be scary.

Knox let the cloak fall open and his body grew to its full size, his golden armor shimmering in the low light as brightly as his own skin and hair. He looked more like a golden statue than he did a man, but it wasn't time to hold back. As they'd planned before, Ramses would do his best to restrain opponents as Knox laid out the runes necessary to multiply his attacks.

Ramses waved his hands and water lashed out, smacking the black armor and attempting to tie him up in ropes of water. Each strike sent the armored figure backwards, but it didn't allow itself to become entangled, smashing each tendril of water with puffs of black smoke.

"I am the Grand Champion of our Lady the Dark Titan, and guardian of her precious artifact. The moment you entered this castle I knew you for what you were. You do not stand a chance against me," the Dark Champion said, a sword appearing in his grasp out of a puff of black smoke. With his other hand black ooze appeared and he pointed at Knox, releasing a spray of it right for him.

Ramses was quicker though, weaving his magical water into a barrier, blocking the ooze and at the same time lashing out with tendrils of water to cut and break the armored man.

Knox finished his Radiant Glyph and released a Luminous Surge into it. The attack blasted forward and threw the knight backwards, his sword falling from his grip. But the fight wasn't over, the guardian teleported forward, his sword returning to his grip, and he slashed for Ramses.

He had just enough time to teleport himself away and lash out with a magical jet stream of water, leaving a noticeable mark on the armor. This guardian was proving to be more of a nuisance than Knox cared to admit, as he used Dimensional Shift on it, switching places and throwing it off its guard.

Pulling his axe out, he ignored the calls for blood from the dragon spirit and focused on attacking in measured strikes. Runeth metal met the black metal of the knight sword, and his arms shook from the power of the blow. Whatever this knight was, it had strength to rival Knox's own, which was saying something.

Reaching forward, he smashed out a Luminous Surge, blowing the knight backward and opened him up for a strike to the chest. Knox siphoned some of its power and the axe screamed for more. The truth of the battle was clear, Knox would win, but it would take some time.

Slamming down his foot he used Radiant Ground, followed by Radiant Rush to meet the incoming knight. His axe cut through his armor like an axe cutting through a fairly difficult tree, but in the end it cut. Back and forth they fought, Knox taking wounds here and there, the black ooze enough to slow him down but he didn't relent.

Lashes of water and all manner of other magics came crashing down on the knight as they fought, weakening him further. It wasn't until the knight turned to challenge Ramses, appearing before him sword raised, that Knox saw his chance.

He stepped forward and unleashed the Luminous Surges he'd collected in his ring, hitting the knight with a combined strike that shook the castle's foundations.

The knight screamed and then went silent, falling before the might of Knox and Ramses.

Something felt off though, pushing himself as he had, his Aurorapex felt off, like it was weakening in a way he'd not experienced for some time. Allowing himself to be suppressed helped, his form shrinking, but he worried about the future and was glad he'd brought his own suppression rings, just in case his artifact gave out on him. He knew all magical items had a limit, he just hoped he wouldn't find it before slaying the Dark Titan.

They made their way past the fallen Knight, taking up their cloaks again as they made their way to the crystal above. The staircase led to a ledge that snaked across toward the crystal. It was a massive thing, at least twenty paces tall and half as wide. And the power coming from it was unlike anything he'd ever felt before.

They needed to act fast, the Dark Titan would know that her champion fell, that her artifact was in danger. The question remained if they'd be able to take it apart though.

It was like staring into the sun when he had his sense active, so he pulled away from it and focused on what he could see with his physical eyes. Only then did he notice a stream of something pouring into the gem from all around, like a siphon of something feeding the gem. Focusing his sense once more but not directly on the gem, he saw waves of power filling it.

Knox couldn't believe where the waves were coming from as

he looked down at the city. Each person down there seemed to be giving up power, slow and steady, to the gem. This thing was a repository of power unlike anything he'd ever encountered, but something was off or wrong about it. There were no signs of runic formations when he chanced to look at it with his sense.

This gem was something different, that he couldn't explain, like a living thing that wanted more and more power, unending in its desire and hunger.

"It's like she captured the void itself," Ramses said, gesturing at the gem. "I can sense the absolute nothingness within it, forever sucking inward and consuming."

"Can we break it?" Knox asked, already he wanted to be out of close proximity to it.

"I think the real question is, do we want to?" Ramses asked. "The power that will be released might very well level the entire castle, if not the city."

"What if we siphoned away the power before it could do that?" Knox asked, he gazed deeper and used his full sight as a Titan to view it, but even in this level of sight, the gem looked foreign and opposite of everything he'd seen so far of magic. Like an antimagic of some sort.

"I wouldn't recommend it," Ramses said. "Something is happening to the power contained within, something dark and terrible."

As Knox peered at and around it, looking far deeper than ever before, he felt a sense of something within. "I think this is an egg," Knox said. "And I'm not sure we can destroy it."

To test his theory, he used Luminous Surge on it and as he'd thought, before the attack could do any harm, the power was siphoned away and into the egg. They were dealing with something far older than he'd imagined, older than even the realm which Gowlen had created. He knew instinctively that if this egg were to hatch, it would be the end of the world as he knew it.

Suddenly, black ooze dripped forth from the egg and formed into several monstrous creatures of tentacles and teeth.

"It is defending itself," Ramses said, lashing out with his water magic. "What do we do?"

"I don't know," Knox said, desperation painting his voice.

Knox engaged the black ooze monsters, slashing through and blasting them away with his light magic. It worked super effectively against them, so he knew his light magic was the key, but what could he do to pierce the shell of the egg, it would just siphon away his magic before it hit.

A hungry voice inside of Knox cried out and a plan began to form. It was taking magical energy, but how hard would the outer shell be against a powerful physical strike?

He cut through more black slime monsters and Ethereal Stepped beside the egg. It pulled at him, wanting all of what he was as he transformed into a full Titan of Light. Knox swung down with his axe, but his strike rattled his bones as the perfect gem of an egg held fast. The hungry dragon screamed in protest, but a physical attack wasn't the answer.

Landing hard, Knox rolled and thought of the final card he had to play, his Radiant Judgement. It was magic, but it was said to bypass all defenses. The attack had its drawbacks though, he knew he could do it once before he'd require a long night's rest. So, if he encountered the Dark Titan, he'd have no way to deal with her without his special talent. But this was the more dire situation and perhaps the key to the Dark Titan's downfall.

Standing firm Knox first activated Dawn's Ascendance, and he felt a pressure remove itself from the Aurorapcx, then he did his ultimate talent, Radiant Judgement.

Light, terrible and brighter than a noon day sun, crashed down all around him as he focused on the target, the egg, the great terrible darkness that lay within. At first, he was sure the spell had failed, its power being leached away as fast as it could manifest, but as his two ultimate abilities merged, he felt something in the egg give.

Until finally the sound of cracking glass could be heard, and the egg shattered, releasing a wave of energy that threw Knox and

Ramses from the top of the castle, while laying waste to most of the structure. Finding a spot on the ground, Knox Ethereal Stepped to safety as debris crashed down all around him. Ramses appeared beside him a moment later, looking haggard.

Then, from above the castle came a roar that shook Knox to the bones. He shrunk as his magic faded, suddenly unable to control the process. The Aurorapex was badly damaged, it leaked light visible to the naked eye now and he could feel he was no longer fighting at full power. Slamming his hand down he flooded it with power and for the moment it stabilized, the artifact as old as the Titans themselves.

Something had come from the egg above them, a terrible beast in the shape of a humanoid but with tentacles coming out in every direction, great swathes of power. Then as fast as it appeared, it was gone, in the literal blink of an eye.

Next came a scream of rage from the castle and a robed figure appeared and Knox got his first sight of the Dark Titan. She was emanating terrible awful power, but not as much as Knox would have guessed when he'd been told the stories of her deeds.

"We've found our opponent," Knox said, turning to Ramses only to find him sitting on the ground holding his gut. "Ramses!"

"A fragment of that shell has pierced me deeply," Ramses said, coughing blood. "I'm afraid I'm going to be of little help, unless..."

"I can heal you," Knox said, summoning forth a Luminous Surge but the power was siphoned away into him just like when he'd attacked the egg. "Here let me pull it out first."

"Not enough time," Ramses said, coughing more blood. "Let me give you my power, combined you will be a match for her."

"You can't," Knox said, knowing the transfer of power between Titan's might be possible, but doing so would end his life.

"I must," Ramses said. "Please let me do this, one final act of heroism and a reason for those old buggards and their kin to remember me."

Knox put a hand on Ramses shoulder, ready to dig in and try to get the shard out, but Ramses looked him in the eyes and then power hit him. Some of it was being siphoned into the gem shard, but most was making it to Knox, and he felt his essence fill and his level hitting new heights.

The power flowed and Knox began to seize up from it, so vast was the essence being poured into him. And with each point transferred, Ramses began to weaken and wither, until he was just a husk of what he once was, and the power transfer ended. The rings around his fingers cracked and turned to dust, followed by Ramses himself, along with all his gear, leaving a glowing purple shard behind.

Just like that Knox had lost his best chance at defeating the Dark Titan, but the power inside of him thrummed. He had reached a point where he'd only need a single ring to repress his power, his level had reached into the eighties, far further than he expected to make it in such a short period of time. He was nearly a full Titan by measure of power and abilities now.

This took a good deal of pressure off the Aurorapex, making him able to access the godlike tier of his attributes all the easier. Letting his true form take shape, he looked down to where Ramses had been and made a silent promise to him.

He would kill the Dark Titan and he would raise up a new Titan Born in her and his place. He would be victorious on this day.

CHAPTER 30
DARK TITAN

WITH RAMSES FALLEN and a crowd beginning to appear around him, Knox wondered at what true chance he had against the Dark Titan.

Shouts of alarm followed, and soldiers began to appear with weapons drawn. It looked like Knox would be fighting a lesser battle first, but he'd need to conserve his strength for when the time came.

The Dark Titan appeared before him suddenly, as if by teleportation, and everyone around went to a knee.

"You dare trespass into my realms, release my prize, and stand in challenge to me?" she asked, her voice rather ordinary and feminine.

Knox, his full Titan appearance shining through, answered her.

"I am Knox, the Titan of Light, here to put out your dark deeds."

The Dark Titan laughed, a wicked sounding noise if Knox had ever heard one.

"Who I am is of no consequence, I've surpassed even the title of Titan, you stand no chance against me little worm," she said.

According to Knox's sense, she was bluffing, he had more

power than her right now, though she would be the strongest opponent he'd ever faced and doing so alone wasn't ideal.

"I believe you are weak, and I'll strike you down," Knox said, stalling for time as he worked out his best path forward. He'd used up his ring, his two abilities that required rest, so he had only his bread-and-butter abilities and they would have to do.

Knox began chanting a spell just as she responded.

"I've been weakened, but when that void beast returns and I gain mastery over it, you will fall before me," she said, barely getting out her last words as a Luminous Surge smashed into her.

The move wasn't the strongest he could muster, but it hit her with a force equal to any that he'd cast before, besides the multiplied force of his ring and runic formations perhaps. Using the time, he'd bought himself he cast Mystic Armor and Mystic Veil over himself.

Next, he used Reality Ripple on her, slowing her response time and buying him a few precious seconds. With that he cast Astral Projection, pushing it beyond the limits of its spell. Several dozen copies of him appeared and he hid among the back of them as he began to charge his ring with a Luminous Surge. The first one locked into place as the Dark Titan shot out a beam of darkness that rebounded back to her as if she herself were being attacked by it.

Knox got two of them locked into place before she'd blown through the majority of his astral projections. Using Dimensional Shift on her, he felt the pull of something hit him, but the spell went through, and they switched places just in time for her to get hit by her own attack.

She cursed and scrambled, her robes moving back to reveal skeletal hands. This surprised Knox as she had no flesh at all, and her bones were milky white, not metallic like he'd expected them to be.

"Why are you obsessed with spreading the darkness, what is the point of that black ooze?" Knox asked, hoping to distract her for another few seconds as he locked in another spell.

It didn't work, she shot out a web of darkness that dripped with the ooze and Knox was forced to Ethereal Step away to avoid getting taken in by it.

However, she did answer after attacking. "Power, I sought power to prevent the ending of our world. This creature," she motioned up and around, but Knox saw no creature, "is the answer to the threat Titan Gowlen presents on his return. It is older than even the Titans, created by the first ones, primordial beasts of death and destruction. If I could harness that power, I would have been successful. But you released the being too soon! It hasn't gathered enough power to slay any Titans, much less the mighty Gowlen."

She was much more talkative than Knox imagined she would be, perhaps he might be able to sway her back to the side of sanity if he tried?

"The path to defeating Gowlen is a united front," Knox said, unleashing a Luminous Surge followed by an Arcane Pulse, that sent her spinning backward and out of range. She flew forward, literally ignoring the laws of gravity as Aetex had on occasions, before speaking again.

"There is no united front that can stand against them," she said, shooting forward a wave of darkness. Knox summoned forth a Prism Ward, golden light surrounding him in a globe and took the hit full on. His barrier held and he activated Solar Wings to take to the sky after her.

Slashing out with his hungry axe, he cut a portion of her robes, revealing more skeleton beneath it. "If all the Titan Engines are linked," Knox yelled as they fought back and forth, the Dark Titan using summoned weapons of darkness to ward off his powerful blows, "then we can stand against what is coming!"

"The Titans here are too weak," she screamed back. "You see how easily your friend fell, his power not enough to even face the void beast."

"But together we can be victorious!" Knox yelled back, as he rained down blow after blow, shattering her weapons of darkness one at a time.

Then a thought occurred to him, that shard that took in energy and killed Ramses, could he use it against her somehow? His Solar Wings faded, though he felt that he could have kept them going for an extended period of time now. He hit the ground near where Ramses fell and picked up the shard of purple glowing rock. It immediately began to siphon away his power, but he focused hard on his left hand, solidifying himself and preventing it from doing so.

With all of his new influx of power he found he had unprecedented control over it as well and he would not be letting it go so easily. Now it was time to see if she had the same kind of control or not.

Despite the cooldown on it, Knox was able to force Solar Wings to activate early, though he could feel it doubled the cost of the spell, and he took off into the sky, slashing away attack after attack.

"You will never get the Titans to stand together," she said as he got within earshot. "The Titan of Death and the Titan of Strength are more powerful than even I, and they have an indescribably firm grip on their nations. Join me and perhaps, once we've recovered the void beast, we can use its influence to bring them to heel as well."

As she spoke, she summoned several copies of herself made of the black ooze and each of them came at Knox with weapons drawn. Knox slashed out, cutting one but it just reformed a moment later and he took a hit to the chest, his barrier already gone. His armor took the hit and he felt it, the black ooze, the influence of the void beast as it tried to take hold of his mind, filling it with thoughts of murder and mayhem.

He slammed to the ground, each of them following, as he cast Radiant Ground, then Aethereal Step, creating a double dose of damaged ground that also healed and purified him. With the effects of his step ability, he was faster in the line it created and he fought with a ferocity that could match the dragon soul within his axe.

His strikes began to glow with light, doing extra light damage with each strike and tearing apart the oozelings that were attacking him. One by one he took them down, just as he felt the influences get pushed out of himself and his mood return to normal.

However, the Dark Titan had not been idle during this exchange. Knox looked up to see several streams of power entering her and all around the mass of crowds were on the ground, unconscious. The sounds of battle could be heard distantly, and Knox spared a glance toward his people.

They were fighting their way through an army of elves to get to him, but why? They knew, certainly, that he alone was the best chance against this Titan, they would only slow him down. But regardless of what he thought, they fought on through impossible odds to try and help him. It warmed his soul to think of their sacrifice and he knew he couldn't let it be in vain.

The Dark Titan also seemed distracted by the new sounds of battle, her stream of power cutting off as she sucked out the essence of all those present. Knox felt with his sense and could feel that she'd grown stronger, so much so that he wasn't sure which of them were more fit.

She began to summon forth a mighty ball of darkness around her and Knox answered her attack with one of his own. First, he threw down the fastest redoubling runic formation that he could with Radiant Glyph, then he unleashed a three times charged Luminous Surge from his ring through the runic formation. He would end this now, or so he hoped, as the darkness around him grew he could feel her pouring every ounce of her power into this attack and he worried if his would be enough.

He cast an additional Luminous Surge right after the next and poured his power into it, pushing the first attack forward and maintaining the second much longer than it was meant to be. The powers clashed in a spray of light and darkness. He felt himself being pushed back, but he somehow managed to cast Solar Wings without the verbal component or cutting off his maintained spell, the wings just appeared and beat wildly to keep him in place.

He felt his Aurorapex begin to give way under the strain of his attack and if he held on any longer, he would break it, but he had to, the darkness was still coming and though he felt himself pushing at the very bounds and rules of the Titan System, he fought onward, pushing more essence into a continuous Luminous Surge.

His focusing band, the Aurorapex, shattered on his arm and he felt the pull once more of the shard he held. His axe lay at his side, and the continuous Luminous Surge came from his right palm, but he transferred it to his eyes, redoubling the attack and blinding himself to everything but what his sense could detect.

Then with his right hand he threw the shard into the mix of magic clashing together and felt as both spells began to get sucked into the shard. Knox finally cut off his spell, using Nexus Shift to leave behind an explosion of light and appear on the ground.

His entire body ached, and he could feel his essence burning away to maintain his increased attributes, but he quickly slipped on the final restraining band, his core stopped shaking and he felt himself grow noticeably weaker, both in Mind, Body, and Spirit. But not so weak that he felt he was out of this fight, he still, thanks to Ramses' sacrifice, had enough essence to stand against any foe he'd ever encountered.

In fact, he felt like he was on the cusp of reaching the power that the Aurorapex had granted him, though he had no way of getting essence enough to make that final jump. Instead, he'd fight as best he could, his powers strong but not so strong as before.

He looked at his hands and was surprised to see most of the metallic sheen was gone, though still there if you knew what to look for, similar to how Ramses had looked. Even his size had diminished by a head or two worth of height. When he tapped into his sense he felt that he could almost see the threads that wove the world together, but it was a distant thing and no longer something he could manipulate.

Seeing the shards of the Aurorapex on the ground he made a mental note to collect them and study their construction if he survived this night.

The cloud of power and haze finally lifted, showing a tattered and ripped robe of the Dark Titan, her skeleton showing through as she floated above. If she'd been hurt or weakened at all, Knox couldn't tell the difference with his sense or otherwise. Between them fell the shard, now sparking with captured potential.

As she began to summon more black ooze versions of herself to do battle against Knox, he had an idea. His spirit enabled him to suck in essence at an increased rate and it was the spirit of a mighty S Ranked Dragon, perhaps even stronger. What if he tried to pull the energy out of the shard, sure the void might attempt to corrupt him, but it would have to be worth the risk if it brought him back to full power.

As if she had a similar plan in mind, or perhaps just wanting to keep the shard away from Knox, her black ooze copies slammed down all around the shard, and she began to cast out smaller globes of darkness toward him.

Knox rushed forward using Ethereal Step to try and bypass the dark figures, but one appeared before him, stabbing low with a dagger. Barely fast enough to dodge the blow, Knox pulled out his axe, cleaving the arm free of the one that had attacked him. This left him not paying attention to the Dark Titan above though and he took a direct hit to the back.

He needed to focus on his sense more than ever now, there were too many strong opponents and if he failed here, he'd be failing not only his friends but the entire world.

"Join me and together we will raise up the strongest generation possible outside the laws of the system and its nonsensical rules," she paused her attack to monologue more which Knox was perfectly fine with as he closed his eyes and let his sense take over.

The dark oozes were harder to sense, but the lack of anything was more a giveaway than anything else, and he weaved through the void, striking out when they got too close as she continued speaking, occasionally throwing out bolts of darkness that he dodged and danced through to get to the center.

"Can't you see that the Titan System is just a way to limit us, this Path of the Titans that they set up doesn't raise us to their power, it pulls us within their grasp. Would you join ranks with one such a Gowlen, to be his servant as he creates and destroys entire worlds on a whim?"

She obviously knew more about Titan Gowlen than he did and if he weren't fighting for his life on the edge of a dagger, he'd ask her more or try to work out a way to get more information, but as it were, he fought to survive. Yet she continued as Knox moved ever closer to his goal.

"I reached the final level, the end of the Path of the Titans just as your predecessor did, we even joined our engines together for a time, do you think that we were a match for Titan Gowlen? No! The powers to create and destroy as he does have remained out of our reach. We could sense the weaves but interacting with them proved too difficult, though your predecessor, my friend, had some success whereas I had none. He created that artifact which you so casually allowed to be destroyed using his talents. Perhaps if I'd allowed him to live any longer, he might have been successful, but I'd found a better way, a path forward that relied not on the System but on true raw power. The void beast will be our savior!"

Knox was barely listening at this point, so close was his goal. He danced through the final of the obstacles, cutting it down with a mighty slash of light and activating Solar Wings, he rose into the air and aimed at the shard with his axe. Releasing the spell, he came crashing down, axe behind him and ready to strike. With a mighty clash he shattered the shard and put a notch in the metal of the axe, but it held together as essence poured out.

The shard had been strong, but the abundance of essence inside of it had weakened it somehow, making it susceptible to a physical attack. It was an imperfect vessel to hold energy now, the full crystal would have been able to reflect his attack without worry, but this piece was left wanting.

Essence poured out all around him and the system guided it into him, but Knox also grabbed hold of some himself, using the last bit of control he had over the weaves of magic. The Dark Titan had spoken of not having control over these threads, but Knox had proven her words wrong. Though his control was limited at the best of times, it only increased with the passage of time.

If he could share this gift with other Titans, then perhaps they could stand against the Titan Gowlen after all. The very power of creation and destruction. It was a shame that he couldn't use it now to take apart his opponent, but he felt himself growing stronger as the essence filled him, then suddenly he hit a threshold, and he knew he was no longer in need of a suppression ring.

Suddenly the world opened up to him as he ripped off the ring and his power bloomed. He'd reached the apex of the system, his walk along the Path of the Titans could truly begin now. He felt more strongly than ever the threads of creations around him as his body grew and his skin turned golden.

He was the Titan of Light, the one to enlighten the way of the rest of the Titans against the forces of evil that would threaten to do harm to them. It was time to show the Dark Titan what it truly meant to be a Titan.

With a flexing of his magical muscles, he strummed the threads of creation and destruction, unmaking her attack she'd begun to gather up and destroying the remnants of her copy spell.

Then he cast Astral Projection, sending out nearly a hundred copies of himself but more than just illusions this time, they had a piece of him. He strummed the threads of creation once more and they all began to cast Luminous Surge. No fancy multiplying tricks for each one, just pure and powerful spell casting all focused on a single point.

"You can't do this," screamed the Dark Titan, "I won't be

defeated so easily! The void will return and then you will know true pain!"

"Yes," Knox said in a hundred different places at once, "you will."

They unleashed their attacks, each one with a measure of his true self, each one with destructive power enough to level a building, if not a keep. Then there was his true blast, one which he threw so much of himself into that it hurt. The attack, his signature Luminous Surge, flowed out of him with reckless abandon and at the same time a level of control that he'd never achieved before.

Instead of a broad beam of light smashing into his target like the rest of the Astral copies, his came out as a perfect bar of white light that pierced the center of the Dark Titan.

Light and power collided as the Dark Titan threw all she had into defending herself, but it wasn't enough. The power reached her, and she was unable to stop it, no void beast came to her rescue and as with all things, she came to an end.

The Dark Titan exploded into a million pieces and Knox fell to his knees, exhausted beyond measure. He'd put literally everything he had into that final blast, so as his many astral projections poofed away, he felt darkness tug at the corners of his vision. He held on just as the fighting in the distance suddenly came to an end, something was happening, but Knox could do nothing more than sit there and wait to see the outcome. He'd truly spent his very all in defeating the Dark Titan and ending her plans.

Though it wasn't a complete victory, there was still a black ooze infecting void beast out there somewhere, a problem for another day.

CHAPTER 31
NEW BEGINNINGS

THE FIGHTING STOPPED in the distance, that much Knox was sure of as his strength slowly began to return. It wasn't a quick process, but it was surprisingly fast compared to other times he'd felt down and out. Before too long he was even able to move, sitting up and looking around. He reached out with his sense just as three powerful figures emerged from the crowd.

Zhul, Tress, and Terris, battle-worn and bloody, appeared through the crowd. The crowd, for their part, were backing away fearfully from them and Knox couldn't blame them, they looked something fierce as they walked ever closer. Behind them, looking even more bloodied and beaten, were some of the rest of his crew, Terrim and Frederick, though Dernal and Henry were nowhere to be seen.

"I see you've fought as hard as we have," Zhul said, his words sounding like a mere casual observance. "Are you injured? Where is Ramses?"

Knox swallowed hard as he stood, stumbling a bit. "Not injured, just weak for a time," Knox said. "Ramses fell in battle, where is Sintra I must speak with her."

The Dark Titan had fallen, but someone needed to take her

place and Knox knew of someone who had the grit and strength to take the role, keeping her people always in the forefront of her mind.

"She lives, but we took heavy casualties, they had some very powerful people on their side," Tress said, injecting her words when Zhul didn't immediately answer.

"It was expected," Knox said, trying not to feel the pain that came with loss, though he knew once he learned of who had fallen, he was sure to feel it. Looking around and not seeing Dernal, a sinking feeling hit Knox in his gut. "Who fell? Where is Dernal?"

For a long second no one spoke, and Knox was sure he knew why. But finally, Zhul spoke up where no one else would.

"He is alive but injured gravely. I've done all I can to heal him, but the internal injuries refuse to knit together as they should. I'm sorry, but he will die soon," Zhul said.

Knox didn't ask where he was, he reached out with his sense and found the man, stretching the limits of his Ethereal Step he appeared before a fallen and bloody Dernal.

"Hhrmm," Dernal said, before falling into a coughing fit of blood and phlegm. "Nice to see you boy." He finally added when he finished his coughing fit.

"Be still so I can heal you," Knox said, he could already sense darkness inside of Dernal, which would be why Zhul couldn't heal him fully. But Knox was limited in pushing out the ooze.

"Just in case," Dernal said, coughing more blood. "Know that I love you boy, you've been a light in my life and for that I can die in peace."

He struggled to get each word out and Knox could see the pain it was taking him to do it. Knox cast Luminous Surge on him, and the darkness was cast out. But in doing so, Dernal fell unconscious and stopped breathing, the pain of it all too much for him.

Knox refused to let him die, not when he was so close to

seeing this through. He cast Luminous Surge again just as a hand laid on his shoulder.

Looking up he saw his mother, battle worn and bloody, beside her stood a ruffled Askar, his own armor rent and bloodied. "He's gone," Scarlet said. "Let him go in peace."

But Knox knew better, and he had hope beyond hope that he could bring him back still. There was a small, tiny measure of him left, the power that was Dernal hadn't yet fled but it was nearly gone. Using his final straw and an ability that he could only do once before resting a long time, he cast Arcane Revelation, invoking the Titan's vast well of knowledge to instantly learn and cast a spell from another pathway for a short period of time. He'd seen the impossible done this way before and he would see that it was repeated!

A portal sprung to life in front of him and out walked a child glowing with white light.

"I told you not to summon me unless the need was dire," the boy said, the king of the Celestials. "What matter requires my attention?"

"Revive him," Knox said, his body, mind, and spirit at the limit having cast such a powerful spell so close to his exhaustion point. "Please." He managed to add as his vision began to fail him. He didn't know what happened next, as he passed out and was met with dreams of dragons, Titans, gods, great beasts, and beings of even more vast power, all battling it out over a singular great black dragon.

A familiar voice came to him then and he welcomed the warm familiar words as relief seemed to wash over him.

"Sometimes people are meant to fall," Mah'kus said, gesturing to himself. "Even in death there are greater quests. Be at peace and know that I take him into my fold, I will harden him and forge him into a weapon that will return to you one day. He is not gone, not truly."

A sudden dread overtook the calmness that forced itself over

Knox and he spoke as if from a great distance while something pulled him closer and closer to consciousness. "You can't have him! Please, I will do whatever you need, just don't take him from me!"

"It is done, already," Mah'kus said. "But stay firm on your path and you will stand strong when the end of the days comes upon us. You've done your part, be at peace and rest a while. Dernal will fight beside me, an agent for my work, just as Aetex is. The physical and the spiritual aren't as separate as you might imagine."

Suddenly a short, stout figure appeared before Knox, a familiar look of consternation on his face. "Hhrmm," he said, then noticing Mah'kus and Knox he added a few words. "I died, now what?"

As straightforward and to the point as always, Knox thought with a smirk and tears running down his face.

"Do you wish to help Knox on his journey?" Mah'kus asked just as Knox began to awake and be pulled away from the dream world or whatever it was that they spoke.

"I do." Were the last words he heard, but he saw a smile on Dernal's face that spoke of the love and caring the man had for Knox. A part of him refused to believe he'd lost his closest mentor and friend, but that damned peace continued to wash over him, deliberate and persistent.

"Dernal!" Knox screamed as he awoke, the small boy over him pouring magic into his chest.

"It was between you or him and I am bound to serve you," the boy king said. "I've brought you back from the brink, but you need rest. I must depart now; my strength has been taxed to its very limit and the Celestial realms are weaker for it. Pray that the demonic forces of the abyss do not attack this day."

"Thank you," Scarlet said, her words filled with emotion and tears pouring down her face.

But Knox barely heard a word of it, instead he reached out and felt for Dernal. Nothing remained of him, and Knox focused hard on remembering the dreams and his interaction with Mah'kus. Perhaps, if he survived long enough and united the Titans, he might see Dernal again, someday. He'd speak with Aetex about it, the man had claimed to have died before, then perhaps this godlike being had taken Dernal elsewhere and he hadn't truly died.

As if in answer to his unspoken question, a force that Knox couldn't begin to understand or feel, came upon Dernal where Knox had been focusing and his body disappeared in a sparkle of white lights.

"What happened?" Zhul said, panting as he made his way into the circle where Dernal had been. "Where did his body go?"

"To fight another day," Knox said, his voice horse and raw. "Bring me Sintra, we have much to speak of."

Knox didn't try to stand, just letting his body try to heal itself further. He had pushed too hard too fast when he was already weak, if not for the Celestial's help, he knew he would have died. But if he'd never cast the spell, he might have been fine, so it was in the end his own rash actions that had caused him harm. He'd be more careful now, more calculated in his responses.

Sintra arrived surrounded by guards some ten minutes later, enough time for Knox to at least stand. Knox informed Sintra of the falling Dark Titan's fate and fixed her with a leveled look.

"Can you be trusted to take up the mantle?" he asked, knowing that he didn't need to explain it to her, he'd informed her of his plan before.

"I believe that it is the best course of action for my people, if you will have me, I'd like to join the ranks of the Titan Born," Sintra responded, taking a knee before the giant metallic man.

Knox gave her a hand up, which she took, and he took a deep breath. "Then let's get this started," he said. He walked slowly, not to build up the moment but because he was so exhausted it was the best he could manage. Even so, his long legs meant she had to walk double-time to keep up.

He had several conversations with Sintra in the past to help figure out where the Titan Engine might be, but now Knox could sense it, deep in the ground some mile or two behind the keep, or what used to be the keep. They found tunnels that led in that direction and soon Knox happened upon the Titan Complex.

It was very cave-like in its construction, a very natural design, but with everything sharpened into points that could kill, from stalagmites to stalactites. He even sensed several wards in place, but with a casual wave of his hand they registered him and didn't try to repulse him. As he'd suspected it was meant to keep anything but Titans, and since Sintra walked with him alone, they were fine. This must have been something from her past, before the discovery of the void egg, for she could not truly be considered a Titan when she fell.

A low purple light filled the entire area and Knox followed the path he knew would lead to the Titan Engine, as all Titan Complex's held similar designs. They reached it and Knox bid Sintra to put a hand on it, she did so.

"It says I will be put to sleep for a time while it uses my power to rebuild my body," Sintra said, a hint of worry in her voice.

"I will guard your body as if it were my own," Knox assured her. "You are powerful, and I would guess it won't take you more than a few weeks for your body to adjust to its new state of being."

"Very well," Sintra said, then she fell toward the ground, but Knox caught her, laying her flat. She'd be safe enough for now, so Knox left while keeping his sense locked on her. He relayed a message to her people and his own. They would be helping with the repair of the city and in the coming weeks they would leave when Sintra was ready.

He hated to have to wait, but he now knew he was strong enough to deal with that pesky dungeon and free Beth, so waiting he would do. But in the meanwhile, he had to practice plucking the threads of creation and destruction, the very powerful magic that lay beneath the system, beyond it.

Knox worked on connecting the Titan engines while Sintra slept, and perhaps that was why it took her a staggering two months instead of the weeks he'd calculated based on her strength, but it was needed as connecting the Titan Engines wasn't as easy as Ramses made it out to be. He did it, but at great cost to his time and a few plucks of magic beyond his understanding.

During this time, he learned of Henry's death, as well as many others he cared for. He collected the shards of both the Aurorapex and the void egg, he had plans for both given enough time. He experimented on them in the workshops of the Dark Titan, while Sintra came into her power. When she finally awoke, Knox had her begin her training with the Gowlen echo, then gifted her various Monster Cores to achieve her first few quests that she'd been granted.

"The Path of Darkness feels like a solitary one," Sintra said when finally, she finished much of her training. "But I will endeavor to stand beside you. When you call, I will come."

"For now, I just need you to grow stronger, fortify yourself and grow your people. You've much to heal from and time is the best medicine sometimes," Knox said, he'd learned to suppress himself enough to look human and less Titan, but he only did it so he wasn't so much taller than everyone else.

Terrim joked that Knox could do better, since he was now equal to him in height even with his power suppressed as it was.

"I will," Sintra promised, and Knox left to gather his people and return home.

"So, it's finally over?" Terrim asked, then seeing Knox grimace he added, "I mean we still need to rescue Beth, but you are basically a god now so that should be easy for you."

"I don't know about easy, but I believe it is within my abilities now," Knox said, a careful smile on his face. He didn't want to appear overconfident, lest some unknowable entity place bad luck on him, but he was sure that this dungeon was going to meet its end and he'd be the one to hand down the final verdict.

"Is Murdoch back on his feet?" Frederick asked, and Knox felt out with his sense to locate his wounded friend. He was indeed back on his feet and heading in their direction.

They all sat around a fire, somewhere halfway to the surface from where their journey had started, several of Sintra's people had come with them to act as guides and eventually ambassadors to Knox.

"The party can begin," Murdoch said as he climbed up to the fire and sat heavily down beside Knox. He'd lost his left leg from the knee down, but Knox had already promised him a replacement when they returned, but wounds such as that had to heal by themselves or risk infections that couldn't be healed.

"If you'd told me," Knox said, looking over his powerful group of old friends, new friends, and allies, "that a mere couple of years ago that we'd be where we are today, I'd never have believed you."

"None of us would," Terrim said, laughing. "You've dragged us into a life full of unwanted adventure and excitement. Shame on you." The jest in his words had them all laughing, Knox included.

Scarlet reached out and put a hand on Knox's leg, beside her sat a quiet but alert Askar. "You've blessed as many lives as anyone could hope. You saved not only us, but the world. Tell me you can rest for a while, after you save Beth of course."

"Rest?" Knox asked, still smiling as he recovered from Terrim's jest. "My journey has just begun. I will unite this world, bring the powers of the Titan Engines together one way or another and when the Titan Gowlen returns, we will wage war against him in a battle of creation and destruction. No, this is not the end, but merely the start of my journey."

CHAPTER 32
BETH

THEY MADE it back to the Titan Complex in the following weeks, happy to find that it was intact and Aetex well. Knox immediately went to work on figuring out the teleportation between the two places. He'd thought to use it from the Dark Titan complex, but the teleportation rings were damaged, and Knox hadn't the expertise to fix them.

It took another couple of weeks to work out how to do it by himself, but finally Knox roared the portal to life and stepped through alone. He'd purposely told no one of his plans to leave that day and left at the deepest part of the night, not wanting anyone else to fall in battle. He was powerful enough now, he'd trained with Gowlen and assigned all his extra points. Nothing would stand in his way.

He walked through the portal into the noonday sun, something that was odd, but not surprising as there was a time difference between the places. What was surprising was the immense power he felt from two beings the moment he arrived.

Pirate corpses lay strewn about all over in various levels of decay and composition. It was the scene of a massive battle and even the complex itself looked to have been damaged here and there.

As Knox made his way outside, he first saw Beth suspended over the pyramid of the main building he exited, wreathed in power. He could feel her connection to the Titan Engine and was confused for only a moment before realizing what must have happened.

Somehow Beth had become the new Titan of Water, but why and how?

"You are probably wondering how your loved one became the next Titan," came a familiar voice. Knox turned to see Izel's voice coming from a sleek golem of black metal with gold swirls and glowing blue runic formations.

"The dungeon," Knox began to say, feeling utterly confused.

"Has thrown off its bonds and become free!" Izel finished.

Knox snarled and began to call upon his power. "You're done for!"

"Wait, wait, you could defeat me, it is possible, but why would you want to," Izel said, raising his hands in a sign of surrender. "I've brought you back your sweet love and, better yet, she is ascending to the same height as you, a Titan among men."

The logic of the statement almost made Knox pause, but he had vowed to take this evil dungeon down and he kept his promises.

Unleashing a Luminous Surge, he blasted away the construct, squashing him under his might like a fly. He felt the thing come apart, but then something moved from behind him. Dodging to the side he missed getting stabbed by yet another Izel golem, this one nearly his size as a Titan.

"I've already multiplied and spread out into the sea," it said as it slashed. "You'll never get all of me."

It took no more effort to dispatch the next, and a dozen more before he was finally sure that the island at least had been purged of the Izel golems. What he could do about a dungeon somehow spreading beyond its confined was beyond him and a problem for another time.

Going down to the dungeon spire he was surprised to find it cracked and broken, his job being done for him. However, he was less happy about finding the dungeon core missing from the pillar. If he could find which golem was using that, then he'd be able to end the dungeon once and for all.

It took another month and a half before Beth came to, her transformation finally complete. He caught her from her suspended state above the island and carried her down to safety.

"So, you're a Titan Born now?" Knox said, smiling ear to ear.

"Looks that way," Beth said, her eyes filled with a familiar glint of defiance. "Sorry about Izel, but I sort of tricked him into freeing me after he said the Titan of Water, Ramses, had fallen. He spoke of being able to replicate himself so much that I egged it on and he used my transformation to power his escape."

"Becoming a Titan Born was your idea?" Knox asked, not really mad but confused at why she'd want such a fate.

"It was," Beth said, her turn to smile ear to ear. "Now we can be equally awesome!"

"We've got a big quest ahead of us," Knox said. "I hope you're ready."

"I am," Beth said.

"Then let's begin by training you up a bit," Knox said, pulling her by her hand down to the Titan Engine. She'd have quests to complete, and he had cores to give.

This was just the first day of a new age for them and all of the world. Much had happened leading up to Knox's defeat of the Dark Titan, but one thing remained consistent. He was surrounded by friends ready to do whatever they could to help him out. He learned the true meaning of friendship and what it meant to love and be loved. This isn't the end of Knox's adventures, but it is the end for now.

The End of the Path of the Titans

Note from Author: If you liked the first Arc of Knox's adventures please rate and review so that we can add more to the story! The more attention these first three books can get, the more I will be able to write in this world.

LEAVE A REVIEW

Thank you for reading. Please leave a review!

If you really liked the book, please consider reaching out and telling me what you enjoyed about it at, Timothy.mcgowen1@ gmail.com.

Join my Facebook group and discuss the books at: https://www. facebook.com/groups/234653175151521/

Join my Patreon at: https://www.patreon.com/ TimothyMcGowen

ABOUT THE AUTHOR

Timothy McGowen, a Kansas-based author, cherishes the joys of family life with his wife and two daughters. His journey in the literary world began in grade school, and it's a passion that continues to flourish. Inspired by the imaginative realms of Terry Brooks and Brandon Sanderson, Timothy endeavors to follow in their footsteps, crafting stories that resonate with fantasy and adventure enthusiasts.

Prior to dedicating himself to the art of storytelling, Timothy honed his skills as a Software Developer, an experience that not only enriched his technical knowledge but also subtly influences his narrative style. This unique blend of technology and creativity is evident in his work, where he seamlessly integrates elements of Fantasy with splashes of Sci-Fi and the innovative concepts of LitRPG/Gamelit.

Timothy's passion for both reading and writing books is the lifeblood of his creative journey. For those who share this enthusiasm, he warmly invites you to join his newsletter. Stay updated with the latest news and embark on an exciting journey with each new book release.

His debut novel Haven Chronicles: Eldritch Knight has sold over a thousand copies of both ebook and audible so far. He writes Fantasy that contains a splash of scifi and Litrpg/Gamelit stories. Consider signing up for my newsletter for news on book releases as they become available.

LITRPG GROUP

Check out this group if you want to gather together and hear about new great LitRPG books.

(https://www.facebook.com/groups/LitRPGGroup/)

LEARN MORE ABOUT LITRPG/GAMELIT GENRE

To learn more about LitRPG & GameLit, talk to authors-myself included-, and just have an awesome time by joining some LitRPG/Gamelit groups.

Here is another LitRPG group you can join if you are looking for the next great read!

Facebook.com/groups/LitRPG.books

List of LitRPG/Gamelit Facebook Groups:

- https://www.facebook.com/groups/LitRPGReleases/
- https://www.facebook.com/groups/litrpgforum/
- https://www.facebook.com/groups/litrpglegends/
- https://www.facebook.com/groups/LitRPGsociety/
- https://www.facebook.com/groups/AleronKong/

www.ingramcontent.com/pod-product-compliance
Lightning Source LLC
Chambersburg PA
CBHW022247020726
47496CB00004B/1105